TO BE SEEN IS TO BE HIT

Horsip went off to see his Planetary Integration staff, ow working happily on plans for final integration of the lanet Earth into the Integral Union, and Moffis went long. Horsip described the appalling number of wrecked nd sabotaged ground-cars.

A precocious-looking individual, with large eye-orrectors and thin hair on his hands, addressed Moffis n a peevish voice. "I fail to understand how it can be ossible for the natives to approach the vehicles with-ut being apprehended."

Horsip put in quickly, "He means, why aren't the umans seen?"

Moffis, whose furry face was glowing red, said fiercely, Because it's night, that's why! They *can't* be seen!"

"A simple solution. Carry the operation out in daytime."

Moffis gritted his teeth. "We *can't*. Every time a car lows down in the daytime, some sharpshooter half a rag away puts a dart through the tires."

Moffis' questioner stared at him. "Oh," he said sud-lenly, looking relieved, "exaggeration-for-conversational-ffect."

"What?" demanded Moffis.

"How far the native's gun could shoot with accuracy," lorsip hastily interpreted. "He thought you meant it."

"I did mean it," said Moffis.

There was a sound of uneasy movement in the room. Theoretically impossible," said someone.

Moffis glared at him. "Would you care to come up and e down behind a tire?"

BAEN BOOKS by CHRISTOPHER ANVIL
Pandora's Legions

BAEN BOOKS BY ERIC FLINT
Joe's World series:
The Philosophical Strangler
Forward the Mage (with Richard Roach)
(forthcoming)

Mother of Demons
1632
Rats, Bats, and Vats (with Dave Freer)
Pyramid Scheme (with Dave Freer)
The Shadow of the Lion
(with Mercedes Lackey and Dave Freer)
(forthcoming)
The Tyrant (forthcoming)

The Belisarius series, with David Drake:
An Oblique Approach
In the Heart of Darkness
Destiny's Shield
Fortune's Stroke
The Tide of Victory

By James H. Schmitz, edited by Eric Flint:
Telzey Amberdon
T'nT: Telzey & Trigger
Trigger & Friends
The Hub: Dangerous Territory
Agent of Vega & Other Stories

By Keith Laumer, edited by Eric Flint:
Retief!
Odyssey (forthcoming)

PANDORA'S LEGIONS

CHRISTOPHER ANVIL

EDITED BY ERIC FLINT

PANDORA'S LEGIONS

This is a work of fiction. All the characters and events portrayed in this book are fictional, and any resemblance to real people or incidents is purely coincidental.

Copyright © 2002 by Christopher Anvil

The various parts of *Pandora's Legions* were previously published in the following: Part I as "Pandora's Planet" in *Astounding*, September 1956. The story was later incorporated as the first seven chapters in the novel *Pandora's Planet*, published by Doubleday in 1972 and reissued by DAW Books in 1973. The remaining portions of that novel, somewhat revised, now constitute Parts II, IV, VI and VIII of this volume. Part III was originally published as "Pandora's Envoy" in *Analog*, April 1961. Part V was originally published as "The Toughest Opponent" in *Analog*, August 1962. Part VII was originally published as "Trap" in *Analog*, March 1969. "Sweet Reason" was originally published in *IF*, June 1966.

All rights reserved, including the right to reproduce this book or portions thereof in any form.

A Baen Books Original

Baen Publishing Enterprises
P.O. Box 1403
Riverdale, NY 10471
www.baen.com

ISBN: 0-671-31861-6

Cover art by Patrick Turner

First printing, February 2002

Distributed by Simon & Schuster
1230 Avenue of the Americas
New York, NY 10020

Production by Windhaven Press, Auburn, NH
Printed in the United States of America

Part I:
Pandora's Planet

Klide Horsip, Planetary Integrator, prided himself on being much more than a jailer. Each advance of the Integral Union meant more occupied planets, and each one of these planets, like a single tiny component in a giant magnet, must be brought into line with the rest. This was Klide Horsip's job, and he settled to it now with relish.

"Phase I is *complete?*" he insisted, emphasizing the word.

Brak Moffis, the Military Overseer, smiled ruefully, "Not quite as complete as it often is on these humanoid planets."

"Then give me a brief summary of the details," said Horsip. He cast a quick glance out the landing-boat's window at the curve of the blue and green world below. "Looks promising enough."

"Well," said Moffis, "as far as that goes, it is. It's a Centra-type planet, mean diameter about 0.8, with gravity, oxygen, and temperature ideally suited to human and humanoid life. The percentage of water surface is higher than on Centra—about seventy-five per cent—but it's well distributed, and helps moderate the climate. There are plenty of minerals, including massive quantities of deep nickel-iron that hasn't yet been touched."

Horsip nodded. "And the inhabitants?"

"The usual types of plant and animal life—and, the humanoids."

"Ah, we come to the main point. What stage were the humanoids in when you landed?"

1

Brak Moffis looked at Horsip and gave a wry smile. "Technologically," said Moffis, "they were very near Centra 0.9, and in some areas higher."

"You aren't serious?"

The Military Overseer shook his head and looked away. "You wouldn't ask me that if you'd been in on the invasion. Perhaps you've heard of *Centralis II?*"

"The hell-planet! Who hasn't heard of it?" Horsip let his voice show impatience. "What of it?"

"Well," said Moffis, "that gives us ground for comparison. This was worse. Thirty per cent of the Initial Landing Parties were vaporized the first day. Another fifty per cent had their sites eliminated by the second day, and were pinned to the earth that day or the day after. The whole second wave had to funnel through the remaining twenty per cent of sites in isolated regions, and of course that meant the natives retained effective control of the situation everywhere it counted. If you'll imagine yourself wrestling one of the giant snakes of Goa, you'll have a good idea of our position." He raised a hand as Horsip, frowning, started to speak. "Let me summarize. Thirty per cent of our selected sites were eliminated, fifty per cent were in desperate straits, and the remaining twenty per cent were jampacked, overloaded, and only meant for secondary purposes in the first place. All this, mind you, despite the fact that the natives let off a couple of incomplete attacks on *each other* during the initial stages."

"Hysteria?" scowled Horsip.

"Regional rivalries," said Moffis.

"Well," said Horsip, "give the censorship another silver nova for efficiency. All I ever heard of this was that it was proceeding 'according to schedule.'"

"It was," said Moffis, "but it wasn't our schedule."

"I see," said Horsip, his face disapproving. "Well, what did you do?"

"Organized our established sites as fast as possible, and improvised new ones in chosen locations connecting the outer sites to form a defensive perimeter."

"Defensive!"

"That was what it boiled down to."

"What about the other sites—the fifty per cent under attack?"

"We supplied them as well as we could. When we were built up enough, we started a heavy thrust to split the enemy—I mean, native forces—and at the same time ordered a simultaneous break-out of the surrounded units toward common centers. The idea was to build up strong enough groups so they could fight their way to the perimeter."

"You were actually *giving up* the original sites?" Horsip looked at the Military Overseer with an expression of offended disbelief.

Moffis looked back coldly. "I'm telling you all this in detail so you'll understand it wasn't the usual matter of slaughtering a molk in a stall, and so you'll be ready in case *you* run into anything. I'm telling you we had a rough tossing around in the beginning. Maybe you'll have a better idea when I tell you one of our northern groups of Initial Landing Parties ran into this routine:

"The natives vaporized the center of each site with a nuclear bomb, contained the troops remaining in each site with minimum forces, then switched a heavy reserve from one Landing Party to the next, slaughtering them one-after-the-other, in succession. This wasn't brilliance on their part; this was their usual level of performance."

Horsip swallowed and looked serious.

Moffis noted Horsip's reaction and nodded. "I'm no more used to being on the defensive than you are, and I can assure you I didn't enjoy a minute of it. But that's what we were up against. We managed to recover just one large group—about eighteen per cent—of the original Landing Parties, then we pulled back into our perimeter under heavy attack. We had to bring the Fleet down into the atmosphere to get at their communications. At that the ships took losses of better than one-in-five despite the meteor guards. It was touch-and-go for three weeks, then we got the edge, and by the end of the month we had them hamstrung. Then we had some terrific fighting when we broke out of the defensive perimeter. But we won. At the end, we crushed them piecemeal."

"How long did this take?" asked Horsip.

"A hundred and twenty-seven of the planet's days," said Moffis. "Their day is roughly the same length as a day on Centra."

"I see," said Horsip, "and ten to twelve days is considered average."

"Averages don't count with something worse than *Centralis II*."

Horsip looked out at the planet, growing big as the landing-boat swung closer. As he watched, he saw a region of pits and craters, a part of the globe that looked as if an angry giant had beat on it with a sledge hammer. He turned away, as if to change the subject.

"What," he asked, "do these humanoid natives look like?"

"A lot like us. They have a pair of anterior and a pair of posterior appendages, one head, eyes, ears, and nose. They walk upright, and have opposable thumbs on the anterior appendages."

"Any significant marking-differences?"

Moffis swallowed. "A few."

"Good," said Horsip, relaxing a bit. "That will save us the trouble of marking them." When Moffis remained quiet, Horsip turned impatiently. "Well, don't just sit there. Enumerate them. What are the differences?"

"A bigger skull," said Moffis, "with a larger brow and a less prominent nose. The females are practically hairless over the greater portion of their bodies, and so are the males, though in less degree."

"Very good," said Horsip, nodding approval. "What else?"

"The vestigial tail is almost completely absorbed. There's no visible stump at all. And the head is set more nearly erect on the body."

"Splendid! Yes, very good indeed." Horsip looked vastly pleased. "You realize the implications?"

"I don't see anything good about it," said Moffis.

"Oh, come, man," said Horsip. "You've had a difficult

experience, but don't let it distort your values. This is a propitious start for Planetary Integration. These folk are self-marked, by nature. We'll have no mixed-race trouble here, nor any of the usual marking difficulties, either."

Horsip paused in thought, snapped his fingers and added, "For instance, look at the words that apply to these natives: big-headed, hairless, flat-nosed—"

"But they aren't flat-nosed."

"What does that matter? Didn't you say their noses were smaller?"

"Well, yes. But not flat."

Horsip waved his hand. "Never mind that. We'll call them flat-nosed. Now let's see. Big-headed, hairless, flat-nosed. Wasn't there another—"

"Tailless," supplied Moffis, without enthusiasm.

"Yes, *tailless*. Well—" Horsip leaned back, and a smile of creative enjoyment crossed his face—"we'll call them 'Puff-skulled, hairless, flat-nosed, lop-tails.' Let's see any of our rowdy young bloods try to mate with them after that."

"They will," said Moffis tonelessly.

"But not officially," said Horsip. "And that's what counts." He looked down with pleasurable anticipation at the planet grown large beneath them. He rubbed his hands. "Well," he said, "this is going to be pleasant work. A treat, Moffis."

Moffis shut his eyes as if to ease a pain.

"I hope so," he said.

A strong guard of heavily-armed soldiers awaited them in the landing area, itself ringed by several formidable lines of spike-bar barriers, thickly sown with leaping-mine trip wires, and covered by deeply dug-in splat-gun emplacements.

Horsip looked the defenses over curiously as he walked with Moffis to a heavily-armored ground-car. He noted that the soldiers carried out their orders readily enough, but without a certain verve usual on newly-conquered planets. "Trouble?" he asked.

Moffis glanced around uneasily. "Roving bands," he said. "You think you've got them wiped out, and they pop up again somewhere else."

They got into the ground-car, an order was shouted outside, and the convoy began to move off. It wound out onto the road like a giant chuffing snake, moving jerkily as gaps opened and closed between vehicles. The going was bumpy till they got out onto the main road, then the cars moved smoothly along. At this stage, Horsip raised up to peer out a shuttered slit in the side of his vehicle. For a hundred yards back from the side of the road, the vegetation was a burnt black. He scowled.

Moffis read his thoughts. "Yes, clearing the roadside *is* an unusual precaution. But it's either that or get plastered with a can of inflammable liquid when you go by in the car."

"Such an unnecessary width might indicate fear to the natives."

Moffis suppressed a snort.

Horsip looked at him coldly. "Isn't that so?"

"Maybe," said Moffis. "And maybe it indicates fear to a molk when you put heavier bars on his stall. But the main idea is, not to get gored."

"We've already conquered these lop-tails."

"Some of them don't know it yet. That's the trouble."

"We won't convince them by being frightened."

"We won't convince them by being dead, either."

Horsip looked at Moffis coldly. His heavy brows came together and he opened his mouth.

There was a dull boom from somewhere up ahead. Their car slowed suddenly, swerved, and then rolled forward so fast they were thrown hard back against the cushions. Something *spanged* against the side of the car. The snapping *whack* of a splat-gun sounded up ahead, was joined by others, and rose to a crescendo as they raced forward and passed to one side of the uproar. Acrid fumes momentarily filled the car, making Horsip cough and his eyes run. Somewhere in the background there was an unfamiliar hammering thud that jarred Horsip's nerves. There was another explosion, and another, now well to the rear. Then the car slowed with a loud squeal from the machinery. Horsip was thrown forward, then slammed back hard as the car raced ahead again. As they settled into a fast steady run, he turned to Moffis with a thoughtful frown. "How much farther do we have to go?"

"We should be about a quarter of the way."

Horsip sat, pale and thoughtful, beside Moffis, who sat, pale and gloomy, all the way to Horsip's new headquarters.

The site of the new headquarters was not well chosen to convey the effect of untouchable superiority. The site consisted of a large, blackened mountain with a concrete tunnel entrance at the base. The mountain bristled with air-defense cannon, was pocked and lined with shell holes, trenches, bunkers, and spike-bar barriers. Around the tunnel entrance at the base, the barriers, cannon, and splat-gun emplacements were so thick as to excite ridicule. Horsip was about to comment on it when he noted a huge thing like a monster turtle some hundred-and-fifty yards from the entrance. He felt the hair on his neck, back, and shoulders bristle.

"What's that?"

Moffis peered out the slit. "One of the humanoids' traveling forts."

Horsip stared at the long thick cannon that pointed straight at the tunnel entrance. He swallowed. "Ah . . . is it disarmed?" The ground-car's armor plating suddenly seemed very thin. "It is, isn't it?"

Moffis said, "Not exactly. Our engineers are studying it."

"You don't mean the humanoids are still in *control* of it?"

"Oh, no," said Moffis. "The concussion from our bombardment apparently killed them. Our experts are *inside* it, trying to figure out the mechanism."

"Oh." Horsip, as his angle of view changed, saw an armored ground-car gradually come into sight, parked near the alien fort. He damned himself for his scare. Of *course*, the thing was disarmed. But he could not help noticing how ineffectual the ground-car looked beside it. He cleared his throat.

"How many of those, ah, 'moving forts' did the human-oids have?"

"Hundreds of them," said Moffis.

They rode in silence through the massive concrete entrance, and Horsip felt an unexpected sense of relief as the thick layer of earth, rock, and cement intervened between himself and the alien world. They rode downward for a long distance, then got out of the ground-car. Moffis showed Horsip around his new headquarters, which consisted of a large suite of rooms comfortably fitted-out; several outer offices with files, clerks, and thick bound volumes of maps and data; and a private inner office paneled in dark wood, with Horsip's desk and chair on a raised dais, and a huge flag of Centra hanging behind it.

Horsip looked everything over in complete silence. Then he looked again around the private office at the desk, dais, and flag. He cleared his throat.

"Let's go into my suite. Do you have the time?"

"I suppose so," said Moffis gloomily. "There isn't a great deal I can do, anyway."

Horsip looked at him sharply, then led the way back to his suite. They sat down in a small study, then Horsip got up, scowling intently, and began to pace the floor. Moffis looked at him curiously.

"Moffis," said Horsip suddenly, "you haven't told me the whole story."

Moffis looked startled.

"Go on," said Horsip. "Let's have it."

"I've summarized—"

"You've left out pieces. Perhaps you've told me the facts and left out interpretations. We need it all." He faced Moffis and pinned him with his gaze.

"Well—" said Moffis, looking uncomfortable.

"You're my military deputy," said Horsip, his eyes never leaving Moffis. "You and I must work together, each supplying the other's lacks. The first rule of planetary integration is to apply the maximum available force, *in line with itself*. If you apply force in one direction, and I apply force in another direction, the result will be less than if we both apply force in the same direction. That can be proved.

"Now," he said, "you have had a difficult time. You hit with all your strength, and the blow was blunted. The natives showed considerable low cunning in using the brute force at their disposal. Because we are accustomed to swift victories, the slowness of your success discouraged you. I was somewhat surprised at the situation myself, at first.

"However," said Horsip, his voice swelling, "a molk is a molk no matter how many bars he kicks off his stall. He may put up a struggle. It may take twenty times as long as usual to strap his neck to the block and slam the ax through. But when he's dead, he's just as dead as if it was over in a minute. *Right?*"

"Truth," said Moffis, looking somewhat encouraged.

"All right," said Horsip, pacing. "Now, we've got the molk into the stall, but apparently we're having some little trouble getting his head in the straps. Now, we can't strap a molk in the dark, Moffis. The horns will get us if we try it. We've got to have light. You've got to light up the beast for me with the lantern of knowledge, Moffis, or I can't do my part. How about it?"

"Well," said Moffis, looking interested and sitting forward on the edge of his chair. "I'm willing, now you put it that way, but where should I start?"

"Start anywhere," said Horsip.

Moffis cleared his throat, and looked thoughtful.

"Well, for one thing," he said at last, "there's this piece-meal filing-down they're doing to us." He hesitated.

"Go on," prompted Horsip. "Talk freely. If it's important, tell me."

"Well," said Moffis, "it doesn't *seem* important. But take that trip from the landing-boat to here. That wasn't a long trip, yet they knocked out at least one ground-car. If it was the same as other trips like it, they would have put fifteen men out of action, and three ground-cars, at least. Suppose we have three hundred men and fifty ground-cars we can spare as escort between here and the landing-boat place. Each time, they're likely to get hit once, at least. It seems like just a small battle. Not even a battle—just a brush with some die-hard natives.

"But in two trips, we've lost one man out of ten, and one car out of eight."

Moffis paused, frowning. "And the worse of it is, we can't put it down. It's like a little cut that won't stop bleeding. If it just happened here, it would be bad enough. But it happens everywhere and anywhere that we don't have everything screwed down tight."

"But," said Horsip, "see here. Why don't you gather together five thousand men and scour that countryside clean? Then you'll have an end to that. Then, take those five thousand men and clean out the next place." He grew a little excited. "That's what they did to our landing parties, isn't it? Why not spring their own trap on them?"

Moffis looked thoughtful. "We tried something like that earlier, when all this started. But the wear on the ground-cars was terrific. Moreover, they moved only a few scores of men, and we had to move thousands. It was wearing us out. Worse yet, as they only had small bands in action, we couldn't always find them. We'd end up with thousands of men milling around in a little field, and no humanoids. Then, from somewhere else, they'd fire into us." Moffis shivered. "We tried to bring the whole army to bear on them, but it was like trying to shoot insects with a cannon. It didn't work."

"Well," said Horsip, "that was too bad; but still, you had the right idea. But you overdid it."

"I wouldn't be surprised," said Moffis. "None of us were in very good form by then."

Horsip nodded. "But look here, take five thousand men, break them up into units of, say, five hundred each. Train the units to act alone or with others. Take six of the units, and send them to troubled places. Hold the other four in your hand, ready to put them here or there, as needed."

Moffis looked thoughtful. "It sounds good. But what if on their way to the trouble place, *these* men get fired on?"

Horsip suppressed a gesture of irritation. "Naturally, the

five hundred would be split up into units. Say it was ten units of fifty men each. One fifty-man unit would clean out the nest of snakes, and the rest would go on. When they were finished, the unit that had stopped would go after the rest."

Moffis nodded. "Yes, it sounds good."

"What's wrong then?" demanded Horsip.

"The natives' stitching-gun," said Moffis dryly.

"The which?" said Horsip.

"Stitching-gun," said Moffis. "It has a single snout that the darts move into from a traveling belt, like ground-cars on an assembly line. The snout spits them out one at a time and they work ruin on our men. If this five-hundred man team you speak of was hit on the road, and just fifty men from it tried to beat the natives, we'd probably lose all fifty. The only way to win would be to stop the whole five hundred, and let the men fire at them from inside the ground-cars."

"But, listen," said Horsip. "Just how many natives would they be fighting?"

"Twenty, maybe."

Horsip did a mental calculation. "Then you mean one of their men is worth two to three of ours?"

"In this kind of fighting, yes."

Horsip made a howling sound in his throat, let out the beginning of a string of oaths and cut them off.

"I'm sorry," said Moffis. "I know how you feel."

"All right," said Horsip angrily, raising his hand and making gestures as if brushing away layers of gathering fog, "let's get back to this stitching-gun. It only shoots one dart at a time. How does that make it better than our splat-gun, that can shoot up to twenty-five darts at a time?"

"I don't understand it exactly," said Moffis, "but it has something to do with the way they fight. And then, too, the stitching-gun shoots the darts out *fast*. It shoots a *stream* of darts. If the first one misses, the humanoid moves the gun a little and maybe the *next* one strikes home. If not, he moves it a little more. This time, five or six darts hit our man and down he goes. Now the humanoid looks around for someone else and starts in on him. Meanwhile, another humanoid is feeding belts of darts into the gun—"

"But our splat-guns!" said Horsip exasperatedly. "What are *they* doing all this time?"

"They're heavy," said Moffis, "and it takes a little while to get them into action. Besides, the enemy . . . I mean, the humanoids . . . have had all night to set *their* gun up and hide it, and now they pick out their target at will. We have to stop the vehicles to go into action. And that isn't the worst, either."

"Now what?"

"The splat-gun operators can't see the enemy. I mean, the humanoids. They'll be dug in, and concealed. When the gunners do realize where they are, as likely as not the splat-guns can't get at them, because there is nothing but the snout of the stitching-gun to fire at. It's likely to be someone firing from inside the ground-cars that finally picks off the humanoids."

Horsip looked at Moffis thoughtfully. "Are there many more difficulties like this?"

"The planet is full of them," said Moffis. "It seems like heaven compared to what it was when the full-scale fighting was going on, but when you get right down to it, it's hard to see whether we've made any headway since then or not. The maddening part of it is, we can't seem to get a grip on the thing." He hesitated, then went on. "It's too much like trying to wear down a rock with dirt. The dirt wears away instead."

Horsip nodded, made an effort, and looked confident. "Never mind that, Moffis. You've got the molk in the stall for us. He's still kicking, but that just means there's so much the more meat on him."

"I hope so," said Moffis.

"You'll see," said Horsip, "once Planetary Integration gets started on the job."

The staff of Planetary Integration came down on the planet the next day. Soon they were coming in from the landing field in groups. They were talkative people, waving their hands excitedly, their voices higher-pitched than most. Their faces were smug, and in their eyes was a glint of shrewdness and cunning as they regarded the new world around them. Moffis did not look especially confident at their arrival, but Horsip brimmed over with energy and assurance. He began to put the problems to them:

First, what to do about the ambushing on the road?

The answers flew thick as dust in summertime.

Small forts and splat-gun nests could be built along the chief roads. Light patrols could scour the fields alongside to seek out the lop-tails before they got their guns in place. Strips of leaping mines could be laid alongside the roads at a distance, so the lop-tails would have to cross them to do any damage. Light airplanes could drop explosives on them. The problem was easy.

What about the stitching-gun?

Simple. Capture as many as possible from the lop-tails, and teach our men how to use them. Find the factories that made them, and induce the manufacturer to make more. And the same for the place that made their darts. Minor details of the gun's outward appearance could be changed, and a big seal attached, reading "Official *Centra* Stitching Gun."

Now, the big question: How to end this creeping war?

The Planetary Integration staff had a simple answer for that one. Every time a human was killed, ten of the lop-tails should lose their lives. If that didn't stop the foolishness, then *eleven* lop-tails should die. If it still went on, then *twelve* lop-tails. Each time the ratio was raised there should be an impressive announcement. Placards should be scattered over the country, saying, "If you murder a Centran, you kill *ten* of your own kind."

The lop-tails should be offered full humanoid equality, local self-government, and all the other inducements, on the condition that they were peaceful, and disciplined the rowdy elements that were causing trouble.

Horsip gave the necessary commands to set the machinery in motion.

For a full week, everything worked splendidly.

Horsip was enjoying a hot scented bath when Moffis came charging in. Moffis had a raised black-and-blue welt on his head, his uniform was torn open at the chest, and he looked furious.

Horsip put his hands over his ears.

"Stop that foul-mouthed cursing," said Horsip. "I can't understand a word you're saying."

Moffis shivered all over convulsively.

"I say, your integration program isn't working, that's what I say!"

"Why not?" Horsip looked stunned.

"How do I know why not? Nothing works on this stinking planet!"

Horsip clambered out of the tub into the drip pan. "What's wrong? What's happened?"

"I'll tell you what's wrong! We built the small forts and splat-gun nests just as you told us to. The crews in them have been living a horrible life. They're harassed from morning to night. And just what is the advantage, I'd like to know, of having five hundred men strung out in two dozen little packets that have to be supplied separately, instead of all together where you can do something with them?

"And then, this stitching-gun business. We can't *find* the manufacturer. Everyone says someone else made it. Or they say they used to make them, but not that model. Or they haven't made them for years. Or we blew up their factory when we attacked. And—hairy master of sin!—by the time we get through going from one place to the other—they talk a different language in each place, you know—we don't know whether we're standing on our hands or our feet. Let me give you an example.

"We took this stitching-gun we captured around to find out who made it. Wouldn't you think they could just look at it and tell us? No, sir! Not them! We showed it to the Mairicuns first. One of them said it didn't look like one of their jobs. He thought the Rushuns made it. The Rushuns said it wasn't one of theirs. Theirs had wheels on them. Try the Beljuns. The Beljuns said they didn't make it. Maybe the Frentsh did. The Frentsh looked it over and said, Oh, no, that was a Nazy job. And where were the Nazies? They were wiped out years ago."

Moffis stared at Horsip in frustration. "Now what do we do? And listen, I'm just giving you a summary of this. You don't know what we went through. Each one of those places has bureaus, and branches, and departments, and nobody trusts anyone else.

"The Rushuns say about the Mairicuns, 'What can you expect of those people? Pay no attention to them.'

"The Mairicuns say about the Rushuns, 'Oh, well, that's just what the Rushuns say. You can't believe that.'

"Now what do we do?"

Horsip decided he had dripped long enough, wrapped a bath-blanket around him and began drying himself. Evading the issue, he asked, "How's the casualty rate?"

"We haven't had a man *killed* since we made the edict."

"Well," said Horsip, brightening, "that worked out, didn't it?"

Moffis looked like he smelled something unpleasant. "I don't know."

"Well, man, why not? What's wrong with that? That's what you wanted, isn't it?"

"Well . . . I guess so."

"Well, then. We're getting a grip on the thing."

"Are we?" Moffis pulled a sheet of paper out of his pocket. "Since we gave the edict, we have had three thousand seven hundred sixty-eight slit or punctured tires, one hundred twelve blown-up places in the road, five unoccupied cars rolled over the side of a hill, eighteen cars stuck in tarry gunk on a steep incline, and a whole procession of twenty-six cars that went off the road for no known reason at the bottom of a hilly curve. We have also had break-downs due to sand in the fuel tank, water in the fuel tank, holes in the fuel tank, and vital parts missing from the machinery. Is that an improvement or isn't it? The tires, injured roads, and damaged machinery have to be repaired. That takes work. In this same period we have had"—he turned over the paper—"one hundred twelve men out for sprained backs, ruptures, and so on, and eight men in bad shape due to heart trouble. Also, the men are getting rebellious. You know as well as I do, Centran soldiers *hate* drudgery. Not only that, but you should see those roads! How do they make them like that in the first place? We *can't* repair them as well as they're made. I tell you I'm getting fed up with this!"

Horsip scrubbed himself dry, then dressed and went off to see his Planetary Integration staff, now working happily on plans for final integration of the planet into the Integral Union some twenty years in the future. Moffis went along with him. Horsip explained the situation.

A precocious-looking individual with large eye-correctors and thin hair on his hands addressed Moffis in a peevish voice.

"Why," he demanded, "do you fail to assure proper protective precautions for these vehicles?"

"Because," snarled Moffis, "we have all these stinking rattraps to supply, that's why."

"I presume your troops are in possession of all their senses? How can damage be inflicted upon the vehicles when your men maintain proper precautions?"

"What? I just told you!"

"I fail to understand how it can be possible for the natives to approach the vehicles without being apprehended."

Horsip put in quickly, "He means, why aren't they seen?"

Moffis, whose face was glowing red, said fiercely, "Because it's night, that's why! They can't be seen!"

"A simple solution. Carry the operations out in daytime."

Moffis gritted his teeth. "We *can't*. Every time a car slows down in the daytime, some sharp-shooter half-a-drag away puts a dart through the tires."

Moffis' precocious-looking questioner stared at him in a daze. "Oh," he said, suddenly looking relieved, "exaggeration-for-conversational-effect."

"What?" demanded Moffis.

"I supposed you to be serious about the half-drag accuracy of the projectile."

"About," Horsip hastily interpreted, "how far the native's gun could shoot with accuracy. He thought you meant it."

"I did mean it," said Moffis.

There was a sound of uneasy movement in the room.

"Theoretically impossible," said someone.

Moffis glared at him. "Would you care to come up and lie down behind a tire?"

Horsip, noting an undesirable effect on the morale of his staff, suggested they put a team to work on the new problem, while the rest continue what they were doing. He ushered the growling Moffis out of the room.

By the time Horsip had Moffis soothed down, and finally got back to his staff, an uproar had developed over the "meaning" of the "significant datum," that the lop-tails could shoot a gun half-a-drag and hit something with it. This fact seemed to upset a great number of calculations, in the same way that it would upset calculations to find two different lower jaws for the same prehistoric monster.

The arguments were many and fierce, but under Horsip's skillful prompting, they seemed to boil down to a choice between two, either: (a) the lop-tails possessed supernatural powers; or (b) the lop-tails used methods of precision manufacture on their ordinary guns and munitions such as humans used only—and then with great difficulty—on their space-ships.

The possibilities resulting from the acceptance of (a) were too discouraging to think about. Those resulting from (b) led by various routes each time to the same conclusion, that the lop-tails were smarter than the humans.

This unpleasant conclusion led to one that was really ugly, namely, of two races having humanlike characteristics, which race is human, the smart race or the dull race?

At this point in the argument, an unpleasant little man in the back of the room rose up and announced that on the basis of an extension of standard comparative physique types from the humanoid to the human, the lop-tails were more advanced than the Centrans.

But that was the low point in the argument. Soon the hypothesis of "pseudo-intelligence" was introduced to explain the lop-tails' accomplishments. Next, a previously undistinguished staff-member introduced the homely simile of passing over the brow of a hill. If, he said, one went far enough in one direction, he at last came to the very top of the hill. Any further motion in that direction carried one down the slope. True, he said, these lop-tails might go further in certain physical characteristics than the Centrans themselves. But to what point? The Centrans were at the peak, and any ostentatious exaggeration of Centran traits was merely ridiculous.

The excitement abated somewhat, and Horsip got his staff back to work on the pressing problem of supplying the road outposts without losing vehicles in the process. Then he hunted up Moffis.

The Military Overseer was in a room with five humans and a number of lop-tails. Plainly, Moffis was trying to question the lop-tails about something. But the lop-tails were arguing among themselves. Moffis left the room when he saw Horsip, first instructing his subordinates to carry on.

Moffis, wincing as if with a severe headache, said: "What a relief! I'm glad you came along."

"What's wrong?" asked Horsip.

"Interpreters," said Moffis. "These lop-tails all have different languages, and interpreters never agree on what is being said."

"Hah!" said Horsip. "You should have heard what I've just been through."

"This was worse," said Moffis.

"I doubt it," said Horsip, and described it.

Moffis looked gloomy. "I don't care what you call it. This pseudo-intelligence is going to be the end of us yet. Of all the planets I've helped capture or occupy up till now, I've generally had the feeling of outplaying the natives. You know what I mean. After the first clash of arms, you play a *deeper* game than they do. You manipulate the situation so that if they go against you they're swimming against the current. When you have that advantage, you can use it to get other advantages, till finally you have complete control of the situation."

"They're integrated," said Horsip.

"Yes," said Moffis. "But it isn't working that way here. Ever since the initial clash, we've been *losing* advantages. We're spread thin. The natives act in such a way that we spread ourselves thinner. I have the feeling *we're* the ones that are swimming upstream."

"Still," said Horsip, "we're the conquerors."

"I just hope they stay conquered," said Moffis fervently.

"I have an idea," said Horsip.

Horsip and Moffis spent the next few hours discussing Horsip's idea.

"It's the best thing yet," said Moffis, as they strolled down the hall afterward. A smile of anticipation lighted his face. "It should tie them in knots."

Horsip smiled modestly.

"We'll need plenty of reinforcements," said Moffis, "so I'll send out the request right away."

"Good idea," said Horsip. They strolled past the office of the Planetary Integration staff. A sound of groaning came from within. Horsip spun around.

"Excuse me," said Horsip. Scowling, he went into the room.

As he entered, he saw the whole staff sitting around in attitudes of gloom and dejection. A number of natives were in the room and one was talking earnestly to several members of the staff.

"No! No! No!" the native was saying. "You can't do it that way! If you do, the cars will lurch or even fly off the track every time you get up past a certain speed. You've got to have a transition curve first, see, and then the arc of a circle."

Horsip stopped, puzzled, and looked around.

Beside him, a staff-member with his head in his hands

looked up and saw Horsip. Horsip glanced at him and demanded, "What's going on here?"

"We got the natives in to study their language, and . . . and to worm their tribal taboos out of them." His face twisted in pain. "And we wanted to find out the limits of their pseudo-intelligence." Tears appeared in his eyes. "Oh, why did we do it?"

"Will you stop croaking?" snapped Horsip. "What happened? What is all this about?"

"They're smarter than we are!" cried the staff-member. "We tested them. And they're smarter. Oh, God!" He put his head in his hands and started to sob. Several other staff members around the room were crying.

Horsip let out a low growl, stuck his head into the corridor, and bellowed, "Guards!"

A sergeant came running, followed by a number of soldiers.

"Clear these natives out of here!" roared Horsip. "And hold them under guard till I give the word!"

The sergeant snapped, "Yes, sir!" and began to bawl orders.

The natives marched past with knives and guns in their backs.

"Listen," said one of the natives conversationally, as he was hustled out of the room, "if you'd just put holes in the guards of those knives, you could slip them over the gun barrels, and it would make it twice as easy—" His voice faded away in the corridor.

Horsip, furious, turned to glare at his staff. With the natives' voices taken out of the room, the sobbing and whimpering was now plainly audible.

"Stop that!" roared Horsip.

"We can't help it," sobbed several voices in unison, "they're smarter than we are."

"Gr'r'r," said Horsip, his face contorted. He reached out, grabbed one man by the uniform top, and slapped him hard across the face. The man stiffened, his eyes flashing reflexive rage.

"Listen to me!" roared Horsip. "You limp-spined, knock-kneed boobs! Pay attention here, before I—"

Slap!

"Look up, you slack-jawed—"

Slap!

"Straighten up, before I—"

Slap!

"Look up, you—"

Slap! . . . Slap! . . . Slap!

Massaging his fingers, Horsip returned to the head of the silent room.

"Morons," he said angrily. "You boobs, you simpletons, you sub-human—"

"That's just it!" cried one of the men. "The things you just said are—"

"Shut up!" Horsip glared at him, then let his glare roam over each of the others in turn.

"Here you sit," he went one, "the elect of Centra. Not the smartest by a long shot, but good enough to be in Planetary Integration. And you moan because the lop-tails are smarter. Do you make your own mind stronger by putting your heads in your hands and groaning about it? Do you make a muscle stronger by complaining that it's weak? Do you climb a hill by lying down, putting your hands over your eyes, and rolling to the bottom—all because someone else seemed to be a little higher up? Do you?"

There was a feeble scattering of "No's."

"'No'!" said Horsip. "That's right. Now you're starting to think. If you want to be stronger, you use your muscles, so if you want to strengthen your grip, do you let things go loose and sloppy through your fingers? No! You grip down tight on something suited for the purpose. And if you want your mind to grip stronger, do you let it stay limp and loose with self-pity? Do you? *No!* You grip with it! You take hold of something small enough to work with and grip it, fasten your attention on it, and then you've exercised your mind and you're stronger. Right?"

"Now," he turned to the nearest man. "Fasten your mind on what you've learned from these natives. Hold it steady and think on it. Nothing else. The rest of you, do the same. What an opportunity for you! Then, when you've squeezed all the juice out of what you've learned, boil it down, and put the essence of it on a sheet of paper so I can look it over. Now I am going to be busy, so get to work."

Horsip stalked out of the room, closed the door firmly, strode down the hall to his suite, and locked the door behind him.

"My God," he groaned. "They *are* smarter than we are!"

He stripped off his wet clothes, soaked himself in a steaming hot bath, fell onto his bed in a state of exhaustion, and slept sixteen hours without a break.

He awoke feeling refreshed, till he thought of what had happened the day before. With a groan, he got up, and some time later appeared in the Planetary Integration offices, smiling confidently. A stack of papers twice as thick as his hand was waiting for him on his desk. He greeted his staff cheerfully, noted that if they were not exuberant, at least they were not sunk in despair, then picked up the stack of papers and strode out.

Back in his private suite, he plopped the papers down, looked at them uneasily, chose a comfortable seat, loosened the collar of his uniform, got up, checked the door, sat down, and began going through the papers, peeping cautiously at the titles of each report before looking further. Clearly, the natives had unburdened themselves of a vast amount of information. But most of it was very specialized. About a quarter of the way down the list, Horsip came on a thick report labeled: "Love Habits of the Lop-Tail Natives." Firmly he passed over the paper, moved on and found one headed, "Why the Lop-Tails Do Not Have Space Travel." He separated this from the rest, put one labeled "The Mikeril Peril" with it, set it aside, and went on.

When he was through, he had a much smaller pile of papers that he thought worth reading, the lot headed by a paper on "Topics the Lop-Tail Humanoids Avoided Discussing." Before starting to read them, he thought he would just glance through the pile to see that he hadn't missed any. About a quarter of the way through the heap, he came on a thick paper labeled: "Love Habits of the Lop-Tail Natives." Hm-m-m, he thought, there might be important information in that. You never knew—

Firmly, he passed over it and searched through the remaining sheets. He set the pile aside, it slipped off the table, and as he bent to pick it up he came across "Love Habits of the Lop-Tail Natives."

He decided to just glance at the first page.

Fifty-one minutes later, Moffis rudely interrupted Horsip's wide-eyed scrutiny of page eighteen by hammering on the door.

"Now what?" demanded Horsip, opening the door.

Moffis strode in angrily, a large piece of message paper fluttering in his hand.

"The double-damned boob won't reinforce us, that's what! Look at this!" Moffis thrust out the paper.

Horsip read through the usual dates and identification numbers, passed through some double-talk that all boiled down to, "I've thought it over," and then came on the sentence: "Requests for such massive reinforcements at this date would create a most unfavorable atmosphere, and in so far as the Sector Conference on Allocation of Supplies is about to begin, it seems highly inadvisable at this end to produce a general impression of disappointment and/or dissatisfaction concerning the performance of any units of this command."

Horsip's teeth bared involuntarily. He took a deep breath and read on. There were vague hints of promotion if all went well, and subtle insinuations that people would be jammed head first into nuclear furnaces if things went wrong. It ended up with double talk designed to create a sensation of mutual good feeling.

Moffis glared. "Now what do we do?"

Horsip controlled his surging emotions, and took time to think it over. Then he said, "There's a time to smile all over and be as slippery as a snake in a swamp, and then there is a time to roar and pound on tables. Go find out when this Sector Conference meets, and where."

Moffis hurried out of the room.

Horsip went into his office, yanked down a book on protocol, and began drafting a message.

Moffis found him some time later and came in. "I've got the location and time."

"All right," said Horsip, "then send this." He handed over a sheet of paper. "If possible, it ought to be timed so it will arrive just as the conference opens."

Moffis looked at it and turned pale. He read aloud:

"Situation here unprecedented. Require immediate reinforcement by two full expeditionary forces to gain effective control of situation, which has exceeded in violence and danger that of *Centralis II.*"

Moffis swallowed hard. "Do I sign this or do you?"

Horsip glared at him. "I'm signing it. And it would be much more effective if you signed it, too."

"All right," said Moffis. He smiled gamely and went out of the room.

Horsip shivered, went back to his suite, wrapped himself up in a blanket, and began reading "Topics the Lop-Tail Humanoids Avoided Discussing."

Horsip was very thoughtful after reading that paper. Apparently the humanoids were slippery as eels regarding any discussion of military principles or problems. They professed also a great ignorance concerning questions on nuclear fission. They were evasive concerning a glaring discrepancy between the numbers of cannon, traveling forts, et cetera, turned over to the Centrans, and the number that were estimated to have been used in action. Horsip made brief notes on a pad of paper, and turned without pleasure to the next report.

This was a paper headed "The Mikeril Peril." As usual, he felt the hair on the back of his neck rise at mention of the word "Mikeril." Uneasy tingling sensations went up and down his back, probably dating from the childhood days when his mother warned him, "Klide, do you know what happens to bad boys who don't do what they're told? The Mikerils get them." The Mikerils ate Centrans. Or, at least, they *had* before the humans wiped them out in a series of wars. Horsip pulled the blanket around him and began reading the paper.

"I was discussing problems in statistics with one of the lop-tails," the paper began, "and searching a test problem to put to him, I came across some old data concerning the numerous outbreaks of Mikerils on Centra and other planets we have occupied.

"On the basis of the partial data I gave him, the native was able to accurately date other outbreaks that preceded and followed the period concerning which I had given him information. I was preparing to concede the correctness of his calculations, when he screwed up his face, put his head on one side, and said, 'I should estimate the next probable heavy outbreak to take place 67 days, 4 hours, and 13 minutes from now, plus or minus 7.2 minutes.'"

Horsip looked up, the hair on his back rose, and he experienced a severe chill as he seemed to see a big hairy Mikeril sinking its poison-shafts into its victim, its many legs spinning him round and round as it bound him helplessly and carried him off inert.

Then Horsip sank down in his seat, looked over the prediction again, and his eye caught on "'plus or minus 7.2 minutes.'" Horsip decided the native was either vastly overenthusiastic, or else just liked to poke people in the ribs to see them jump. He turned to the next paper.

This one, on "Why the Lop-Tails Do Not Have Space Travel," made difficult reading. Horsip could not reconcile the straightforward title with the involved argument and minute dividing of hairs in the body of the paper. After a hard fight, Horsip got to the last paragraph of the report, which read:

"Summary: In summary, this author states the conclusion that the beings provisionally known as 'lop-tailed humanoids' failed to acquire space-traversing mechanisms owing to a regrettable preoccupation with secondary matters pertaining principally to interests other than those regarding the traverse of interplanetary and interstellar regions, primarily; and secondarily, owing to use of that characteristic provisionally known as 'pseudointelligence,' the aforesaid beings were enabled to produce locally satisfactory working solutions to certain difficult and specialized problems the solution of which, in a different state of affairs, might well have eventuated in the discovery of the principle known briefly in common professional parlance as the positive null-void (PNV) law. With these conclusions, the native known as Q throughout this paper was in complete accord."

Horsip, dazed from the rough treatment the paper had given him, stared at it in vague alarm. Unable to pin down the exact point that bothered him, he moved on fuzzy-brained to the next report.

This one started off as if it consisted of vital information about the very core of lop-tail psychology. But on close inspection, it turned out to contain a collection of native fairy tales. Horsip read dully about "Pandora's Box, the highly-significant, crystallized expression of the fear-of-the-unknown syndrome, the reaction of retreat-into-the-womb; the tale symbolizes the natives' attitude toward life and their world. The protagonist, Pandora, receives a box (significance of angular shape of typical native container), which she is not supposed to open (see taboo list, below), and a variety of afflictions emerge *into* the world (Pandora's world)—"

Horsip looked up angrily to hear a knock sound on the door. He let Moffis in.

"I sent it off," said Moffis.

"What?" snapped Horsip.

"The message to the Sector Conference, of course." He looked sharply at Horsip. "What hit you?"

"Oh, these stinking reports," said Horsip angrily. "Come in and lock the door."

Horsip went back to the reports and told Moffis about them.

"Some are good, and some are bad," said Horsip, "and some are written so you need a translator to explain them to you. It's always been like that, but on this planet, it seems exaggerated. I suppose for the same reason that a ground-car makes more trouble in rough country."

"Well," said Moffis, "maybe I can help you. Let me look over that bunch you've finished. That business about the significant quantities of guns, et cetera, that are missing, makes me uneasy."

"Help yourself," said Horsip.

Moffis picked up the pile and leafed through it. He paused at one report, looked at it, started to pull it out, put it back, scowled, looked at it again, shrugged, pulled it out further, held his place in the pile with one hand, and pulled it out all the way to look at it.

Together they read the reports, Horsip uttering groans and curses, and Moffis saying, "Hm-m-m," from time-to-time.

At last, Horsip threw down several reports with a loud *whack*, and turned to speak to Moffis.

Moffis was absorbed.

Horsip looked impressed, turned away considerately, stiffened suddenly, turned back, got down on his hands and knees, twisted his head around and looked up from below at the title of what Moffis was reading. The letters stared down at him:

"Love Habits of the Lop-Tail Natives."

Horsip untwisted himself, stood up, brushed himself off, and disgustedly left the room. He strode down the corridor, resolved on action. He was fed up with this feeling of struggling uphill through a river of glue. He was in charge of this planet and he aimed to make his influence felt. The first thing obviously was to take these natives the staff had been questioning, get one of them alone with some guards, then put the questions to him. This business of getting it second or third hand was no good.

He turned a corner, strode to a door marked "Prison," said, "At ease," as the guard snapped to attention, and started in.

"Sir," said the guard desperately, "I wouldn't go in there just now. Things are a little confused right now, sir."

Horsip's brows came together and he strode through the doorway as if propelled by rockets. He halted with equal suddenness on the other side.

Several dazed-looking soldiers were working under the direction of a red-faced officer who was barking oaths and orders in rapid succession. The general direction of the effort seemed to be to get three soldiers who were tied up untied. The trouble was that the three were off the floor, strung by their middles to the upper tier of bars in a cell. When one soldier was successfully pulled to the floor, overenthusiastic soldiers working on the other side of the bars would make a leap upward, seize one of the other soldiers, and haul him down, whereupon the first soldier would fly up out of the hands of the men trying to untie him.

"Captain," said Horsip dryly, "concentrate your effort on one man at a time."

The officer was apparently shouting too loudly to hear.

Wham! Down came one soldier and up went another.

The officer paid not the slightest attention to Horsip's order.

Horsip noticed one of the three tied soldiers slowly bending and unbending from his middle.

The first soldier came down. The second jerked up.

The officer screamed in frustration, threats, oaths, and orders mingled together in a rage that drove the soldiers to jerking frenzy.

Down came the second soldier. Up went the first.

Now the first was down again. Now he was up. Now down again.

Up . . . Down . . . Up . . .

Every small detail of the scene was suddenly crystal clear to Horsip, as if he were seeing it under thick glass. He felt detached from it all, much like a third person looking on. When he spoke, he did not feel that he gave excessive force to the word. He was hardly conscious of speaking at all. He merely said:

"CAPTAIN!"

The officer halted in mid-curse. He turned around with the glassy-eyed expression of a fish yanked out of the water on a hook.

The soldiers froze in various postures, then jerked to attention.

The outer door opened up and the guard presented arms.

Horsip said, "Captain, take the two nearest soldiers. Have them pull down that man on the *outside* of the cell. Now have them hold tight to the rope that's looped up over the bar. Now, take the next two nearest soldiers and have them untie that man. All right. Now, have those next two soldiers stand on the opposite side of those bars, *inside* the cell, ready to catch that other soldier when the rope is lowered."

The captain, using his hands to move the soldiers around, was following out Horsip's orders in a sort of dumb stupor. The first soldier was untied. The second soldier was cut down. The second soldier was untied. The third soldier was untied, and sat chafing his wrists and hands, and massaging his abdomen.

Horsip motioned the captain into a little cubicle containing a desk and a filing cabinet.

"What's happened here?" said Horsip.

The captain merely blinked.

Horsip tried again. The captain stood there with an unfocused look.

"Report your presence," said Horsip.

The captain's hand came up in a salute, which Horsip returned.

"Sir, Captain Moklis Mogron, 14-0-17682355, 3rd Headquarters Guards, reports his presence."

The captain blinked, and his eyes came to a focus. He seemed to really see Horsip for the first time. He turned pale.

"What happened, Captain?" said Horsip.

"Sir, I—" the captain stopped.

"Just tell me what you saw and heard, as it happened," said Horsip.

"Well, I . . . sir, it all boils down to . . . I just don't remember."

"What's the first thing you do remember?"

"I opened that outside door, and I came in and—Wait. No. The guard came to me and told me the prisoners needed attention. I came in, and . . . and—" He scowled fiercely. "Let's see, I came in, and, let's see, one of the prisoners—yes! The prisoners were out of their cells! . . . But they said that's what they called me in for. The lock design on the cell was no good, and they wanted to show me a better one. One of them was holding a shiny key on a string in the bright light from this desk light . . . now, what was that doing out there? . . . and he said to look at it, and watch it, and keep my eye on it, and he'd explain why I should . . . should—"

The captain looked dazed.

"Report your presence!" snapped Horsip.

The captain did so. Horsip tried several times, but could not get past the point where the natives showed the captain the shiny key in the bright light. Horsip became vaguely aware that he was wasting his time on scattered details, and, as usual on this planet, coming away empty-handed. He sent the captain out to learn from the three soldiers how they had come to be tied up in the air that way. The captain returned to say the natives had told the soldiers about a rope trick, had gotten them over to the bars with a coil of rope, and that was all the soldiers remembered.

Horsip sent out orders to comb the place for the prisoners, and for anyone who had seen them pass to report it.

The prisoners weren't found, and everyone was sure *he* hadn't seen them.

Horsip went back to his rooms feeling more than ever as if he were struggling uphill through layers of mud.

The next day passed in a welter of sticky details. The staff had finally figured out how to get supplies to the outposts without having the tires shot out in the process. An armored ground-car towing a string of supply wagons was to approach the outposts, traveling along the roadway at high speed. As the cars passed the outposts, soldiers on the wagons were to throw off the necessary supplies, which the men from the outposts could come out and pick up. In this way, the staff exulted, there would be no need for the cars to slow down; as the natives seemed reluctant to fire at moving vehicles—lest they kill someone and invoke the edict—there should be no more trouble from that source.

To protect vehicles from sabotage at night, the staff proposed the construction of several enormous car parks, to be surrounded by leaping-mine fields and thick spike-bar barriers.

Meanwhile, another convoy of eighteen cars had shot off the bottom of the hilly curve with no known explanation. The staff advised the building of a fortified observation post, with no fewer than two observers on watch at all times, so it could at least be found out what happened.

But the old troubles were not the only ones to deal with. Just as the Planetary Integration team triumphantly handed out answers to thorny problems that had confounded them in the past, word came of something new and worse. The soldiers were getting hard to manage.

Always in the past, on conquered planets, the troops had had *some* sort of female companionship. The natives had often been actually glad to make alliances with their conquerors. But here, such was not the case. The females of the local species ran shrieking at the approach of a love-starved soldier. This had a bad effect on morale. Worse yet, the lop-tail authorities had been offering to help matters by showing the soldiers instructive moving pictures on the topic, these pictures being the very same ones used to instruct the lop-tail soldiers on how to act toward females. Since seeing these pictures, it was a question who was more afraid of whom, the soldiers or the women. Now there was a sort of boiling resentment and frustration, and there was no telling where it might lead to.

While the staff, under Horsip's direction, was thrashing this problem out, Moffis, red-faced and indignant, came charging into the room.

Horsip sprang from his seat and rushed Moffis out into another room.

"Hairy master of sin!" roared Moffis. "Are you trying to ruin me?"

"Keep your voice down," said Horsip. "What's wrong now?"

"Wrong? That stinking idea for feeding the outposts, that's what's wrong."

"But—Why?"

"Why?" Moffis growled deep in his throat. He stepped back, his teeth bared and one hand out to his side. "All right. Here I am. I'm on one of these stinking supply-wagons your bright boys say ought to be hooked up to the ground-cars. We're racing along the road at high speed, like we're supposed to. We go over a repaired place in the road. All the wagons go up in the air. I have to hang on for dear life or *I* go up in the air. Now someone yells, 'Three barrels of flour, a sack of mash, three large cans Concentrate B, and a case of .33 splat-gun darts.'"

Moffis glared. "I'm supposed to get this stuff unstrapped and pitched out between the time we bounce over the repaired place and the time the outpost shoots past to one side?"

Horsip hesitated.

"Come on," roared Moffis. *"Am* I?"

"Well, now, look," said Horsip. "You're not going at it the right way."

"Oh, I'm not, am I?"

Horsip flared: "If you had the sense an officer's supposed to have, you'd know better than to have the stuff strapped in helter-skelter. You'd have a supply schedule strapped to a wagon post, and the supplies all loaded on in reverse order, so it would be no trouble at all—"

"But," said Moffis, "I'm not playing the *part* of an officer here! I'm one of our *soldiers*! I'm irked and griped because here I am, a soldier of the Integral Union, and I don't even dare speak to any of the native girls running around. There's no fighting going on—nothing definite—just an endless folderol that isn't getting anywhere. I'm about fed up with the thing. Every time I turn around there's some new make-shift."

"Yes, yes," said Horsip. "I see that—"

"All right," said Moffis, "the point is, the soldier is no mathematician in the first place. If you explain every point of the routine to him—O.K., *maybe*. But if he isn't used to it, things are going to get snarled up. Well, he hasn't had any training for this routine and it's a mess."

"In time—" said Horsip, groping his way.

"In time, nothing," said Moffis. "It won't work, and that's that. I haven't even had time to tell you everything wrong with it. What do you suppose these barrels and cans *do* when they hit the ground, anyway?"

"Well—"

"They *burst*, that's what they do! And I'm here to tell you a soldier that sees his barrel of flour come out the side of a wagon, hit the ground, fly to pieces, and then get swirled all over the road by half-a-dozen sets of wheels is in no frame of mind worth talking about."

"For—"

"He has to sweep it up with a broom!" roared Moffis. "And by the Great Hungry Mikeril, I tell you, *I* don't want to be around trying to give that soldier orders until we've unloaded his gun and got his knife away from him. There's got to be some other way of supplying these outposts or I pull in every one of them and to *hell* with sharp-shooters along the road. At least the men will be able to eat."

"Yes," said Horsip, feeling exhausted, "I see you've got a point there."

"All right," said Moffis. He stopped to swallow and massage his throat. "There's another thing. This car-park idea."

"Surely there's nothing wrong with that."

"No, the *idea* is all right. The plan on paper looks good. But how many million gross of spike-bars do your people think an army is equipped with, anyway? You're an officer. You know that. We have just so many for ordinary require-ments, plus a reserve for desperate situations. And that's it. Well, this planet has been nothing but one big desper-ate situation since we landed on it. We just don't have the material to make any such big things as these car parks."

"Couldn't you," said Horsip, desperately, "collect a few here and there from your fortifica—"

"*No!*" roared Moffis, his voice cracking. "Not on your life! Once we start gnawing holes in our own defenses—"

"All right, then," said Horsip, straightening up, "what about the natives? They had armies. *They* must have used spike-bars. Or, if they didn't, we can teach them how they're made, buy them from them—"

Moffis looked down at the floor gloomily.

"What's the matter?" said Horsip.

Moffis shook his head. "They didn't use spike-bars."

"Well, then, we can teach—"

"They had their own stuff."

Horsip looked apprehensive. "What?"

"Fang-wire."

Horsip felt himself sinking into a fog of confusion. With an effort he struggled clear. "What did you say?"

"I said, they had their own stuff. Fang-wire."

"What in the world is that?"

"Thick twisted wire with teeth on it."

Horsip goggled. "Is it as good as our spike-bars?"

"As far as coming up against it, one is about as bad as the other."

"Then—why don't we use it?"

Moffis shook his head. "If you ever saw our soldiers laying the stuff out—it comes wound up on little wire barrels. You have to take one end of the stuff, without getting the teeth in you, and pull if free. It comes off twisted, it jumps and vibrates, and the teeth are likely to get you if you try to straighten it out. I saw half a company of soldiers fighting three rolls of fang-wire the only time we ever tried to use it. The wire was winning. The natives were dug in on a hill opposite from us, and they were having hysterics. No, thanks. Never again."

"Listen," said Horsip doggedly, "if *they* use the stuff, there must be some way to do it."

"That's so," said Moffis, "but if we take the time to train the army all over again in new ways of fighting, we aren't going to get anything else done."

Horsip paced the floor. "I hate to say this, Moffis, but it appears to me to be a plain fact that this victory is tearing the army to pieces."

"I know it," said Moffis.

"Everywhere we come in contact with the natives, something goes wrong."

Moffis nodded.

"All right," said Horsip, his voice rising. "What we need here is drastic action, striking at the root of the trouble."

Moffis watched Horsip uneasily. "What, though?"

"Reconcentration," said Horsip. "The iron rusts fast when it's cut in bits where the air can get at it. Melt it back into a bar and only the surface will rust. Then the bar will keep its strength." Horsip looked hard into Moffis' eyes. "We've got to mass the troops—not just the road outposts, but the occupation districts. Everything. Take over a dominating section of this planet and *command* it."

"But regulations—in Phase II we *have* to do it this way!"

"All right," said Horsip, "then we'll go back to Phase I."

"But . . . but that's never been done! That's—" Moffis paused, frowning. "It might work, at that. The devil with regulations."

They gripped each other's arms. Moffis started for the door and walked into a hurrying messenger. They exchanged salutes, Moffis took the paper, looked at it, and handed it to Horsip. Horsip looked at it and read aloud:

"Hold on. Arriving in thirty days. Twenty million troops in motion. Your plan good. Argit, Supreme Integrator."

"I guess we'd better stay put," said Moffis.

Horsip frowned. "Maybe so."

It was a trying thirty days.

The outposts took to buying food direct from the natives. The road-repair crews fell into an ugly habit of getting out of work by exposing arms or legs and daring the lop-tails to shoot at them. There were so many flesh-wounds that the aid stations began running out of supplies. Troops in the remoter sections began drinking a kind of liquid propellant the lop-tails sold in bottles and cans. It was supposed to cure boredom, but the troops went wild on it, and the reserves were kept bouncing and grinding from one place to another, thinking the war had broken out again.

Planetary Integration did have a few victories to its credit. The trouble on the hilly curve, for instance, proved to be caused by a gang of native boys who came out every few days and stretched a cable across the road at an angle. The speeding ground-cars spun around the curve, slid along the cable and went over the edge. The boys then came out, rolled up the cable, and went home for breakfast. By the time this was discovered, the situation was so uneasy no one thought of asking any more than that the boys be spanked and the cable confiscated.

At intervals, by now, large concentrations of humanoid soldiers were observed in open maneuvers; their troops were fully equipped with stitching-guns, cannons run from place to place by their own engines, and traveling forts in numbers sufficient to turn a man pale at the mere mention.

Horsip watched one of the maneuvers through a double telescope in an observation post on his fortified mountain.

"Is that what you had to fight, Moffis?" he asked, his voice awed.

"That's it," said Moffis. "Only more of them."

Horsip watched the procession of forts, guns and troops roll past in the distance.

"Their airplanes," said Moffis, "were worse yet."

"Then how did you ever win?"

"For one thing," said Moffis, "they weren't expecting it. For another, they wasted energy fighting each other. And our troops were in good order then. They were used to victory, and they were convinced they were superior. Then, too, we used the Fleet to cut the natives' communications lines."

Horsip looked through the telescopes for a while, then straightened up decisively.

"Well, Moffis," he said, "we're in a mess. We're like a man in an ice-block house when the spring thaw sets in. We don't dare step down hard anywhere lest the whole thing fall apart. We've got to walk easy, and just hope the cold wind gets here before it's too late. But there is one thing we ought to do."

"What's that?" said Moffis.

"The reserves. They aren't committed anywhere. We've got to hold them in hand. And if we need them, we want them to be a club, not a length of rotten wood. We've got to train them so hard they don't have any time to get flabby."

"Truth," said Moffis. "There are so many leaks to patch, one forgets other things."

The occupation army got through twenty-four of the thirty days like a ship sinking slowly on a perfectly even keel.

On the twenty-fifth day, however, a procession of native military might passed by Horsip's mountain headquarters in such strength that the ground was felt to tremble steadily for three hours and a half.

On the twenty-sixth day, a native delegation called on Horsip and politely but very firmly pointed out to him that this military occupation was disrupting business, and was causing all manner of trouble to everyone concerned; it should, therefore, end. Horsip was very agreeable.

On the twenty-seventh day, three hundred traveling forts blocked traffic on one of the main highways for more than two hours.

On the twenty-eighth day, a flying bomb came down a mile-and-a-half from headquarters, and left a hole big enough to hide a rocket fleet in. The ground shuddered and quaked with marching feet. That evening, the native delegation called again on Horsip and stated their position in short pithy sentences, and words of few syllables. Horsip pleaded that he was tied up in red tape. The natives suggested the best way to get rid of red tape was to cut it with a knife.

In the early morning of the twenty-ninth day, a flight of Centran airplanes, trying to scout the strength and direction of the native movements, was forced down by humanoid aircraft, that flew at and around them as if they were standing still. Horsip ordered the rest of his airplanes grounded and kept hidden till he gave the word. The observers of the planes forced down straggled in to report massive enemy concentrations flowing along the roads past the small forts and splat-gun nests as if they did not exist. The troops in the forts and nests were apparently afraid to fire for fear of being obliterated.

Horsip received the reports while Moffis carried out a last minute inspection of the fortifications at and around headquarters. Late that morning, a hot meal was given to all the troops.

At noon, a traveling fort of a size suitable to have trees planted on it and take its place among the foothills was seen approaching headquarters. It moved into range, came up close, and swung its huge gun to aim directly at the concrete doorway heading down into the mountain. Horsip ordered his gunners not to fire, his unexpressed reason being that he was afraid it would have no effect. He then bade Moffis a private farewell, walked out the concrete doorway in full regalia, glanced at the huge fort, laughed, and remarked to a white-faced man at a splat-gun that this would be something to tell his children. He carried out a calm, careful inspection of the fortifications, reprimanding one gunner mildly for flecks of dirt in a gun barrel. He glanced confidently up the mountainside where ranks of cannon-snouts centered on the huge fort. The gunners around him followed his gaze. Horsip returned the salute of the officer in charge and went back below.

On the plain before the mountain, hundreds of traveling forts were grinding across-country, clouds of dust rising up behind them.

"We should open fire," said Moffis.

"No," said Horsip. "Remember, we're playing for time."

The traveling forts swerved and began approaching. Behind them, the hills were alive with troops and guns.

Horsip gave orders that a huge orange cloth be unrolled on the far side of the mountain. A landing boat circling far above did a series of dips and rolls and rose rapidly out of sight.

The traveling forts came closer.

The monster fort just outside headquarters debouched one native who came in under guard and demanded Horsip's surrender.

Horsip suggested they hold truce talks.

The native returned to his fort.

The troops in the distance began spreading out and crossing the plain.

The huge fort moved its gun a minute fraction of an inch, there was a blinding flash, a whirl of smoke. The tunnel entrance collapsed. There was a deafening clap and a duller *boom*. The ground shook. Tons of dirt slid down over the entrance. There was a fractional instant when the only sound was the last of the dirt sliding down. Then the earth leaped underfoot as the guns on the mountain opened up.

The traveling forts roared closer, their firing a bright winking of lights at first, the boom and roar coming later. The troops behind followed at a run.

Horsip ordered the planes up, to ignore the forts and attack the troops.

Humanoid planes swooped over a nearby hill.

Life settled into a continuous jar that rattled teeth, dulled thought, and undermined the sense of time. Things began to seem unreal and discontinuous.

Reality passed in streaks and fragments as Horsip ordered the movement of cannon by prepared roadways to replace those put out of action. There was a glaring interval where he seemed to live a whole lifetime while reports came in that enemy troops were swarming up the hillside to silence the guns by hand-to-hand fighting. When the attack slowed he sent a body of reserves to drive the attackers back down and away. But more came on.

The enemy planes began a series of dives, unloosing rockets that bled his troops like long knives stabbed into flesh. Moffis ordered the highest guns to fire on the planes and the rest to carry on as they were. Horsip spent a precious second damning himself for not making that arrangement prior to the battle, and then a yell from the enemy sounded as they surged through the doorway Horsip had thought blocked. He sent a few troops with splat-guns to fire down the corridors, then had to turn his attention to a rush up the reverse side of the hill that had captured a number of the lower gun positions there. He sent in a picked body of the Headquarters Guard he had ordered concealed on the side of the hill for that very purpose.

Evening had at last come, and with it a steady rumbling from the near distance, where the sky was lit with a blue and yellow blaze. Centran ships were pounding the gun positions on the opposite ridge, and their screens were flaring almost continuously with the impact of missiles slammed against them.

The fighting had died out around the mountain, and Horsip and Moffis went out with a small guard to inspect the positions personally. The air was pungent and damp. Their ears felt as if they had layers of cloth over them. There was a thin moon, and here and there on the ground pale glimmerings could be seen as wounded men moved. There was an almost continuous low moan in the air. A soldier with his back against a gun feebly raised a hand as Horsip came near. "The Great One bless you, sir," he said. "We threw 'em back."

Horsip went back to his command post after ordering several guns moved and some spike-bar barriers set up. He felt dazed. He lay down on a cot for a few hours sleep, and was wakened in the early morning to be told an important message had arrived.

On the thirtieth day, five million reinforcements landed.

Horsip spent the day explaining the situation to Drasmon Argit, the Supreme Integrator.

Argit paced the floor, ate meals, lay down on a couch, stretched, pounded out questions, gave orders to hurrying subordinates, and listened, questioned, listened, as Horsip in a desperate urgency to get the situation across, explained and expounded, using charts, maps, diagrams, and photographs. He tried to get across the sensation of struggling uphill through a river of glue, and was gratified to see that

Argit seemed to be getting the idea faster than he—Horsip—had.

After the evening meal was eaten and cleared away in the privacy of a small office, Argit got up and said, "All right, I think I see your point. The natives are technologically more advanced than we are. By a freak, they don't have space travel. We beat them for this reason and because we caught them off guard and they attacked each other. There is also the possibility that they are more intelligent than we.

"All these things are possible. In the course of occupying a million worlds—and there must be that many—who could hope we would not find beings more intelligent than we? Yet these intelligent beings had not yet succeeded in integrating their own planet, much less whole star systems, as we have done. On the contrary, they were about ready to blow their own planet apart when we landed. Why was that?

"You know the principle of the nuclear engines. There is a substance Q that flings out little particles. These little particles strike other atoms of Q which fling out more particles. There is also a substance L which absorbs these particles. Success depends on the correct proportioning of Q and L. There must not be too much L or the particles are absorbed before things can get started. There must not be too much Q or the particles build up so fast that suddenly the whole thing flies apart.

"Now, consider these natives. What are they like? An engine with too much Q, is it not? And what are we like? To speak frankly, Horsip, we have a little too much L, don't you think?"

Horsip nodded reluctantly, then said, "I think I see your point all right, but what are the flying particles in this comparison?"

Argit laughed. "Ideas. From what you tell me of these people, they fairly flood each other with ideas. Horsip, you and I and others in our position have had a difficult time. We are like atoms of Q tearing ourselves apart to try and fling enough particles—ideas—through the general mass so the thing won't all grind to a stop. We only half succeeded.

At intervals these Mikerils come along and hurl us halfway
back into barbarism. We should be able to merely raise the
speed of reaction a little and burn them back into outer
space. But we haven't been able to. The machine was running as well as it could already—not enough Q. Horsip, this
planet is a veritable mine! There are vast quantities of Q
here. It is just what we need!"

Horsip scowled. "Getting it out may be another matter."

Argit nodded. "We only arrived just in time. A little
longer and it might all have blown up. We have to fix that
first."

"How?"

"Your idea, first. You intended to mix whole populations
up, because the language and customs difficulties would
cause much confusion and tie them in knots. That is very
good. That would act, you see, to slow up the spread of
particles—ideas. But we want these people on our side. To
that end, we must first help remove their own difficulties—
while serving our own purposes, of course. We couldn't
stand too many eruptions like this.

"Horsip, with due consideration for their various levels
of civilization, we must transfer groups of young people,
and various professional groups, from one region of this
planet to others. We will not insist that they mix races or
customs; but chemicals react best when divided in small
lumps, so—who knows—perhaps it will bring an *end* to
some of these enmities.

"Meanwhile, they are bound to pick up our language.
And we will pick up such of their technological skills as
we can make use of. They need a universal language. We
need new discoveries. Both will profit.

"And then we will offer posts of importance, trade
agreements, raw materials—"

"How do we know they are going to accept this?" said
Horsip, remembering his own eagerness.

"Ha!" said Argit. "You showed me yourself. They are a
born race of teachers and talkers. Every time they've been
in here, what has it been? —'Let me show you how that

should be done.' 'No, look, you have to do it this way.' 'Put a hole in the guard of that knife and you can slip it over the gun barrel.'" Argit laughed. "I will bet you the hairy arm of the first Mikeril that attacks us after we get this settled that half the trouble with these people is, they can't find anybody to listen to them."

Argit opened the door. A number of Centran troops were squatting in a circle outside, where a medical aide was bandaging a wounded native. The native was talking eagerly in the Centran tongue that appeared to seem simple to them, compared to their own languages.

"Now," he was saying, "see here. Put a heavy bolt through this place where these bars come together, and you can vary the focus from here, with one simple motion. See? What's the advantage of having to swing each of these barrels around one at a time? It takes too long. You waste effort. But from *here*, you just loosen the nut, swing the barrels close, tighten it with the wrench, and you're all set. It'd be easier to carry, too."

The circle of Centrans looked at the native, looked at each other, and all nodded.

"Truth," said one of them somberly.

Argit closed the door.

"You see?" said Argit. "They're born Q material."

Horsip sadly shook his head. "It seems so. But what are our men? Damper rods."

The sound of tramping feet sounded outside in the corridor as the leading elements of more reinforcements marched past.

"That's all right," said Argit. "*We* need Q material."

The tramping rose to a heavy rumble. Horsip felt reassured and Argit nodded approvingly.

"And more than anything else I can think of," said Argit, speaking over the noise, "these people need damping rods.

"You have to have *both*."

Part II:
Able Hunter

Some days later, Horsip found himself studying the maps, where bright orange symbols showed the disposition of fifteen million fresh Centran reinforcements, with another five million standing by in their transports.

"I think," said Horsip, "that we can finally say that we have conquered this planet."

Moffis looked at the map skeptically. "That's what *I* thought, about a million and a half casualties ago."

"There's no armed resistance."

"There wasn't then, either."

Horsip nodded moodily. The effect of Argit's enthusiasm had worn off somewhat, and Horsip was again bothered by the natives' exasperating mental superiority. Horsip was now inclined to think that instead of merely mixing the natives up on their own planet, it might be a better idea to scatter them all over the universe—too much Q material in one spot could be dangerous.

Horsip, however, didn't want to make Moffis feel any more discouraged than he already did, and so, after a few comments recognizing the seriousness of the situation, Horsip shifted gears:

"However, thanks to numbers and surprise, we *have* conquered this batch, Moffis, and now we have to figure out what to do with them."

Moffis glanced at the maps.

"Let's just make sure they don't heave us right off the

planet. I don't want to go through what we've just been through all over again. We need the rest of these reinforcements down here where we can get some use out of them. The longer we leave them in those transports, the more stale they're going to get."

"All right," said Horsip, "where do we put them?"

"Some place where the country is rugged, so we can defend it, and where the natives are scarce, so our men don't have too much contact with them, and get depressed by the comparison."

They pored over the maps, and Horsip said, "This Main-Base Defense Zone A looks as good as any—and we've already got it fortified. The main supply dumps are there, and the country couldn't be much more rugged. It's the least bad place to be if the enemy has any nuclear bombs left. But we can't cram *all* these reinforcements in there. Let's spread them around in these other main-base zones. The country there is fairly rugged, too, and the zones support each other."

Moffis looked relieved. "Good . . . Now, will Argit go along with it?"

Horsip thought a moment. Argit had understood the situation quickly, and even got along well with the tailless, furless inhabitants of the planet, who, in turn, appeared to forget that Argit was a Centran, the Chairman of the Supreme Staff, and the ultimate Centran military authority on the conquest of new planets.

"H'm," said Horsip. "That's the place where the troops will hurt the natives least, and help us most. I think Argit would be all in favor of it. But he's leaving these details to us. *His* problem is to figure out how to fit these loptails into the Integral Union without wrecking it, and I think he's busy enough with that. He's already mentioned some ideas to me."

Moffis grunted.

"Then let's get the troops down here. If we're going to keep this volcano from blowing up again, we need more weight to hold down the lid."

"Oh," said Horsip, glancing at the map, with all its

reassuring orange symbols, "things aren't that bad, Moffis."

Moffis failed to look convinced.

The following days passed with great activity on everyone's part. Horsip's troops worked as if inspired—as they were, by Horsip, Moffis, and the other survivors of the first expedition. The natives, for their part, carried on an enormous trade. Argit, too, was busy.

One day Argit summoned Horsip to his office. Looking as if he had gone through several weeks of penance and fasting, Argit nevertheless spoke with satisfaction.

"When you want a stubborn, headstrong individual to do something," said Argit, "one way is to argue *against* it. Think up plausible reasons why you might want him *not* to do it, and act accordingly. The odds are good that he will end up doing what you tell him not to do, which, of course, is what you really want him *to* do."

Horsip thought it over. "You've persuaded the natives to—"

"They have persuaded me to open up the Integral Union to them. Believe me, Horsip, there is all the difference in who persuades whom."

"Now it's *their* idea?"

"Exactly."

"But why *wouldn't* we want them to spread out?"

"Obviously—from their viewpoint—our supposed fear that they might take over the Integral Union. Of course, I never mentioned it. They deduced it."

Horsip thought of the number of star systems in the Integral Union, and his mind boggled.

Argit smiled. "Remember, Horsip, they have no real feeling yet for space. They've had no experience. They don't appreciate the order of magnitude involved. But they're moving in the direction we want. Now, for the first benefit of this policy, I will want your help, Horsip, in attending a meeting of the Supreme Staff, where we will evaluate a new military department, and the . . . ah . . . man in charge."

Horsip looked interested.

"Who is he?"

"His name is Towers. Let's see, *John* Towers."

"A lop-tail?"

Argit winced. "If we are going to get desirable results, Horsip, I think it would be just as well for us to call them 'Earthmen.'"

"He's one of the locals?"

"Yes. And as nearly as we can discover, his ideas, directly and indirectly, have cost us better than half a million casualties."

"He must be one of their highest officers."

"No. Ideas are not so rare with them as with us, so they don't value good ideas properly. This officer is appreciated only by a few loyal followers. He has the temporary rank of brigadier general, and the permanent rank of major. He is outspoken, and he has highly placed enemies. To get him out of their way, these enemies have cleverly decided to unload him on us. I think we can use him. We are going to have a special meeting of the Supreme Staff to consider the matter. We will need someone with firsthand experience of these Earthmen.

"And," added Argit, frowning, "we may run into opposition on the Staff itself. I'll appreciate your support."

Horsip considered what it would be like to have some Earthmen on *his* side for a change.

He nodded cheerfully. "I'll do my best."

Horsip, aboard the warship that served as their headquarters, looked on with awe as the generals of the Supreme Staff settled into their massive seats around the oval table. There was a creak of leather, the rustle of paper, the snap of lock-levers as the seats were adjusted. Then, halfway down the long side of the table, Argit, Chairman of the Supreme Staff, cleared his throat.

"The fourth meeting of the twentieth session of the present cycle is hereby opened. This meeting was called to consider a new military department. The secretary will note that all members are present, and will read the summary of the previous meeting."

A thin, nervous-looking individual at a small side table rose to his feet.

"Summary, third meeting, twentieth session. All members were present, two regional seats unfilled due to vacancies. Business at hand was to evaluate performance of General Klide Horsip, Planetary Integrator of Earth. Testimony of General Argit favorable. Records and reports examined. Exhibits: stitching-gun, portable; several rolls four-tooth fang-wire; flying bomb with Q-metal warhead; disassembled warhead mechanism; scale models, traveling forts; other exhibits, listed in full minutes. Much discussion. Examination of casualty figures. Lively discussion. General Takkit moves for censure of General Horsip. Motion defeated. General Argit reprimands General Maklin for referring to General Takkit as a 'brainless molk.' General Argit reprimands General Roffis for correcting General Maklin, to say General Takkit is an 'addled molk.' General Maklin moved for approval of General Horsip's conduct. Motion passed. General Argit raises question of empty regional seats. Lively discussion. General Roffis proposes General Horsip to fill vacancy. Motion passed. General Argit raises question of second vacancy. Much discussion, no agreement. General Argit closes meeting."

The secretary sat down.

Horsip, dazed, was escorted to a seat at the table. Argit cleared his throat.

"We welcome our new regional member, and trust he will add to the wisdom and harmony of these meetings. Horsip, we need your experience on this next item of business. Now, we have approved the plan, and the High Council has sanctioned it, to give every opportunity to these Earthmen to disperse. We have now been offered use of an Earth military unit—"

A bull-necked general seated to Argit's left cleared his throat.

"Gride Maklin speaking. Let the secretary get it in the minutes that I'm opposed to arming native troops. The Great Records show we've already had two revolutions and an interstellar war out of that."

Argit said politely, "General, there's no need to interrupt. You'll have full time, during the discussion."

"I want it in the minutes before you get us convinced in spite of ourselves. We don't control a gun some native's got in his hands. Out men get soft, and theirs get tough. Next they jam our tail in the meat grinder. No, thanks. *We'll* keep the guns, and *we'll* do the fighting. That's simpler."

Argit growled, "You've got it into the minutes now, General."

Maklin nodded. "It had to be said. Armed natives are poison."

A slender general near Horsip snarled, "Secretary, note that Dorp Takkit opposes Maklin's giving the background discussion."

A white-furred, steely-eyed general at the far end of the table looked around.

"Sark Roffis. Note, Secretary, that I back General Maklin's opposition to native troops, and I back it to the hilt."

Takkit snarled, "We have one chairman. We don't need three."

Another general growled approval.

A murmur arose like a hornet's nest when someone jars the tree.

Argit said, very courteously, "The opposing viewpoints are now on record. I hope that any further comment can wait until we reach the discussion. Otherwise I will have to censure it, and the censure will go in the condensed summary. The High Council always reads the condensed summary."

There was a silence that bulged with unspoken comment, and Argit went on.

"These Earthmen have technological ability demonstrated in action, and shown in previous exhibits. They have been granted *full partnership* with Centra. 'Full partners' have to do their share of the fighting. The Earthmen are *not* going to be armed by us. Despite everything we can do to disarm them, they are still armed to the teeth, by their own efforts, and this unit in particular has a method of fighting that ought to be put to use for Centra's benefit.

"The question," said Argit, "is not of arming native troops, but of putting the prowess of this special unit to work for Centra. We have already suffered severely from the operations of this unit, and now, since the unit's commanding officer is unpopular with his short-sighted superiors, we can whisk this unit out from under the control of the Earthmen and put it to use ourselves. The general in charge of the unit is right outside, and we can call him in and evaluate the man and his methods."

There was a silence when Argit finished, and then the discussion began. General Maklin still opposed the idea, but he and everyone else wanted to see this native general. Argit turned to the guards.

"Show in General Towers."

The guard escorted into the room a trim Earthman, whose uniform bore a double row of ribbons, wings, and other emblems. The officer's bearing was quiet, but there was an indefinable something about him that made Horsip uneasy.

Around the table there were creaks, scrapes, and snaps as those with their backs to the door craned, shoved their chairs back, or pivoted around. Then came a grunt and murmur at the sight of the tailless, almost furless alien.

It came to Horsip that the indefinable something about this native was his quiet unimpressed look. There was no need to put him at his ease. He *was* at his ease.

Argit was saying, "Members of the Supreme Staff, this is Brigadier General John Towers. General Towers, we are considering the suggestion that you and your Special Effects Team serve as part of the Centran Armed Forces. What is your view of this?"

Towers said warily, "It's an idea."

Argit frowned. "Perhaps you'd care to give us your opinion?"

Towers looked stubborn.

"It all depends on who is over us, and how he operates."

Towers, narrow-eyed, looked over the Supreme Staff, and, for an instant, Horsip seemed to see how he and the others must look to the Earthman:

Furry creatures, like some kind of blend of Earthmen and the furry animals they called *lions*.

Towers suddenly grinned.

"I don't know *how* it would work. We've got some ideas we'd like to try out, but if I'm given orders what to do, and then when I start to do it some blockhead starts telling me I can't do it that way, or if I get orders to stick to my headquarters so I can fill out all the forms and be there when the phone rings, why, we're going to have trouble, and we might as well find it out right now. Give me a job— I'm not worried about how *hard* it is—but then leave me alone. Let me know what the problem is at the *beginning*. If I'm given to understand that the problem is such-and-such, and then, every time I try to move, some new condition is added, it isn't going to work. And there's something else. We might as well have this out in the open, too. I figure there's no special break in the chain of command between top sergeant and second lieutenant. I don't see any unbridgeable gap there. If that's the wrong attitude, get somebody else for the job, because that's the attitude I'm going to have, whether I'm a buck private in the rear rank or the man in charge. What counts isn't rank, so far as I can see, but whether the man can and does do the work."

Towers looked at them, started to say more, then changed his mind, and waited attentively.

The clear impression came to Horsip that whether or not Towers was on trial before the Supreme Staff, the Supreme Staff was, in effect, on trial before Towers. Horsip, though agreeing with what Towers said, began to see why Towers was unpopular with his superiors.

Near Horsip, the slender general named Takkit said, "You know, Towers, there are many unpleasant jobs in the Integral Union. An officer who failed to show a cooperative frame of mind could find himself with a succession of rather unpleasant assignments, with no advancement, and with—shall we say—a somewhat *tedious* life ahead of him. But life can be quite pleasant for those who are cooperative."

There was a sudden tense silence, with every eye on Towers.

Towers' eyes glinted, and then he smiled and faced Takkit.

"Oh, I will cooperate, General."

Takkit said coolly, "I rather thought you would."

Towers added, "I just won't cooperate with a blockhead, General."

To Argit's left, the bull-necked general named Maklin suddenly grinned.

Takkit said coldly, "I trust—what is your actual rank?—Major, isn't it?—I trust, Major—line your hands up along the seams of your trousers, there—I trust that you understand the penalties for even the hint of discourtesy to superiors?"

Again there was silence, with every eye watching Towers, who clicked his heels, stood at stiff attention, and said, "Yes, sir."

Takkit said lazily, "Oh? Is that so? I'm surprised. I thought you had been in the lop-tail—pardon me, *Earth*—armed forces. How would *you* know *what* our regulations are?"

"Because, sir," said Towers, "when offered this opportunity to transfer to your armed forces, I naturally studied your regulations first."

"Is that so?" said Takkit, sounding somewhat foolish.

"Yes, sir," said Towers, without intonation.

At the far end of the table, the white-furred General Roffis looked at Takkit's expression and began to grin.

Towers remained at stiff attention.

Takkit said, "At any rate, *Major*, whatever order I directly give *you*, you *will* at once, and without hesitation or question, obey that order, *won't* you?"

"I will not, sir," said Towers matter-of-factly.

"WHY NOT?" roared Takkit.

"Because, sir," said Towers politely, "I am not yet a

member of the Centran Armed Forces, and your authority over me is nonexistent."

At the far end of the table, General Roffis was beaming.

General Maklin, grinning, banged his fist on the table. Takkit opened his mouth and shut it again.

Towers remained at stiff attention, waiting.

The silence stretched out, and Argit, with the urgent distracted look of someone groping for a way to cover up someone else's peculiarly stupid blunder, said, "Were there any more questions that you wanted to ask General Towers, General Takkit?"

Takkit let his breath out with a hiss.

"That will be all for now."

Towers turned to face Argit, and relaxed from his posture of stiff attention. He now looked alert and attentive, but at ease.

Argit said uneasily, "I think we understand, and are sympathetic with your ideas of command, General Towers . . ."

Horsip, watching, did not know how the Earthman's face could express, with scarcely a movement of the muscles, such a profound lack of agreement.

Argit studied Towers' face, cast an irritated glance at the fuming Takkit, and then suddenly glanced around at the other generals, a large number of whom were watching the scene with expressions of profound gratification. Argit seemed to come suddenly to a decision.

"General Towers, if you want the job, and are agreeable, we will, first, support your complete force, allow initially for recruitment to three times its current level, and give you a completely free hand in its organization."

"*That* part is more than satisfactory, sir," said Towers, plainly reserving judgment.

"Now," said Argit, "some of our men—even occasionally general officers—are not always receptive until they get their minds on the track. Even highly able officers occasionally make errors . . . We all do it . . . And there are always clashes of personality amongst able men. You will need plenty of authority to get the proper cooperation. We cannot give you high rank in the beginning, until your method proves itself clearly. What I propose, to bridge the gap, is a device we have used occasionally in the past. This is the 'code name,' and its associated rank. If my colleagues agree, your regular rank with us will be that corresponding to the Earth rank of colonel. This rank is solid, not temporary, but it is insufficient to deal with a hard-headed general in a tight spot. We therefore offer, if the majority of my colleagues agree, a code name—say, 'Able Hunter'—together with the rank of general, grade III, and—again if the majority of my colleagues agree—a regional seat for Able Hunter on the Supreme Staff. You see, General Towers, we cannot give *you* this rank, but we can give it to the code name, and then, at our will, assign the code name to you. You can then use the code name whenever you find it advisable. As code names receive no pay, you will suffer a disadvantage in pay for every day you assert this rank. However, once your method proves its worth, there should be little difficulty."

Argit looked around. "What do you say, shall we give General Towers the rank and code name, with the particulars I've just mentioned? Secretary, note the votes."

A rumble of Yes's followed, and Argit turned to Towers, who cheerfully accepted the offer.

Horsip, smiling, considered the situation. The Integral Union was so big that there were always upheavals of some kind going on somewhere.

If Towers, code name "Hunter," needed a place to try out his special methods, the Integral Union could certainly use someone who could straighten out problems.

The question was: *Could Towers do it?*

As Horsip asked himself that, there came a rap at the door, and the guards let in an officer who bent by Argit's chair with an air of gloom.

Horsip braced himself.

Argit looked up.

"Another revolt on Centralis II. This time, they've managed a *total* surprise."

There was a groan, then Argit, and everyone else, turned to the Earthman.

"Towers," said Argit, "if you want to test your methods, here's your chance. Get your troops together. We are sending you to Centralis II as fast as we can get you there."

Part III:
Pandora's Envoy

Tark Monnik, Planetary Integrator of Centralis II, looked out through his twin telescopes at an early-morning panorama of tracer bullets, blazing cannon, and geysers of flying dirt. The solid mountain trembled under his feet. The air reeked of gun powder. Monnik and his occupation army, settled down comfortably just a few weeks before, now found themselves bled white, cornered, and fighting for their lives. Monnik looked up angrily and gestured to a nearby officer with the staff's morning summary of the situation.

"Sir," said the officer, "in the north, the enemy—"

"Never mind that," said Monnik. "The other day I sent out a call for reinforcements. Everything depends on whether or not we get them. Has any answer come in yet?"

The staff officer looked unhappy. "Yes, sir. We've had a reply from Drasmon Argit himself."

"Good," said Monnik. "Let's hear it."

The staff officer separated one sheet of paper from the rest, and read: " 'Monnik—Owing to complications elsewhere, we find it impossible to properly reinforce you in less than sixty to eighty days. To tide you over till the reinforcements arrive, we send you "Able Hunter"—this is his code name—who is a member of the Supreme Staff, and a genuine Earthman. Hunter is bringing his Special Effects Team, with full field equipment. You may find Hunter's methods of war somewhat unconventional and even eccentric, but we would advise you not to underrate either him or them. As we mentioned before, he is an *Earthman*. Good luck, Argit.'"

The staff officer stopped reading, and Monnik said, "Let's see that." He read it over, then looked up blankly.

"What's an 'Earthman'?"

The officer looked perplexed. "Sir, we've had our hands so full here, I guess I haven't kept up with things. It sounds like some kind of alien to me, sir."

Monnik, puzzled, ran his hand through the fur at the base of his neck. "If I remember correctly, we have a few men in the Headquarters Guard who were transferred from a planet called 'Earth.' Get hold of them, and see what they can tell you."

"Yes, sir."

"When is this 'Able Hunter' going to get here?"

"His ship came down at the spacefield a few hours ago, sir. He's on his way out here by ground-car right now."

"All right. Give me that summary, and go find out about Earth."

"Yes, sir."

Monnik braced himself, and looked over the sector-by-sector summary of the situation. Not much had happened overnight, but the new day was starting with a bang. Monnik's defense rested on a network of improvised fortifications in the south, and a river along most of the rest of his front. Behind the river was a chain of formidable mountains, a strip of coastal lowland, and the sea. Monnik was fighting to hold the river line. The enemy was using every stratagem and maneuver to pry him out of it.

Last week, the enemy concentrated his artillery south of the big bend of the river, and under protection of the artillery swung a pontoon bridge across. Monnik rushed reinforcements to the scene, and concentrated his own artillery. The enemy established a bridgehead. Monnik blew up the bridge, and plastered the bridgehead with a heavy bombardment.

Now, though the firing from both sides still went on, the summary in Monnik's hands told him that the enemy had secretly started the bulk of his artillery south during the night, and was at present rushing this rolling concentration of firepower down the river road at all possible speed.

Farther to the south was Monnik's network of improvised fortifications. If the enemy could get there first with his artillery, it would mean serious trouble for Monnik.

Monnik gave the necessary orders to start the bulk of his own artillery moving south. He then went inside to study the map table and was confronted with a bulging excess of symbols on the other side of the river, and a depressing scarcity of them on his own side. Venturesome plans just starting to germinate deep in his consciousness withered at the mere sight of the map.

Monnik was moodily contemplating the superiority of enemy numbers and equipment when he heard a ground-car come slamming up the trail of ruts and potholes that served as the road to his headquarters.

A few moments later, the door opened up to let in a strongly built alien with the insignia of a general—grade III—and member of the Supreme Staff. Monnik was absorbing the sight of this tailless, practically furless, wide-browed creature, when the creature looked directly at him, and said, "I'm Able Hunter."

"Tark Monnik," said Monnik automatically.

Able Hunter handed over his identification and a set of vague orders assigning him to Monnik's command "for purposes of consultation and technical assistance."

Hunter remarked, "I understand you've got a little trouble here."

Monnik grunted. "They've got us with one hand, and they've got an axe in the other hand. All they need is to get our neck on the block for about five seconds."

"Is that the present situation on the map table over there?"

"That's it."

Hunter looked over the map intently. After a while, he walked around and looked at it from the other side. He grunted and said "How did this mess come about?"

Monnik scowled, then glanced at the silver emblem of the Supreme Staff on the Earthman's jacket. Monnik said, "We made a serious error of judgment. Before we landed, the planet was run by a caste system that was pretty unfair to the governed classes. After we finally managed to smash their military resistance, we also smashed their caste system. We thought the majority of the natives would be grateful. What we overlooked was that their philosophy stated that the lowest member of their caste system was still higher than any other species in creation. They call themselves 'kingmen,' and I guess they'll fight to the finish to stay 'kingmen.' They feigned obedience to us, fooled the attitude-testing technicians, and at a given signal there was a simultaneous uprising all over the planet. Now, if we don't get reinforcements soon—"

There was a faint rapid tapping noise to one side. Monnik glanced around. The staff officer he'd sent to get information about Earth was standing a little back from the doorway, out of Hunter's range of vision. He looked urgently at Monnik.

"If you'll excuse me," said Monnik, "one of my officers wants to see me for a moment."

"Go right ahead," said Hunter.

Monnik went outside and moved away so they wouldn't be overheard.

"Sir," said the staff officer excitedly, "the men who were on Earth said the fighting here is like a vacation by comparison. They—"

"Keep your voice down," growled Monnik. "How reliable did these soldiers seem?"

"Sir, several of them have the platinum nova for extreme bravery in action. But then, they said the platinum nova was issued to whole units on Earth."

Monnik blinked. The platinum nova was given out with grudging restraint, and only after investigation by half-a-dozen separate teams of examiners, all of whom had to be satisfied or the award was withheld.

"Listen," said Monnik, "I don't want to leave him in

there too long. For now, just give me a quick summary of these Earthmen. What's their strong point?"

The staff officer thought intently. "They're original thinkers, sir, and they're mechanically ingenious. The soldiers said they'd come to the conclusion an Earthman must be born with a tool kit in one hand."

"I don't see how that can help us in the present situation."

"I don't know, sir. The soldiers said it was no fun at all fighting them. They said—"

Monnik nodded. "Tell me that later. I'm going back inside now."

"Yes, sir."

Monnik went back and found the Earthman leaning over the map table, contemplating the big bend of the river near the center of Monnik's line. He said, "I suppose you're hanging onto that riverbend to cramp the enemy's movements from north to south?"

"Well, yes, and also because it would be a lot harder to stop him once he got across that river anywhere."

The Earthman nodded thoughtfully, and Monnik cleared his throat. It had just occurred to him that there might be advantages to the Earthman being "mechanically ingenious." Monnik said, "I imagine you've brought along special equipment. Any . . . ah . . . new weapons?"

Hunter's face took on a blank uninformative expression. "We have some exceptionally powerful weapons, but they're only for use as a last resort. My men and I aren't operating as regular troops. We're irregulars, and work on a special theory of war."

"What's that?"

"An army, like a person," said Hunter, "has certain special points of vulnerability. Strike these at the right times and in the right sequence and the whole thing will collapse of its own weight."

Monnik looked at the map, at the symbols of the tremendous power massing against him across the river. Where, he asked himself, were the weak points in that bristling array of helmets and guns? He looked at the Earthman without enthusiasm. "Maybe," he said.

"Well," said Hunter, "if you'll get me some passes, so my men and I can operate on all sectors of the front—"

Monnik nodded. "I can do that easily enough."

A little while later, the Earthman was on his way back down the mountain, and Monnik was listening to his staff officer describe the war against Earth, as told to him by those who had been there.

" . . . Traveling forts," the staff officer was saying, "ships with guns big enough to hide in, bombs that flew under their own power; why, sir, the place sounds like a nightmare. They had guns that squirted out fire—"

"Fire?"

"Yes, sir. And if it hit you, that was the end. They say it took thirty-five million troops before they got the place more or less under control, and all they really ended up with then was a compromise."

Monnik scowled. Automatically, he discounted fifty per cent for exaggeration. But, even so—

"Sir," the staff officer finished, "the Earthmen have a fairy tale about somebody called 'Pandora,' who opened up a nice-looking box, and all sorts of horrors came out. The soldiers say Earth is like that box. They call it 'Pandora's Planet'!"

Monnik thought that over. "All right. Set up a team to report to me everything these Earthmen do. And I'll want to know *fast*."

"Yes, sir."

As this staff officer departed at a run, another bolted out of the headquarters building.

"Sir, the kingmen are trying another crossing!"

Monnik stared. "Where?"

"Sir, that artillery they were moving south along the river—they've swung it off the road and opened fire on our observation posts along the opposite bank. We thought all the wagons they had with them were part of the ammunition train, but they've got a disassembled pontoon bridge on some of them. They've got a column of troops marching up the road toward them. We've got practically *nothing* on the opposite bank because we sent everything north to fight at that first bridgehead. We can't pull those troops back yet because they're still fighting, and they're about worn out."

"Where's our artillery?"

"Coming south on the road. But, sir, they're bogged down in a terrible stretch of road."

"How long till they get to the new crossing-place?"

"Tomorrow afternoon."

Monnik felt as if he had been hit over the head with a club.

"Sir," cried the staff officer, "the kingmen will cross the river, go straight through us, and split the front in two halves. They'll—"

"Shut up," snarled Monnik. "Bring Karrif up from the south and block the crossing."

"Sir, it was quiet on Karrif's sector, so his transport was pulled out to help move the reserve. He has no transport."

"Then he'll have to do it on foot. Get moving."

The staff officer sprinted away. Monnik considered the Earthman and his theory. He hoped there was something to it because the fight was getting to the point where the moves were forced, and there didn't seem to be too many moves left.

For most of the day, the situation wavered and hung fire. Then a fierce attack opened up before his fortifications in the south. The kingmen in the original bridgehead tried hard to break out. As both these attacks were held, the enemy engineers assembling the new pontoon bridge lagged and bungled in a suspicious way. Meanwhile, on Monnik's side of the river, General Karrif's troops alternately marched and ran, marched and ran, the general himself at the head of the column, as they raced north toward the crossing.

As evening approached, Karrif's troops, bone-tired but triumphant, marched up opposite the crossing-place.

The enemy artillery instantly swung onto the road and headed south again. With smooth efficiency, the engineers loaded the pontoon bridge back onto its wagons and followed the artillery.

"They'll cross farther south, sir," said a worn-looking staff officer. "We can't move anything north because of the attack at the fortifications. Even the general reserve's committed—what's left of it."

"Give Karrif two hours rest. Then start him south again."

"Sir, the men will drop like flies."

"It will be worse than that if the kingmen get across that river. How's the artillery coming?"

"Axle-deep in mud, sir. The men are moving the guns but it's hellish work."

"How did this come about? That road was all right earlier."

"Yes, sir, but some rubbish plugged up a culvert under the road. The water backed up, overflowed the ditch, and soaked the roadbed. The dirt turned into mud, and when the weight of those guns hit it, they ground it into bottomless slop."

Monnik shook his head in weary disgust. "They've got the culvert unplugged by now, I hope."

"Yes, sir, and they're laying down planks, but it's a mess."

"All right. Get that order out to Karrif."

"Yes, sir."

Monnik stood still for a moment, considering how the fate of an army could rest on a few puny branches drifting into the mouth of a culvert and catching a pile of miscellaneous trash that could indirectly halt a whole column of artillery, without as much as a shot fired or a hand raised in anger.

He scowled suddenly, and sent one of his officers to find out what the Earthmen were doing. The officer came back with a blank look.

"Sir, they're flying kites."

"They're what?"

"Flying kites, sir. The reports say they're very pretty kites. And they're also floating little rafts down the river."

Monnik shook his head in disgust. There, he thought, went his last hope. Grimly, he braced himself for the morrow.

It was a bad night for Monnik. And then he woke to confront a gray-faced staff as the reports came in.

"Sir, Karrif is back in position."

"Good."

"And there's about a third to a fourth of the enemy artillery opposite him."

Monnik started. "Where's the rest of it?"

"They apparently pulled it off the road soon after dark, sir. Now it's back where it was yesterday. They're putting the pontoon bridge together with record speed, and the first enemy troops are waiting to cross. We're back where we were before, only now Karrif is too worn out to be able to intervene either in the north or the south. His troops are exhausted."

Monnik made a hard effort to keep his equilibrium. "How's the fighting elsewhere?"

"The enemy has made a little dent in the south, but it isn't bad. The reserve has stopped them. Further north, they've been driven back into their bridgehead with heavy losses. We've stopped them elsewhere, but there's nothing left to stop them at the crossing." The officer managed a faint imitation of a smile. "Except the Earthmen, sir. They're there."

"What are they doing?"

"Flying kites, sir. And floating rafts."

Monnik grunted. "Where are our guns?"

"They're just dragging the first of them out onto the solid road. But they can't get into position before this afternoon, and with no infantry support, we'll just lose them to the kingmen."

"Keep dragging them out," said Monnik, "and move them south as fast as possible. Pull out Hossig and his best units and send them south."

"Sir, they'll never make it."

"They've *got* to make it."

"Sir, it just isn't possible. If there were anything, of any size, to slow down the kingmen when they cross, it *might* work. But there's nothing left there except the remnants of our observation posts. There's just nothing to delay them, sir."

"Then there will be," said Monnik. "We'll delay them

ourselves. The Headquarters Guard is an elite unit. Assemble them outside."

For the first part of the trip, over the miserable trails that wound around horseshoe curves and plunged up and down long steep grades, Monnik used what remained of his pool of headquarters transport. When they had delivered Monnik and the first section of the Headquarters Guard to a specified point, they went back for more. Monnik started off cross-country with the men he had.

On the map, it had looked to him like a possible thing. Monnik had thought he knew all about maps, and their little tricks, until he came to the third of the ravines that weren't shown on the map. Sweating and furious, he led the men as they scrambled and slid down to the bottom, stumbled through the tumbled rocks and rushing water, and laboriously hauled themselves up the other side. In time, they emerged on an open hill, to see in the distance below them a pontoon bridge, with a steady stream of enemy soldiers crossing and fanning out on the near side of the river. To Monnik's left, far down the road that wound along the base of the hill, his own guns were approaching.

Monnik looked over the ground carefully. He turned to the captain of the guard.

"You see that ridge above the road? If we spread out along it, and switch our men back and forth as we fire, we can give the impression of a much larger body of troops. Come on."

The captain passed the orders back, and they spread out along the ridge. In the distance, the kingmen approached. From somewhere out of sight, the Earthmen drifted pretty kites over the battlefield. Monnik and his men began to fire.

The kingmen continued to advance.

Monnik braced himself for the unavoidable end. He hoped Hossig would make good use of the delay.

Suddenly, from the direction of the river came a white flash, followed by a terrific concussion.

From the drifting kites dropped little gray packets.

The captain put his hand on Monnik's arm.

"Sir, their bridge is gone! And look there. *Great hairy master of sin! Look at that!*"

The kingmen were rushing in all directions, thrashing their arms wildly. Abruptly they all bolted for the river. The huge array dwindled into a mob that vanished headlong over the river bank.

Monnik said suddenly, "The Earthmen dropped *something* from those kites. But what could—"

From the distance came a faint whining sound that grew to a speeding little speck, and was joined by other whining little specks.

Monnik looked at the fleeing kingmen, then at the growing multitude of specks traveling in his direction. His mouth felt dry. He turned to the captain of the guard.

"We've done our duty here, captain. I don't know what that is coming. We'd better withdraw."

"Yes, sir." The captain flung back his head.

"RUN FOR IT!"

Monnik suddenly found himself alone on the battlefield. The kingmen had vanished into the river. His own troops were so many pairs of heels dwindling fast up the hillside. The multiple whine was closing on him like a cyclone. A sudden sense of urgency gripped Monnik and moved him up the hillside in a blur of speed.

A whining noise followed right behind him and suddenly caught up.

A red-hot knitting needle seemed to pass back and forth through Monnik with simultaneous discharges of about twenty thousand volts.

Monnik let out a yell and suddenly began to *really* move. He passed his men as if they were standing still, miraculously bolted uphill between innumerable tree trunks without hitting any, and plunged down a steep ravine. Ear-splitting yells burst out to the rear, and on the way down the ravine, his men started to pass *him*. Then Monnik hit the water amidst a whining noise, screams, the roar of guns let off in panic, flying rocks, chunks of dirt and moss, and somebody's left boot with no foot in it. The water suddenly went up his nose, a submerged rock hit him on the chin, and a sensation like fifty poisoned fishhooks passed through his exposed right shoulder.

When Monnik came to, he was done up in bandages, and lying on a cot somewhere in the pitch blackness.

"Great space," he croaked. He sat up, and somewhere in the distance he could hear intermittent dull explosions. He tried to get up, felt dizzy and nauseated, and sat down again. He leaned back, and never even felt himself hit the cot.

The next thing he knew, it was broad daylight.

An orderly with a bulging white patch over his face brought him in some hot broth. Monnik forced down the broth and sent for a member of his staff. A staff officer came in looking as if he had spent the night being rolled around in an oil drum.

"Good afternoon, sir," said the staff officer shakily.

"*Afternoon?*" growled Monnik.

"Yes, sir."

Monnik squinted around. He had some trouble seeing, as his face and one side of his head was swollen up. "What happened?" he said, propping himself up.

"Well, sir, the second section of the Guard found us in the bottom of the ravine and dragged us out. At that, we lost about half a dozen men drowned."

Monnik lay back dizzily. "What about the kingmen?"

"*Some* of them made it across the river, sir. The ones on the other side, at the guns, ran away when the kites started drifting over them. After they ran away, a man-sized thing with flippers came up out of the river, set down a cylinder, took off the flippers and a kind of face mask, and turned into an Earthman that walked past the line of guns carrying a sack. As he passed the guns, he reached into the sack and slapped something onto the left wheel of each gun-carriage. He went back into the water, and all of a sudden a section blew out of each left-hand wheel of the kingmen's cannons." The officer paused and added, "The kingmen aren't going anywhere with those guns, sir, till they get the wheels fixed."

"Where are our guns?"

"In position, sir. Dropping whip-shot on the other side of the river every time they try to get at *their* guns."

A pleasant warm sensation built up in Monnik. "Well," he said, "what was it that blew up the bridge?"

"The Earthmen drifted some explosives under it in a little raft."

Monnik's bruised lips creased into a grin.

"And what was that racket last night?"

"That was the Earthmen, too, sir. They were on the other side putting bombs in culverts and setting off fuel dumps. The kingmen were a little rattled from what had happened earlier in the day, it was a dark night, and they couldn't do much to stop it. The patrols are boiling over there today, though, and I'd hate to set foot on the other side tonight."

"Help me up," said Monnik. "A situation like this should be taken advantage of."

With one arm across the staff officer's shoulders, Monnik got out of the room. He was vaguely conscious that it took three of them and a swearing doctor to load him back on the cot again.

After a nightmarish interval, Monnik awoke to again find it dark. A distant uproar suggested to him that despite the bristling patrols, the Earthmen must once more be busy on the enemy side of the river. Feeling that things were in good hands, Monnik drifted into a deep, restful sleep.

The next morning, Monnik awoke feeling refreshed. He found that if he moved slowly, and was careful not to touch or bump various parts of his body, he was able to get around with only an occasional spell of dizziness. He went to his headquarters, to find worried officers clustered around the map table. A brief glance showed him the reason. The kingmen were gathering in great force around the wide loop of the river near the center of his front.

"What's this about?" he demanded.

"Sir, the Earthmen have been operating from that river bend. Last night, there was a terrific uproar on the kingmen's side of the river. It sounded like they'd split up

into two teams and were having a private war. I guess they
were, too. The Earthmen told us they let animals called
'rabbits' loose over there, with 'noisemakers' strapped to
them. Every ten or twelve bounds there would be a loud
bang from the noisemaker. Then the rabbit would run and
there would be more bangs. In the dark, the kingmen fired
at the rabbits, and there were so many kingmen on patrol
they couldn't help firing near each other, and a few of them
got hit, and others fired back, and one thing led to another
and pretty soon they were calling out the reinforcements.
Well, sir, as we see it, their commander has had about all
he can take, and he's going to end everything by brute
force. The troops were coming in from all over this morning. They're a little short on artillery, but they've got a lot
of transport, even if they do have to use alternate roads,
and they're massing fast."

Monnik glanced at the map. "You think they'll try to
smash through our center and crush each half in turn?"

"Yes, sir. You can see, here, they've brought up some
more pontoon bridges. They must be bringing those in from
all over the planet. And they've got what artillery they can
still move. If they once get a good grip on this side of the
river, it's going to be rough."

"Can we bring our artillery back along that road to the
base of this loop of the river?"

"Not too well, sir. That road hasn't drained dry yet. We'd
get bogged down again. Sir, the Earthmen asked us to pull
back, fortify these hills back here, and fight to the death
on that line if the kingmen get over. But we aren't to
advance in any circumstances. We couldn't do it, sir, on
our own authority, but if you think—"

Monnik nodded. "Pull them back. Once that attack opens
up, they'll never stop it." He frowned. "What about the
old bridgehead—the first one? Is that still holding out?"

"No, sir. The Earthmen flew their kites over it yesterday, and that caused so much panic our men got in and
cleaned them out."

"Good. Then we don't have that to worry about. All
right, we'll have to thin our men out some to the north,

and rush all we can down here where the kingmen are going to get through. Get the artillery ready to move on short notice. Switch Karrif and Hossig to the south and put Karrif in overall command. When the kingmen come over that river to crack our center, I want to smash their left, swing around and hit them from the rear. We've got to give Karrif the bulk of our transport, and check with our observation posts and the Earthmen to see what roads on the other side are usable."

"Sir, we can use our transport to switch troops down from the north, and at the same time our other trucks and ground cars can be rushing back and forth from the south, too. But the men can lie down while the trucks are headed south, and coming north we can set up dummy props like the Earthmen use, and then the kingmen will think we're moving troops north, instead of south."

"Good. All right, get to work." Monnik glanced at the map, and then the phrase "dummy props like the Earthmen use" really penetrated his consciousness. Puzzled, he asked the nearest officer about it.

"Oh, yes, sir," said the officer. "You see, sir, they're trying to bluff the kingmen. They've got a lot of dummies made out of rubber that they blow up to large size, and weight down with dirt. Why, there are dummy guns, dummy soldiers, dummy ground-cars, and imitation marching sounds coming out of loud-speakers. They said, sir, it was one of their favorite effects."

Feeling somewhat dizzy, Monnik went outside to peer at the river bend through his double telescopes. As he bent at the telescopes, he instantly recognized the signs of a mammoth troop movement. Clouds of dust trailed across the jutting salient of the river bend. The roar of engines, rumble of rolling guns, tramp of feet, and murmur of mingled voices rose to meet him. He could just detect the chink of picks and shovels as the troops dug in, the called orders of officers, and distant blast of signal whistles. Through the dust and haze, he seemed to see the moving shapes of columns of ground-cars, and the dull flash of the sun on the shiny scabbards of masses of marching troops.

Monnik straightened in wonder. It hardly seemed possible to him that a troop movement of that size could be counterfeited. But then, almost everything was shrouded in the dust and haze, and besides, he knew it *had* to be fake. With the meager stock of transport he had available, his men just couldn't have been concentrated that fast.

Monnik took another look at the scene, and could find nothing wrong with it. If he hadn't known that it was impossible, it would have fooled him. He went back inside, and watched as the kingmen piled up more and more power around the loop of the river, while his own men pulled out to fortify the hills further back. The map took on a fantastic appearance. With a crushing superiority on one side, and nothing on the other side, the enemy was afraid to move.

As a staff officer remarked, "They're completely fooled, sir."

"Yes," said Monnik cheerfully, "at this rate, we'll have things in good shape by tomorrow or the next day." He felt a sensation of warm friendliness for the Earthmen.

Just then, the solid mountain seemed to jump under his feet. There was a concussion that stunned him for an instant. Then they were all running outside.

Down below, within the bend of the river, a great column of black smoke boiled toward the sky. Then a second and a third explosion shook the ground.

Monnik whirled and shouted:

"Get inside! There'll be a flood of reports any moment now. And we have to know what's going on."

As the officers ran in, Monnik took a closer look at the river bend. The wind was slowly moving the column of smoke, and through it he could vaguely see burning ground-cars, overturned cannon, and flickering bits of wreckage.

Monnik groaned. He didn't know what had caused the disaster. But he knew what the result would be.

A little later, an officer ran out to him.

"Sir, the kingmen are swinging their pontoon bridges across!"

Monnik watched the map as the enormous enemy force

funneled unresisted across the pontoon bridges and began to surge toward him. "How," he demanded of his officers, "is that defense line in the mountains coming along?"

"Slow, sir. There just hasn't been enough time, and there aren't enough men there yet. It will *probably* stop the first attack. If they don't hit it too hard, or in the wrong place."

Monnik swore, went outside, and got the captain of the guard. "I hate to do this to you," said Monnik to the bandaged figure, "but I've got another job for you."

As the guard roared off to help dig and man the defense line, Monnik once more became conscious of his aches and pains.

Late that afternoon, he received word that the advance scouts of the kingmen had reached the defense line, with the swarming army not far behind them. Able Hunter had by then installed a television command post in Monnik's headquarters, so Monnik could see the advancing scouts on one of the screens. Hunter was talking into a headset. On the screen, the enemy scouts moved toward the defenses.

A few moments later, the hidden troops higher up opened fire. There was a roar of cannon, and the scouts dove for cover. There were shouts and the blasts of whistles from the rear.

One of Monnik's staff officers said, "That line will never hold them."

Able Hunter was saying into his headphones, " . . . The 000 Canadian first. The jumping, crawling, and burrowing later . . . Now, I should think it's about time to try the Spider Special and a couple cases of Sparky Willie on that pack before they get spread out too much—"

One of the other screens showed the first of the main force of kingmen coming up well spread out. Further back, hosts of kingmen advanced in little groups. It was on these groups that miniature planes suddenly dove, trailing long pale strands that stuck and clung as the planes whipped around the groups, shot up, exuded more of the pale substance, and dove again. Behind the planes were left knots of men struggling with clinging filaments like so many flies trapped in webs. During the confusion this caused, a number of pale blue parachutes drifted to earth, burst into flame and disappeared on touching the ground. Small devices with caterpillar treads and long whiplike antennae crept out toward the kingmen, who were now broken up into innumerable knots of individuals stuck together in a complex pattern with strands running in all directions. Just then, the long antennae of the creeping devices approached the struggling soldiers.

Monnik watched as the kingmen's triumphant army began to retreat.

One of Monnik's officers said dazedly, "It's victory, sir."

Monnik grunted. "If it lasts. Signal Karrif to open the attack in the south."

"Look there, sir," cried an officer.

Monnik looked around to see on another screen, a huge host of kingmen spread over the land within the river bend. Beneath the cloudy sky, some were still grimly coming forward. Others were hastily going backwards. These men were not stuck by sticky strands, but appeared to exist in the center of a faint swirling gray haze. The majority of them appeared demented, and shrugged their shoulders, coughed, nervously reached down inside their jackets, batted the air, slapped their wrists, necks, and ankles, gritted their teeth, hopped, rushed in and out of stalled ground-cars, climbed on top, sprang off, and then began to dig as if their only hope was to melt into the earth.

Monnik looked up in awe. "That's nerve-gas, isn't it?"

"No," said Hunter, "that is a brand of tiny black fly, selected from a type found in northern swamps and forests on Earth, and specially bred for biting power, hardiness, and ease of incubation. You'd be surprised how many can be packed into the space occupied by a single bullet, and these things *seek* their targets. We're also dropping other insect pests to vary the agony."

Monnik squinted at the screen. "But—mere bugs can't stop an army."

Hunter turned away and said into his headphones,

"Bombing raid, eh? Good. Get our plane with the enemy markings up, and see if you can sneak into their formation and go back with them—don't complain. You volunteered. A few of our Superstrength hornets and yellow-jackets will keep the enemy pilots away and their planes down long enough for us to make a leaflet raid on the nearby cities and villages."

"Leaflet raid?" asked Monnik.

Hunter wordlessly handed him a neatly-printed oblong of paper. At the same moment as Monnik started to read it, an officer rushed in.

"Sir! The wind's shifted! *Bugs*—"

"Aah!" said Monnik irritably. He waved the officer to silence, and began to read the paper.

A kind of swirling gray fog came in the door. Monnik ignored it. The staff officers looked to Monnik for guidance, and stood firm. Hunter went straight out a window on the opposite side of the room.

Monnik was reading in astonishment:

CITIZENS!

For reasons of strategic rearrangement, your victorious army will, within the next day or two, move back through certain towns and villages in rear of the present lines.

You will, of course, firmly assist the military authorities in every way possible. For example:

1) Soldiers who have gone violently insane under pressure of enemy action will be cared for.

2) Troops suffering from vicious insect pests will be treated at houses designated by troop commanders.

3) Infested civilian houses will be burnt to the ground.

4) Citizens will borrow the guns of soldiers temporarily out of action, and turn out to resist roving bands of savage enemy.

Monnik became conscious of a peculiar fuzziness. The air before him seemed to be filled with innumerable tiny gray specks. He swept his hand through the air, and that rearranged the specks. He felt a surge of irritation and decided that the thing to do was to ignore the presence of the creatures. He looked up.

An officer with one hand across his face and the other fanning the air gave a guilty start. The room was filled with officers turning round and round, slapping wrists, necks, and ankles, snorting, coughing, and hopping from one foot to the other.

"Here," snapped Monnik. "Ignore these irritations. There's work—"

Something went down his throat to the entrance of his lungs. Monnik coughed desperately. That only made things worse till he remembered to keep his mouth shut as he inhaled. Meanwhile, from those few spots where he wasn't liberally covered by bandages, came an intense itching, and a sensation of being crawled over by countless tiny feet. Monnik grimly tried to ignore it. Now the things were going up his nostrils, crawling out onto his eyelids, and buzzing around inside his ears.

From outside came Hunter's voice.

"Anyone who wants repellent, come on out here!"

Various officers began to edge for the door.

"None of that!" snarled Monnik. "Back to work!"

The officers milled around, futilely making an occasional grab at a report or fumbling with a movable symbol on the map.

The things were now biting Monnik on the eyes, on the face, in the ears and nostrils, on the lips, the backs of his hands and his wrists, and were working in from all directions to bite him through his thick fur, so that while it was bad now, it was bound to get worse shortly. Monnik estimated that he had killed possibly twenty of them, and the space around him plainly contained thousands eager to land.

Monnik told himself that a good general knows when to retreat. He growled, "Follow me, men!" and headed for the bug repellent.

❖   ❖   ❖

It was only a few days later that the kingmen, their troops in flight before Monnik, and their civilians in flight before their troops, sent Monnik an emissary.

The emissary, his face puffed and bandaged, with eyes swollen nearly shut, stood swaying uncertainly as he glanced from Hunter to Monnik. The feathers at the back of his neck were badly rumpled—a sure sign of illness amongst the kingmen—and he looked as if he might collapse at any time. In a croaking voice, he said, "Where's the surrender terms? I want to sign."

Monnik had his staff draw up a suitable document, and meanwhile the kingman sat dozing in a camp chair, his head nodding forward and snapping upright, with one hand gripping the edge of the chair and the other swishing the empty air like a traveling fly-swatter.

The sight was beginning to unnerve Monnik when the document was brought over. He checked it carefully, then had an orderly shake the emissary awake.

"Here," said Monnik, "you can read this, and if—"

"Don't want to read it," the emissary interrupted. "I just want to sign it. *Then* you'll get rid of the bugs, won't you?"

Monnik glanced at Hunter, who nodded. "Yes," said Monnik.

The emissary scratched the pen rapidly across the bottom of the paper, then said, "We'll need another signature." He stepped to the door.

A dignitary covered with poultices was carried in on a stretcher, and allowed his hand to be guided across the page. The kingmen then shambled back to their ground-car and were loaded in.

"Great space," said Monnik, "isn't that a pathetic sight?"

"They'll recover," said Hunter. "If we'd blown the battle-field off the planet, they might have cause for complaint."

Monnik watched the wavering ground-car for a moment.

"Well," he said, "we beat them, all right, and I'm glad that's settled. But I can't help wondering."

"About what?"

Monnik said uneasily, "Was it *war*?"

"An interesting question," said Hunter. "And if a 'layman'

makes a new discovery or invention, a host of profession-als will ask, 'But is it *scientific*?' "

He pointed down the road, where the kingmen's ground-car weaved around the corner and crept out of sight.

"As I told you when we got here, we aren't regular troops. We're irregulars. And there's only one yardstick you use to judge a job done by irregulars."

"What's that?" said Monnik.

"The simplest yardstick of all," said Hunter. "The per-formance test:

"Did it work?"

Part IV:
Pandora's Unlocked Box

After Towers' departure, Horsip remained on the warship that housed the Supreme Staff. He had his own room and his own office, but spent much of his time working on a special three-man committee formed to keep track of the Earthmen's activities.

General Maklin and General Roffis sat with Horsip amidst growing stacks of papers, which they read with profanity and bafflement.

Horsip exasperatedly read of one Q. Zoffit, who had illegally bartered a Class VI landing-boat for a "classic Packard in mint condition."

General Roffis smoothed back the thick white fur of his head and neck.

"While you were on this planet, Horsip, did you happen to have any experience with a . . . ah . . ." Roffis glanced at a document flattened onto his desk—" 'glorious sun-drenched quarter acre on the warm sandy shores of a hidden inlet on Florida's unspoiled west coast, all conveniences, golf course, pool, garbage pick-up, and exclusive clubhouse'?"

Horsip looked blank. "No, sir, I never ran into anything like that."

"XXth Rest and Recuperation Battalion," said Roffis, "purchased some of these 'sun-drenched quarter acres' for a rest and recuperation center for IInd Western Occupation Command."

Maklin scowled. " 'Purchased'? Why not requisition them?"

"According to this document, the commanding officer intended to do just that, but got into a conversation with the 'sales manager' of the HiDry Land Reclamation Corporation, and the result was that the battalion bought the land 'on time.' " Roffis glanced at Horsip. "What is 'on time'?"

"I suppose . . . h'm . . . 'on time' would mean 'without delay,' wouldn't it?"

"To get the 'down payment,' the commanding officer got talked into going to a 'loan company.' "

"Loan company," said Horsip. "That sounds like a usurer."

"This outfit," said Roffis, "charged 25 percent. The battalion pledged its space transport as 'collateral' for the loan."

Maklin growled, *"Then* what happened?"

"The battalion couldn't repay the loan—naturally, where would they get local currency, unless they stole it—so, the loan company claimed the transport. Then the HiDry Land Reclamation Corporation 'repossessed' the 'sun-drenched quarter acres.' The result is that the Earthmen have the space transport, and the XXth Rest and Recuperation Battalion has insect bites, sunburn, and three men 'presumed eaten up by alligators.' "

Horsip nodded moodily.

"That sounds familiar."

Roffis said, "When we have dealings with these Earthmen we get carried off in a basket."

"Yes, sir."

"How do they do it?"

"When they get through talking, everything looks different."

"How do they accomplish *that?*"

"They seem to emphasize one point, and slant everything to build up that point."

"Do they see what we overlook? Or do they take some unimportant aspect and puff it up out of proportion?"

"I think they emphasize whatever favors their argument."

"Then they have a weakness. If they restricted themselves to truth, they would be strong. With this procedure, they will take up false positions."

"Still, they pull our men off-base."

Maklin's eyes glinted. "They won't pull *all* of us off-base."

General Roffis said, "Nevertheless, we have a serious problem. They have gulled our men into giving up valuable space-ships in return for—let's see—fancy ground-cars, cabin cruisers, vacation trailers, sauna baths, undeveloped real estate, a 'private ocean backyard swimming pool' . . ." Roffis looked up. "This isn't very promising."

Maklin growled, "And all this is against regulations. Every one of these transactions is a capital offense. Yet the punishment is light. Here, for instance, is a report on an individual who traded a supply ship for a 'Complete Library of the Works of the Leaders of World Communism.' On going into this further, I find that 'communism' is a scheme for overthrowing one ruling class to install another. What did the fellow *want* with this collection anyway?"

Roffis tossed his list on the desk.

"What we have here is trouble, now and in the future, on a scale we never saw before."

"We could eliminate some of it," said Maklin. "Hang the offenders. Then we'll have an end to this business."

Roffis picked up a slip of light-blue paper, and read aloud: "All offenses relative to the providing of space transportation to the local inhabitants will be dealt with leniently, as it is High Policy to disperse the Earthmen as rapidly as possible throughout the Integral Union . . .'"

Maklin said, "Argit is behind that. All right, *disperse* them. But *this* means of doing it violates discipline!"

Horsip was again getting that sensation he'd first had on Earth—the feeling of struggling uphill through layers of glue.

Roffis looked as if had a headache. He glanced at the stacks of unread reports.

"Horsip, you've had experience with these Earthmen. What do *you* think of our policy?"

"It won't work. I thought at first that it would, but I don't think so now."

"Why?"

"The Earthmen are too smart. Somehow they'll take over the Integral Union."

"But they'd have to get control of the High Council. The High Council hasn't got an Earthman on it."

"No, sir, but they may not do it that way."

Maklin snarled, "I've run into three separate reports here on how to overthrow governments. It looks to me as if they've had practice."

Roffis massaged his chin. "There must be some way to put the Council on guard—"

There was a rap on the door, and Maklin called, "Come in!"

Half a dozen armed guards came in, escorting an officer and a sergeant. The officer saluted, and put an envelope and receipt form on Horsip's desk.

Horsip signed, and officer and escort went out.

Horsip broke the heavy wax seal, and took out a sheet of thick paper, to read:

By Command
The High Council

Distribution:
>   One (1) copy to Chairman, the Supreme Staff.
>   One (1) copy to Earth Surveillance
>   Subcommittee of the Supreme Staff, through
>   General Klide Horsip.
>   One (1) copy to the Commanding Officer,
>   Special Group "B."

Circulation:
>   All members present of the Supreme Staff;
>   C.O. and C. of S., Special Group "B."

Disposition:
>   Read and return, within the day of receipt.

A. Effective immediately, the Integral Union is divided into two zones:
    (1) Open Zone—That portion marked in red on the enclosed section charts.
        This zone will be open to penetration by the inhabitants of the planet Earth.
    (2) Sealed Zone—That portion left unmarked on the enclosed section charts. Earthmen will be discouraged from entering this zone. Any Earthman who enters this zone will be killed and his body and effects destroyed.

B. Effective immediately, all personnel of Information Facilities in the Open Zone will be withdrawn to the Sealed Zone, and replaced by new personnel.

C. Effective immediately, all Official Charts of the Integral Union in localities within the Open Zone will be delivered to representatives of the High Council, to be replaced by new charts issued by the High Council.

D. Effective immediately, Special Group "B," under the direct control of the High Council, will put in effect all measures necessary to detect and destroy any inhabitants of the planet Earth who penetrate the Sealed Zone.

E. Effective immediately no member of the Supreme Staff will volunteer to any Earthman any information regarding the Sealed Zone, nor acknowledge its existence as an inhabited region.

The punishment for disobedience to any of the above commands will be death, preceded or not preceded at the discretion of the High Council by whatever degree of torture may be deemed to suit the offense. The purpose of these commands is to restrict the influence of the inhabitants of the planet Earth to a limited, although vast, region, so that the nature of that influence may be determined before permitting it to extend over the whole of the Integral Union.

Any failure to obey the spirit as well as the substance of these commands will be dealt with summarily, as the existence of the race is at stake.

> By command of the High Council,
> J. Roggil
> Vice-Chairman

Horsip whistled.

Maklin, reading over Horsip's shoulder, grunted. Roffis said approvingly, "They aren't asleep."

"But," said Maklin, "just how do we keep the Earthmen from getting information that's so widespread?"

Horsip looked inside the envelope, and fished out a set of charts on fine paper. As he leafed through the charts, gradually a picture began to form in his mind. The Council, in dividing the Integral Union, had made use of every hazard and particularly large distance separating one part of the Union from another, to pass a border between two regions in such a way that passage from one region to another not only would appear difficult and unattractive to one not used to space travel, but also that the loss of a ship on such a route would seem understandable.

Roffis straightened. "Maybe it *is* possible."

Maklin nodded. "This is a masterpiece. This Open Zone even has roughly the shape of the whole territory. It's only the scale that's off."

Roffis reread the orders.

"If they've prepared everything this carefully, a trip to an information center would probably convince an Earthman that he had the facts. But what do we do about scholars who know differently?"

Maklin said, "They must have thought of that. What *we* have to do is to make sure our own arrangements don't give us away. For instance, we've already got this Earthman,

Towers, on the Staff with us. He has a perfect right to see our documents and charts."

Roffis said, "We'll have to split the Staff, one part for the Open Zone, and one for the Sealed Zone. The Records Section will have to be split too."

"This could make trouble."

"These Earthmen could make more."

"Well, if Towers should fail, we'll dump him."

Some weeks later, Horsip, methodically working through new reports, pulled out one titled:

Rebellion on Centralis II
Handy Methods and Devices
by Able Hunter.

Able Hunter, of course, was John Towers' code name. Horsip flipped pages, and nodded approval. The report gave the facts plainly and then stopped.

Horsip cleared his throat.

"Towers hasn't fallen on his face yet."

He handed the report to Roffis and Maklin.

As they read, Horsip had a vision of what cooperation with the Earthmen could mean.

While gripped with this enthusiasm, his gaze happened to fall on the upturned title of an unread report:

Entrapment Into Communist Cells—
A Serious and Growing Problem
What is Communism?

The headache that had disappeared with Towers' report came back as Horsip looked over this document. Then there came a sharp rap at the door.

Maklin barked, "Come in!"

Armed guards entered to present Horsip with a sealed envelope.

Horsip drew out a crisp slip of paper reading:

By Command
The High Council

The High Council requires the presence of General Klide Horsip, at once, to report his experiences on the planet Earth, and recent relations between the Integral Union and the inhabitants of the planet Earth.

> J. Roggil
> Vice-Chairman
> The High Council

The High Council was on board a massive warship designed for their use, accompanied by a formidable fleet. Horsip walked down a corridor lined with guards, passed through a door emblazoned with the emblem of Centra in gold, and found himself suddenly in a small room in which sixteen men sat around an H-shaped table, hard at work. One of the men glanced up.

"Ah, General Horsip. Pull up a chair."

In a daze, Horsip heard himself introduced, replied to the brief comments, smiles, and intent glances, then he was seated at an end of the H, explaining Earth to the man who had greeted him, and whose name Horsip in his confusion had already forgotten.

"Then," the member of the High Council was saying, "you believe the Earthmen, on the average, are more intelligent than our own men?"

"No question of that, sir."

"You have no doubt of it?"

"None, sir."

"Now *in what way* are they more intelligent?"

Horsip sat blankly, aware of his questioner's keen gaze, but unable to grasp the question. Then his experiences on Earth came back to him.

"You mean, sir, is it a question of some special skill—"

"Exactly. Intelligence is not an undifferentiated quality, any more than physical strength. If you feel that the

Earthmen are the same as we are mentally, but stronger in every respect, why say so. I want your impression of the strong and weak points mentally."

"They seem to have two strong points—but it may be that they boil down to one—their ability to make clever devices, and their ability with words. Their weak point . . ." Horsip groped around, and shook his head. "I can't think of any weak point."

"You feel that their strong point is a technical skill in handling words, and in handling tools and materials?"

"Yes, sir."

His questioner was intently still for a moment, then sat back.

"Now, Horsip, let's hear your experiences on their planet. I am familiar with your reports, but I'd like to hear it firsthand. Please be frank, and complete. I want your feelings, as well as what happened, and I don't care how long it takes. I want the full account."

Horsip, faltering at first, then gathering confidence as the memories came back, told of his first sight of the planet, and of his irritation with Moffis' description of the difficulties. He described the confident arrival of the Planetary Integration staff, their brisk plans for integrating the planet, and their troubles later on. He described the recovery of the Earthmen's military power, their revolt, and the struggle it took to put that down. At last he described the most recent reports, which fit in with past experience.

Now and then during the long account, Horsip was vaguely aware of continuing activity around him. But his listener, silent and intent, seemed to miss not a word as people came and went, as notes passed around the table, as at a far end of the H a huge map was unrolled and intently examined. A sense of harmony and singleness of purpose was gradually borne in on Horsip. Through the seeming confusion, there seemed to loom underlying order. Then at last he came to the end of his account.

"That," he said, "is all I can tell you, sir. It seems to me that the Earthmen cut deeper than we do, their people are smarter, and they tie us in knots." Horsip glanced around, and added wonderingly, "But I don't think they would tie many people in *this* room in knots."

For an instant Horsip saw the High Council as the Earthmen might see it, and even so, the Council looked formidable.

Some sense of nagging apprehension suddenly evaporated. The name of the man opposite him popped into his head. Jeron Roggil. The names of the people he had been introduced to came back. He had a sudden feeling of confidence.

Roggil said, "Earth may have a higher *average* intelligence, but Centra has a far greater population. In such a population, the number of outstanding intellects is greater, and we value such intellects. Moreover, from what you tell me, the Earthmen *do* have a weakness."

"What's that, sir?"

"A man who does not have much money, Horsip, but who is sensible, tries to use that money wisely. He learns to distinguish between what is truly useful and satisfying, and what rouses his desire but gives no real benefit. A person who has much money is in a different situation. If he is so inclined, he can spend freely, and acquire all manner of possessions. What is showy but worthless does not deprive him of something useful. He can have *both*. What's more, he may not realize, since he is not driven to analyze the situation, what it is that gives him satisfaction. A fool's money may surpass by a hundred or even a thousand times, at the beginning, the money at the disposal of a wise man. And yet—despite this difference— the difference in actual use and satisfaction is nowhere near so great, because a wise man in such a situation will use his money to the greatest effect, while the fool will waste his. Is this not so?"

"Truth," said Horsip, nodding.

"Well, Horsip, we should not be made overconfident by the fact, but from what you have said, it appears to me that these Earthmen are like rich men, in that they have much brainpower—more by far than they strictly need—and the larger part of them have not analyzed what they should spend their brainpower *on.* They do not use it methodically and consistently, as *we* are compelled by brute necessity to do. They *squander* it. Look at this General Towers you speak of. If he were a Centran, he would be on the High Council, never doubt it. We may put him there yet. Already his ability has been recognized, and he is a member of the Supreme Staff. But, with the Earthmen, rather than recognize such ability, his competitors use their mental skill to confuse the issue. We have obtained a good deal of information on the history of the Earthmen. Horsip, the recorded instances in which superior Earthmen, of no matter what degree of ability, have been beaten into the muck by jealous competitors would make you dizzy. The Earthmen squander their mental wealth. They do it as a group, and the bulk of them seem to do it as individuals."

"Nevertheless, sir, when they have as much as they have—"

Roggil nodded intently.

"True, Horsip. But we must bear in mind that there are, in effect, *two* different kinds of brainpower. One is what we ordinarily think of as brainpower—raw intelligence. The other is that directing faculty that guides the *use* of raw brainpower. Both levels must be considered, and we are not inferior on this second level. Moreover, very few contests are contests of intelligence alone. The elements of will, and of pure physical power, for instance, cannot be ignored."

Horsip thought it over. "Truth. But—having fought them—that does not give me as much comfort as it might."

Roggil smiled. "We must certainly do our best. One of the most important things is to keep close track of these Earthmen, and what they are doing. We want an organization devoted entirely to that job. I can think of no one better fitted to head it than you, and you will have a free hand in setting it up."

Roggil reached around to a set of pigeonholes against

the wall behind him, and handed Horsip a slip of crisp white paper.

Horsip read:

By Command
The High Council

By command of the High Council, each and every person without exception in the Integral Union, whatever his rank may be, is required to assist General Klide Horsip in the gathering of information concerning the activities of new citizens of the Integral Union, that their activities be mutually beneficial to the Union and to themselves.

The High Council holds this commission to be of such importance that in carrying it out General Horsip is empowered to act with the inviolable authority of a Full Member of the High Council.

By command of the High Council,
J. Roggil
Vice-Chairman

Horsip swallowed, and looked up at Roggil.

Roggil said seriously, "What we are giving you, Horsip, is no perfumed hammock of sweet flowers, believe me. But the job is urgent, and we aim to see that you get cooperation. As you are a member of the Supreme Staff, few would dare block you. If you should run into opposition on the Staff itself, however, the work could be stopped. In such a case you have the authority to do whatever you choose. You need justify your actions to no one but us. And all *we* are interested in is results. We want a clear picture of what these Earthmen are doing, and we will have it, or the firing squads will go to work."

On the way back in his ship, Horsip worked out the organization he wanted, and decided that what he needed more than anything else was someone he could trust absolutely. At once he thought of Moffis, his military deputy back on Earth.

Once back in his office, Horsip glanced over the bank of phones on the wall, each connected to a different department, and picked up the phone marked "Personnel."

A small voice said, "Personnel, Major Dratig."

"General Horsip speaking. I'd like to know the whereabouts of General Brak Moffis, formerly Military Overseer of the planet Earth."

"Just a moment, sir." There was a sound of file drawers sliding out, and of paper being riffled. "General Moffis is now assigned to the personal staff of General Dorp Takkit of the Supreme Staff as a confidential adviser."

Horsip looked blank. "Confidential adviser?"

"That's what it says here, sir."

"What might that be?"

"I don't know, sir. I never heard of it before."

"How can I get in touch with General Moffis?"

"You'd have to ask General Takkit, sir."

"Is there," growled Horsip, "some reason why I can't reach Moffis direct?"

"Well, sir . . . there's nothing listed here."

"I see. Thank you."

"Yes, sir."

Horsip's teeth bared in a snarl. He was taking down a second phone when there came a rap on the door.

Horsip looked around. "Come in!"

The bull-necked General Maklin stepped in, leather belt and insignia shining.

"Sorry to bother you, Horsip. I can come back later."

"This can wait, sir."

"I'll take the molk by the horns, Horsip," said Maklin. "We're all curious to know what the Council had to say."

"The Council wanted me to set up an organization to keep an eye on the Earthmen."

Maklin looked approving.

"How did they seem?"

"All business, sir."

"Then, at least, there's no softness there. Well, Horsip, I won't take your time. I imagine you're setting things up already."

"Trying to, sir."

"What's wrong?"

"Someone has a man I need."

"Who?"

Horsip hesitated.

Maklin pinned him with his gaze.

Horsip explained the situation.

"Takkit?" Maklin's face darkened. "What does he want with a confidential adviser. What *he* needs is a brain." Then he shook his head. "Once they get on Takkit's personal staff, Horsip, you don't see them again. He gets them working on some private fantasy, and that's the end of them."

"Moffis is just the man I need."

"That won't bother Takkit."

Horsip reached around to his bank of phones, and took down one marked "Sup. St.—Takkit."

A voice spoke, cool and remote:

"Office of Colonel Noffel, Staff Secretary to General Takkit."

Horsip growled, "General Klide Horsip speaking. May I speak to General Takkit?"

"General Takkit is not available."

"Then may I speak to General Moffis?"

"Who?"

"General Brak Moffis."

"Just a moment . . . Now, just what is your name again?"

Across the desk, Maklin, overhearing this, growled under his breath.

Horsip said shortly, "Who am I talking to?"

"I *beg* your pardon?"

"*Who are you?*" snarled Horsip.

There was a *click*, a *buzz*, and a new voice.

"Colonel Noffel speaking."

Horsip said evenly, "This is General Klide Horsip."

"Oh, yes, General Horsip. Congratulations on your appointment to the Staff. General Takkit is tied up, I'm afraid, and won't be free today. If there's anything I can do for you, General Horsip, please feel free to ask. Call me Radge."

Horsip opened his mouth and shut it. He took a fresh grip on the phone. "I want to speak to General Takkit about General Brak Moffis. Moffis is a confidential adviser, as I understand it, to General Takkit."

Noffel's voice became wary.

"What did you wish to speak to General Takkit about General Moffis *for*, General Horsip?"

"I'll make that clear to General Takkit."

"I'm afraid I may not have made the situation clear myself, General Horsip. General Takkit is most particular regarding the protection of his personal staff from outside distractions. I'm afraid if you should raise this question with General Takkit, you might run into—there might be a good deal of—a certain *unpleasantness* which could all be avoided by simply mentioning the matter to me . . . You see?"

Horsip said shortly, "I want to ask General Moffis to work with me in an organiza—"

"Quite out of the question, I'm afraid. General Moffis' time is fully taken up at present. . . . And for the foreseeable future, I might add."

"This organization is—"

"No. I'm *very* sorry, General Horsip. This is a matter of standing policy."

Horsip spoke very politely.

"The High Council has given direct orders to set up this organization. The matter is urgent."

"And *you* are to head this new organization?"

"That's right."

"You are certainly to be congratulated, General Horsip. Permit me to be the first to extend my felicitations to you on this auspicious assignment. But as a new member of the Supreme Staff, you are, of course, junior to General Takkit."

"That's beside the point."

"Not at all. This is quite central to the issue. You wish to—forgive the term—'raid' General Takkit's staff for personnel. General Takkit is your superior officer. Moreover, General Takkit has a prior claim on the individual in question. You wish to use this assignment you have been given by the High Council as a lever to—forgive me—'pry' General Moffis loose from General Takkit's personal staff, disregarding both General Takkit's superior rank and his prior claim on the man in question. We've experienced this sort of thing before. General Takkit's policy is quite clear. Your request, if it is a request, is refused. Pardon me if I speak frankly, General Horsip, but you see, it is much better that I make this clear than that General Takkit be disturbed with this matter . . . Was there anything else?"

Inside Horsip, something wound tighter and tighter, and then snapped.

Horsip suddenly felt very relaxed and at ease.

Horsip said, quietly, "Get Takkit on this line, Colonel."

"The general does not wish—"

"I don't care what he wishes. Get him."

"General Takkit is in confer—"

"Where?"

"In his conference room, and left explicit—"

"Is he in easy reach?"

"Physically, I suppose, but—"

"Get Takkit on this phone."

"The general left specific ord—"

"I don't care what he left. I said get him, and you will get him," said Horsip, pleased that he could be quiet and reasonable about this, "or I will step down the hall and get him myself."

Horsip took down another phone marked "Provost."

A brisk voice came out:

"Provost Marshal's office. Major Rokkis speaking."

Across the desk, General Maklin looked alarmed.

From General Takkit's phone, Colonel Noffel's voice said, with a faint quaver, "I certainly can't carry out this request. It is contrary to General Takkit's specific order."

Horsip spoke into the phone marked "Provost."

"Send a section of guards to my office, equipped to smash down a door."

"Yes, sir! At *once!*"

From Takkit's phone, Noffel's voice cried, "What? What?"

Horsip hung up the phone marked "Provost," and spoke to Noffel.

"You have now put General Takkit in the position of refusing to cooperate with an order of the High Council. Just incidentally, you are defying me by calling a direct order a request. Get Takkit to that phone or face the consequences."

There was silence from Takkit's phone, and then a heavy tramp of feet in the corridor. There was a rap on Horsip's door.

"Captain Bokkil! Guard Section B, at your command, sir!"

Maklin said urgently, "Listen, Horsip, do you know what you're doing?"

"Come in," called Horsip. He pulled open a drawer of his desk, and took out Roggil's order. As the burly captain saluted, Horsip held out the order. "Here's my authority. Now, just wait a minute, while I see if I have to use it."

"Yes, sir!" The captain read the order, saluted, leaned into the hall, and shouted, "Splat-gunners to the front! Hurry up with that ram!"

A grating voice spoke from Takkit's phone:

"This is Dorp Takkit speaking. I will say this only once. Your request is refused. That is final."

There was a *click*.

Horsip turned to the guard captain. "Knock on General Takkit's door. If they don't open, order it opened in the name of the High Council. If they refuse, smash it down. Ask General Takkit to get on the phone to me here, and if he refuses, put him under arrest, by authority of the High Council, and bring him down here."

A few minutes later, the guards smashed down the door, and dragged a furious Takkit into Horsip's office.

Horsip showed the struggling Takkit the order signed by Roggil, and Takkit knocked it from his hand. Horsip read it, and Takkit shouted so loudly that neither he nor anyone else could hear it. Takkit commanded the guards to release him, and one of them, awed by Takkit's rank and fury, let go. The guard captain himself pinned Takkit's arms,

Horsip said, "I shot him, Moffis. He was making off with your bag."

"What's he doing now?"

"Don't ask me."

As Moffis came back with his bag, a small man emerged from the crowd wearing a tag reading "Press," and bent beside the nearer thief. A second person, taller and carrying a camera, pushed through the crowd. The man wearing the "Press" tag spoke sympathetically to the thief.

"What happened, fella?"

The thief said eagerly, "It was terrible. One of them held me while the other shot me and beat me up. I got a real wound. Do you suppose you could get a doctor?"

"Not now. What happened?"

"Will this come out with my name on it and everything?"

"Sure, don't worry."

"Can I sue?"

"Of course you can sue. Come on, come on, let's have it! I haven't got all day!"

"This hurts awful."

"It can wait. Here we go. What happened, fella? Did the beasts get you? Speak right into the mike."

"Yeah. They ... they shot me. They held me. They beat me. I ... I'm weak."

The Centran reporter raised the microphone, and spoke into it smoothly. "In the Integral Union, here in a main thoroughfare of a principal city on the planet, even here citizens are not safe from the attacks of the murderers. They learned to kill on foreign planets, and now they bring their blood-lust home with them. . . . Fella, I don't know what to say to you. I . . . I guess *all* of us are guilty. . . ."

Moffis glanced at Horsip.

"Which one is the thief?"

"The one on the ground."

Moffis looked baffled.

The Centran reporter gestured to the photographer, and rose from beside the thief.

"Yes, we all are guilty, for allowing *beasts* to walk among us like *men*. There!" He pointed dramatically at Horsip and Moffis.

"There they are!" cried the reporter. "The kill-crazed murderers! This time the people must rise against the cowards!"

There was a murmur from the crowd.

Moffis gave a start.

"Cowards?"

He dumped his bag on the sidewalk, and stepped forward.

The Centran reporter backed up into the crowd.

The crowd looked interested, and shoved him forward.

"Wait a minute," said the reporter. He glanced at the photographer. "Help!"

The photographer eagerly raised his camera.

Moffis smashed the reporter on the jaw, knocking him back into the crowd. The crowd, cheering, heaved him forward, and Moffis knocked him flat.

Someone pushed past Horsip, and from his long brown robes, Horsip recognized a Centran monk.

The monk, tall and severe, loomed over Moffis, who gave a guilty start.

The monk looked at the outstretched reporter, then smiled benignly upon Moffis. "Son, do not let me disturb your righteous work."

He turned to Horsip. "I see you are both new here, my sons. If you will get your baggage together, perhaps I can be of assistance."

Horsip, who could use any assistance anyone could offer, nodded agreement. He and Moffis got their bags.

The monk looked grimly at the reporter, then glanced at the pickpocket and thieves.

"So, this is the latest benefit you have derived from the search after money without work? Put your ingenuity to use finding a way you can help someone, then sell your service to *him*. . . . And, why not pray a little now and then? What hurt can it do?"

The pickpocket and thieves looked embarrassed and muttered incoherently.

The monk nodded to Horsip and Moffis.

"This way, my sons. As you see, I have no truck with these new inventions, but use sensible transportation which should suffice for any man."

Horsip, carrying his bag under one arm, waited till the traffic let up, then followed across the street, with Moffis right behind him. On the far side waited a four-wheeled coach drawn by a creature whose long powerful body appeared built to deliver dazzling bursts of speed. Its large paws were armed with sharp, partially retracted claws, and, as it cleaned its short black fur, its blood-red tongue licked out past teeth like daggers.

The monk opened the door on the left side of the coach. "After you, my sons."

Horsip uneasily climbed in, but Moffis paused. "Your . . . ah . . . loadbeast, Reverend Father—what breed is that?"

The monk beamed. "That, my son, is a man-eating gnath. Gnaths, you know, are said to be killers by nature. Their reflexes are so fast it is impossible to follow their motions. Their teeth are very strong, of a hardness which rivals diamond. The jaws have compound leverage, with an action similar to a ratchet, and can bring terrible pressure to bear on the prey. Few zoos can hold the gnath. It has been known to chew steel bars into bits to exercise its jaws. See the size of its head? It is highly intelligent, but much of that head is skull, of unusual thickness, armored with the substance that makes its teeth so tough. A single gnath has been known to slaughter almost a whole company of soldiers before one managed to hit the heart with a lucky shot. The ribs of the animal are flat, they overlap, and, like the rest of its bone, they are exceptionally hard and tough, so that the bullet must penetrate the abdomen at just the right angle to reach the heart. Since the gnath moves so fast, it is, of course, difficult to make this shot while being attacked by the beast."

Moffis uneasily put his hand to his holster, then let go with a dazed look.

The monk, beaming benignly, said, "I have raised this

gnath from a cub, feeding it vegetables and milk, and radiating thoughts of universal love and brotherhood in its presence. By kind treatment, its manners have been transformed." He lowered his voice. "Get in, brother, or the bystanders over there—what are left of them—may think you do not trust the Great One to protect you."

The monk followed Moffis in, shut the door, and swung around a kind of semicircular latch that snicked into its rests like a bolt.

He seated himself, and took the reins, which went out two vertical slits under the thick front window. He gave the reins a light shake.

The gnath leaned forward.

The carriage jerked into motion.

The gnath lazily stretched out his legs. The carriage rolled briskly behind.

After traveling some time in silence, the monk said, "There are now those on this planet who would not hesitate to take advantage of the Brotherhood. . . . Look there!"

Up ahead, the huge factory was coming into view. An elaborate ground-car, with a silver bird on the front end, was starting out onto the road.

The monk slapped the reins.

The gnath leaned into the harness. The carriage picked up speed.

Up ahead, the ground-car came to an abrupt stop, backed, turned, and headed for the factory, a cloud of dust stretching behind it.

The gnath sniffed and growled as he passed through the dust cloud from the car.

The monk slowed, to turn off onto a narrower road.

"That ground-car back there," he said, "belongs to the manager of the factory. Some weeks ago he tried to force me off the road." The monk gave a spare smile. "He was not yet acquainted with the nature of the gnath."

Horsip thought this over in silence. Such conduct, toward the Holy Brotherhood, was almost inconceivable.

"Is it only the factory manager who is responsible or—"

"It is anyone who submits to the teachings of the Earthmen."

"Perhaps there is some misunderst—"

"Bah! We understand each other well enough. Either the Earthmen's system or ours must break, and they well know it. Yet, bad as the Earthmen are, they are as nothing compared to our own people, once converted to their ways. That gossip-mongering 'reporter' is an example of it. We had an Earth reporter here not long ago, teaching how it was done. The fellow was unbearable. But not as unbearable as our own men when they do the same thing. The Earthmen have *some* restraint."

"Yet they break down our ways?"

"Their theories twist facts, present the doer of evil as a harmless fellow, and the honest man who does his duty as some kind of fiend. They make the average person uncertain where to turn. He is hag-ridden by all their conflicting subtleties and false guides. I tell you, these Earthmen—"

Moffis gripped Horsip by the arm.

"Look—behind us."

Horsip turned. Coming along the road behind, an armored ground-car trailed a cloud of dust, and gained steadily on them. Behind it, at an angle, as if to block the other side of the road, came a second armored ground-car.

Horsip looked around. The road was narrow, bordered on both sides by rows of trees.

The armored cars closed the distance fast.

From the nearest of the cars came the flat commanding blast of a horn.

Moffis drew his gun.

The monk smiled. "No, my son, trust that those who do evil will be punished."

There was a slight *bump*, and the carriage tilted. Through the carriage's rear windows, only the flat gray tops of the armored cars could now be seen.

The ground-cars dropped back again, then surged forward.

The monk, watching, gripped the brake lever, drew it

back with a loud ratcheting click, and shoved it over and back. He jerked a knotted cord on the dashboard, and gave a penetrating whistle.

With a loud scream from the wheels, the carriage slowed. The gnath bounded free of the traces. There was a thud-*click*, as padded meal shutters dropped over the windows.

The horn blast grew suddenly loud. There was a slam, a crash, and the carriage tipped heavily.

The world seemed to turn over as the carriage careened to a stop. There was the sound of smashing glass, screams and curses, and then a bloodthirsty roar that startled Horsip out of unconsciousness. The carriage was bobbing slightly, the inside dark. Horsip unlatched a shutter and looked out.

Jammed between two trees was one of the armored ground-cars. The other was on its back, wheels up, The gnath, one end of a metal plate in his mouth, rivets sticking out like torn threads, muscles standing out on his big forelimbs, slowly straightened up to a loud *ik-ik-ik* noise and the scream of straining metal.

There was a loud snap, and the gnath tossed the massive plate into the air. Gears and shafts flew in all directions. Then the gnath worried the engine out of the wreckage, peeled back the firewall, crouched, lashed his long tail, and insinuated his head into the ground-car's passenger compartment. There was the banging of a pistol, then screams.

Horsip tried to get up, saw the whole world turn end-for-end, and everything went black.

Somewhere there was a murmur of voices, the slam of a door. Horsip opened his eyes, to find himself looking up at the lower limbs of a big tree. Propping himself on one elbow, he could see a shambles of metal plates, gears, axles, a shaft with steering wheel on one end, wiring harness with the generator still attached, fan belts, coolant hoses, bandoliers of ammunition, strewn over the road, hanging from the lower branches of trees, or scattered in the grass. The largest piece he could see was a length of I-beam two feet long, with the sun glinting on a freshly sheared end.

A third ground-car, this one not armored, had stopped in the road, and Moffis was standing beside it talking to an individual with broad shoulders and brawny arms, who beamed expansively upon Moffis.

"Honored sir, I shall be happy to welcome you to my dwelling, and if your superior is hurt, we may summon a healer, as I have a long-talker hooked up right in my own house. I am off work for the day, and will help you all I can. Let's see, you say there was a whole ground-car here— in one piece—when the wreck happened?"

Horsip looked around, to see the carriage still in good shape, but with an outline in crushed wood at the rear. Looking at the carriage, Horsip became aware of a steely glint from underneath the splintered wood.

At the far end of the carriage, the gnath placidly cleaned itself, radiating contentment and well-being.

Horsip got to his feet, and saw the monk sitting up. Horsip helped him up. The monk's eyes glinted.

"There," he murmured, "is *more* work of the Earthmen. You see that fellow? Sark Rottik is a good honest work-man, skilled at his craft. But if he has two brass halfpennies to scrape together, I will be surprised. . . . He has every-thing else, I'll grant."

The workman called, "Greeting, Reverend Father. What happened? It looks as if a junk wagon ran into you."

"The last I knew, there were two armored ground-cars behind us. Luckily, our workshops build strong."

"I see no one lying hurt from the other vehicle, at least," said Rottik.

"No?" The monk looked momentarily blank, glanced at the gnath, looked serious, and turned to Horsip and Moffis.

"I had intended to offer you hospitality. But . . . this situation requires attention. Perhaps . . ." He glanced ques-tioningly at Sark Rottik, who beamed.

"I have already invited them. My ground-car is right here. We can go at once."

Horsip and Moffis said good-by to the preoccupied monk,

and their new host ushered them to a ground-car with leather seats, folding top, and an impressive array of instruments. The ground-car gave a whine, then a howl, shoved them back in the seats, and was moving fast before Horsip could get the door shut. Rottik grinned.

"The Earthmen designed it, but I helped build it. Observe the floating action. The Earthmen are wonderful! . . . My house is just up ahead, conveniently close to my work."

They rounded a curve, shot up a side road, braked, rounded another curve, and there loomed in front of them a kind of palace, administration building, or headquarters of the planetary governor, with flagpole, swimming pool, mansion of gray stone trimmed with yellow wood, neatly mowed lawn, graveled walks, and avenues of flowering trees.

Radiating pride, Rottik drove up the broad driveway, to stop under an overhanging roof supported by stone pillars and wrought-iron lattice up which vines of purple flowers climbed.

As Horsip and Moffis stared around, Rottik got out, beaming, felt through his pockets, pulled out a small gold key ring, and bent briefly at a massive paneled door. The door swung noiselessly open.

Rottik grinned, and bowed to the speechless Horsip and Moffis.

"I am as yet unmarried, so that my hospitality is limited. But you will find the stocks of foods and beverages complete, as they came with the house. Also the linens. Everything is included on the Revolving All-Payment Plan. Please make yourself at home, and if you want anything, just ask for it. I am sure I have got it here somewhere."

A few minutes later, in a palatial guest room on the second floor, Horsip and Moffis stood at a big window.

"If this is what comes of cooperating with the Earthmen," said Moffis, "I can see why anyone would cooperate with them."

Horsip looked out at the water sparkling against the pale-green tiles of the swimming pool.

"I have to admit, Moffis . . ." He paused, frowning. "On

the other hand, I wonder what a 'Revolving All-Payment Plan' is?"

Moffis looked thoughtfully at the walks, pool, bathhouse, green lawns, and statue of a demure female with water spurting out the top of her head.

"H'm," he said. "We will have to ask about that."

Part V:
The Toughest Opponent

Colonel John Towers, personally commanding Independent Division III of his Special Effects Team, whose modest name gave little indication of its ability to create pain and suffering amongst its enemies, had learned from long experience that danger did not come just from those enemies.

Towers heard Logan's sharp intake of breath, and the *snap* as Logan's holster-flap whipped open. Towers knew that his second-in-command, right behind him, could have his service automatic in action in a fraction of a second. The scene around them flashed through Towers' mind, his eyes and memory showing him the massive wall of logs and stone, the orderly rows of barracks, and the Centran guards that had been standing on the wall, glancing idly down as Towers' landing-boat settled into place. In that instant Towers realized where the danger must come from.

He abruptly straightened, the cloth of his uniform tightening as he drew his breath in sharply, and pivoted on his heel to face the Centran troops on the wall.

In the same instant, his suddenly keyed-up mind separated from the meaningless gabble around them a string of words in Centran, and gave him the translation:

" . . . Furless, tailless aliens impersonating officers. Shoot the . . ."

As Towers turned, he could see in sharp detail every tiny fold of cloth, and every facial line of the soldiers on the wall, their guns raised and aimed at him.

From Towers' right came the faint *click* as the safety went off on Logan's automatic, and the fusion charges needed only a slight touch on the trigger to release their bolts of controlled destruction.

Towers had just time to notice, in the faces of the Centran troops, a trace of hesitation.

"You there!" he barked in fluent Centran. "You men on the wall! *Who's in charge there?*"

Towers saw the hesitation waver into uncertainty. He realized he had unconsciously gripped Logan's arm in warning, and now released the pressure. Glaring at the Centrans, who still looked at him over their guns, he roared, "What the devil is this nonsense?"

Abruptly, he ignored the rest of them, and focused his gaze on the uneasiest face.

"Sergeant!"

"S-Sir?" The Centran noncom glanced uncertainly at Towers' insignia.

Towers demanded, "Are those men off-duty?"

The sergeant hesitated.

"Answer me!" roared Towers. "Are they off-duty?"

The other Centrans glanced at each other, and lowered their guns unhappily.

"No, sir," said the sergeant.

"What *are* they supposed to be doing?"

"Watch and guard, sir," said the sergeant.

"Watch and guard!" said Towers. He stared at the sergeant as if he couldn't believe it. Then he exploded. "By the Great Hungry Mikeril! Get those men back to their posts, or I'll have those stripes of yours nailed to the latrine door, and you'll spend the next six months inside with a scrub brush!"

The sergeant jumped as if he'd been touched with a live wire. He gave Towers a lightning salute, then all but threw the men off the wall in his haste to straighten things out.

Narrow-eyed, Towers looked around. The Centrans on the wall were now earnestly going about their duties. Directly in front of Towers, in the space cleared for landing-boats, was an unhappy Centran captain, his arm raised in a salute. A pace behind stood a paralyzed lieutenant. Towers looked them over coldly.

Beside him, Logan murmured a low oath, and Towers heard the faint slide-snap as Logan shoved his automatic back in its holster and shut the flap. Towers looked hard at the Centran captain, then returned his salute.

"S-Sir," stammered the captain, "General Klossig, Military Overseer of the planet, requests that you see him immediately. I can take you to him at once, sir, and if you wish to arrange barracks space for your men—"

Towers glanced at Logan, who said promptly, "I'll take care of it, sir."

"Good." Towers went off with the captain. A backward glance showed him Logan following the lieutenant toward a far corner of the camp.

"Sir," said the captain walking beside Towers. "I'm sorry about that business back at the wall. The men are jumpy. They've never seen Earthmen before. And to tell the truth, this planet is driving us all out of our heads."

"What's the trouble?"

"The natives just won't give up. I was in on the invasion of Earth, and I remember what *that* was like. But at least we could respect our opponents. Here . . . well, it's like fighting humanoid gnats. No matter how many you kill, they never quit. You can't make any treaty with them. They don't catch on. You can't win, and you can't end it. It's—" He shook his head, led the way up a flight of steps, and down the hall to a door marked, "Maj. Gen. Horp Klossig, Military Overseer."

The captain held the door open. "If you'll just step right in, sir. General Klossig wants to see you at once."

Towers passed through a small anteroom, and found himself before a desk stacked with papers. On the other side of the desk sat a powerfully built Centran in major-general's uniform, irritably flipping through a report. On the desk was the nameplate: "H. Klossig, Overseer."

"Ah-h," rumbled Klossig, and loosened his collar with a furry hand. He slammed the report backhanded against the wall, where it hit with a sharp *whack* and fell to the floor. Without looking up, he reached out and jerked a fresh report from the nearest pile. He flipped through it. "Junk, junk, junk," he muttered.

Towers hesitantly cleared his throat.

The general gave an automatic flip of his hand, and slung the report across the room into the fireplace. He jerked another from the pile, glanced at the title, and stiffened. He pressed the report flat on the desk, read for a few moments, and swore in a low voice. He looked up, furious.

Towers saluted, and reported his presence.

Klossig looked blank for an instant, then sprang to his feet. His face lit up. He reached across the desk and gripped Towers by the hand. "I've heard of your Special Effects Team!"

"Sir, I just have Independent Division III with me."

"But you're the ones with the motto, 'We'll Find a Way'?"

"Yes, sir."

"Good enough. That's just what I need." Klossig waved a hand at the stack of reports. "The motto of these people is, 'There is no way. It's too hard. Let's all jump off the cliff together.' Here"—he snatched up the report he'd just been reading—"take a look at this. Read the heading, then look at that first sentence."

Towers glanced at the heading, which read, "The Invariant Law of Growth and Decline."

Towers frowned, and read the first sentence: "To all societies, as to all creatures, comes at last the realization that the knell of their greatness has sounded, and some outwardly small sign or omen reveals to them the irreversible nature of their imminent decline; just so, to we of the Integral Union, who perhaps with greater percipience than our forbears, and a wiser maturity, may accept as we must with undismayed resignation the portents of the disintegration of our society which are revealed to us by our experiences upon this planet."

Towers had the sensation of being mentally treated with perfumed mustard gas.

"That," said Klossig, "was written by a prominent sociopsychometrodiagnostician on the Planetary Integration staff. Read some more. It will give you a good idea of morale here. Morale is half my problem."

Towers flipped back through the report. Phrases like "inevitable rise and decline," "the dark forces of destiny," "immutable laws of historical development," "the hour of a culture's foreordained passage into the limbo of the past," flew at him like so many bats out of a cave. At the end came the summary: "And so, like all the societies of the past, at last we find ourselves before the fatal door. Not ours the choice to enter or refuse. Ours only to choose whether we shall go quietly, retaining for a time, perhaps, our dignity if not our power; for the implacable laws of historical development have laid down their verdict, and there can be no choice save to comply. We can determine not our fate, but only how we accept our fate. As it comes upon us, then, let us accept it humbly, with such of dignity as we can muster. For this is enough in the face of the immutable laws. It is enough. It is enough."

Towers looked up, and took a breath of air. Leaving the report open to the summary, he handed it back to Klossig. Klossig glanced at the summary, read it, and changed color. He balanced the paper in his hand, as if undecided what he could do to it that would do it justice.

Towers said thoughtfully, "People like that sometimes found schools."

Klossig nodded gloomily, and tossed the paper onto his desk. "He has already. But what can I do with him? To begin with, the fellow has a reputation. And he's not basically bad-intentioned. He's just cracking up under the strain of this planet. The attempt to get a solution to the problem has overloaded his circuits. If I come down on him as I could in the ordinary kind of situation, the whole Planetary Integration staff will resent it. How the devil do I shut him up, and break up his defeatist ideas, without tearing my organization apart in the process?"

Towers considered the question. "Would he still be competent to handle a simpler problem?"

"If it were reasonably straightforward? Yes."

"Why not take him off your problems with the planet, and assign him to the problem of tracing down *the causes of bad morale?*"

Klossig blinked. For a moment, he stood with his chin in his hand, then suddenly he grinned. "You've got it. He'll hang onto the problem till he traces down every cause of bad morale, and sooner or later he'll discover amongst the causes certain reports written by associates of his. The associates will explain that they were only following his lead. But he will be immersed in the new problem and he will think that they are trying to saddle *him* with the blame for what *they* did. Then the sodium shot will really hit the lake. Excuse me just a moment."

Klossig went outside, and Towers could hear him on some kind of personal intercom system, praising the scientist for his good work, and urging him to take on the problem of isolating individual causes of deterioration of morale. In the moments of comparative silence when Klossig was not speaking, Towers could hear a sound he hadn't noticed before—a distant sound of almost continuous rifle fire from somewhere outside.

Then Klossig came back in. "That takes care of that," he said. "But that's just a drop in the bucket. Come on. There's something out here you've got to see."

Klossig led the way out, down the front steps of the headquarters building, and along a well-traveled walk toward a side of the wall that ran at right angles to that where the Centran soldiers had taken aim at Towers and Logan. As they walked, Klossig was saying, "The trouble with life, Towers, is that it presents an endless selection of choices between undesirable alternatives. For instance, if a man wishes to act sensibly, he should first understand the situation thoroughly. But, if he waits till he understands the situation thoroughly, the opportunity for action passes. The result is, we have to make a quick estimate of the most important factors, then act fast while we have the chance. This means we have to take certain elements of the situation for granted. Every now and then, this taking things for granted lands us in a mess. That's what has happened on this planet."

"How so?" said Towers.

Klossig paused at a strip of ground paved with crushed rock, glanced in both directions, and waited while a ground-car bounced past pulling a four-wheeled trailer filled with ammunition cans. Then he started forward, saying, "We assumed all humanoid races would develop the same way—from family to tribe to city to nation. From hunters to farmers to builders. It never dawned on us that we were taking for granted the basis of this process, which is poor adaptation of the race to its environment."

"But that process of development *is* an adaptation of the race to its environment."

"A *roundabout* adaptation. It presupposes the failure of more direct methods of adaptation. What do you suppose happens when a humanoid race is, for instance, so well-adapted to its environment that *the search for food presents no problem?*"

Klossig paused at the foot of the stairs that led to the top of the wall and glanced at Towers. "That's not just a hypothetical question."

"Well," said Towers, after a moment's hesitation, "it would certainly result in a terrific population growth. But the result would still be, sooner or later, that food *would* present a problem."

Klossig started up the steps. "The trouble is, we've always taken it for granted that that problem would turn up sooner, not later. Assuming there is an abundance of food to begin with, what type of social organization will come about?"

Towers thought it over. "Unless there were some powerful predators to contend with, all that would really be needed would be the family, to care for small children."

Klossig nodded. "But remember, if you have the mental picture of a family huddled in a cave in the middle of the wilderness, with another family squatting around a camp fire somewhere on the horizon, you are forgetting the abundance of food. What is going to happen as these families multiply with no restraint save that of occasional plagues and natural disasters?"

Towers frowned. "If the food were really abundant, there would be a—" He hesitated as the picture dawned on him.

"Yes," said Klossig. "Now you see it. The result would an unprecedented situation—a planetary mob."

"But there *couldn't* be that much food!" Towers regretted the comment as soon as he'd made it, but Klossig merely nodded in understanding.

"The trouble," said Klossig, "is that we automatically take for granted a maladaptation of humanoid to environment. Of *course*, there isn't so much food that fruit cascades continuously from the trees, and small animals present themselves eagerly to be eaten. That's the way it would have to be for *us*, who can eat only certain rare parts of the environment. Here, it's different."

Klossig and Towers were almost at the top of the stairs. Klossig paused to break from the log wall beside the steps a large chunk of thick corky bark. He looked at it with a peculiar exasperated expression, and handed it to Towers.

Towers scowled, and studied it. The bark was heavier that it appeared, dark gray, and apparently homogeneous. He sniffed it, and noticed no scent. He squeezed it, and it yielded slightly to his pressure, than recovered elastically as he loosened his grip. He glanced curiously at Klossig.

Klossig nodded sourly. "That chunk of bark represents nothing but inert matter to you and me. The natives find it highly nutritious, if not tasty." Klossig pointed the length of the wall, and Towers looked at the mass of thick gray bark that covered the big logs. "Think of that," said Klossig, "not as 'bark,' but as so much steak or root crops. There are whole forests of those trees down there. You and I can't eat them. But the natives here *can*. They have a digestion that can cope with just about every plant and animal they come up against. They are *adapted*."

Klossig and Towers climbed to the top of the wall, where there was a flat walk about fifteen feet across, with a parapet not quite waist high at the edge.

Klossig walked to the parapet, and pointed down. "And here," he said, "is the result of that adaptation."

Towers looked down, through rows of spike-bar barriers, so that his gaze traveled down the wall to the sheer cliff on which the wall was built, and down the cliff, where thin clouds drifted by, to the dense forest, small and hazy down below.

On the cliff face, something moved. Towers looked closely, and suddenly realized that a small humanlike figure was climbing the cliff. There was another motion, and Towers saw another figure, to one side, and lower down.

The firing he had heard earlier was louder now, and the wind brought a sharp smell of gunpowder. Towers looked up.

Projecting out from the wall on log struts and braces, a covered wooden platform hung far out over the edge of the cliff, connected to the top of the wall by a swaying catwalk across which two Centran soldiers carried a load of ammunition cans. On the platform lay several Centran soldiers, aiming at the wall.

Towers glanced down. One of the little figures he'd seen earlier suddenly jerked, lost its grip, dropped down the face of the cliff, struck it and bounded back, to fall, tumbling over and over, and dwindling in apparent size, till it was lost from view against the hazy forest far below.

Towers glanced at the outthrust platform, where the soldiers had ceased fire. Suddenly one of them pointed. They shifted their position a trifle, and opened fire.

Klossig said, "Population pressure, Towers. On the top of high buttes such as these, there are often forests of old gnarled trees, lichen, moss, and other things useless to most races, but a family or two of these humanoids could live up here."

"And what would they do when the others climbed up?"

"Throw them off. Or get thrown off themselves. What else could they do?"

Towers looked down at the forest far below. "What's it like down there?"

"Alternate paradise and hell. When a plague goes

through, it cuts the population to the bone. Then, till the population builds up again, there's overflowing abundance for all. But then, the population *does* build up. There's food for a thousand people to subsist on, but there are twelve hundred people there. The result is chaos, slaughter, and cannibalism. Whoever doesn't shove his neighbor to the wall gets shoved to the wall himself. Think what it's like down there to make a climb up that cliff seen attractive by comparison."

Towers glanced down at the cliff face. "What happens if one of them *does* get up here?"

"Hell on wheels," said Klossig. "They're savages—as who wouldn't be in that spot?—but that doesn't help us any. They attack on sight."

"What if you meet them down below?"

"Same thing. They see us. *Wham!* They attack us."

"Are they dangerous to well-armed troops?"

"Not in a cleared space, no. In the forests, they're dangerous enough. We've had a number of clashes with them under both conditions, and it was no fun, I can tell you that."

"What's it like?"

"Men, women, and children take part in the attack. There's no warning. There's no organization. They may use their bare hands, sticks, or rocks. If they get you—then you're dead. There's no mercy. If you get them, that's just a temporary expedient. It doesn't mean much. There are others to step right into the place of those you've killed. All you accomplish by killing them is to relieve the population pressure a trifle."

Towers said, "From the way they act, how do we know they're humanoids? That presupposes some brains on their part."

"They're humanoids, all right," said Klossig. "We've tested individual captives, and they have brains enough to qualify—as individuals, that is."

"Yes," said Towers slowly. "I see. You aren't up against them as individuals."

"Exactly," said Klossig. "That's the whole thing. We are

up against them as a mob. We can't make peace with them. There's no organization to deal with. It's just one huge mob. Now, what do we do?"

Towers looked out at the forested land mass stretching into the distance.

Klossig said, "The purpose of the Integral Union is to unite all human and humanoid races in an interstellar organization for mutual benefit and defense. That's our reason for existence, and the justification for our actions. If *we* don't do it, somebody else may, and not for mutual benefit, either. Now, here we are, up against it. Either we solve this problem, or at the same time we lose a rich planet, and fail a humanoid race that's caught in a truly vicious trap."

From somewhere in the distance, Towers heard a shot. Dimly, the thought went through his mind that the platform thrust out from the wall here was badly located. The outer edge of the wall itself, like the walls of ancient cities back on Earth, did not run a perfectly straight line, but was set out at intervals to allow a view of adjacent sections of the wall. The outthrust platform should have been built twenty feet or so farther to the left, to allow a view of the corner made by the edge of this set-out part of the wall. This thought passed through Towers' mind as the thought may occur to a man that a picture is a trifle off-center. He would have forgotten it, but at that moment he heard the shout from somewhere along the wall, glanced around, and chanced to look down at the corner of the parapet.

A large hand, covered with coarse reddish-yellow hairs, gripped the edge of the parapet.

What happened next took place almost too fast to follow. A second hand joined the first at the edge of the parapet. Towers reached for his gun, and at the same time shouted a warning to Klossig. The two hands atop the wall tensed, and abruptly a head of wiry tangled hair above two frenzied eyes thrust up into view. Towers had the impression of a mouth full of bared teeth, a shout with an almost physical impact, a fluid blur of motion, and he was knocked back against the parapet.

For an instant, Towers was at the edge of the parapet, a little less than waist-high. Then something hit him and heaved his legs roughly up and over. A shout of triumph followed him into empty space, and then he was falling, too far out to have any chance to catch the wall.

An instant later, something smashed into the back of his left shoulder like a sack of cement. He flung his arms out, felt himself whirl, then wall and sky pivoted to show him nothing but the cliff and the sheer drop through the cloud to the forest below.

His left arm was around something solid.

Towers gripped with convulsive strength, his heart pounded, and a second later, he saw that he had hit one of the log struts that supported the outthrust platform.

The triumphant yell was still echoing from the wall above, and Towers' sudden fear abruptly changed into rage. He twisted around, heaved himself up onto the strut, and went up it as an island native on Earth goes up a palm tree. He went from the strut to the platform, from the platform to the catwalk, and from the catwalk to the wall.

Before him was an open ring of soldiers with guns raised, but afraid to use them, as Klossig and a hairy muscular yellow-red form spun in a grapple that whirled them from the parapet to the unprotected inner edge of the wall.

Towers dove for the pair, shot his right arm around the humanoid's neck, clamped his right hand at the inside of his left elbow, and shoved his left hand against the back of the wiry head. Then he tightened the grip with every ounce of strength he had.

Abruptly, he was whirling through the air again, but this time all he felt was a grim satisfaction that the cause of his trouble was locked fast in his grip, its bones and joints straining under the compound pressure.

There was a sudden terrific impact, then blackness.

Towers slowly opened his eyes, and there was a circle of Centrans around him, the wall rising nearby. The massive furry figure of Horp Klossig was bent over him anxiously.

It dawned on Towers that this time he had landed on the

inside of the wall. He took a slow breath and felt carefully for broken bones. He seemed to be all right. Carefully, he rolled to one knee, waited a moment, then stood up.

Klossig steadied him. "Are you all right?"

Towers nodded, then remembered something and looked narrowly around.

Two Centran soldiers were lugging an inert figure up the steps. They reached the top and stepped onto the wall.

As they approached the parapet, they vanished from Towers' view, because of his angle of vision, then reappeared, empty-handed. They glanced at each other with pursed lips, then started back down the steps.

Klossig said, his voice tense with emotion, "Towers, listen—"

Towers noticed the circle of Centran troops standing around.

"Sir," said Towers, "are these men supposed to be on guard duty?"

Klossig looked around. His brows came together. "What the devil is this?" He sent the men scurrying back to the wall, then turned to Towers, and said fervently, "If you need anything, Towers, just ask for it."

"Thank you, sir."

The two men looked at each other a moment, then Towers saluted, Klossig returned the salute, and Towers set off to get hold of Logan and arrange to bring the first of his men down.

Towers met Logan, coming from the corner of the camp where the Centran lieutenant had taken him to arrange for barracks space. Logan's expression was set and angry. He saluted as soon as he saw Towers, then his expression changed to concern.

"What happened, sir?"

Towers was thinking over what had happened back at the wall, and was trying to figure out how the native had managed to climb up and heave him over the edge before he could even get his gun out of its holster. The memory made him angry, and his voice came out in a rasp that made Logan wince.

"Not a damned thing happened," said Towers. "Have we got the barracks space?"

"Sir," said Logan, coloring, "the Centran colonel in charge of the arrangements has allowed us six double bunks in one corner of one barrack."

Towers had felt nothing but a kind of light-headed vagueness when he got up after the fall, but he was now beginning to ache all over, and on top of that, a hammering headache was just getting started.

"Six double bunks in one corner of one barrack," said Towers tonelessly.

"Yes, sir. And to top it off, he says we will have a certain amount of 'good-natured hazing' from the Centran troops in the barracks. He says they aren't accustomed to associating with 'alien entities.' "

Towers' left side and shoulder felt as if a large iron hook was imbedded in it. His head throbbed painfully.

"Where is this Centran colonel?" said Towers.

Logan hesitated.

"Where is he?" said Towers.

"I suppose he's still in his office, sir."

"Lead the way."

Logan paled, and started toward the large headquarters building where Towers had seen Klossig. As Logan turned, the sun shone briefly on the cover of something clamped to his belt. Through the headache, it took Towers an instant to realize that that was the cover of the case that held the little transceiver Logan had brought along to keep in touch with Towers' division of the Special Effects Team.

"Wait a minute," said Towers. "Have you gotten any of the men started down here yet?"

"No, sir. With only a corner of a barrack—"

"All right. Order down a dozen men, all controllers or operators, with squads of close-trained wolves, lions and armored gorillas. Also the biggest superconda we've got in running order. Bring them down as soon as possible in the nearest landing space to that barracks, and move in."

Logan enthusiastically repeated the order into the transceiver, along with detailed instructions for locating the barracks. Then he started toward the headquarters building.

Towers said, "I thought you went right over to the barracks with the lieutenant after we landed?"

"I did, sir. Then after I'd picked out suitable barracks space, he brought me over to fill out forms and took them in to the colonel. The colonel crossed out everything on the forms, wrote in 'six double bunks northeast corner Barracks A12 will be sufficient,' read the riot act, and that was that."

They climbed the stairs of the headquarters building, and Towers' headache developed an effect similar to that of being struck at the base of the head with a sledgehammer at every step. When he could force the words out, Towers said, "What was his reason?"

"He doesn't like our table of organization. I tried to explain to him that a Special Effects Team unit doesn't have as many *men* as most organizations of similar size, but that we have a lot more equipment, so one of our twelve-men companies takes just as much space as the usual company. But I couldn't get started. Every time I opened my mouth, he'd demand to know whether twelve soldiers weren't twelve soldiers regardless what race they belong to. Next he wanted to know how big our men were that they took up so much room. That's how it went."

Towers said nothing as they walked down the hall, and Logan opened a door and stepped aside. Towers stepped in, and nearly walked into a desk set so close to the door that there was room for just one straight-backed chair between it and the door. A somewhat querulous-looking sergeant glanced up as he came in.

"Yes?" said the sergeant, his voice rising.

Between blinding flashes from the headache, Towers looked the sergeant over. When he had memorized his features so that he would never forget them, Towers glanced down at the desk. A little wooden picket fence, with a closed narrow gate, ran from the outer corner of the desk to the wall, so that it was necessary for Towers and Logan to stand in a space about four-and-a-half feet by three feet. Beside the desk where the sergeant sat was a large filing cabinet. Across the room in the corner was a hat-stand, and against the inside wall was an overstuffed armchair. At the far wall of the room were two doors, with a water cooler near the right-hand door. The rest of the room was bare.

Towers turned his head to glance at Logan, and was rewarded by a white-hot flash of pain over the eyes.

"This is the place?" said Towers.

"Yes, sir," said Logan. "This is the place."

The sergeant shoved his chair back, stood up, made as if to go to the inner office, turned back, and said sharply to Logan, "I think the colonel has already given you your orders, Major."

Towers' headache abruptly died away to a faint throb. He looked at the Centran.

"Say, 'sir.'" he said, in a grating voice.

"I used the correct form of—"

"I said, say 'sir.'"

There was a brief pause.

"Sir." said the sergeant. The word came out with a squeak.

"Now," said Towers, "go in and inform the colonel that the commanding officer of Special Effects Team, Division III, is out here and wishes to speak to him immediately. The matter is urgent."

The Centran turned without a word, and Towers said in a flat voice, "Sergeant—"

The sergeant swallowed, came back, said "Yes, sir," turned and disappeared through the right-hand door.

A loud voice said from behind the door. "Tell them to sit down and wait."

Logan swore.

Towers smiled.

The sergeant came out, closed the door with reverent softness, and said in a tone of triumph, "The colonel is busy now. You may wait, if you wish, sir."

"I see," said Towers. You told him the matter was urgent?"

"Yes, sir."

"I believe I heard him say we should sit and wait?"

The sergeant glanced at the straight-back chair behind the door and smiled briefly, "Certainly, sir. You may sit down if you wish."

"It's not a question of 'wishing' it," said Towers, the rasp returning to his voice. "The colonel invited us to. Is that correct?"

The sergeant frowned. "As a matter of fact, sir, I believe so."

"Did he, or didn't he?"

"Yes, sir. He did."

"Since there's only one chair here, I assume he meant us to use the armchair also?" Towers looked pointedly at the armchair against the wall behind the fence.

"No one but permanent party is allowed back of the gate, sir," said the sergeant positively.

Logan glanced at his watch and said uneasily, "Sir, it's about time for the men to start coming down."

"Yes," said Towers, "but since the colonel may be ready to see us at any moment, and since he invited us to sit down and wait, I think we should do it. Sergeant—"

"Sir?"

"Bring that chair out here." He glanced at the armchair.

The sergeant blinked, and looked at the desk, the little gate in the picket fence, and the narrow space between the desk and the wall.

"But it won't fit," said the sergeant, his voice climbing.

"That," said Towers, "is a matter of perfect indifference to me. I've been invited to sit, and I will sit."

Just then, the sound of a descending landing-boat passed overhead and dwindled away in the direction of the far corner of the camp.

"Sir," said Logan, in a low voice, "that will be about half-a-dozen armored close-trained gorillas and their controller. Right behind them come a pack of close-trained wolves and *their* controller."

A second landing-boat whined overhead.

"The next one," said Logan, "has about a forty-foot

superconda in it, with operator. Sir, when they go in that barracks, all hell will—"

"Exactly why I wish to speak to the colonel urgently. But he tells us to sit and wait." Towers looked at the sergeant, and his voice when he spoke had the crack of a high-voltage discharge. "I said, *move that chair!*"

A third landing-boat passed overhead, and its sound dwindled off in the direction of Towers' barracks.

The sergeant wrestled the chair over to the narrow gate.

Logan mopped his brow with a sweaty handkerchief.

"It won't go through," said the sergeant.

Despite this obvious fact, he tried ineffectually to fit the bulky chair through the narrow opening in the picket fence.

"Lift it," said Towers irritably, "or move the fence, or do whatever else you have to, but hurry up."

The sergeant tried to lift the chair over the fence. The chair slipped, fell, and with a loud cracking sound split the fence at the base and knocked it outward.

The sergeant dragged the chair back, propped the fence upright, and then tried pulling the desk back out of the way. The desk was screwed to the fence, the lower screw broke loose, the top screw held, and all the pickets in that end of the fence leaned over at a forty-degree angle, with the baseboard pulled free of the floor and a row of nails sticking out.

The sergeant moaned, went around to the other end of the desk, and tried to swing it around instead. To do this, he had first to drag the filing cabinet out of the way. When he had the filing cabinet out in the middle of the floor, he swung the desk around, and found that it and the filing cabinet together now blocked the chair into the far half of the room. When he made this discovery, something seemed to pop within him. Working like a madman, he now succeeded in blocking himself and all the furniture in front of the colonel's door. Then, desperate, he wrestled the bulky armchair onto the desk, where it tipped off and hit the floor with a crash that shook the room, and was followed shortly by the sound of the filing cabinet tilting back against the wall as the sergeant hastily squeezed past it. The feet of the filing cabinet then slid, and the whole works slammed down on the floor like a dropped boulder.

The outer door opened up, and a neatly-dressed Centran brigadier-general stepped in. At the same moment, the door to the colonel's office came open. The general looked around at the overturned furniture. His face perfectly blank, he went out again. From somewhere outside there came the sound of shouting.

Towers shook his head. "Well, it's too late, now. They seem sort of disorganized in here, anyway. Come on."

He and Logan stepped out in the hall, and hurried outside.

As they neared the barracks, Towers saw a large crowd of Centran troops staring at a deserted part of the camp. In the middle of this deserted section was the barracks to which Towers' men had been assigned. There was nothing exceptional about the appearance of this barracks, except for about twenty feet of oversize python gradually disappearing through the nearest doorway, a gorilla in plate armor walking out a doorway at the opposite end of the barracks, and a yawning lion looking out a window.

In the front of the barracks was a stack of crates about twelve feet high and twenty feet long. A couple of Towers' men were outside the barracks, scratching their heads in apparent perplexity, and glancing back and forth from the heap of crates to the barracks. As Towers approached, they saluted, and one of them said in a carrying voice, "Sir, there are exactly six double bunks in that barracks that aren't taken. How do we fit all this stuff in?"

Towers said, "Wait a little."

There was the sound of another landing-boat coming down, and a few minutes later an electric truck delivered another load of crates in front of the barracks. Half-a-dozen armored gorillas marched past under the command of a heavily-armed human. Stepping carefully around the python, they disappeared into the barracks.

Towers glanced around.

The Centran brigadier-general, who had looked in at the chaos in the office a little earlier, was thrusting his way through the crowd. As he approached, twelve huge gray dogs or wolves came out the far door of the barracks and trotted past in single-file, to disappear in the direction of the place where the landing-boats were coming down. From that direction, another half dozen armored gorillas marched past, and into the barracks.

Logan said uneasily, "You don't think we're laying it on too thick do you?"

Towers glanced in the direction of the landing-place. "Something will snap shortly, and then we'll know. Look there."

The Centran brigadier general was staring at the electric truck, as it trundled up carrying a big transparent case full of water, inside of which a large bulbous creature floated amidst a tangle of flexible arms.

"Great," said the general, "hairy master of sin! *Who's in charge here?*"

Towers saluted. "I am, sir."

"What *is* this?"

"Advance Unit I of Independent Division III of the Special Effects Team, landing at the request of Major-General Horp Klossig."

The general walked over, frowning. "You're Towers?"

"That's right, sir."

The general looked around. "Let me see your barracks assignment sheet."

Logan handed the papers to Towers, who handed them to the general. The general leafed through them. "How are you going to get all this stuff into one corner of one barrack?"

"I've been trying without success to get an answer to that question, sir," said Towers angrily. "These sheets of paper show our requirements for space. Six double bunks is what we were allotted."

"But this sheet of paper says 'Advance party. Twelve (12) men, and equipment.'"

"That means, sir, twelve human beings. Amongst the equipment, which there is no place on that form to specify, is everything else you see here."

The general pointed to the last ten feet of what looked

like an oversized python, now disappearing through the doorway. "You call that 'equipment'?"

"Certainly, sir. Equipment shaped as an animal form is often far less conspicuous than the usual equipment. That is a Mark III Superconda with hydronic drive, twin fusion guns at the nostrils, scraper jaws, and adequate specimen storage compartments just aft the muzzle. It can be controlled remotely, or from a sealed compartment in the forward third. Among other things, it's extremely useful for scouting dense brush, swamp, and rain forest. It looks like an oversize constrictor. It's actually a highly-specialized vehicle."

"What about that?" The general pointed to a lion trotting past. "That's no vehicle."

"No, sir. But we find that in ordinary close combat, certain animals, when properly trained and disciplined, are hard to beat. By the use of surgical implants at selected nerve-centers, we can cause the animal in training to feel an instantaneous sharp pain. We can also initiate slight impulses for the motion we desire the animal to make. To a degree, the trainer can create a pleasurable sense of well-being. With such immediate prompting and guidance, with swift reward for the right responses, and instantaneous punishment for the wrong responses, the animal learns very rapidly. We call this 'close training.'

"For long periods, we put such close-trained animals in a state called 'deep sleep,' in which their bodily functions and food-requirements are depressed to a minimum. When we need them, we awaken them. We need them now. They aren't, strictly speaking, 'men,' but they do require barracks space."

Towers glanced at Logan. "My second-in-command, here, tried to explain this matter to the colonel in charge of allotting barracks space, but he wasn't allowed to explain it. I tried to avert this mess, but the man declined to discuss the matter. Sir, I am here at General Klossig's urgent call. But if colonels are allowed to countermand the orders of generals, we may as well all pack up and go home. This mess here is going to snowball rapidly unless one of two things happens. Either my forces will reverse their direction and leave this planet. Or they will be given adequate barracks space."

The general's face darkened. He glanced at the papers again, then said, "All right. Pull your men out of that barracks long enough for the troops to move in and take out their footlockers and bedding. Anybody with the brains of an oyster ought to be able to see that you're going to need plenty of room. I never saw a division yet that could be squeezed into one barrack, and this is no exception." He turned, and gave a sharp blast on a whistle. Towers sent Logan to clear out the barracks.

Approximately forty-five minutes later, Towers found himself in possession of twelve barracks.

"Now," said the general, "I know this isn't enough, but it's the best I can do."

"For our purposes," said Towers, "this will serve very well, sir. But I wonder what effect the sight of our equipment will have on your troops, particularly at night. A close-trained animal, properly controlled, is no danger to speak of—but this can be hard for regular troops to believe."

"I've been thinking the same thing. What if we put up a wall and gate around your section of the camp?"

"Fine. And I can put up an electric fence on the inside, to reassure the guards on the wall."

"Good. Anything else?"

"Yes, sir, there is. It would be a big help if we could have a few prisoners to examine."

"Nothing easier. But look out for them. They're tough, fast, and violent. If they get loose, you've got galloping hell on your hands till you blow their brains out."

"I'll remember it. And sir, my talk with General Klossig was interrupted, and there were a few questions I neglected to ask."

"I'll tell you whatever I can."

"Sir, is this the only garrison on this planet?"

"Oh, no. We have a fairly sizable force on the planet, but it's just a dust mote in space compared to the planet's population. Our men are all in inaccessible spots, but every garrison except those on some large islands in the middle of the ocean—where we raise our food—is under continuous attack."

"Sir, is there any need for hurry in solving your problems here?"

The general hesitated. "Yes, there is, I'm afraid. There are two reasons. First, morale is cracking up badly. Second, we are largely dependent on locally-raised food and locally-manufactured gunpowder. Our powder works are cut off from time to time by bad weather. So are our shipments of food. The only feasible transport on the planet is by air or sea, and when our reserves of food and powder get low, as they are right now, it takes only a brief interruption to bring on a crisis."

"I see," said Towers. "Thank you very much, sir."

"You're entirely welcome. If I can help, let me know."

"I will, sir."

The two men exchanged salutes.

Logan came over as the general left.

"Sir, the men are settled, and we can bring down the second unit any time."

"Good. And if we can get half-a-dozen scouts down in that forest with supercondas, we can get a clearer idea what's going on down there."

"Yes, sir. I'll get them down right away."

"Meanwhile," said Towers, "we're going to want to examine some humanoid prisoners the Centrans will send over. We'd better get construction started on a concrete blockhouse to house them. For the time being, we can fit out a barracks with heavy mesh, and look them over in there."

Towers walked into a barracks which had been hastily fitted out with partitions to serve as his headquarters. One of the rooms had a couple of desks, chairs, several telephones, and a filing case, and was plainly his office. He had just looked the room over, and sat down at his desk, when the door opened up, and a Special Effects Team man said, "Sir, there's a smug-looking Centran captain out here who wants to see you."

Towers frowned. "Send him in."

A Centran with a self-pleased expression came in, saluted, and said, "Sir, it has occurred to the Chief of our Planetary Integration Section that you will need to be briefed regarding the situation here."

"Thank you," said Towers coolly, "I have already been briefed."

"By whom, if I may ask?"

"By your commanding officer, General Klossig."

"Oh, well, but if I may say so, sir—"

Towers narrowed his eyes and looked the captain over coldly. The captain frowned, blinked, paused, gave a little laugh, and visibly shifted gears. "Well, then, sir, certainly at least you will want to examine the available literature—"

"It's quite extensive, I imagine?"

"Oh, exhaustive studies have been carried out. The correlation of data must, of course, reach a certain critical point before those charged with responsibility for administrative action may be . . . ah . . . educated—" he hesitated and studied Towers' expression—"I mean, sir, *enabled*, to—"

"Educated to the point of being enabled to make intelligent decisions," said Towers helpfully.

"Well, that wasn't precisely what I had in mind, sir, but"—Towers was watching him with a cold, calculating look—"but, I'm sure, sir, that's close enough."

There was a little silence.

Towers said, "I wouldn't want to keep this valuable literature out of circulation."

"Oh, but we have copies."

"Then, by all means, send them over."

The captain blinked. A look of relief passed across his face. "Yes, sir. Thank you, sir." He saluted. Towers returned the salute. The captain faced about and went out. Towers picked up one of the phones on his desk.

"Get me the labor detail."

"Yes, sir." A moment later a new voice said, "Labor detail."

"How is the blockhouse coming?"

"We're laying out the plans, and we've sent for a load

of fastset from the supply ship. It won't take us long, sir."

"Good. Let me know when it's finished. What about the barracks?"

"We're working on it now, sir. We should have it ready before any prisoners get here. Major Logan sent for the electric fence, and we think we can get that set up tonight, too, so that by tomorrow, we should have everything in shape."

"Fine."

The door opened up, and the same Special Effects man who had shown in the Centran captain said, "Sir, did you want some Planetary Integration reports brought in?"

Towers scowled. "Already? Yes, send them in."

The Special Effects man glanced back in the hall, nodded, and opened the door wider.

A squad of Centrans came in, each carrying a tall stack of reports, set the reports down along the opposite wall of the room, and went out. As they went out, Logan came in, squinted at the stack of reports, and said angrily, "Sir, did that bootlicking captain from Planetary Integration wish this junk on us?"

A puzzled voice from the phone said, "Sir?"

Towers looked at the heaped reports, and spoke into the phone, "That about covers what I wanted to know. Thank you."

"You're welcome, sir."

Towers hung up, and glanced at the stacks of reports. Then he looked up, to see that the Special Effects man was still holding the door open.

The squad of Centrans came back in again, each with his tied stack of papers. They halted, turned, bent, straightened, turned, and went out empty-handed.

The Special Effects man continued to hold the door open.

Logan swore under his breath.

The Centrans came back in again, left another load of reports, and went out.

The Special Effects man waited a moment, then closed the door.

Logan spat out a livid curse, drew a deep breath, and said, "Sir, listen, there's enough stuff there to last us six months easy if we try to absorb it. And we'll end up with a case of mental constipation that will—"

"I didn't realize there was going to be *that* much."

"Now what do we do with it?"

"We certainly can't fight our way through all that stuff. The devil with it." Towers looked away from it. "What's going on outside? Are the Centrans started on their wall?"

Logan turned his back on the reports. "Sir, the Centrans are working like madmen to get that wall built. They've set up searchlights, and they're going to work all night. I've got our men going in shifts, so we'll be all set by tomorrow morning. But, what are we going to do next?"

"Test the prisoners and find out what they're vulnerable to," said Towers. "The Centrans are short on ammunition. Well, as we know, one Selected-Strain yellow jacket takes up less space than a bullet, but it doesn't miss its target. Evasive action and obstructions don't trouble it at all. The first thing we want to do is to ease the strain on the Centran ammunition supply. A few nests of these hair-trigger yellow jackets, halfway up the cliff, should settle the problem with great economy of force."

"H-m-m," said Logan. "Yes, we can put the feeder units about halfway between nests, and a little higher up, and the bugs will patrol the whole circumference of the cliff for us. Why not do that now, sir?"

"Because first we want to test these natives to be sure of their reactions. It might be, for instance, that a few dozen giant bumblebees will do the job better. There are a number of tests we have to make, then we'll have a better idea where we stand. What we particularly want to avoid is any big crisis before we have a clear idea of what to do."

Logan nodded thoughtfully. "I can take care of the arrangements for the first tests." He looked at Towers and added apologetically, "If you don't mind my making a suggestion, sir—"

"What?" said Towers, scowling.

"Well, you look a little tired, sir."

It dawned on Towers that he *was* tired. He glanced out the windows, and saw that it was dark. He nodded, thought a moment, and got up. "I guess we can take care of the rest of this tomorrow."

Towers slept long, and, till a little before daybreak, he slept fairly well, considering the number of bruised places it hurt to lie on. Some time before daybreak, however, he had the impression of something unpleasant just beyond the edge of his consciousness. He woke up, went back to sleep, woke up, rolled over, dozed, woke up again, dozed fitfully, woke up, and exasperatedly tried to locate the cause of the trouble. The cause eluded him. He got up in the darkness, and looked out at the gray light just starting to seep over the camp. An edge of the outer wall of the camp, visible from where he stood, was lit by a faint glow, apparently from searchlights shining down onto the cliffs. The room was cold, and in the faint light, the camp outside had a frosty look. In the sky over a nearby barrack glittered an unfamiliar constellation.

The light from the wall shone dimly on the roof of the barracks nearby, and Towers frowned and leaned forward, trying to make out what appeared to a be a short, slanting chimney-pipe thrust out of the roof at an angle.

Not far away, a board creaked.

Towers froze. Behind him, the latch of his door clicked.

Towers turned, felt on the stand by the head of his bed, and pulled his service automatic from its holster.

There was a sudden crash.

The door slammed in, smashed against the wall, and sagged by one hinge.

In the hall, dimly lit by the light at the far end, crouched a hairy primitive figure. Its face, half-obscured by shadow peered into the room. It took a little step forward, bent—

Towers squeezed a little tighter on the trigger—

There was a bellow that seemed to burst his eardrums.

The figure blurred.

The thin dazzling line from Towers' fusion pistol vibrated in space before him.

Something slammed him heavily against the wall. There

was the smell of burnt flesh, a tinkle of glass, and a sharp crack. For an instant, Towers saw something against the dim square of the sky, then it was gone. He felt carefully along the wall, holding the gun close to him, and snapped the room light on.

Lodged in the window, its back steaming and ruined from the fusion charge, was a humanoid.

Towers swallowed, studied it for an instant, noted the widening pool of blood on the floor beneath it, then stepped out in the hall, and glanced in both directions. The hall was empty.

From the end of the hall, where Logan's room was, came a heavy crash.

Towers glanced up the hall, in the opposite direction, saw nothing, and sprinted down the hall toward Logan's room.

Logan's door was knocked from its hinges, the room was dark, and from inside came a grunt, a thump, and a straining, choking sound.

Towers felt for the room light, and couldn't find it. He groped his way into room, reached out, felt a tough, hairy hide—

There was a yell that deafened him, and something smashed him across the side of the head. He saw an explosion of sparks, then was knocked back by a heavy numbing blow in the center of the chest. He hit the wall as if he had been thrown out of a second-story window, dropped to the floor instantly, and heard something slam into the wall over his head. He reached out, and his left hand closed around a thick-boned ankle with a coat of wiry hair. He gripped the ankle, levered it up, and with his other hand slammed back the knee of the same leg. The humanoid struggled to recover his balance. Towers lifted harder, and still gripping the ankle with one hand, sprang to his feet as the humanoid went over.

There was a loud crash.

Towers dropped the ankle, jumped for the spot where the humanoid had fallen, and smashed down hard with both heels as he came down.

There was an agonized grunt.

The lights came on.

On the floor lay a humanoid, staring up with an unfocused gaze.

Logan, one eye puffed nearly shut, a set of striped pajamas hanging from him in shreds, with blood running from a set of long gashes across his chest, had his right hand on the light switch, and his left arm dangling unnaturally at his side. His unswollen eye studied the humanoid.

"Look out," said Logan hoarsely, "he's going to—"

A hairy hand shot out to grip Towers' left ankle like a vise. There was a fraction of a second's hesitation. In that instant, Towers bent slightly at the knee, brought up his right foot, and smashed his right heel down on the humanoid's head. The hand gripping his ankle relaxed. Towers spotted his gun across the room, and picked it up.

The humanoid started to sit up.

Towers smashed him across the head, and he fell back.

Towers straightened.

The humanoid's eyes came open. He fixed Towers in a momentary unblinking stare, then his eyes fell shut, his head lolled to one side, his muscles relaxed—then abruptly he rolled over, sprang to his feet . . .

Towers shot him.

"Good," breathed Logan.

From somewhere upstairs came a heavy crash, and an unearthly scream, followed by a rumbling grunt, then a heavy pummeling sound, as if a human body were being bounced off a wall like a handball. The barracks shook.

Towers saw a battered flashlight on the floor by an overturned table, grabbed it, snapped it on and went into the corridor, around a corner, and up the stairs to the second floor. He rounded a corner and found himself facing a short hall.

At the end of the hall, a door was slowly opening.

Towers stepped forward, and felt suddenly dizzy. He eased back around the corner, steadied his gun hand against the wall, and covered the door. The flashlight dimmed, and brightened again.

As he stood, tensely watching, Towers' chest hurt so that it was hard to breath. His left ankle felt as if a vise were methodically crushing it, and every separate bone, muscle, and joint seemed suddenly to have developed its own individual ache. He thought dazedly that he should go down the hall to help whoever was in trouble there, but the sensations of his body told him that he was dangerously close to his own limits.

The sound of choked breathing came from the room in front of him, and it dawned on Towers that he could, at least, shout for help. He drew in a painful breath, then paused as a huge humanoid, larger than any of those he'd seen earlier, moved back-first and slowly out the door in the flickering flashlight beam.

In the dim light, Towers could see the humanoid's arms stretched out, as if he were choking someone and pulling him out into the corridor.

The sense of weakness passed, and Towers stepped forward, to get a clear shot from the side.

The humanoid stumbled backward, and slammed into the wall of the corridor.

For an instant, Towers looked on blankly, wondering which of his men had the physique to shove back one of these creatures by raw strength.

The flashlight lit up more brightly, to show Towers the dark broad chest, huge arms, and massive head of a male gorilla, its big hands clamped around the humanoid's throat, as it forced it down.

There was a brief violent struggle, a grim thrashing, and then the gorilla straightened up. The humanoid remained on the floor.

Towers found the hall light, and snapped it on.

The gorilla saw Towers, and automatically snapped to a posture as close to attention as its physique allowed.

Towers bent over the inert hairy form on the floor. Seen in a good light, it looked considerably worse for wear than Logan did, and it showed no visible sign of life. Towers felt around till he located an artery. There seemed to be a very faint pulse.

He straightened up, and glanced at the gorilla. "Watch. If move—kill."

The gorilla grunted obediently.

Towers went downstairs.

Logan was lying motionless at the bottom of the flight of steps, a gun near his hand. Towers shook him gently by the shoulder.

Logan grunted, and opened his eyes.

Towers said, "Who's in charge of the guard detail tonight?"

"Cartwright," said Logan, sitting up. He picked up the gun.

"Stay there," said Towers.

"No, I'm coming, too." Logan stumbled to his feet.

They went down the hall, past Towers' office to an office marked "Guard and Security Detail." They opened the door. Across the room, stretched out on a cot, lay a tall, uniformed figure with first lieutenant's insignia.

Towers and Logan glanced at each other. Towers crossed the room, looked the figure over, and observed no marks or bruises. He took hold of a shoulder and gave it a rough shake.

Cartwright's eyes came open. He groaned, looked at Towers, and abruptly sat up. His glance darted from Towers to Logan.

Towers looked at Logan. "Get the next man on the list."

Logan gave Cartwright a long look, crossed the room, set his gun on the desk, and jerked open a drawer.

"I—" groaned Cartwright.

"Shut up," said Towers.

Cartwright swallowed.

Logan was speaking into the phone, turned so he could keep an eye on the closed door.

Out in the hallway, an alarm bell set up its jarring clutter.

Towers looked at Cartwright. "Name for me the precautions you've taken since you came on duty tonight."

"Sir, we're inside a friendly camp. With guards all around us."

Towers said, his voice grating, "Name for me the precautions you've taken since you came on duty tonight."

Outside, there was a sound of something large and heavy running swiftly past. An instant later, the sound was repeated. Then repeated again.

Cartwright said, "I put a half-squad of gorillas in each end of the barracks where the captives are tied up. There was a little disturbance there around two o'clock, then everything settled down. I checked everything at four, then around half-past four—everything was quiet. I felt awfully tired and just lay down for a moment. I must have fallen asleep instantly."

The door opened up and a strongly-built man in first lieutenant's uniform came in, frowned at Cartwright, looked at Towers and Logan, froze and swallowed.

Logan had set down the phone and aimed his gun at the door, but now put the gun down and picked the phone up again. He hung up the phone, spoke briefly to the lieutenant, then turned to Towers.

"Nobody else heard anything. The Centrans had no trouble on the wall last night."

"That leaves the prisoners," said Towers.

"Sir," said Cartwright earnestly, "the prisoners are guarded."

"I'm going over there now, and see how they're guarded," said Towers. "Wait right here till I get back."

Logan got up, and went out with him. When they were out in the hall, Towers said, "Hadn't you better get that arm taken care of?"

"I want to see these well-guarded prisoners first," said Logan.

They walked out into the gray light of dawn, and up the steps of the barracks across the way.

Towers opened the door, and a corporal nodding at a table in a small anteroom shot to his feet. "Atten*shun!*"

Six massive hairy forms in body armor snapped erect.

"Where are the prisoners?" said Towers.

"In the next room sir."

"Quiet, aren't they?"

"They settled down after they got a taste of that wire."

"Let's see them."

The corporal opened up the door, and snapped on a light.

Towers stepped into a long room divided into three parts by a heavy wire mesh fence, with mesh carried across the walls, ceiling, and floor, and covering all the windows. The central portion of the room had a pile of straw on the floor and could be entered by a steel-and-wire door from either end.

"You see, sir," said the corporal, "they can't get out unless they spring the gate on this side, or the other gate. Then they have to come out the doors. We're waiting for them."

"Fine," said Towers. "Where are they?"

"Under the straw, sir. That's where they were the last time." He took a long pole from the corner of the room, and rammed it through the heavy mesh into the pile of straw. "Funny," he murmured.

Logan said, "Sir, that wire is stretched out of shape here and there, but I don't see any break."

"Neither do I, but there's one somewhere."

The corporal was getting frantic with his pole. "I *know* they're here somewhere!"

"Look there," said Towers. "At the ceiling. In the far corner."

"It looks like a hole. But the wire isn't broken."

"Sir," said the corporal. "They're gone."

"Open that gate," said Towers.

The corporal unsnapped the lock, and lifted a bar that fastened the gate to its frame at several points. Towers and Logan walked in and looked up. In the far corner was a rough hole in the ceiling with wire stretched across it.

"Yes," said Towers, studying it, "the edge of the wire on the ceiling was fastened to the wire of that fence with a kind of heavy loop, like a hog-ring. Look there." On the floor nearby lay a thick piece of wire bent in the form of an open U. "They sprang the fasteners, got up between the two pieces the fasteners held together, tore the ceiling boards loose—then they were upstairs." Towers glanced at the corporal. "Who told you to have half your squad in one end of the barracks and half in the other, with no one outside, or in here watching these prisoners?"

"Lieutenant Cartwright, sir. But about watching the prisoners, sir. If any of us were in the room with them, it seemed to drive them into fury. And that was getting through to the gorillas. We *had* to get out."

"Was there anything to prevent you from drilling a peephole through the wall, so you could watch them without being seen?"

The corporal opened his mouth, then shut it. He shook his head dazedly.

"Next time," said Towers angrily, "*think*." He turned, left the prisoners' cage, and with Logan close behind, went outside and back to the headquarters barracks. He paused at the door marked "Guard and Security Detail," turned to Logan, and said, "You'd better get yourself taken care of."

"Yes, sir. I'll go see the medic right now."

Outside, a Centran bugle was rousing the troops in the other part of camp. The day was just starting, and Towers felt as if he'd been rolled down a mountainside in a barrel. He opened the door, glanced at the perspiring Cartwright, and motioned him to come out. Towers shut the door and looked at him. There was a painful silence.

Towers said, "People in the Special Effects Team are not supposed to be stupid, Lieutenant. We've been on this planet not quite twenty-four hours, and we have had more dislocation from two officers who refused to think than from any other cause whatever. Major Logan and I were almost killed this morning. The Centran position here may break down anytime, so we've got to find a solution as quickly as possible. But thanks to your witless arrangements to guard the prisoners, and to your going to sleep when you were supposed to be awake, the whole business has been thrown into confusion. What do you have to say for yourself?"

"Sir . . . there isn't anything to be said."

"What was the cause of this trouble?"

"I . . . I went to sleep . . . I—"

"Nuts," said Towers furiously. "*Why* did you go to sleep?"

"I was tired . . . I didn't—" He hesitated.

"Go on," said Towers tensely.

"I didn't think, sir."

"All right. You've hit on the answer. Now, for the love of heaven, *start thinking*. If we don't think in the Special Effects Team, *who will?*"

"Yes, sir. I'm sorry, sir."

"You'll be more sorry, yet, before this is over. And every time you're sorry, remember it's because you didn't *think*. Now, down this hall about halfway is my room. You can recognize it because the door is knocked in, and there's a dead humanoid halfway through the window. Down at the end of the hall is Major Logan's room, which you can recognize because it's a shambles, the door is knocked off, and there's a dead humanoid across a table knocked upside down. Clean up both rooms, deliver the humanoids to the medic for examination, and replace the doors, windows, and anything else that's damaged. Do it yourself, with no help, then report to me. Don't eat any breakfast. Don't eat any lunch. Major Logan and I lost the benefit of sleep, and you are going to lose the benefit of those two meals. If I learn that you had anything whatever to eat before the evening meal, I will see to it that you wish you had never been born."

"Yes, sir."

"All right, get started."

"Yes, sir."

Towers went into the Guard Detail office. "There's a wire mesh prisoners' cage on the barracks across the way. It's been broken out of. Have it repaired with more and heavier fastening rings to bind the sections of wire together, and put in some arrangement so prisoners can be watched unseen. See that the prisoners *are* watched unseen. Put a patrol outside, just in case. Also, there's a humanoid upstairs in this building, with a gorilla on guard. The humanoid is either dead or playing possum. If he's dead, blow his head off just to be on the safe side, and deliver the body to the medic for examination. If he's alive, stick him back in the cage. And see that he's *watched*."

"Yes, sir."

"Then check up on exactly how the prisoners got out, and let me know."

"Yes, sir. I'll take care of it as soon as possible."

"Good."

Towers went back to his room, washed, dressed, went out to eat breakfast, then walked back to his office. He felt like a man after a two-week binge, but he had accomplished this overnight, and without benefit of any pleasure in the process.

As he entered the office, Logan, one arm in a sling, was just putting down his telephone.

"Sir," said Logan. "The Centran ammunition supply has been cut."

Towers shut the door, and nearly fell over a tied stack of Centran reports that lay tipped over on the floor. Logan sprang up, and heaved the stack back against the wall. The whole long row of stacks teetered precariously, and two at the end tipped out and fell over with a heavy crash.

Logan spat out an unprintable oath. "That thing," he added, "was tipped over when I came in, and I no sooner sat down then it fell over again. I'll—"

Towers said, "Wait a minute. The trouble is, when they brought these reports in, they just *set* them here. They should have *leaned* them against the wall. Or at least set them close enough to it so—" he heaved a stack upright, and leaned it back. He heaved the other stack upright, and wrestled it into place. Everything now seemed to be in order, save that the whole row was slumping a little toward the door. Towers scowled, then shrugged. "Good enough. Now, what was that about the Centran ammunition supply?"

"A bunch of humanoids got into one of their biggest munitions works, and raised so much hell that the garrison got excited and forgot where they were. One thing led to another, and the place blew up."

Towers pulled out his chair and sat down.

"What did that take out?"

"Thirty per cent of the Centran ammunition capacity.

They'll feel the pinch in three or four days, which is about all the local reserves are good for."

Towers' phone rang, and he picked it up.

"Sir," said a voice, "you wanted me to let you know when the blockhouse was finished. It's finished now, and ready to take the prisoners."

"Good. Thank you." Towers hung up and glanced at Logan. "The blockhouse is ready. Now all we need are some prisoners to put in it."

Logan said exasperatedly, "Well, at least, the Centrans ought to be able to give us some more of *them*."

"Call up and see. We may still have one alive, anyway." Towers called up the Guard Detail.

"Yes, sir," said a voice on the other end. "That one upstairs with the gorilla watching was alive, all right. When we went to pick it up, it almost put Private Higgins through the wall. That big gorilla on guard went to work before we could stop him, bashed the humanoid through the fiberboard, and wrapped him around an overhead beam. Doc's working him over now. About how they got out of the barracks, sir—"

"Wait a minute. Doc's working *who* over now?"

"Sir? Oh, Higgins."

"What about the humanoid?"

"Dead. As you suggested, sir, we blew his head off for good measure. I guess that takes care of the four of them."

Towers looked at the phone. "The *four* of them?"

"Yes, sir. The one dead in your room, the one dead in Major Logan's room, the one we killed, and the one Doc was dissecting when we got Higgins over there."

"Wait a minute. Do you mean to say there were *four* prisoners?"

"Yes, sir. I have the receiving sheet right on my desk here. There were four male humanoid prisoners, all captured yesterday, delivered at 10:58 last night, signed for by Cartwright, also by Meigs, private in charge of temporary detention barracks."

Towers glanced at Logan, but Logan was busy on the phone. Towers thought a moment, then said, "Listen, I think you've counted one of the dead humanoids twice. One was killed in Logan's room, one in my room, and one upstairs. Cartwright had orders to take the one in Logan's room and the one in my room over to the medic for examination. I think you saw the humanoids in those rooms, then had the fight with the one upstairs. Meantime, Cartwright brought the one in Logan's room over to the medic. Then you took Higgins over there, saw the one Cartwright had brought over, and counted it again."

"Then one's still loose. I'll get right at it, sir."

"How did they get out of the detentions barracks?"

"Through a join in the wire, through the first-floor ceiling, up through the second-floor ceiling, and out the roof."

"O.K. Find out about that other humanoid."

"Yes, sir."

Towers hung up. Logan said, "Sir, the Centrans say they can supply us with all the humanoids we want. But it will take a half-hour or so before they can get us one. What they do is to let him climb up to the top of the wall, then knock them over the head with a big hammer, grab them with hooks, and strap them up."

Some kind of oddly-shaped bug droned past Towers' head, distracting him for a moment, then settled on the opposite wall.

"Well," said Towers, bringing his mind back to business, "the blockhouse is finished, and we'll have some prisoners in a little while. Better get the arrangements for testing set up."

"I've taken care of it, sir. They were all set up even before the blockhouse was ready."

"Good work," said Towers approvingly.

The phone buzzed, and he picked it up. "Hello?"

"Sir, the first of the scouts is back from observing that jungle down below. We thought you'd want to hear his story."

"Fine. Send him in." Towers turned to Logan. "They're sending in one of the scouts. And just incidentally, Logan, how many of those humanoids did *you* think we had around this morning?"

"Well," said Logan. "There was a dead one halfway through your window when I got back from getting patched up. There was the one in my room. And there was that terrific fight going on upstairs after those two got finished. That makes three."

"The guard detail has record of four being delivered to us last night."

"Four." Logan glanced around, the hair at the back of his neck seeming to bristle.

There was a respectful knock on the door, and a tired-looking Special Effects lieutenant of about average height came in, and saluted. "Sir, second Lieutenant James Andres, in charge of Scout Unit One—two Wings and six Mark II Supercondas."

"You were down in the forest."

"Yes, sir. It's actually more of a jungle down there—the growth is luxuriant. Sir, we were supposed to observe particularly the humanoids. When we got down, it was approaching dusk, and as it got light this morning we had to pull the 'condas back into a swamp. The jungle growth is so thick that from the Wings it's next to impossible to see what's going on, while from the supercondas we had a splendid view, but were attacked on sight by any humanoid that happened along. What I mean, sir, is that I can give a fairly clear report of what we saw, but during daylight we couldn't get into the place where the humanoids were really thick, without creating such an uproar that it defeated our purpose."

Towers nodded. "Go ahead. I'd like to hear your impressions."

"Sir, the place is a hellhole. There are humanoids all over, crouching on limbs, behind tree trunks, and hiding in the brush. We saw them eat just about everything in sight, but they seem to prefer—from our short observation—a kind of berry on a thorny vine that grows up high into the trees."

"They spend most of their time eating?"

"No, sir. That just seems to be their objective. They actually spend most of their time creeping up on each other, and bashing each other's brains in. When they're not attacking, they're looking over their shoulder for fear somebody's going to attack *them*."

"That's in the daytime?"

"Yes, sir."

"How is it at night?"

"They climb trees, hide under fallen logs, or somehow get out of sight. Most of them, that is. We did see some of them work their way up a giant tree at night after what we think was an insect nest of some kind. They broke off the limb the nest was on, then came down again."

"Eat the insects? Or find honey on the nest?"

"No, sir, they just threw it down. But it landed out of sight, and it may be that later on they got it. The way we figure it, sir, is that the nest belonged to some pest that couldn't see at night, and they were getting rid of it. The humanoids seem to have some night vision. Only a few seem to have the courage to move around much, but we noticed a number waiting to brain anyone that did."

"Cannibalistic?"

"Not that we saw last night, sir. The idea seems to be, to wait till somebody else has a delicacy, then kill him and eat the delicacy. The place seems to abound in food. We saw them eat chunks of thick bark right off the trees. But the foods they really like seem to be rare."

"What happens to any humanoids that are sick, or injured?"

The scout lieutenant shook his head. "All the ones we saw were healthy. I imagine any sick or injured ones get killed off pretty fast. The strange part is, with all this fighting amongst themselves, they unite the instant they spot anything different. There are scavenger birds that come down at night, and live on the dead from the previous day. One came down a little early last night, before it was really dark, and a bunch of humanoids tore it to shreds. Whenever they saw us, they attacked us, even though one superconda—even if it had been just a big snake—could have slaughtered dozens of them before being finished. And yet, we were glad to get out into the swamp. There are so many of those humanoids, they are so fast and so violent, and their reactions seem to be on such an instinctive basis, with no time wasted on thought, that to tell the truth they scared the living daylights out of us, and some of those supercondas have the outer camouflage casing around the snout pretty well beat up. It's an awful place down there."

Towers imagined a jungle alive with creatures like the ones he and Logan had fought with that morning. "Yes," he said, "it must be."

"In order to get some good out of the trip, we each jammed a couple of humanoids into the forward sample pouches on the supercondas. But we'd better do the rest of our scouting remotely, by planting hidden TV and radio pickups down there. We can use the 'condas to do that at night."

"Good. Now, did you say, you'd brought up some humanoid prisoners?"

"Yes, sir. A dozen, all told."

"Fine. Go down the hall to the Guard Detail office, and arrange to unload the humanoids under guard, half at the blockhouse, and half at the detention barracks, as soon as you can."

"Yes, sir. I'll do that right now." The lieutenant saluted, and went out.

Towers and Logan glanced at each other.

Logan said, "I don't care much for the sound of this. We're up against a kind of situation I don't think we ever ran into before. These humanoids aren't stupid, actually, but they're completely oriented toward combat. They all gang up on any different life form that raises its head. When they don't have any alien life form to fight, they fight each other. It's an ingrained instinctive-traditional reaction backed up by the sheer mechanics of the situation. They've got to fight, because with unrestricted reproduction there just can't be enough food for all. But as long as they *do* fight all the time, every man's hand against every other man's, they can never develop any organization or technological skills worth mentioning. They'll just go by a process of natural selection getting tougher, faster, and trickier, till they reach the limit, and the slaughter will just go on by itself with no more sense or reason than a chemical reaction. But how do we end it? There must be plenty of surplus birth rate down there, and we have a huge mass of these humanoids to contend with."

Towers watched the odd-shaped bug he'd seen earlier buzz across the room, and hover outside the door of a small storage closet in the corner of the room. The bug hovered by the crack at the top of the door, its buzz rising to a whine, and dying away again. Towers stared at it in puzzlement, then with an effort dragged his mind back to the problem at hand.

"Maybe," he said, "these tests will give us some idea."

The first series of tests, carried out at the specially fitted blockhouse, took all afternoon, and were designed to find which of a great variety of available insects and arachnids the humanoids might be most susceptible to. The tests showed conclusively that the humanoids were untroubled by—among others—gnats, flies, ticks, and several sizes and varieties of mosquitoes, all of which lost interest after a taste of humanoid blood. The humanoids seemed vaguely aware of attacking yellow jackets, hornets, giant bumblebees, and tarantulas, which they squashed absent-mindedly when they chanced to notice them. The only thing that seemed to cause the humanoids any real trouble was a selected strain of scorpion, which succeeded in raising a dark pink bump about half the size of a man's little fingernail, which disappeared in an hour.

Towers and Logan, considerably depressed, went through the motions of eating a hasty supper, paused briefly at their office, then watched tests designed to determine the limits of the humanoid's tolerance for various foods. These tests revealed that the humanoids could eat all bark, root, branch, leaf, grass, moss, fungus, and lichen samples given to them, together with leather, rubber, cotton, wool, synthetic fiber, chalk, every kind of normal food, spice, and flavoring in the camp, plus soap, grease, wallboard, a variety of plastics, and engine oil. The humanoids drew the line at gasoline, which made them sneeze, but gnawed and sucked on nails, tin cans, rocks and the concrete walls of the blockhouse.

The medic now reported that he had examined the specimens given him for dissection, had dulled a large number of knives in the process, but had succeeded in finding out that the humanoids had an exceptionally powerful digestive system, including a small gizzard, a "selection chamber" where food was apparently split into digestible and occasional indigestible portions, and a "bypass" by which the rare nondigestible or poisonous portions were routed around the ordinary digestive system through several valves and disposed of with no wasted effort. The medic also mentioned that he had passed along portions of the humanoids' tissues for chemical analysis, and gotten back a report that the tissues contained an unusually large amount of silicon. The medic hazarded the guess that just as certain silicon coatings were tougher than ordinary organic coatings, so the body tissue of the humanoids was tougher than ordinary tissue.

In a state bordering on shock, Towers and Logan went back to their office. Nothing much had changed here, save that the piles of Centran reports were gradually slumping more steeply, and the odd-looking bug was perched over the door of the storage closet, giving an occasional buzz from time to time. The guard detail reported no sign of the missing humanoid, and Lieutenant Cartwright, looking exhausted, reported that he had cleaned up and repaired Towers' and Logan's rooms, had eaten no breakfast or lunch, but had eaten some supper, and he was ready for the next stage of his punishment, which he knew he well deserved.

Towers told him to report back the next morning, then sent him to bed, and looked over a report from one of his men on possible ways to slow down the attacks on the Centran camps. He approved for immediate action the measures it suggested, then after a half hour of futile wrestling with the problem, he turned out the lights, and he and Logan went off to try to catch up on sleep.

Towers was in the middle of a nightmare, with half-a-dozen escaped humanoids lurking all over the barracks as he stood paralyzed in a hallway, listening for telltale signs, when there was a crash that shook the room and jolted him awake. Towers was out of bed, gun in hand, crouched in a corner of the room, with his heart hammering and the blood pounding in his ears, before he was fully awake. He heard a door come open somewhere, there was a thunderous crash, the sound of running feet, another roar, the sound of splintering wood, a yell and a hideous worrying sound.

A lifetime of devotion to duty moved Towers across the room, and out the door into the dim-lit hallway before he had time to really consider the matter.

As he stepped into the hall, there came a growl from the direction of his office, a heavy grunt, and the biggest humanoid he'd seen yet exploded at him out of the shadows.

Towers squeezed the trigger, whipped back against the wall, and fired again as the humanoid veered toward him, gripped him around the waist, and threw him down the hallway. Towers lost his footing, slammed down on his back, the humanoid landed on top of him, and with a heavy smash a lion landed on the humanoid. There was one chaotic instant full of claws, teeth, and noise, then Towers was on his feet, the badly-wounded humanoid was in a corner, and the lion was mauling the humanoid with terrific blows from his paws.

There was a sound of running feet, and a strongly-built private with a guard detail armband, a thick smear of dirt across his face, and a bloody nose, ran up and shouted, "Back! Sit!"

The lion, growling, backed from the shambles of the humanoid, and with his right forepaw raised and the claws out, the paw making tentative motions in the air, sat, crouched forward on his haunches.

The guard shone a powerful light in the corner, murmured fervently to himself, and said in a clear steady voice, "Good boy. Good. All right, now."

The lion abruptly sat back, gave a final growl, and began to clean himself.

"Sir," said the guard, "do you know where that thing was?"

"Where?"

"In your office, sir!"

Towers limped down the hall, took a look in his office, which was a shambles, and waited while the guard detail checked, and reported that no new captives had gotten loose, so this latest humanoid must be prisoner number four, missing since last night.

Towers went back to sleep, and after what seemed only a few minutes, woke up exhausted and aching from head to foot, with someone gently but insistently shaking him by the shoulder.

Logan was saying, "Sir, I'm sorry. The situation's gotten worse."

Towers opened his eyes. The room was light, and from outside came an almost continuous firing.

Towers sat up. "What time is it?"

"Almost ten."

Towers swung out of bed, winced at a sharp pain in his side, splashed cold water on his face, and dressed rapidly. "What's happened?"

"A searchlight on the wall burned out late last night, and in trying to light that section of wall, the soldiers on duty stepped up the current at the two neighboring searchlights, and burnt them out, too. Before they got them back in operation, some humanoids climbed over the wall. They killed about a dozen Centrans in their sleep, and there was a reign of terror in the camp till sun-up. Now," Logan stepped to the window and raised it, "listen out there."

Towers stepped to the window and listened.

Clear and distinct, a chant came through the window: "*Home . . . We want to go home. Home . . . We want to go home.*"

"That's the Centrans?" said Towers.

"About half of them, sir. Klossig's deputy was just on the phone, and says General Klossig is out there with the Headquarters Guard, trying to break up the mob. Anything we can do to support the general, to distract, to—"

The crash of a volley of gunfire came through the window, followed by another crash, and another. Then the chant rose up again, "Home! Home! We want to go—"

Towers shut his eyes and tried to think. Again there was a crash of guns, this time followed by screams and yells.

Towers said, "Where are the bugs we were using to test the humanoids?"

"There are whole cases of them in the Special Devices barracks next to the blockhouse."

"Break out the all-purpose bug spray, and be sure everybody—and all the animals—gets a good dose. Then turn loose the Jersey Special mosquitoes, the yellow jackets, the hornets, and all the other flying pests on hand except the giant bumblebees. We'll make this the shortest rebellion in Centran history."

Logan left the room at a run.

Towers strapped on his gun, went down the hall to his office, and looked around. All the stacks of Centran reports were out flat on the floor. Logan's desk was knocked over on its side, and Towers' desk was slewed around five feet from where he had left it. The door of the storage closet was open, with half-a-dozen empty cans and a brass belt buckle lying on the floor. Over the door, smashed flat on the doorframe, was the bug that had been flying around the room the day before. Towers went into the closet, and looked around. Bottles were empty, cans were licked clean, a large section of wallboard was eaten away from the floor halfway to the ceiling, exposing the studs. Towers stepped back and looked up at the bug. He gave a low exclamation, and turned at the sound of the door opening.

One of his men burst in, carrying a formidable gun with a number of outthrust nozzles.

"Bug spray, sir! Don't move!"

Towers shut his eyes. He was enveloped in a cloud of fine stinging spray that seemed to hit him from all directions at once. From somewhere, he could hear the clanging of an alarm bell, and the booming of loudspeakers warning that there was just ninety seconds left to get sprayed with repellent.

"Done, sir!"

The door opened and slammed shut. There was the pound of feet hurrying down the hall, and the bang of doors being thrown open and shut again as the hunt went on for anybody who needed bug repellent.

"Sixty seconds!" roared an amplified voice.

Logan came in as Towers was choking in a breath of air that stank of repellent. Right behind Logan came Cartwright. Clouds of vapor rose from both men.

"We're about set," said Logan, stepping around the fallen stacks of Centran reports. "The bugs are ready, and we've got plenty of them."

"O.K.," said Towers. "Now—"

"Thirty seconds!" roared the loudspeaker.

"Sir," said Cartwright hopefully, "is there anything I can do?"

Towers said to Logan, "Listen—"

The phone rang, and Logan, still facing Towers, scooped it up. "Yes, sir . . . Yes . . . Yes . . . In about half-a-minute, sir." He hung up, and said to Towers, "General Klossig's deputy, sir."

"O.K.," said Towers. "Now—"

"Fifteen seconds!" roared the voice from the loudspeaker.

The door flew open. A set of nozzles thrust in. A voice shouted "Here are some!"

"No, no!" said Towers. "We've already—"

A blast of spray enveloped him.

"Ten seconds!" boomed the loudspeaker.

Logan swore, and gagged.

"O.K., now!" The door banged shut.

Towers groped his way to a window, and savagely threw it up.

"Five seconds!" boomed the loudspeaker. "Four! Three! Two!"

"Sir—" choked Cartwright.

"Open that door," said Towers, "and get a little air in here."

"Zero!" screamed the loudspeaker.

Cartwright threw the door open.

There was a buzzing, droning noise from outside. Towers looked out to see a tornado of hurrying black dots rise over the human section of the camp. The air filled with buzzing, droning, whining sounds, and little darting shapes.

Logan was furiously wiping his face. "Thank God that's over."

"Yes," said Towers, "as long as some fool didn't—"

There was a thunder of feet that shook the building. Towers shouted, "Look out!"

A huge gorilla burst into the room, and whirled around. A black-and-yellow thing about the size of a one-inch cut off the end of a lead pencil, flew in right behind and dove at him. The gorilla let out a roar of terror and heaved a chair at it. The chair smashed through the ceiling, legs first, and hung there. The black-and-yellow thing reappeared from the side, and darted for the gorilla.

A set of nozzles poked in the doorway.

"Spray him!" yelled Towers and Logan simultaneously.

The gorilla streaked around the room.

Towers, Logan, and Cartwright bolted to get out of the way.

There was a crash that shook the building.

Towers whirled around. There was a big hole in the opposite wall of the room. Logan and Cartwright were hastily picking themselves up. The gorilla was gone. At the door, the nozzles now thrust in decisively.

"*No!*" shouted Towers. He's *gone!*"

There was a rolling cloud from the nozzle, then a yell. The spray gun flew in the doorway followed by a shouting figure with half-a-dozen yellow jackets swirling around his head. The gun landed against the wall, and the figure went out the open window, hit the ground in a somersault, and streaked across the open space.

Towers shut his eyes.

Logan picked up the spray gun. "The total, one hundred per cent, witless damned fool. He was so busy spraying everyone else, *he didn't get sprayed himself.*"

Towers said, "Just so long as they didn't miss any more gorillas."

Cartwright cleared his throat apologetically, "Sir, excuse me. If there's anything else I can do to clear myself?"

"There is." Towers took him by the arm. "You see that bug, flattened on the doorframe? Odd-looking bug, isn't it? It appears to have a sting on one end, and a sucker on the other end. Now, look in this supply closet. Obviously from all this stuff that's eaten up, the escaped humanoid spent a long time in here. Now, this bug didn't pay much attention to us yesterday, but flew around the room, hovered outside the door to this closet or sat on the doorframe over the closet, buzzing from time to time. Now, *our* insects don't trouble these humanoids, but *something* kept that humanoid from coming out till after we closed up and snapped off the lights in here."

"Yes, sir," said Cartwright, frowning at the squashed bug. "It must have been that insect."

Towers nodded. "And the sooner we find out what that insect is, the better. The obvious way would be to get the information from some expert in Planetary Integration, but" —he listened for a moment to the distant shouts and screams coming from the Centran part of camp—"I'm afraid they're not going to be available for a while."

"Yes, sir," said Cartwright. "So I should—"

"Go through these papers," said Towers, pointing to the stacks of Centran reports on the floor. "As soon as you find out what this bug is, your punishment's over."

Cartwright whipped out a pocket knife, cut the strings binding the end stack of reports, pulled out the top one, and started to read. Abruptly he stopped, and looked intently at the thousands of reports waiting to be read.

Logan said to Towers, "Sir, if we *do* find the right kind of bug, and can mass-breed it, that should take care of protecting the Centran camps. *After* we have enough bugs."

"We might be able to do more than that with them," said Towers, frowning. "We have to be very careful about spreading complete colonies of our own insects over a planet. But *this* bug is native to the planet, and on top of that it doesn't seem to bother us." He slewed his desk around to something like a normal position, and amidst the shouts, buzzing, droning, and whining sounds, sat down and tried to think.

"But, sir," said Logan apologetically, "*first* we've got to get around this ammunition shortage."

The days blended into weeks as they struggled with the ammunition shortage, and a host of miscellaneous problems.

Klossig's part of camp was like a city after a siege. The buildings were shot up, dead and wounded were strewn around indiscriminately, the air was choked with smoke from small fires that threatened to get out of hand and burn up the whole camp. The Centrans not hurt in the shooting were dazed from the shock of the revolt, and half-dead from the attacks of the insects that broke it up. Powerful insecticides had disposed of most of the insects, but a few kept reappearing from unlikely places, to add a pall of nervous dread to the desolation.

To keep the camp from being overrun by the humanoids, Towers had to rush his own men onto the walls as sharpshooters, backed up by roaming squads of close-trained wolves, big cats, and gorillas. The other Centran camps pleaded for help as their munitions supply dwindled, and this strained Towers' manpower to the limit. Just as he reached the point where he had nothing to spare, Cartwright discovered in the Centran reports a reference to an odd bug that terrorized the humanoids in the daytime, and was destroyed by them at night, the nests being thrown down, ripped open, and the young bugs torn out, to be eaten as a special delicacy.

By degrees, Towers managed to straighten out the worst of the mess, getting automatic devices into operation to ease the strain on his men. The scouts then went into action, and brought back several nests of the insects. But now, one of the random eddying migrations of the humanoids produced a surge of population below Klossig's camp, and the number of desperate climbers coming up the cliff rose to an unprecedented flood.

At this point, Klossig fortunately was able to get back onto his feet. A sudden burst of energy swept through the Centran part of camp. The troops, jolted into action by the sight of dead mutineers dangling from gallows, took over from the Special Effects men on the walls, and savagely knocked the humanoids off with clubs, axes, and sledge hammers.

This desperate effort gave Towers and his men just time enough to study the main routes up which the humanoids climbed, and to put some Special Effects into operation. The mountain suddenly blossomed out in live wires, strips of rock polished mirror-smooth and greased, and sets of handholds that supported a climber's full weight for a brief moment, then snapped out on forty feet of cable, stopped with a jolt, and wound up ready for the next climber.

Towers, mopping perspiration from his brow, returned to his office to find a report stating that the local bugs were now being propagated successfully by mass-breeding. The report stated: "Initial efforts at fractionation suggest that in no very great time we will have on hand a spectrum of strains ranging, in their effects on the local humanoids, from very moderate to near-lethal virulence."

"In other words," said Towers, in relief, "we'll have strains of bugs capable of hitting the humanoids with everything from annoyance to terror."

"Well," said Logan, "that's a relief. We've about stopped the humanoids coming up the wall, but the Centran troops are dead on their feet, and I hate to think what will happen if more humanoids *should* climb up. With the bugs, we can stop them."

Towers was drawing a careful sketch on a pad. "The original problem wasn't just to stop them," he said. "That will leave us, Klossig, and the humanoids, right in the same hole we were in to start with. The problem is to somehow break the humanoids out of their planetary mob. See if you can find one of our men who's ingenious at construction."

Logan went out, and came back with a thin, wiry individual with capable hands. Towers pointed to several sketches. "We're going to plant nests of bugs down there in the jungle. The bugs will frustrate and terrorize a large proportion of the humanoids by day—which, we hope, will tend to break up their instinctive-traditional pattern of living in an endless cycle of eat, reproduce, and kill. But at night, the humanoids will go up after the nests, and only a few that happen to be located in particularly inaccessible spots will survive. Unless we take precautions."

The technician looked over the drawings. "You want a kind of cage, or barrier, with knives and other stuff sticking out, so the humanoids can't get at the nests?"

"No," said Towers, "so the humanoids can't get at the nests *as the humanoids are now*. These cages have to be of various kinds, requiring different degrees of ingenuity to open, the mechanism has to be out where it can be seen, and some of the doors are to have widely-separated releases, so they can be opened by cooperative effort."

The technician frowned, then straightened up as a light seemed to dawn on him. "I get it. I'll start right to work on it, sir."

"Good."

The technician hurried out with the sketches.

Towers, feeling exhausted, pushed back his chair and got up. He thought he would go outside, take a little walk, and get some fresh air. He opened the outer door and froze.

Coming straight for him, a wild-eyed hairy figure burst across the clear space between the barracks. Right behind sprinted a crowd of Centrans with clubs, axes, and sledge hammers. But the humanoid was gaining.

Towers barely had time to reach for his gun.

There was a terrific burst of lights, then spiraling blackness.

Towers was on his back, vaguely aware of a soft covering over him. He opened his eyes.

Daylight hit him with a hammering shock.

He waited a moment, and tried opening his eyes

gradually. By degrees, he succeeded, until in a half-squint he could look around.

He was lying in his own room with a medical orderly watching him tensely.

Towers tried to sit up. The room wavered around him.

"Careful, sir," warned the orderly.

Towers waited till the room steadied, then sat up further. The orderly propped him up with a pillow.

Towers said, "Where's Major Logan?" His voice came out in a whisper, and he had to clear his throat and try again.

"I'll get him, sir." The orderly went out.

A few minutes later, Logan came in.

Towers said, "What day is it?"

"Sir, you've been out for nearly ten days. The doctor thought you were done for."

Towers grunted, and swung carefully to sit on the edge of the bed. He felt light-headed, but otherwise all right. It came to him with a shock that he actually felt better than he had earlier. He no longer ached all over. He glanced at Logan.

"What happened while I was out?"

"We got into production on the barriers and cages to protect the nests. We've got a pilot project going down there."

Towers got carefully to his feet. "How's it working?"

"Inside the test area, the insects knock the humanoids' normal daytime procedure to bits and pieces, and the more virulent ones create a terrific casualty rate. At night, a few individuals and little groups of humanoids hunt out the insects. At first the cages cut the humanoids to ribbons, and we thought it was going to be the same procedure as outside on the cliff. The ones in front rush on because they're pressed from behind, and the ones behind neither know nor care what happens to the ones in front. But apparently the humanoids that hunt the nests at night have a little more initiative than the rest."

"What happened?"

"Early the other night, we were watching a scene on

infra red, and one of those scarred-up humanoids got into a terrific fight with two others, finally beat them into a stupor, dragged them around to opposite sides of a fence of knives protecting the base of a pole with a nest on it, and by sheer persistence finally got the others to press down the two separated release-levers simultaneously. The fence collapsed, and the three of them got the big nest for their reward. The next day, these three stayed together, and a couple of nights later, they got at a trickier nest. Now there are half-a-dozen humanoids in this group, they generally stick together in the daytime, and they don't get broken up by the others. Swarms of the less-virulent bugs create so much distraction that not many of the humanoids can spare the patience to stalk the others. What's getting formed down there is a tribe, with a leader."

Towers breathed a sigh of relief. "When that process picks up enough speed, we should have something it's possible to deal with."

Logan said, "Klossig thinks so, too. When we started the second test area—a ring of virulent bugs on the outside to stop migration, with the less virulent ones scattered around the interior—he insisted on having special briefings for his troops. It's boosted morale terrifically, and the Centrans are in high spirits." Logan glanced out the window and added, "Most of them, that is." Then he said, "I think these humanoids are the toughest opposition we've ever run into."

Towers glanced out the window to see what Logan had seen that made him add the qualification "Most of them, that is."

Outside was a Centran colonel, in charge of a small crew of Centrans led by a private wearing a uniform with threads sticking out in the form of sergeant's chevrons. Towers leaned forward, and recognized the colonel and the sergeant who had caused Logan and him so much trouble when they first landed on the planet.

The colonel gloomily led his little band slowly past the barracks, where they picked up cigarette butts, chewing-gum wrappers, odd bits of string and broken rubber bands, and other miscellaneous junk.

Towers laughed. "Klossig's caught up with the colonel."

"Yes," said Logan, glancing out the window, "the colonel's in charge of the worst foul-ups in camp. Last week Klossig had the colonel and his boys putting new crack-filler between all the boards in the main hall of the Headquarters Building. It's only about two hundred feet long."

Towers grinned, then said suddenly, "As a matter of fact, these humanoids *aren't* our toughest opponents. They're just one minor variety of our toughest opponents. Think of the colonel. Think of Cartwright, before he started to use his head. Think of either of us sitting in that office, seeing the antics of that bug without realizing something was wrong."

"What do you mean?"

"Our toughest opponents," said Towers, "are all those who have the capacity for thought, but—for some reason— *won't think*."

Towers and Logan looked out the window, glanced from the colonel to the humanoids to Cartwright, just crossing the yard below. Then they cast a furtive glance at each other.

An object across the room caught Towers' attention. He cleared his throat.

"Look there, Logan. There's the worst offender of all."

"Who?"

"Right there. Look." He pointed.

Logan glanced around, then growled under his breath. Towers laughed.

Then he paused, and thought the matter over carefully. *He* was right there in the mirror, too.

Part VI:
Contagious Earthitis

Horsip and Moffis, on returning from their trip to Adrok IV, were a little dazed. Their heads whirled with details of installment loan contracts, franchises, interest compounded at 24 percent, inflation increasing at 8 percent, and riches for everyone, with poverty in lock step close behind. But before leaving, they had made arrangements with the Holy Brotherhood and others to transmit information on the planet; so that, at least, was accomplished. Their organization was now sending the High Council information on the numerous activities of the Earthmen. Horsip, however, was dissatisfied.

"Moffis, do you *understand* this stuff we're sending out?"

Moffis hesitated. "To tell the truth—no."

"Me either," said Horsip. "We have this report we sent back about our own visit. Consider the oil production information alone. By the time figures are on hand, it's obvious the Earthmen are increasing oil production at a fantastic rate. Despite an inflation on the planet, the price of oil has *dropped*. That benefits everyone who buys it. Despite big taxes on the oil, the drillers and refiners are getting rich. That's to *their* benefit. Apparently *everyone* benefits. But—meanwhile—there's this 'Society for a Livable Environment.' They claim that if something isn't done quick, the air will be unbreathable in twenty-six years and a half. They've got the facts to prove it. Then there's 'Concerned Citizens for Community Conservation.' They say the oil will run out in 24.7 years, unless rationing starts now; they've got figures to prove *that*. Next there's the 'Oil Industry Research Council,' and they claim that if they're allowed to push their production to the limit, that will give them money for research, and they'll be able to make oil out of rock inside of twenty years. They've got the figures for *that*. Each one of these organizations is run by an Earthman, and they all disagree. Moreover, each one can prove he's right. But, at best, only one *can* be right, because they contradict each other."

Moffis looked harassed.

"It's even worse than it seems. I just got a batch of reports wherein our people disguised themselves as 'newsmen,' and questioned some of these Earthmen. The Earthmen were all glad enough to answer questions.... Listen to this."

Moffis separated a bulky sheaf of papers from a bulging stack of reports, leafed through the sheaf, and read aloud:

"Mr. Smith was checking over his company's figures as I came in. He was beaming with good nature. He motioned me to sit down while he totaled up a column of figures, and murmured, 'Sixty million two hundred eighty-six thousand four hundred seventy-two. *That* checks.' He looked up, smiled broadly, and said, 'What can I do for you, young fellow? You aren't here to tell me your government has come out with an income tax, I hope.' He looked worried, and said, 'You aren't, are you?'"

Moffis paused, and scanned the pages rapidly. "*Here* we are. This is the part I wanted.... Mr. Smith stated, 'Our purpose, young fellow, is to press back the frontiers of poverty and the wilderness of despair. We can do this through sheer *productiveness*. Produce!—That's the answer to the problem! Make, build, produce, build, and produce again! Pile it up! Poverty can't stand up against it! That's the way to do it! With our methods of production, we can turn out ten, a hundred, a thousand items while the hand-laborer is working on one. Ours may not be quite as good as his, at first, but that's the next step. *Produce*, that's the first step. *Improve,* that's the second step. The more you make, the cheaper it gets to make it. Just let the forces of the market guide production into the right lines, and keep the producers unhampered, and the problem's solved. Nobody can be poor when he's got everything he needs. And he isn't likely to be despairing, either. As the stuff piles up, the price on it gets cheaper. It's bound to. Then everybody can afford it. This way, everybody gets rich. There's only one thing—keep the government out of it. Once they start sucking the profit out, all the prices go up. And they aren't subject to the laws of the market, either. They'll push production into the wrong lines. Then they've got a special bag of tricks to keep away any depression. A depression, you know, is when all the mistakes add up, and the something-for-nothing crowd gets taught what the truth is. A little depression puts everyone on his toes, after he's got fat and lazy from too much easy living. . . . So, you've got to keep the government out of it. And one other thing— you got to put some kind of limit on the number of college professors there are running around loose. You get a lot of funny things out of college professors. I don't understand it, but that's how it is.' "

Moffis put the report down, and Horsip frowned and massaged his chin.

Moffis said, "You see what I mean. He didn't hold anything back."

"But," said Horsip, "what does it mean?"

Moffis nodded. "That's it."

Horsip said, "Let's see that."

Moffis handed it to him. Horsip sat back, scowling, and leafed through the report.

"It appears to me, Moffis, that Smith has already been through a lot of things we've never dreamed of."

"Yes, but with Smith putting his solution to our problems into action, maybe now we *will* experience these things."

"H'm. I wonder what a 'depression' is?"

"I don't know, but I don't like the sound of it. It may not bother Smith, but it doesn't sound good to *me.*"

"Whoever made up this report should have had the sense to find out what the words he put in the report meant."

"A lot of these reports don't add up, even *with* explanations. Here, let's have that one. . . . Now, here in back—here we are. 'Depression: A state of acutely depressed business conditions. In a "depression," there is no money. Except for the urgent necessities, the means of production are idle. Nearly everyone is filled with gloom and despair. The future looks dismal. People kill themselves from lack of hope. Objects worth large sums of money can be had cheaply by anyone with the money to buy them. But nobody has any money.'" Moffis looked up. "That's a depression."

Horsip said fervently, "It doesn't sound good."

"No," said Moffis, "but how does the money disappear? Here, under 'Boom,' it says, 'Exuberant state of the economy. Everyone has money. Prices are high, but no one hesitates to buy, as everyone expects conditions to be even better in the future.'"

Horsip shook his head. "This is as hard to figure out as an 'installment loan contract.'"

"And it's only the beginning. Here, for instance, we have a report titled 'Hairwire Finetuning of Planetary Economic Systems.' I haven't found a complete sentence in it anywhere I can understand. My mind sort of slides over the surface, and can't get a grip."

"This is another interview with an Earthman?"

"Yes, this one is a famous economics professor. He even impresses the Earthmen."

Moffis reached into his stack of reports, and pulled out another sheaf. "Listen to this. 'Economic Systems—Their Sabotage and Overthrow. How to Do It.' Take a look at this."

After the first three sentences, Horsip had an attack of chills, but he read through to the end.

Moffis said, "How do you like that one?"

Horsip reread the summary, then looked up.

"Do you notice, Moffis, that when one of our men interviews an Earthman, he comes away talking like the

Earthman? Here, for instance, our man is describing what's the best thing to blow up. That's all right, because this interview was his job, and he's summarizing it. But listen to this: 'By this stage, the capitalists and their lackeys will lie awake nights drenched in sweat and shaking with fear. In their nightmare, they see the Revolution approach.' And so on. What's this?"

"Let's see that," said Moffis. He looked it over, frowning. "I didn't notice that when I was reading it. I suppose after reading that interview, this seemed mild by comparison. It's as if this Earthman had a bad case of something, and our man caught it from him."

"Let's see that first report again—the one on production. . . . Let's see, now." Horsip settled back, and turned to the summary. "Here we are. 'In summary, then, the important thing is, *produce*. Turn out the goods so fast and in such quantity that poverty and need are overwhelmed, swamped. Then, if too much is produced, the price goes down so anyone can buy the goods, and there is no harm done. Produce! That's the important thing! From high production, *everybody* profits.'"

Moffis sat up. "You're right! He caught it too!"

Horsip, scowling, weighed the reports in his hands.

"All these Earthmen, each with his special theory, are spread out through the Integral Union. That much we foresaw. But now—you remember, our men are supposed to make more fanatical 'reporters' than the Earth reporters who taught them. Apparently an Earthman can convince our people, and then they are stronger believers than he was. Can that be?"

Moffis was thinking it over. He said, "But, in that case . . ." And that was as far as he got, because at this point he stared across the room and stopped talking.

Horsip said, "Well, whether it's so or not, there's nothing we can do but improve the information network, hang on tight, and hope the High Council has some plan for taking care of this."

He became aware that Moffis was watching someone thread his way through the desks of busy workers and team supervisors, striding fast toward their slightly raised cubicle at the corner of the room. Horsip recognized Nokkel, the Security Chief.

Nokkel, looking as if he were suffering from a bad case of indigestion, opened the door of the cubicle, stepped in, and saluted.

Horsip studied Nokkel's expression, and returned the salute.

"Sir," said Nokkel, "we've turned up a communist cell in the Communications Section. And I—we—don't know what to . . ."

Horsip glanced out at the room full of desks and apparently busy individuals, where an intense silence suddenly reigned.

Horsip smiled, and spoke so his voice would carry. "Good news, Nokkel! That's fine work! Have a seat, and we'll work out the details."

The morbid interest on the watching faces turned to boredom, and the volume of noise in the room started to return to normal.

Horsip growled in a low voice, "Pull up a chair, Nokkel. Now, what's this? Let's have the details, and keep your voice down."

Nokkel leaned forward on the edge of his chair.

"Sir, what happened is that we got a tip from one of the men in the Communications Section that something suspicious was going on. We've used a new . . . ah . . . 'bug' and we've got evidence against the assistant chief of the section, two of the shift supervisors, and three of the men. The six are members of a 'cell,' and the leader is one of the men. He reports to someone else, and we're trying to trace that down, but we haven't got it worked out yet. They use 'drops,' code words, transmitters, something called 'microdots,' and ciphers that have driven my best men half out of their heads—and, well, frankly, sir, it's a mess. Somewhere there's an Earthman giving them instructions, but we don't know how he gets the information to them. We can't leave them where they are, because they will eventually trace down our sources and expose them to their own people. Moreover, they're trying to recruit new members. So we've got to stop them. On the other hand, if we close in now, we won't find out who they're reporting to, and it may be someone high in our own organization. We'd shift them onto less important work, but if we do they'll know we've found out. Every minute they're where they are, they do damage. But we don't dare touch them, because they're our only link to someone who may be doing more damage yet."

Horsip glanced at Moffis, who looked serious, and said nothing.

"So," said Horsip, turning to Nokkel, "you need to know what to do about this 'communist cell,' is that it?"

"Yes, sir."

Horsip again had that melting-ice sensation he'd had back on Earth.

Nokkel said jitterily, "I have the feeling that once I rip the cover off, there's no telling *what* we'll find. I'd have trusted these men anywhere. But they're all corrupt. My own assistants could be in on this. The whole organization could be . . ."

Horsip watched Nokkel alertly.

Nokkel gave a shuddering sigh. "No matter what you do, you can't beat the Earthmen. Some of those ciphers— I tried to show my men how to do it, but I got in a worse mess than they were in. You can't win. They're too smart. You—"

Horsip spoke confidently.

"You're overstrained, Nokkel. Now, don't worry about beating the Earthmen. It's true, they're clever, but they work against each other. Just bear in mind, there are a lot more of us, and we *don't* work against each other."

"But that's just it! Now we *do*. We—"

"Keep your voice down." Horsip looked into Nokkel's eyes. "All this is part of a great plan worked out by the *High Council*, Nokkel. It *looks* as if the Earthmen are making progress. But you know the High Council. The Earthmen see deep, but the Council sees deeper. Now, I can't tell you what the plan is. I don't claim to know more than a small part of it. But I can tell you the Earthmen are like a newly caught wild molk running around in a pasture. The molk looks ferocious. He *is* ferocious. But the herdsmen are watching him, and when the right time comes, they will throw out the tangle-ropes, and the molk will go down. Now, when I say *we* don't work against each other, naturally I mean our *top men*. Our top men are just like one man. But what of the leadership of the Earthmen? They are working in all directions. They are wasting their strength strangling each other. They *can't* win, Nokkel. Their strength is subtracted from each other. Not so with the High Council. Our strength is one, united, all working in the same direction. You and I may have a difficult time, but that doesn't matter. We will win in the end."

Nokkel's expression wavered through various shades of doubt and hope, but, as Horsip confidently approached the conclusion, Nokkel heaved a great sigh of relief.

"That's true," he said. "I've been so close to the details I've missed those points." His brow furrowed. "But now—on—this business with this 'cell'—what do we—"

"Clean them out," said Horsip firmly. "Arrest them, and put them to the question."

"But we'll lose the only link to their superior!"

"True, but every moment we leave them where they are, they do damage. And we can't move them without warning them, which would be worse. So, if we wait for them to give some lead to their superior, we may have a considerable wait, and the damage they do will offset what gain we make by capturing their superior, *if* we capture him."

"Truth," said Nokkel. He was silent a moment, his expression distracted and his lips working. Then he nodded again, and beamed. *"Truth,"* he said briskly. "I will take them in at once."

He came to his feet, saluted, and went out. Horsip, watching him leave, saw one of his men study Nokkel alertly, then pick up a telephone. Horsip glanced over his staff. No less than three were speaking into phones while watching Nokkel.

Horsip noted their names on a slip of paper.

Moffis watched Nokkel go out.

"I just wonder if we have the man for this job."

"He seemed all right when we were setting up the job."

"I'm talking about *now*."

"Who would you suggest?"

After a lengthy silence, Moffis nodded. "That's so. At least Nokkel does do the job *somehow*." Moffis picked up a slim report, and tossed it over to Horsip.

"*Someone* is doing his job right."

Horsip glanced at the title of the report: "The Planetary Mob, and Its Control," by John Towers. Scowling, Horsip opened up the report, to read of a planet populated by huge numbers of humanoids that could digest practically everything that grew on the planet, and hence created population problems such as he, Horsip, had never conceived. Towers had gotten the Centran expedition on the planet out of a very tight spot, and yet the report was straightforward and free of poses of superiority.

Moffis said, "Just as I give up hope, another report from Towers comes in."

"Well, let's hope Nokkel cleans out that 'cell.' Maybe then things will come back to normal—whatever *that* may be."

Several hours later, Nokkel came in, to tell Horsip the members of the "cell" had been caught, along with enough evidence to shoot the lot. Better yet, one of them had folded up under questioning, and revealed the name of their highly placed superior, who had also been seized.

"So, sir," said Nokkel, his face glowing, "this foreign influence is wiped out, and everything is now in good order."

"That's good," said Horsip. "Now, Nokkel, there is just one thing that bothers me. This . . . ah . . . informant who uncovered the 'cell' . . . ?"

"Yes, sir. He will be rewarded, sir. We will take him into our organization, and give him staff rank."

"H'm . . . yes, but—how did he uncover this 'cell'?"

"By informing us, sir. He came right to us with the information. That broke the whole thing."

"Yes, but how did he *find out* about it?"

"He . . . ah . . ." Nokkel looked blank. "Let's see, now. He . . . h'm . . . it seems to me that what happened was that he came to us without anything specific, he just was worried and . . . these people acted suspicious to him, and he . . . well, he thought it was his patriotic duty, even though they *were* colleagues of his, and . . . well . . . it turned out he was right."

"I see," said Horsip, with no great air of conviction.

"Often these things depend on intuition," said Nokkel, looking wise. "It isn't the kind of thing you can lay your hand on, but there's just something that your . . . ah . . . clinical sense," he tapped his head and smiled expansively—"fastens on and says to you, 'Nokkel, my boy, there's something about this fellow that isn't right.' And then there's nothing to do but keep an eye on him, and often as not it's the dull unspectacular routine that gets him in the end."

Moffis cleared his throat coldly.

Horsip squinted at Nokkel, who was looking yet more expansive, and seemed about to let loose a new flood of wisdom. Gently, Horsip said, "Well, now, Nokkel, what does your intuition tell you about someone who comes to you and gives you a hint to watch someone else, and manages to get away without giving you any information at all as to how he knows what he knows?"

Nokkel, leaning back and twirling a little chain with some kind of watch charm that wound up on his finger, suddenly straightened up and looked awake. A hint of intelligence showed in his eyes.

"If you look at it *that* way . . ." He frowned, then shoved his chair back. "I'll check on it, sir." He saluted, and went out in a hurry.

Horsip, looking out over his staff, saw three of his men pick up their phones as Nokkel went out.

Moffis said, "Nokkel's clinical sense must have got chloroformed sometime."

"Either that," said Horsip, "or it's getting so many signals it can't handle them all. Don't look too interested, but in the Correlation Section there are two people on the phone, and in the Abstracting Section there's another."

"I see them," murmured Moffis. "That bird in Abstracting was looking at Nokkel's back as he went by."

"It doesn't seem to make much sense," said Horsip, "but the same three did the same thing the last time Nokkel went out."

Moffis scowled. "It must mean something."

"Someone," said Horsip, "must want to know as soon as Nokkel is on his way back to his office."

"But why *three* of them?"

"I have an idea," said Horsip, "but it's going to have to wait until Nokkel takes care of this informant of his."

It didn't take long for that to happen.

Nokkel, looking haunted, settled into the chair opposite Horsip.

"You were right, sir. I sprang a surprise on him, told him I'd known all along, and he'd better come absolutely clean if he expected to get his sentence lightened. The shock jarred everything right out of him. *He* was working for MI-5."

Horsip felt queasy. " 'MI-5.' Let's see, that's—"

Nokkel said exasperatedly, "There's this island down there on Earth, it's just a little place, but we've got so much information on it no one actually knows anything about it. . . . Anyway, MI-5 operates out of there."

Moffis frowned. "If you've got so much information, how is it you don't know anything about it?"

"Because, sir, we can't digest it all. For one thing, we don't know what's fact and what's imagination. If we only had a tenth of the information, we'd be better off." He thought a moment. "A hundredth would be better yet. We could handle *that*."

Horsip said, "At least you've discovered that this fellow who gave you the information about that 'cell' was an agent for MI-5? . . . That's settled, at least?"

Nokkel looked jarred. "Did I say that? No, that one was the agent for the CIA."

Moffis swore.

Horsip said, "I understood you to say you questioned him, and he was an agent for MI-5,"

"Yes, sir . . . ah . . . I see what happened. There are so many of them, it's hard to keep track. He—the CIA agent—was the one that told me about the 'cell.' I got at him through this other fellow on our staff that I was suspicious of. *He* was working for MI-5."

Horsip squinted, started to ask a question, and thought better of it.

"*Anyway*," he said, "you got both of them?"

Nokkel said doggedly, "There were *three* of them by the time we got it all taken care of."

Moffis massaged his temples.

"At any rate," said Horsip, "they're all taken care of *now?*"

"It's like a weed with a taproot," said Nokkel. "I got the part I could get a grip on. But it looks to me like maybe it broke off further down."

"Just get all you can," said Horsip stubbornly. He had the impression that he was walking forward fast and nevertheless going slowly backward. "Now, while you're in here, Nokkel, is it possible that something could be taking place behind your back—something that would have to end when you leave—so someone would want to be warned *when* you leave?"

Nokkel said uneasily, "Well . . . there are only three possibilities. But I'm sure each of them is well guarded against." He glanced from Horsip to Moffis. "Why, what . . ."

"Three possibilities?" said Horsip.

"Yes, sir. First, there's my secret file. Second, there's my quarters. And third, there's the Master Control Center Surveillance Cubicle. But the file has a special lock, and I have the only key. My quarters can only be reached by a corridor that's always guarded by very trustworthy guards. And the Surveillance Cubicle has a special lock, extra trustworthy guards, and a secret camera and recorder that start as soon as anyone enters." Nokkel looked briefly smug, and then uneasy.

"Why?"

Horsip said, "Don't turn around, or give any sign, but each time you leave here, three of our men out there get on the phone."

Nokkel looked shocked, then mad.

"If I could borrow your phone for just a minute, sir? . . . The one that connects up with Internal Security?"

Horsip reached out to the bank of phones, and handed it over.

Nokkel sat back.

"Hello, Groffis. Nokkel speaking. I want special details sent to surround and break into my quarters, the secret file room, and the Control Center Surveillance Cubicle. . . . I don't care what it makes us look like if there's no one there. You'll either carry out that order without delay, or I'll have you strung up by the heels, my boy, and what will people think of that, eh? . . . That's better. Now if no one is there, it was just an exercise, but if anyone *is* there, capture them, and if they resist, shoot them. The main thing is, *get* them one way or the other."

Nokkel's voice, instead of getting louder, stayed at the same level, but seemed to get more intense.

Horsip and Moffis looked approving, then Nokkel handed back the phone, and Horsip hung it up. Nokkel gave a shuddering sigh.

"But I can't believe that anyone could be in any of those places!"

"Let's hope not," said Horsip. "But, in that case, we have the problem of why these three in here are on the phone when you leave."

"Well," said Nokkel grimly, "I've had plenty of practice lately shaking information out of people, and we can do the same to this bunch. The trouble is, I can get only so far. Even if they're willing to talk, there's a limit. These Earthmen apparently have more spies on that one little planet than we have in all the Integral Union. As nearly as I can figure it out, every dot of land down there has a spy system stealing information from everyone else. The result is, they know just how to do it. They've had so much practice the thought of it weighs me down. I feel out-classed."

"Luckily," said Horsip, "it's easy to tell the difference between one of them and one of us. Otherwise, they'd be all over the place. Now, as soon as we clear this up, there's another problem." Horsip was talking about this when there was a sharp ring, and he turned, to see the little metal flag raised beside the "Internal Security" phone. He took it off its hook, and handed it to Nokkel.

Nokkel listened intently to a voice that squawked excitedly as it ran words together. Finally, whoever was on the other end ran down, and Nokkel said, "All right, lock them all up separately, and get started on the questioning. . . . Yes, I'll be there, but not right away." Scowling, Nokkel handed the phone back to Horsip, who hung it up. "Sometimes," said Nokkel, "I wonder if I should trust *him.*"

Horsip said, "Exactly my own feeling, Nokkel, about almost everybody in this room. I suggest you go back early, to just find out if you *can.* Now, here are the names of the three who watched when you went out. It might be a good idea to pick up the lot, as soon as possible. Then, since we've got things moving, I think we should search everybody's quarters while we're at it, and get a look at *anything* that seems suspicious."

"When, sir?"

"As soon as you can get things in order."

Nokkel shoved back his chair.

Horsip said, "Before you go—what did your men find in your three safe places?"

"Spies," said Nokkel. As Nokkel went out, the same three members of Horsip's staff watched alertly, and picked up their phones. Looks of puzzlement, then horror, crossed their faces. Hastily, they hung up. Furtively, they glanced toward Horsip, then busied themselves at their work until Nokkel's men suddenly came in and dragged them all out.

By that same evening, Horsip was examining a collection of code books, miniature transmitters, propaganda leaflets, instructions for spies, false teeth with poison pellets inside, and numerous copies of *The Works of Mao Tse-Tung Translated Into the Centran.* Nokkel, obviously suffering from a headache, reported that he had so many prisoners he had run out of jail cells, and had put a lot of them in the same cell, whereupon a ferocious squabble had broken out, with prisoners accusing each other of being "imperialists," "commie goons," "revisionists," "lousy bloodsuckers," and other names that had so far proved impossible to translate.

The meaning of what was taking place suddenly dawned on Horsip.

The Integral Union was being turned into a battleground for all the conflicting opinions represented on the planet Earth.

And those conflicting opinions had come close to blowing Earth to bits.

That same day, Horsip put his conclusions into a report to the High Council, and grimly braced himself for the reply.

In the next few days, with a considerably smaller staff, Horsip got the routine moving again, and waited for the High Council to reply to his message.

The High Council took its time about replying. Meanwhile, Horsip's system for gathering information had gotten into high gear, and the reports flooded in. The trend on the planets became glaringly plain, and the more Horsip saw of it, the less he liked it.

He tossed over to Moffis a report titled "The New Planetary Arms Race—Who's Ahead?" Moffis tossed back a report headed "Superneonazi Culture on Maphrik II— the Deification of a Racial Hero-Type."

Moffis groaned and Horsip snarled as he read:

" . . . thus in the launching of the first squadron of this formidable space fleet, the Warrior Hero of Ganfre's Cult of the Supreme is become the central *point d'appui* of the Total State. Vowing total conquest of the universe in twenty years, Guide Ganfre was cheered by a crowd of half a million as—"

Horsip looked up, to see a messenger salute, and present a sealed envelope and receipt. Horsip signed, the messenger went out, and Horsip read:

"You and your second-in-command are required to report at the earliest practicable moment, to give your personal assessment of the situation. . . . J. Roggil, Vice-Chairman, the High Council."

"At last," said Horsip. "Here, Moffis, read this."

Moffis growled, "One of these reports at a time is enough."

"No, Moffis. The message."

"What message?"

"Here."

"Ah, I thought it was another report. Let's see . . . good! Good! Now maybe we can get some action!"

"Phew!" said Horsip. " 'Ganfre's Cult of the Supreme,' 'Moggil's Totalization of the State,' 'The Free Life on Qantros III,' 'The Dictatorship of the Proletariat on Gengrak IV,' 'Maximedimastercare Programs on Stulbos VI'—if I never see another of these things, that will be soon enough."

"Too soon," said Moffis. "I hope the Council is satisfied we have the Earthmen spread out enough by now."

"Moffis," said Horsip fervently, "when we get through describing this mess, I'll be surprised if the High Council doesn't squash some of these maniacs before the day is out."

The trip to report to the High Council took longer than Horsip or Moffis had expected. The High Council was in the far end of the Centran system, well beyond the line of demarcation of the Sealed Zone. In getting there, the contraction of time known to the Centrans by experience, and predicted in theory by the Earth mathematician Einstein, came strongly into effect. While the trip seemed long enough to them, from the viewpoint of a person back at their headquarters, far more time had passed. But, finally the trip was over.

This time, the whole Council listened as Horsip and

Moffis, in turn, gave their reports, and answered questions, and Horsip summed up:

"The Earthmen have split up, as expected, but instead of quietly supplying useful leavening for our own people, they have converted large numbers of them to *their* viewpoints. Now, this might not be too bad if only successful Earth viewpoints were put in action. Instead, every collection of fanatical believers has settled a planet of their own, and converted the populace to their own ideas. We now have all kinds of fanatics, all over the place. We're overrun with spies, dictators, weird philosophies, and little space fleets turning into big space fleets.

"These Earthmen are brilliant, but they have a capacity for being one-sided such as no Centran ever dreamed of. They can take a philosophy that's insane on the face of it, and make it work—for a while, anyway.

"I think we should straighten this out while there's still time to straighten it out.

"I respectfully submit that we should divide the planets taken over by the Earthmen into two categories—those anyone can see are the work of maniacs, and those that offer hopes of improvement. The first, we should take over by force."

Horsip became aware that the High Council was not being swept off its feet.

Roggil said thoughtfully, "An accurate presentation, General. But applying force right now won't work."

"Sir, we can't stand by while power-hungry madmen get started piling up space fleets. A lunatic is serious business once he's got a gun in his hand. As it is now, we can smash the lot of them."

"Whereupon, the trouble would spread. No, Horsip. It has to come to a head first."

Horsip felt a powerful impulse to disagree, but suppressed it.

Roggil studied Horsip's expression.

"There are some facts, General, known only to us and to the highest religious authorities. I can't say any more that that."

"Yes, sir."

"We are not necessarily unanimous. But many of us believe something very useful may come out of this situation. That, in fact, something useful is *bound* to come out of it. Accordingly, you are to continue to observe and report to us. When and if the time comes, we won't hesitate to use force in whatever way is necessary. Meanwhile, for your personal safety, we are assigning a unit of highly trained shock troops, and a reinforced squadron of the Fleet, to act under your direct command. You are answerable to no one but us for the way you use this force. We trust you to use it in strict accord with our expressed wishes."

Horsip, beginning to have visions of laying a few dictators by the heels, got control of his imagination, and said stoically, "Yes, sir."

And that was the end of the interview with the High Council, though some of them nodded in a friendly way as Horsip went out.

After the lengthy trip back, Horsip and Moffis found themselves once more at their desks, where things meanwhile had progressed. Although the trip had seemed long enough to Horsip, he hadn't realized how much more time had passed here.

The first report Horsip opened up suggested the change:

Summary: In summary, it appears safe to say that Premier Ganfre, in creating for himself (through his rubber-stamp cabinet) the post of Unified Planets' Guide, has solidified his absolute control over the six planets now subject to him. Guide Ganfre is thus well placed to protect himself from any attack by the comparatively split home planets of the Space Soviet. He can also, if he chooses, attack with the bulk of his forces any one of the planets of the Soviet. Intensive analysis of the situation suggests that either Ganfre or the Soviet can be expected to move soon against the various Free Planets, the Farmers Union planets, and the fantastic Free Life worlds. However, as all these planets are under the control of various Earthmen, no certain prediction can be made, only estimates based on analysis of the relative military power of the various planets, and on intensive study of parallel situations on the Earthmen's home planet. No exact analogy to this present situation can be found, partly because of the control thought to be exercised over the Space Soviet from one nation on the planet Earth. But the apparent probabilities are those given above.

Horsip looked up dizzily, "Six planets." He turned to Moffis, who was studying a thick report he had doubled over, and which was threatening to spring shut at any moment.

Horsip started to speak, changed his mind, and looked sourly at the stack of reports on his desk. He told himself that, after all, he could consider the trip to the High Council as a kind of vacation. But the fact now had to be faced that, to write the overall summary of the situation at regular intervals, he had to keep track of what was happening. He took the top report, and looked at the title: "Agriculture in the Farmers Union."

Horsip opened it up, looked surprised, then began to relax. The report described friendly cooperation between farmers of various kinds from Earth and the Centran farmers. Photographs and sketches showed farm layouts, schemes for returning all the by-products to the soil, new breeds of molk and Earth cattle, ponds, orchards, descriptions of Earth fruits, vegetables, and grains, and Horsip, reading this, fell into a happy frame of mind.

And then he discovered that *this* planet was not armed.

Horsip sent for a copy of the Articles of Union between Earth and Centra, and discovered that Centran Armed Forces could be used to protect, attack, or otherwise regulate a planet only by approval of the Control Committee. The Control Committee was made up of the three representatives from Centra, and three from Earth. The three from Earth were picked by the various power

blocs on the planet. The three from Centra, in the last
analysis, were appointed by the High Council. The decision of the Control Commission had to be unanimous to
be effective. If any member voted against the others, the
decision was nullified.

Checking the records of the Control Commission, Horsip
found a long list of resolutions:

Resolved: That the Snard Soviet be warned against
aggression. 5–1
Resolved: That Dictator Ganfre be seized and shot.
5–1
Resolved: That the Rogebar Soviet be occupied
militarily. 5–1
Resolved: That Dictator Schmung be arrested. 5–1
Resolved: That the Snard Soviet be disarmed. 5–1
Resolved: That free elections be held on Snard.
5–1
Resolved: That Snard be warned against aggression.
5–1
Resolved: That Snard be forced to cease its military
action. 5–1
Resolved: That help be dispatched to Lyrica against
Snard. 5–1

Horsip looked up in disgust. All these resolutions were
waste paper because they weren't unanimous. Checking
further, he discovered that every time the vote was 5–1,
it was some Earth representative who objected. When Centra objected, the vote was generally 3–3. Horsip nodded
approvingly. That was more like it. But the Earthmen, naturally, couldn't even agree with each other. He shook his
head, sent the records back to the files, and reached for
the next report. This proved to be about a planet renamed
"Cheyenne" by the Earthmen:

    . . . inhabitants all wear guns strapped around their
    waists, and excel in drawing the guns rapidly, in
    "horsemanship" (the horse is a beast imported from

Earth—like a slender molk with no horns), and in
games played with cards (like our Grab but more
complicated), and by means of various contraptions
intended to provide unpredictable chance. Exactly
who set up this set of customs is not known, the first
immigrants having long since been shot by later
arrivals. While there is no visible reason for contentment, rough humor and good nature for some reason prevail . . .

Horsip scratched his head, sifted through the report, and
read:

. . . somewhat over three thousand volunteers are
believed to have gone to Lyrica during the Snard
invasion. A resolution to punish Cheyenne was introduced in the Control Commission, but vetoed by the
Euramerican representative. Upwards of ten thousand
casualties are believed to have been inflicted on the
Snard troops, who were baffled by the Cheyenne
method of fighting. Survivors of the Cheyenne expedition are believed to have settled into rough broken
country on Lyrica, from which they still raid the Snard
troops. They are said to be led by an "Apache Indian."
What that is, is not known, but it appears effective,
as Snard is compelled to maintain a huge garrison . . .

Horsip skimmed farther, then picked up a paper headed
"A Study of Conditions on the Planet Bibedebop."
He murmured the name to himself, weighed the report
in his hand, told himself he would have to read it to report
on it, flipped through it rapidly, and was not encouraged by
the dense mass of print that looked up in one solid block
of technicalities. Horsip turned to the summary:

Summary: To summarize, in the simplest possible
terms, the inhabitants of Bibedebop, believing in the
vanity of any expectation of future reward or punishment, and the inapplicability of conventional mores

to the human condition, strive to maximize the input of pleasurable sensation, while severely restricting the output of conventionally so-regarded productive effort. "Maximization of satisfaction with minimization of effort" might be regarded as the life-goal of the inhabitants. Indeed—

Horsip looked up angrily. From Moffis' desk came a thump as he set down the massive report. Horsip tossed his own report on the "Outgoing" heap. "Do you have one worth reading?"

"Yes," said Moffis, "but it isn't pleasant."

"If you're through, let's see it."

Moffis handed it over. Horsip pried it open to read "Armament Rates of Earth-Dominated Planets."

Horsip felt a chill as he looked at charts marked "Weapons Production, Overall," "Space Ship Production," "Growth of Technological Production." Toward the edge of each chart, the curves climbed like ships headed for outer space.

Absorbed, Horsip was only vaguely aware of exclamations of astonishment from Moffis. When Horsip, skimming fast to get the highlights, which fit together like a well-made gun, finally came to the end, Moffis was just looking up.

"Well, Moffis," said Horsip, "that *does* make unpleasant reading."

"This is almost as bad. Would you believe that there is actually a planet where *everything* man-made is barred? And they've made the rule hold!"

"What do they eat?"

"Nuts and berries. Roots. Snigglers and wrettles. Thousand-bristled thread-spinners. Anything that's *natural.*"

Horsip thought of the discipline that would have to be imposed to enforce such a rule. But the Earthmen had doubtless accomplished it by putting across a *theory*.

Horsip shook his head.

"This is worse. All these dictators arm themselves at top speed, while most of the other planets don't arm at all—"

"Of course," said Moffis, "the other planets shouldn't

have to arm. They have a right to look to the Fleet for
protection."

"Yes, but with this Control Commission, what use is the
Fleet?"

Moffis said thoughtfully, "If the Fleet would just blow
up the Control Commission . . ."

Horsip looked shocked.

"We couldn't have that. That would be a . . ."

He paused, considering it, then shook his head.

"That would be a breakdown of discipline. We couldn't
have that—unless higher authority *ordered* it."

Moffis nodded.

"Just let them order it *soon*."

Before the eyes of Horsip and Moffis, the changes took
place, and if the High Council was disturbed by it, they
gave no sign. Day by day, the control of the Earthmen
broadened and tightened. More and more planets fell under
their sway, and instead of being slowed by the sheer bulk
of Centrans who had to be persuaded to new ways, their
progress seemed accelerated by the Centran respect for
ideas. The Earthmen, apparently used to more stubborn
argument, seemed to organize whole planets overnight. Only
where the Holy Brotherhood was exceptionally strong, or
the Earthmen very weak, were the Earthmen defeated.
With these exceptions the peaceful conquest of Centra by
Earth swept forward, with the differences amongst the
Earthmen extended to the Centrans. Horsip and Moffis,
aching for action, varied their monotonous scrutiny of
reports by occasional visits to planets.

"Ah, yes, my son," said a beaming priest, cracking his
knuckles as he stood overlooking a spaceport where large
numbers of dejected Earthmen were trooping out to waiting space-ships, "The Earthmen came, and the Earthmen
went, and the planet is still the same, and the Brotherhood
remains. Bad luck attended the Earthmen wherever they
turned, dear me! The design of the Great One, I think, was
plain in the way their factories burned down and their plans
blew up, whatever they did. Would you believe it, they had

a usurious scheme by which a person might squander money yet unearned on wasteful self-indulgence! They then aimed to sink wells deep in the ground to suck out the lamp oil reserved to future generations, and burn it up in a rush. If once they had got started, there is no telling what deviltry they might have brought to pass! But the Brethren were alert. We clung to them close, and inflicted on them the Judgment of the Great One. The loss the Earthmen suffered on this planet was fantastic! Look at the sorry crew! They may, of course, be back. We are busily spreading tales of their evil designs so the people will be ready. If truth were told, there were one or two little . . . er . . . instances of excessive zeal amongst our own people. . . . But in a good cause."

"Phew," said Moffis, when they were on their way again, "did you notice the look in that priest's eye when he told about the Earthmen's factories burning down? By the way, the back of his robe, along the edge, looked scorched."

"It seemed to me," said Horsip, "that every one of the Brotherhood smelled of smoke—except the saintly High Priest, himself, of course."

"Yes, but what a crafty look his assistant had!"

Horsip nodded. "The Earthmen ran into it that time, all right."

Horsip and Moffis then went over the latest batch of reports, and had any sense of pity for the Earthmen knocked to bits.

"Look at this. The Snard Soviet has got *another* planet."

"So has Ganfre—and he's armed to the teeth."

Soon Horsip was reading a report of disasters and calamities that were hard to believe until he realized this was about that planet he had heard of before—where everything man-made was banned. Wide-eyed, he read:

> . . . as no food had been stored, this frost in the Radigg region was a disaster. Coming on top of the floods, which have occurred periodically throughout the planet's history, they aggravated the food shortage into a famine. Meanwhile, the planetary government issued assurances that all would be well. As the

famine worsened, a delegation of leading citizens demanded a return to systematic storage of food, at least. The planetary government assured the delegation that the Bounty of Nature could be relied on, and that all man's troubles had come from eating artificial food, artificially raised by man. The tilling of the soil was unnatural, the government asserted, man having been meant to find his food in the field like other animals. If there was need, Nature would provide. If Nature did not seem to provide, then it was because the population was too high, and the thing to do was to let Nature adjust the population downward. The result of this pronouncement was revolution, and the planet, its population considerably shrunken, has returned to traditional Centran methods. Although it was only one particular kind of Earthman who caused the trouble, the population now does not like Earthmen, and in the past month two innocent tourists have been dipped in hot tar, while another was only barely rescued from being thrown headfirst into a volcano. The planet was a popular stop on the Nature-Lover's Tour before the food ran out, but . . .

There was the *whack* of paper on a desk top, and Horsip turned to see Moffis shake his head.

"No matter what you say, these Earthmen have increased production. They do it on the 'free-enterprise' planets. They do it on the dictator planets. They make a *fantastic* increase."

"But," said Horsip, "they aren't looking very far ahead. The waste is terrific."

"That isn't going to help us when we run into this concentration of space-ships."

"But they don't agree with each other."

"Let's hope they never do. They're going to be as big as the Fleet soon."

Horsip nodded moodily, and pulled a fresh report off the stack: "Disaster on Bibedebop."

"Ah," he murmured, "that's where they minimize work

and maximize pleasure." He opened up the report, to read of whole sections of the population stupefied by drugs while others stole their possessions. He read of an arrangement whereby volunteers tried out new drugs without charge for a generous drug-manufacturing cartel operating out of Dictator Ganfre's home planet. There were so many volunteers that distillery owners and beer-parlor operators were virtuously trying to end the arrangement. Meanwhile, the cartel was testing a superhallucinant that provided the illusion of fulfilling the user's wants so vividly there seemed no need to *really* fulfill them. To get a satisfying banquet, it was only necessary to snort up the nose a quarter teaspoonful of green powder. So why bother with food? As the population starved and the cartel's scientists methodically took notes, something else came along:

> . . . wave after wave of Mikerils, without warning, each successive wave more powerful than the last, struck the main population centers . . .

Horsip, startled, read a grisly description that brought back the fears of childhood. But then he relaxed. . . . After all, this was the account given by the survivors of a tremendous overuse of hallucinants.

Horsip turned to the next report. This told of " . . . an amalgamation of these worlds that would have seemed unlikely only a short time ago. The various varieties of planetary Soviets, for instance, are now combining with the Snard Soviet against the Free Planets Union, formed to resist the National Racist Planetary Alliance dominated by Dictator Ganfre. Ganfre, meanwhile, is successfully wooing more planets that are alarmed by the conglomeration of soviets. Confronted by these gigantic combinations, the Free Planets Union has formed an alliance with the agrarian planets still uncommitted, but it is unknown how the balance of power will be affected by . . ."

Horsip read on, report after report, and when he finished he shook his head, pulled over a blank sheet of paper, and began to write:

To the High Council:
Sirs:
I send herewith summaries of reports which
describe typical situations we are now facing.

I again urge the use of force in the greatest possible strength, to smash the armed combinations now
formed within the Integral Union. I urge the use of
the Fleet, reinforced to the maximum possible extent
regardless of dangers elsewhere, in a surprise attack
against either Ganfre or Snard. Immediately following the elimination of this opponent, I urge that the
Fleet at once be placed in the most favorable position to attack with its full remaining strength the
other combination, whether headed by Snard or
Ganfre.

If this attack is made at the earliest possible
moment, and if all available force is used against each
opponent singly, it may still be possible to destroy
these combinations.

> Respectfully,
> K. Horsip
> Member, Supreme Staff
> Director of Surveillance

Horsip handed the message to Moffis, who was moodily eyeing a large chart headed:

Order of Battle, the Nationalist Racist
Planetary Alliance, Compared with:
Order of Battle, the United Socialist Planets Soviets

Moffis was grumbling to himself when Horsip handed
the message to him. He read in silence, then slammed his
fist on the table.
"*Good!* But there's no time to lose."
Horsip nodded grimly, and sent the message.

The rough idea of Horsip's recommendation found its
way into general knowledge among his staff, so there was

a tense silence as a messenger brought a sealed message
to Horsip.

Horsip dismissed the messenger, ripped the envelope
open, and read:

By Command
The High Council

The High Council believes that any interference
in the situation at present would defeat its purposes.
What is needed instead is fuller information.

You are hereby requested to review the whole
situation, basing your report as far as possible on firsthand information.

J. Roggil
Vice-Chairman

Horsip looked up in disgust. Moffis read the message,
sitting tense and alert as he started, and slumping as he
read. He handed it back to Horsip.

"Now what?"

"Now we look over *more* planets."

"What would happen if instead of waiting for the Council, the Supreme Staff ordered the attack?"

Horsip felt the electric jolt go through him. Then he
found himself mentally counting votes. Argit would be
opposed. Maklin would very possibly agree. Roffis would
do what he thought was right, but would he go against
the High Council? And what about the High Council
itself? Horsip suddenly laughed.

"It would be a disaster, Moffis. The High Council
wouldn't stand there with its tail wrapped around its ankles
while we flouted its authority."

"But if we let this go on, *that* will be a disaster."

"I know it. But I know it wouldn't work to go
against the High Council. . . . Besides, it would be
wrong."

Moffis said unwillingly, "I know *that*. But something has
to be done. This is almost out of control."

"Maybe the Council does know something we don't know."

Moffis showed a flicker of hope.

"In that case—if we keep looking, we should find it."

But no matter how they traveled, the situation was now developing so fast that the impression of its hopelessness had to be revised upward from day to day. They had traveled quietly on earlier visits, but now commerce raiders preyed on the shipping lanes, and terrorists amused themselves by planting bombs on passenger ships, and taking pot shots from the shrubbery around spaceports. This time Horsip brought along the guard allotted him by the High Council, along with the reinforced squadron of the Fleet that the Council had provided. Horsip spent his spare time, while not reading reports and writing summaries, making sure his force was in good order; and the effect created by this show of strength brought home to Horsip how long it had been since the central authority of the Integral Union had made its will felt.

As his reinforced squadron, its guns and launchers bared for action against the raiders, flashed past planets and space depots belonging to various authorities, its presence acted like a hot poker on tender hide. Through the big screens in the flagship's command center, Horsip could see the hasty departure of questionable ships, the scattering of convoys, and the hurried deployment of warships off the planets of dictatorships. Occasionally a challenge flashed in:

From: Supreme High Command
National Racist Planetary Alliance
Supreme Commander
Region of Snarlebat II, Shock Combat Legion of Space

To: Unknown Fleet
Message:
     Identify yourself at once, or withdraw from NRPA territory, subject to attack by NRPA combat forces at full condition of readiness. Your reply is demanded immediately.

Signed:
Q. Drekkil
Supreme Commander
Shock Combat Legion of Space
Region of Snarlebat II

"What do we do about that, sir?" inquired the squadron's communications officer, as Horsip looked up from the message.

Horsip, itching to flatten Q. Drekkil, and sling the Shock Combat Legion of Space into the nearest sun, reminded himself of the High Council's instructions, and asked himself whether Drekkil could be induced to attack. Whereupon Horsip, of course, could defend himself.

"H'm," said Horsip. "This is an important matter. It will require some time to think of a suitable reply."

"Yes, sir. But . . . ah . . . beg pardon, sir, it says here an *immediate* answer is necessary."

"It does, doesn't it? Possibly I'll have it ready after the evening meal."

The communications officer blinked, and pulled out his watch. He looked up at Horsip, and just at that moment the squadron commander stepped in.

"Sir, we've got two squadrons of warships closing in on us. I've just had a point-blank warning to stop at once."

Horsip considered coldly what would happen if he were now attacked and he and the squadron wiped out while he was attempting to get information for the High Council. What would the Council do?

Horsip glanced at the communications officer.

"Send: 'This is General Klide Horsip of the Supreme Staff. These are Fleet ships of the Integral Union. We will neither stop, alter course, nor answer questions. You are required to stand aside and cover your guns in the presence of the Fleet.'"

The communications officer blinked, scribbled on his pad, and rushed out. The squadron commander stared at Horsip a moment.

"If they open fire—"

"We'll see how many we can take with us."

The squadron commander bared his teeth in a grin, saluted, and stepped out.

The big screen showed the onrush of the two squadrons of the Shock Combat Legion. From the angle of view and comparative velocities, it was evident that Horsip's squadron had not altered course or speed in the slightest. The Shock Combat Legion continued to close in. Then the view in the viewscreen turned into chaos as the ships of the oncoming squadrons clawed to get out of the way, broke formation, gun covers sliding over the turrets, the still uncovered guns and launchers deflecting in any direction to avoid aiming at Horsip's ships. The long-range detector apparatus of the scattered ships swung around in all directions, obviously seeking what might be coming along behind Horsip.

Horsip shook his head. The ships of the Shock Combat Legion were now straining to form a guard of honor.

The communications officer came in, looking dazed.

"Sir, we've got a reply."

He held out a slip of flimsy paper. Horsip skimmed the heading, and came to the business part of the message:

> High Admiral Querk Drekkil, Supreme Commander of the Shock Combat Legion of Space in the Region of Snarlebat II, extends respectful greeting to General Horsip of the Integral Union. High Admiral Drekkil wishes to assure General Horsip of the kind regard in which the Integral Union is held by the National Racist Planetary Alliance. If High Admiral Drekkil may assist General Horsip in action against any common enemy, General Horsip has only to request assistance, and High Admiral Drekkil will give the request his most careful consideration.

Horsip scowled, glanced at the screen, where the two squadrons had formed a guard of honor and were falling behind as they altered course to align themselves with

Horsip's ships. The speed with which they maneuvered showed good discipline and good ships.

All the weapons of Drekkil's squadrons, as the individual ships were picked out under high magnification, were covered. Drekkil had obeyed Horsip's demand, but the message showed that he regarded the Integral Union as a foreign power, not a central government. The precision of handling of Drekkil's ships demonstrated the force supporting his position. Drekkil, however, had no way to know what might be coming along after Horsip. Possibly that was his reason for being so agreeable.

Horsip growled, "Let's have a message blank."

The communications officer handed over his pad. Horsip wrote:

> General Klide Horsip expresses his thanks for the offer of that assistance which is required of every citizen of the Integral Union, to whatever planetary group or association he may belong.
>
> As this is not the advance element of a punitive expedition, but merely General Horsip's personal guard, no such assistance is required.

Horsip considered the message narrowly, then handed it to the communications officer. The communications officer looked nervous and went out.

The squadron commander passed him on the way in.

"I don't like to say it, sir, but they handle their ships very well."

"Better than our own?"

"There isn't much to choose."

"You'd say they have the advantage?"

"Absolutely. We're outnumbered almost two to one."

"We may have a fight with them shortly."

"We won't come out of it alive, sir."

"But it's important that we give the best account of ourselves we can."

"Yes, sir."

The communications officer stepped in, looking bemused, and held out a slip of message paper.

Horsip read:

> High Admiral Querk Drekkil of course recognizes the superior position of General Horsip in the hierarchy of the Integral Union, and respectfully offers salute as the Fleet passes.

Horsip's lips drew back from his teeth. A crawling sensation traveled up and down his spine. The squadron commander looked uneasy.

The large-scale magnification on the screen showed the long-range detection apparatus of Drekkil's ships searching in every direction.

Horsip shrugged in disgust, reached out for the message pad, and wrote:

> *The Fleet returns the salute.*

The communications officer hurried out.

Horsip handed Drekkil's latest message to the squadron commander, who said, "In case they change their tune, the gunnery officers have their targets selected."

Horsip nodded, but had given up hope of any such result. Drekkil had sensed Horsip wanted a fight, and Drekkil was having nothing to do with it.

Drekkil's next message wished Horsip a fine journey, and Horsip could only return the good wishes. But while Horsip was disappointed, everyone else in the squadron seemed exhilarated. The substance of the messages leaked out, and was duly distorted, the resulting version being that Drekkil had warned Horsip he was outnumbered, and must stop, and Horsip had replied, "This is the Fleet, and the Fleet stops for no one. Stand aside or be destroyed." Instantly, Horsip's squadron was transformed into a crack unit that drilled continuously, willingly, with no hint of complaint.

And then, ships and men in perfect order, they began to see what the Integral Union had been transformed into, as one by one they visited the planets.

✧ ✧ ✧

Looming through smoke and fumes, Horsip, at the bridge of the flagship, could see a thing like eighteen roads crisscrossing one atop the other. Vehicles of weird design careened around the numerous curves, while in the background loomed a giant city. Beyond the towers of the city there rose up, slightly to one side, a cone-shaped mound of peculiar reddish tinge mingled with all sorts of other colors in a vertical patchwork.

"Ah, that," said the planetary governor, perspiring freely, "that, now, is a . . . well . . . that's where we put the vehicles when they are . . . ah . . . used up. Yes, sir."

"I see," said Horsip, frowning. He had invited the governor aboard on a courtesy visit, according to hallowed custom of the Centran Fleet. The arrival of the Centran squadron had produced a sensation, as if a rug made out of some defunct wild animal had stood up and roared.

The governor, turning to Horsip, said hesitantly, "But that . . . ah . . . dump you refer to is just a by-product. There, you see, rising over the city, is the great tower where Mr. Schmidt rules over the planet through his gigantic enterprises. And that tower to the left, a little lower—that is the Consolidated Credit Building. Off there in the distance is Monopoly Motors. You see, it is not quite so high, but it is a very impressive building. And over there is the Intercontinental Construction Cartel. . . . They built this multilevel here—one of the biggest on the planet." The governor peered around the control room furtively, and lowered his voice:

"Ah, General Horsip, if I might ask . . . who . . . ah . . . who is your Earthman?"

"My what?" said Horsip, looking blank.

"Your Earthman, sir. Who gives *you* your orders?"

"The High Council gives me my orders."

"Ah, of course. Are they still in existence, then?"

"Of *course* they are in existence! Why not?"

"But what purpose do they serve, *Earthwise*."

Horsip grappled with the word "Earthwise."

"*No* purpose," said Horsip, flatly.

The governor looked nervous. "Have you *no* Earthman, sir?"

Horsip said shortly, "I take my orders from the High Council, and I am a member of the Supreme Staff. There is no Earthman on the High Council, and only one on the Supreme Staff."

The governor blinked, then suddenly looked relieved. "Ah, then it's all right. . . . Well, well, that's *fine.*"

Horsip eyed the governor with no great affection.

"And just who do you take *your* orders from?"

The governor thrust out his chest.

"From Mr. Schmidt. *Personally.*"

"Earthmen run this planet, then?"

"Definitely, sir. How else?"

"What are all these fumes?"

"A . . . well . . . you see those factory chimneys down there, and all those ground-cars too. I suppose, plus . . . well, there's that dump over there, at the edge of the city. All those gas tanks are draining slowly, and . . . well I imagine that's where it comes from. Yes, sir. . . . *Most* of it, anyway."

"Isn't it hard to breathe down there?"

"Incidence of respiratory diseases was up 2 percent last year."

"What is the advantage of all that smoke?"

"We are making more ground-cars. Mr. Schmidt has announced that this year, for the first time, everyone, on the average, will have a new ground-car before the year is out."

The governor beamed. "A new ground-car a year for everyone on the planet, on the average. *Think* of it!"

Horsip's mind boggled.

The governor banged his fist into his hand.

"And soon we may have a new ground-car twice a year! I have it from Mr. Schmidt—*himself.*"

"I see," said Horsip. "But what will you do with two of them a year? And what about the old one?"

"Why, we will put them on that pile there that you just asked me about. What else?"

Horsip glanced back at the odd-looking mound.

"That is a heap of *used-up ground-cars?*"

"Yes, sir."

"Well, now, look here . . . You mean to say these things *wear out in a year?*"

"Certainly. We have to use them very hard to get back and forth over the roads to work and still live in the country and at the sea shore."

"In order to get out of the smoke, eh?"

"Well, that's *one* reason, yes."

"Certainly they don't wear out all at once. Why not just replace the parts that wear out, and save all that work?"

The governor looked at him fishily.

"That would be *very* bad for business."

"To make these things so you have to throw them away every year is wasteful. They should be made so you could hand them down from generation to generation. *That* way a man could save a little money. As for using them to go back and forth from home to work—that is ridiculous! You should use iron roads—"

The governor muttered, "Mr. Schmidt would not approve of *this* . . . Sir, we do not have iron roads. They do not exist."

"Then," said Horsip, "you are progressing backward. All this murk is created, you say, by these factories and ground-cars. There's the answer to your problem. Make the ground-cars so they last, put in iron roads, and you can shut down the factories except for making replacements and spare parts. Then you will be able to breathe again. See, the answer is right in front of you."

"We could *not* do that," said the governor angrily. "*Everybody's* work and income is connected with the making ground-cars. That was Mr. Schmidt's first stroke of genius when he first came to this planet. No, General Horsip. You would create *unemployment* if you closed down the factories. If people received no pay, they could not only buy no ground-cars, but they could buy no other improvements, and they could buy no food. It would be a disaster. Mr. Schmidt would never allow it."

Horsip angrily began to speak, but then shrugged.

The governor said tolerantly, "Ask your Earthman about it sometime, General Horsip. He will explain it to you."

Horsip's next visit took him to a planet where the air was relatively pure, but hosts of iron-helmeted troops marched by as a beaming trio returned the salutes from a reviewing stand. Guns and armored ground-cars rumbled past in such profusion as to bring back memories of the invasion of Earth. Clouds of air-planes swooped overhead, to be followed by a formidable fleet of space-ships. The dictator himself, an Earthman, kindly explained to Horsip, "You see, Jack, I got the idea out of this book I read when I was a kid. *My Battle*, or something like that. But I'd have never had the chance to try it out if you hadn't come down on Earth, and given us a chance to spread out, like, and get a little elbow-room. Our people are kind of stubborn. These people here, though, they lap it up. Can't say I'm as big as Ganfre, but I'm doing all right."

When Horsip got back to his flagship, he found Moffis going through the latest batch of reports in silence. Horsip groped for a chair, and sat down. Moffis reached out with the look of a punch-drunk fighter for another report, turned the pages automatically, put the report in another pile. He reached out for another report, turned the pages automatically, set the report in another pile, and reached out for a fresh report. He turned the pages automatically, and—

Horsip said, "Moffis."

Moffis set the report in another pile, reached out for a fresh report, turned the pages automatically, put the report in a separate pile, and—

Horsip said, *"Moffis!"*

Moffis looked up, and his eyes came to a focus.

"It's too late," he said.

Horsip said, *"What's* too late?"

"We'll never stop them now."

Horsip leaned forward and said sharply, "Stop *who?*"

Moffis shoved the reports back.

"We now have planets run by communists, planets run

by capitalists, planets run by lunatics, planets converted entirely into factories—that's what it boils down to—for some one specialty or to follow some one fad of the Earthmen. They could never have done it on their own. They're too quarrelsome. We would never have done it ourselves. We don't have that many ideas to try out. Argit thought the two of us would make a good combination and supply each other's lacks. It has worked exactly the other way around. We have given the Earthmen the opportunity to bring into existence every kind of one-sided stroke of genius that occurs to them. Do you realize we now have *one whole planet* devoted to nothing but *horse races?* The thing is inconceivable, insane! Worse yet, there's even a planet—a whole planet—devoted to what *they* call 'higher education.' I tell you, it's ruinous! But it's too late now. We can't stop it. It's gone too far. We might as well—"

Horsip said, angrily, "Stop that! There's no use moaning over it! What's done is done."

He paused, frowning. "Wait a minute, now. What was that again? A whole planet devoted to *what?*"

"Higher education," said Moffis wryly. "That's what they *call* it. As a matter of fact, it's a pesthole of subversion. The students are complaining because of the 'monotonous quality of life,' and the 'repressive narrowness of Centran institutions.' *Narrowness! Repressive!* They're running wild, like a molk with the bloat! And they don't know it! The professors on this planet are all terrorized. They teach what they think the students want to hear. I tell you, the thing to do is to land about six divisions of the Suicide Corps, and . . ." Then he shook his head. "But it's too late. There's no hope now. The damage is done. We might as well—"

Horsip said impatiently, "Wait a minute, Moffis. Back up. You said there was some planet devoted entirely to *what?* There was something else you mentioned."

Moffis said dully, "Horse racing. The horse is like a molk, only skinnier, and with no horns. The Earthmen used to ride around on them before they had ground-cars. Now they race them for fun, and to bet on which one is going to win."

"How could they possibly use a whole planet for a thing like that?"

"It's a small planet, and the gravity is low. These horses can go fast because of the low gravity. The Earthmen have figured out a way to get oxygen to the horse even though the atmosphere is thin. Any kind of special training, special drugs, special apparatus is all right, as long as the animal is a horse. There are special farms on the planet where they acclimate the horses to the low gravity. There are stud farms there, where they breed horses with bigger lungs. There's a gigantic rolling casino—"

Horsip said blankly, "A *what?*"

"The track—the race course—is enormous. These horses travel at terrific speed. There are cameras spaced along the track to bring the race, in three dimensions, to people who watch it at 'horse parlors'—central places on other planets where they show the race for a fee. For people who come to watch the race on the spot, the whole central building travels around a track set inside the curve of the race course itself. The building is on wheels with some kind of frictionless bearings. When they aren't watching the race, the patrons gamble in this casino, or . . ." Moffis shook his head. "Maybe what *you see* is encouraging, but not what I get from these reports."

Horsip wavered, thinking of the possibility of raising Moffis' spirits. Then moodily he shook his head. "It's a mess, Moffis. I know what you think of those reports, and I've thought of trying to find someone else I can trust to work up the summaries while we're visiting these planets, but I can't, and the reality is no improvement, believe me."

Moffis nodded. "From what I've seen of it, that's what I thought."

"It's almost a relief to get on our way again, so I can go back to reading reports. It was a dream to think we could get away from this mess. It's everywhere you go."

Moffis nodded moodily. "I had the idea of getting a little relaxation after I read that report on the 'planetary university.' One of ship's officers had bought an omnivision set on one of the planets we've visited. He wasn't using it, so I borrowed it." Moffis shook his head. "That was worse than either the reality *or* the reports."

Horsip looked around blankly, and saw a sizable grayish cube with crackle finish and a row of knobs under two small lenses thrust out on shiny stalks.

"Is that the thing, Moffis?"

"That's it."

Horsip said, "I've never used one."

"Try it if you want to. You put the eyepieces up to your eyes, and there are little plugs that come out and fit in your ears. There's another thing like a cup that fits over your nose. Naturally, that model is outdated already."

"What are those knobs for?"

"Don't touch them. I bumped one by accident, and thought the ship had run into a planetoid. Just work this knob off to the side. That makes the sound louder or fainter. And this rim that sticks out this slot and has numbers on it—that selects the signal you receive. You tune that to pick up different signals."

Horsip nodded, pulled over a chair, and sat down. He adjusted the eyepieces, found the earplugs, and swung up the little cup that fit over his nostrils. Nothing happened.

Moffis' voice reached him dimly. "I forgot. You have to push this switch."

Horsip heard a faint click. Then chaos sprang into existence around him.

A screaming mob armed with clubs and torches hurtled straight at him. The smell of hot metal and burning rubber filled his nostrils. An unkempt maniac with blazing eyes gave a piercing yell, and sprang for Horsip with hands outstretched like claws.

Horsip lashed out, his fist exploded in pain, the maniac dwindled and vanished, and there was a violet yank at his ears, as his head was pulled forward.

Horsip looked around blankly.

The omnivision set was leaning over on its little table, held from smashing to the floor by the cords of the earplugs.

Horsip glanced around furtively, and saw that Moffis was

again going through reports like an automaton. Horsip massaged his fist, and hauled the set back up onto its table. No damage appeared to have been done. The sound was loud and clear. A wisp of smoke was drifting out of the nosepiece. A whining voice came across, and Horsip peered into the eyepieces.

Instead of a mob, there was a desk, with individuals hurrying in and out to lay message blanks on the desk. Behind the desk an unprepossessing-looking individual talked earnestly:

"Despite Planetary Premier Grakkil's speech, the disturbance still has not quieted, and it is feared that the Mekklinites will accept no accommodation short of unconditional surrender to their demands. Already the Mekklinites have razed the western portion of the city. Injuries have occurred, and this has angered the Mekklinites further. The mayor and other hostages, who were shot earlier by the Mekklinites, have been found buried under a cement wall. Panic rules this planet as the Mekklinites turn, no one knows in what direction, to avenge injuries to their people, to destroy the capital city as they have vowed to do if their demands are not met, and there can be no doubt now but that Premier Grakkil miscalculated badly when he failed to accede at once to their demands. Don't you think so, Sike?"

Horsip was suddenly looking at an individual with large eye-correctors and a look as if he had just been awakened out of a sound sleep.

"Yes, Snok, I believe implicitly in the law of instant acquiescence to the stronger force, and that's what we've got here. The Mekklinites obviously believe in death and destruction, and will stop at nothing to get their way. That's pretty plain by now, don't you think so, Snok?"

"It certainly is, Sike, it certainly is. And this should have been obvious to the premier, don't you think?"

Now the second individual was back again.

"It is to *us*, after seeing this precise thing happen so many times before. But the political animal doesn't learn except through kicks administered to his hide. That's a quote from Gek Kon, the Mekklinite leader, by the way, Snok."

"I know it is, Sike. But now, the question is, what's going to happen here? The mayor and the rest of the hostages are dead, of course. This in itself isn't surprising, because of course the Mekklinites are believers in violence. But couldn't it cause the premier to take the advice of the more warlike of his advisers and . . . say . . . use sleepy gas on the mob?"

"I *hope* not, Snok. But the premier might lose his head and attempt to do some such thing. Of course, since the passage of the No-Violence Act as an attempt to appease the Mekklinites, this would involve the immediate fall of the government."

"Yes. The premier is in a situation, Sike, that calls for the utmost political finesse, and I'm just afraid that he doesn't have that magical presence or *zeerema* or whatever it is that would enable him to pull it off. We'll be back with you again later, Sike. Thank you for a truly impressive analysis of the situation."

Horsip muttered to himself, groped for the signal-change switch, and was at once treated to a smell like dead fish.

Before he could get at the signal-change switch again, an impressive voice intoned in his ear: "This is the smell—or 'bouquet' in the words of the *aficionados*—of the drug garazal, or 'green drops.' Those of you who have the latest Constituex sets with full panoply of newsworthy scents will feel the actual effects of this drug as the room begins to rotate around you. We are now in an actual 'green-drop heaven' where the *aficionados* gather to experience what is said to be an elevation of the sense of awareness—far superior to ordinary experience, because the green-drop experience is 'genetically coded on the tissues of the brain.' The superiority of dream experience to real world is said to enable the *aficionado to* 'block out' the real world and its experiences, which become irrelevant as he withdraws into green-drop heaven and its far more attractive—"

Horsip connected with the controls, switched to another signal, and was rewarded by the sight of an individual with large teeth, bared in a smirk, who was saying " . . . superiority of the immoral tridem to the moral tridem is that the immoral tridem simply immerses the viewer in a world he might otherwise never have known, and he can't—simply can't—get out of it if it's really well done. This gives the tridemist a real lift—a real *boot*—I simply can't describe it. It's a sense of power"—the recording camera zoomed in to enlarge his face until it filled the field of view—"a really *god-like* sensation, to use an antique term—"

Horsip's groping hand found the signal-change switch, and now he was looking at three people seated on three sides of a table, facing each other as Horsip viewed the scene as if sitting slightly back from the table on the fourth side. Two of the faces showed expressions of cynical disbelief, and one had a defiant, somewhat maniacal air. The two with the cynical expressions were seated to right and left. The defiant one was saying, "In this year of indecision, I have been visited by a vision of the way things have been and the way things shall be." His eyes seemed to drill into Horsip's head. "Today I have a special message—"

Horsip located the signal-change switch.

Through the earplugs, like some voice of doom, came a monologue in which one word followed fast on the heels of another:

" . . . situation has deteriorated badly in the last several days. Brog Grokig, new member of the Board of Control, suggests that in future it may be necessary to allow criminals to determine their own punishment. 'They will not accept it from anyone else,' Grokig warned . . . Mroggis New College has found a way to cope with the dissatisfaction of its students in today's changing universe and maladjusted environmental situation. Mroggis now offers Certificates of Achievement Specializing in Revolution, in addition to the more traditional subjects. 'We do not prejudge the situation,' said Administrator Gurnik. 'One specialty is as specialized as another. Merely a different viewpoint is involved. Everything is relative.' On Darg III, it is reported that the planetary president has been impeached for suggesting that weapons be supplied to the planetary constabulary . . .

Occupation of Dione IV by forces of the Snard Soviet is now reported to be complete . . . Dictator Ganfre has warned against further aggression by Snard, and has also issued an ultimatum to the president of the planet Columbia, warning that Columbia must join with Ganfre or be subject to precautionary occupation to prevent seizure by Snard . . . A force of unknown size, but said to be powerful, and bearing the emblems of the defunct empire known as the Integral Union, is reported in the vicinity of the planet Hinkel. This force is under the control of a general named Orsip, who is believed to have drawn together the last shreds of the dying empire, and is now rumored seeking alliance with Dictator Hinkle . . . Those of you who missed 'Makers of the Problems' today will be interested to know that Sedak Goplin, the religious so-called prophet, had a seizure during the show, but was revived promptly by administration of oxygen . . . On Atrinx III, the agricultural planet, where 90 percent of all grain for this region of space is produced, the new outbreak of green armyweevils has been contained, under the super-powerful spray Arsoxychlorphosthicide. However, it is reported that the action of the spray has shriveled up the grain, and caused the soil to break up into little lumps of clay and water . . . On Moxis II, where the weather-control satellites are now in action, a new series of disastrous floods has been followed by a plague which—"

At what point it happened, Horsip didn't know, but suddenly he felt like shooting himself. Even when things had been at their worst in the invasion of Earth, he hadn't felt like this. Dazed, he shoved back the eyepieces, pushed down the nosepiece, and pulled out the earplugs, through which came the words, " . . . and that's the news. Stay locked to this signal from morning to night. An informed citizen is a . . ."

Horsip staggered to his feet, passed Moffis, still working like an automaton on the reports, shoved open a hatch, and stepped out on a kind of balcony, rigged for the occasion, that looked out over the spaceport where the ship had set down.

Horsip had scarcely pushed the hatch half-shut behind him when a movement in the brush at the edge of the spaceport caught his attention.

His mind a maze of hopelessness, Horsip watched a hideous hairy creature emerge from the brush, crouch, and spring directly for him, claws outstretched.

Horsip watched it loom larger, knew it meant the end, and didn't care. What was the use? Why bother?

His hand happened to brush the holster of his service pistol, and through tortuous channels of his mind, the sensation operated to rouse his stunned faculties. Abruptly, he whipped open his holster-flap and yanked out the gun, to fire point-blank.

There was a high-pitched squeal, then a clutching of claws all around him. Horsip fired again and again, discharging one barrel after another.

There was a hideous chattering sound.

The gun was empty, but Horsip, suddenly furious, raised a booted leg and rammed the creature in the midsection, knocking it off the balcony.

Moffis, gun in hand, was suddenly beside Horsip, and took aim as the thing streaked for the brush. He missed it three times in succession, then hit it as it dove into the bushes.

Horsip said, "That was a *Mikeril*, Moffis!"

"I saw it! But it *can't* be!"

"Nevertheless," said Horsip, "it was. *Mikerils!* That's all we need! All right, let's go back in before another one shows up. We've seen all we need to here, anyway."

Part VII:
Trap

Colonel John Towers, commanding Independent Division III of the Special Effects Team, drifted down through the moist air with the sun hot on his back, set the gravitor pack to hover, and looked down through his binoculars at a chain of low dark-green equatorial islands that stretched due east to the distant horizon. To the north and south, a placid ocean shimmered unbroken as far as the eye could see.

Scattered along the island chain lay many Centran spaceships, and Towers studied the identifying letters and numbers on a ship almost directly below. This was the command ship of Major General Sark Glossip, Centran Military Overseer of the planet.

Towers, in his many tricky and deceptive assignments for the Centra-Earth alliance, had acquired a knack for recognizing particularly bad situations. He turned back the flap of his holster, and made sure his service automatic slid easily to hand. He glanced up at a glint of reflected sunlight high overhead, and took a small communicator from its case on his belt.

"Logan?"

"Sir?" came the voice of his second-in-command.

"Drop the landing-boats another thousand feet."

Overhead, the bright glint began to change form and position.

Logan's voice came through again. "How do things look?"

"About the same as on the screen. Nothing moving. No Centrans, humanoids, or animals in sight anywhere. But I have the sensation of a hundred sets of unfriendly eyes watching. Do you see anything?"

"No, sir. Nothing worth mentioning."

Towers pressed down the knob of the grav pack's control rod, felt mounting pressure against his eardrums as he dropped, and yawned and swallowed to ease the pressure.

He looked down at the Centran command ship lying on dark sand near the edge of a patch of dark-green brush. The ship had a low bulge along its upper flank, and rising from this, two big thick vertical fins one behind the other. These fins, oval in cross-section, bristled with gun muzzles, spike-bars, and nests of sharpened blades, and were crowned by metal cages backed with mesh.

Logan's voice came through reassuringly.

"Still nothing moving down there, sir. It *looks* O.K., at least."

"Hm-m-m," said Towers, unconvinced, looking over the guns and spike-bars.

Logan said, "What do you plan to do, sir?"

"Obey orders—when Glossip condescends to give them to me."

Sark Glossip, who had brought Towers to this planet by his call for help, had provided an explanation that was a model of its kind:

"So," Glossip had said, looking out intently from the communicator screen, "the Special Effects Team can straighten out planetary revolts?"

"We've certainly had experience at it," said Towers. "What's the trouble, sir?"

"How about planets that haven't yet been . . . ah . . . fully integrated?"

"You want the Special Effects Team for the initial conquest?"

"Well," said Glossip defensively, "we've run into an unusual situation—"

All Towers handled were unusual situations. But he nodded sympathetically, and looked receptive.

Glossip doubled back on his tracks.

"*Is* the Special Effects Team used in the initial conquest?"

"Not in the actual landing. But sometimes later on, if the situation is bad enough."

"It's bad here."

"What's wrong, sir?"

"It's an extremely serious situation. Very serious, Towers. Very serious indeed."

Towers listened patiently.

Glossip said, "We're in a tough spot here." His eyes strayed to Towers' insignia of rank. "Colonel—if I understand you correctly—you will give assistance, if I request it."

"Yes. But—"

"Very well. I *do* request assistance. Now, Towers, I want to discuss this with you."

"Yes, sir," said Towers exasperatedly.

"Down *here*. So, the first thing for you to do, Towers, is to come down, and we will go over this."

"General, I can do a better job if I have some idea what the mess is before I'm in it."

The Centran thrust out his jaw. "I think this is a much wiser way to handle this, Colonel. And the sooner you get here, the better."

"I can get to the planet—"

Glossip interrupted. "In no circumstances are any of your ships to actually *touch down* here. This is the first thing you have to remember."

"General, if you'd give me a few details, I could decide much better what—"

"Exactly why I want to discuss this with you, Colonel. As soon as possible—just as soon as you can get here." Glossip frowned thoughtfully. "There isn't any truth, I suppose, in the rumor that your people have developed a one-man gravitor pack?"

"Yes, we—"

"Splendid! Then you can come down using that, and you won't need to bring even a landing-boat to the surface."

Towers opened his mouth, and shut it again.

"Fine," said the general. "Then that's settled. Now, then, we'll want to know exactly when you can get here . . ."

Now, thinking back on this conversation as he drifted down toward the Centran ship, Towers felt again the urge to profanity.

"Logan."

"Sir?"

"I'm going down there now."

"Yes, sir. Good luck."

"Thanks."

Towers dropped more rapidly, scanning sea and island, and seeing nothing move.

Suddenly, Logan said, "*Sir—*"

"Yes?"

"On high magnification, we've found a great many small translucent objects of some kind, barely afloat—in the water around the island below you."

Towers looked down intently. "Any motion from these things?"

"No, sir. But we don't see any such numbers anywhere else."

"Maybe jellyfish of some kind."

Towers dropped straight for the ship. From here, he could see the gun muzzles in the foreshortened upright fins. The guns pointed not only at sand, brush, and sea, but also at the dented armor of the neighboring fin. Was that to protect against an enemy too close to be reached otherwise? But then, why was only *this* part of the ship protected against attack?

From below, a voice boomed in Centran:

"Colonel Towers! When we open the bars, drop fast toward the red hatch! When you're four or five reaches away, swerve for the green hatch. We'll drop it as you come through. Don't hesitate, and don't shoot."

The cages atop the big fins swung open, to show beneath them small chambers with large hatches at the bottom. The hatch in the forward fin was painted green, and in the aft fin red. Towers shoved down on the control, and plunged toward the aft fin.

The island, and the Centran ship, sprang up at him, enlarging in a rush.

He yanked the control sidewise and forward, and shot toward the forward hatch.

Suddenly, the air was filled with blue-green flippers, white teeth, and flying slivers of pointed shell.

There was a whine of bullets, the green hatch fell open underfoot, and he yanked up on the control as he plunged into thick darkness and a hammering clang shook the air. The deck sprang out of the gloom, and a voice roared, "Shut and lock! Report!"

Towers landed hard, sank down on his knees, felt the crushing pressure grow light, and barely managed to snap the control to neutral before it threw him back up at the hatch.

From overhead came shouts.

"Green clear!"

"Red clear!"

"Cease fire! Check your walls! New guard, by the red gate!"

Directly before Towers in the sweltering dimness, a Centran captain raised his hand in salute.

"The general's waiting, sir. Follow me."

Towers was barely able to breathe in the overpowering heat. He glanced around, to make out vertical bars that divided the space under this fin from a corresponding space farther aft. On each side, armed Centran guards, stripped to the waist, watched the opposite compartment.

Ahead of Towers, the Centran captain dropped through a hatchway, and Towers followed.

He found himself walking along a narrow corridor cooled by a faint current of air. The captain rounded a corner, and halted at a doorway where a Centran sergeant stood on guard. The guard boredly presented arms, the captain knocked, and a gruff bark answered from within. The captain opened the door, spoke briefly into the room, then turned to Towers.

"Go right in, sir."

Towers stepped in. The heat, in here, was the worst yet.

Across the far corner of the room, under a sluggishly-turning four-bladed ceiling fan, was a desk. In back of the desk was an overturned pivot chair, one clawed foot upraised. Seated at the desk was a burly Centran stripped to the waist, his fur plastered to him as if he'd just stepped out of a shower. A glance was enough to show Towers that this was General Glossip.

General Glossip's frame of mind was evident in the abrupt way he toweled the condensation off a pitcher of ice water, and slapped the towel over the upraised claw of the pivot chair, then glanced to the other side of his desk where a tub of ice trailed streamers of fog in the stifling heat, while condensation trickled onto a sodden bath towel, a thin stream of water curled out toward Glossip's desk, and the general cast a venomous glance at it before looking up at Towers.

Towers, who had crossed the room to stand at attention before the desk, was momentarily distracted by a small green-and-brown striped lizard lying atop one of the broad sluggishly-turning fan blades. This lizard, a blissful expression on its face, apparently had the advantage of the only breeze in the room.

Towers became aware that the general was following his gaze. Towers saluted, and reported his presence.

Glossip's face was expressionless as he returned the salute. "Well, Colonel," he said dryly, "I see you got here safely."

"I'd have had a better chance with a little more information, sir."

"And just how the devil was I supposed to explain a thing like that to you or anyone else?"

"Exactly what *did* happen when I was coming in?"

Glossip squinted at him, then nodded sourly. "Happened so fast you didn't have time to see it? Well, Towers, far be it from me to try to explain it." He glanced at the wide harness of the gravitor pack. "Is that the only one of those one-man packs you have?"

"No, sir. We've got others." Towers' voice was unintentionally sharp.

Glossip looked at him coldly. "Do you have any in those landing-boats you're bringing down?"

"We have several of them, sir."

"Could you have one dropped to this ship?"

"Yes, sir."

"Then go out, have an extra pack dropped down, and bring it in here."

Glossip reached back and took hold of a brass knob dangling on the end of a slender chain, and there was a *bong-bong* on the far side of the bulkhead behind him.

The corridor door opened up and a somewhat dull-looking Centran lieutenant saluted.

"Sir?"

"Take Colonel Towers here to the entry port. Inform the officer of the hatch that the colonel is to have every consideration, and may leave by the red or the green as he chooses. He—"

General Glossip paused abruptly.

The lieutenant had suddenly forgotten Glossip, and was looking at Towers' completely furless face and hands. Next he stared to right and left of Towers' ankles. He had that characteristic look of a Centran—one possessing poor manners and dubious intelligence—seeing an Earthman for the first time, and trying to locate the tail.

General Glossip's teeth came together with a snap.

He turned to Towers, very politely.

"Colonel—"

"Sir?"

"If you would just step outside for a moment, while I give Lieutenant Molgrim a few final instructions—"

"Yes, sir."

Towers stepped outside, and could feel the lieutenant's gaze on him the whole distance.

Towers pulled the door shut and stood to the other side from the sergeant on guard.

From behind Towers, the general's voice came through the door, low and angry:

"You sickly lump of Mikeril bait! Stand up! Eyes front!

Get that silly look off your face! Was that the first Earthman you ever saw?"

The Centran sergeant glanced up and down the hall, then, strictly contrary to regulations, murmured confidentially, "I was on Earth in the invasion."

Towers hesitated. He should deliver a stiff reprimand. But here at last might be a source of information.

"Yes, sir," murmured the sergeant. "I was only a cub, but I was at General Horsip's headquarters when the counterattack hit. Believe me, *there* was something. Whatever else they say, I know Earthmen can *fight*. Anything I can do for you, sir, just send the word for Klas Makkil. In a place like this, we have to stick together, or we're finished."

Towers dumped regulations overboard.

"What is it you're up against on this planet?"

"The toads go through the air so fast you can't see them. That's the worst. Next is that they float underwater with just the curve of their eyes awash. They can spot *you*, but you can't spot *them*. By the hairy arm, sir! It's not safe to set foot outside in the daytime, and it isn't much better at night."

"Thanks, Makkil. That's more than the general told me."

"General's all right, sir. But this place has him whipped, and he's too mad to talk about it." The sergeant stood straighter as footsteps approached from the general's office.

The door opened, and the lieutenant came out, trembling all over. "Please follow me, sir."

As Towers started down the hall, the sergeant hissed in his ear, "Go *fast*, from red."

Beneath the closed red hatch in the aft fin, Towers dropped to a low crouch.

The Centran officer in charge bellowed, "Raise the bars! Drop the hatches!"

Towers glanced up at the disk of dazzling sky directly overhead, snapped the pack control to full lift, straightened his legs in one violent thrust, and shot though the hatch. Abruptly he was in bright sunlight, breathing air that seemed fresh and almost cool.

From the ship dwindling below came a clang as the hatches slammed shut.

Towers glanced up, to see that Logan was evidently alert for treachery. The landing-boats were in a formation of open concentric rings, lowest on the outside, and progressively stepped up toward the center. From this formation, they could open fire on the Centran ship without obstructing each other, or close on it simultaneously from all sides.

Towers slipped his belt communicator into his hand.

"Logan."

"Sir?"

"Lift formation a thousand feet."

From below came a roar, and Towers recognized Glossip's voice:

"Colonel Towers! Your orders were to bring no ship or landing-boat to the surface!"

There was a momentary silence, and Towers deduced that Glossip could see the boats lifting, and realized Towers must already have given the order.

"Very good," came Glossip's voice. "See they don't come within a hundred reaches of the surface, Towers."

"Yes, sir," called Towers obediently. He had the growing suspicion that he and Glossip were going to have a head-on collision soon.

He described Glossip's order to Logan, and asked. "Do we have an extra gravitor pack handy?"

"Yes, sir," said Logan, "though how we'll get it into the ship I don't know. I'll set the pack to descend slowly."

"Good. But—wait a minute."

Towers looked around exasperatedly. Glossip didn't bother to explain. He just gave orders. It was, therefore, a little hard to improvise if his orders turned out to be impractical.

Glossip had ordered Towers to *bring* the extra pack into the ship. Of course, to do that, Towers had to go through the same thing he'd gone through the last time, with the added handicap of the extra pack. Was there some reason why Glossip wanted Towers himself back in the ship, or would the pack alone be enough? The devil with it.

"And Logan—"

"Sir?"

"Put a coil of fishline and a couple of lead weights, from the survival kit, in the pocket of the pack. Maybe I can guide the pack down to the ship from up here."

"Yes, sir."

A moment later, a dark object detached itself from one of the landing-boats, and began to drift down.

Towers, hovering, could feel the sun through his uniform, and every breath of air seemed to stay where he exhaled it. He lifted up on the control, and climbed toward the pack.

He still had to get that pack into the Centran ship, and before he tried that, it might not be a bad idea to get a little more information.

"Logan, what happened when I went down to the command ship?"

"I wish I knew, sir. It *looked* like twenty to thirty blue-green mermen materialized around that pair of conning towers."

"Materialized?"

"Well, sir, if they flew, they were too fast to follow."

That, thought Towers, *was what Makkil had said*. He cleared his throat.

"They materialized *over the fins*—the 'conning towers'?"

"Well, not *over* them, at first. They—*clumped*."

"They *what*?"

"Well, they—piled up. The impression most of us got was that they didn't appear all at once, but in rapid succession. It seemed that the first ones were lower than the ones that followed. Then they—dematerialized—disappeared and were gone."

Towers shook his head. No wonder Glossip hadn't wanted to talk about it. He looked down at the water, then up at the landing-boat.

"You've got this recorded?"

"Yes, sir. But we haven't had time to check it over."

"Do you have any idea where these things came from, or where they went to?"

"We don't know where they went to. But they apparently came from the water around the island. First, a series of splashes and then they appeared over the ship."

"Splashes?"

"Yes, sir. As if something had just been dropped into the water. I suppose if something came *out* of the water, fast enough, it would make a splash, too."

"Hm-m-m," Towers thought it over, saw that the pack was close, caught it, and reached into the pocket for the fishline. Just as he drew it out, something in the placid water below threw back a flash of reflected light.

Four feet of glistening teeth and crocodilian head split the water in a streak of foam. There was a wild thrashing, and a humanlike upper body came into view, muscular arms wildly beating the water, mouth wide open and features contorted, the whole body—head, limbs, and torso—blue-green in color. Then the huge jaws twisted sidewise, and there was just a long swell of smooth water marked by a whitish rush of bubbles. Then the distant piercing scream reached Towers, like a reflected flash of agony.

Around the island, a series of low spouts of water flung up and fell back in a splash.

Logan said, "*That's* roughly what happened before."

From the Centran ship came Glossip's voice:

"Colonel Towers! Bring down the pack!"

Towers started down, counting seventeen places in the sea marked by circular ripples.

Logan was saying, "But the last time that happened, the mermen showed up over the ship."

"The splashes came from the places where you'd noticed some kind of translucent objects?"

"Yes, sir. We were apparently seeing the eyes and maybe part of the brow."

Again, that fit with what Makkil had said. It added up, but what did it add up *to?*

"Do you still see any in the water around the island?"

"Quite a few. Around on the other side."

Towers slipped the fishline out, and tied one end tightly

in a shallow groove in the rod below the control knob. To the other end of the line, he tied one of the small lead weights.

From the ship boomed Glossip's authoritative voice: "Start for the green hatch, Towers, then swerve for the red!"

Logan said, "Sir, there's another bunch in that inlet south of the ship."

That decided Towers, who hovered above the ship. He roughly centered himself over the red hatch, lowered the weight on the fishline, peered along the swaying line, then called, "Look out below! Keep back from under the red hatch!"

"Towers!" boomed Glossip's voice.

Towers, sighting along the line, seemed to be directly above the hatch, but he needed a check. He released the other small lead weight, and watched it dwindle. It seemed to be dropping straight for the hatch opening.

Glossip's voice roared, "Start for the--" The instructions were interrupted by a bellow of pain and rage.

Towers carefully pressed down the control, and let the pack go. The pack accelerated for the ship.

"General," he called, "I can't swerve in time carrying the pack! I'm dropping it through the red hatch. Have your men grab it, *and center the control knob!*"

The pack was dwindling fast, headed for the hatch opening.

Near the top of the aft fin, there appeared half-a-dozen blue-green forms, each holding up what appeared to be a kind of large shell. From Towers' angle of vision, these mermen seemed to abruptly displace themselves upward. Then he realized that the first were still in the same position, but more had appeared.

The coiled fishline was leaping from Towers' hand and now he clapped his other hand on it to put a drag on the line, to yank the pack's control to full lift. If he had gauged it properly, the Centrans should be able to grab it once it got in. But would it get past the blue-green forms around the fin? Towers' service automatic was in his hand before he remembered the earlier warning not to fire. Before he could decide whether to squeeze the trigger there was a yell from below, and the blue-green forms were gone.

The pack shot in past the edge of the hatch opening, trailing the fishline. On full lift, it should, according to Towers' estimate, lose enough accumulated momentum so the Centrans could grab it.

From below came a roar, yells, bellowed curses and orders, a loud crashing noise, then a momentary silence. Then there was a burst of ferocious profanity, and the pack shot up out of the hatch, a large furry form clinging to the straps.

For an instant, Towers was paralyzed. Before he recovered, Glossip went past like a rocket headed for outer space, the fishline trailing straight out behind.

Towers grabbed at the line, missed, yanked his own pack control to full lift, took another grab at the line, caught the weight for a moment, then it snapped free.

Towers was rising fast now, and swallowed to equalize the falling pressure against his eardrums. He looked up, and could see that he was gaining. Possibly Glossip had managed to center the control. Towers squinted against the wind, and abruptly shoved his own control all the way down.

Glossip had dwindled to a speck, but this speck was now enlarging like an onrushing meteor.

Glossip went past in a streak, upside down, hanging to the straps, accelerating straight for the island.

Towers shouted, *"Center the control!"*

Apparently, Towers had caught the weight for just an instant, but that had been enough to snap the control all the way down. Glossip had then continued to pull ahead on accumulated speed, while he and Towers were building up a big acceleration in opposite directions.

As the thought flashed through his mind, Towers was urgently looking for the line. Something blurred toward him, and he seized it and tried to hang on. It yanked his arm straight down, and shot free.

Towers snapped the control knob of his own grav pack to nearly full lift, and peered down.

Below him, Glossip appeared centered over the hatch.

Towers prayed fervently and watched. Now there was a twisting motion that Towers hoped meant that the pack had started up again. Now a swarm of blue-green blurs appeared around the fin, apparently trying for a grab at the Centran general. Now they vanished. Glossip was still there. Carefully, Towers eased his pack control down a little to slow the ascent, felt the painful sense of pressure deaden his ears, yawned and swallowed, and got out the communicator.

"Logan—"

"I'm watching, sir."

"If he gets by me, have a landing-boat match velocities over him and brake."

Carefully, Towers gauged speed and position, and, as Glossip climbed past, Towers reached out intently and centered the control. Only when he'd done this, did he spare the attention to look at the general himself.

Glossip, the straps crushed in his hands, eyes tightly shut, had a look of pure bliss on his face.

For a dazed instant, Towers couldn't remember where he'd seen that expression before. Then it dawned on him. He'd seen it down in Glossip's office—on the face of the lizard swinging around on the fan blade.

With the packs slowing to an upward drift, Glossip now opened his eyes.

"Great, Towers! By the hairy arm of the first-born Mikeril!" He beamed as he looked all around. "How do you work this thing?"

Towers dazedly pointed out the control knob. "You move this whichever way you want to go. At the center, you hover. When you move it farther, you get higher velocities. When you move it some more, you get rapid acceleration. At the extreme position, you get maximum acceleration. You don't have to worry about a change in attitude of the pack, because that is internally compensa—"

Glossip let go of the straps with one hand, took hold of the control, and before Towers could stop him, shot for the sky, whirled around as the landing-boats scattered, then plunged for the ocean. Towers snapped the communicator to his lips.

"Logan!"

"Sir?" Logan's voice was that of one earnestly awaiting orders.

Towers started to speak, then stopped. Glossip was now in a steep dive. Now the steep dive stretched out into a shallow dive. Now Glossip was streaking along horizontally, almost skimming the open water. Now the water foamed ahead of him, and a huge snout lifted up, to open out a gigantic set of jaws. Glossip whipped around to one side, reappeared, and streaked in a shallow climb toward the nearest island, where he disappeared against a mottled background.

"Sir?" repeated Logan.

"Just stand clear," said Towers. "Where is he now?"

"Climbing—right in line with the islands. *Here he comes!*"

Towers looked all around, saw nothing, then there was a roar from overhead. Glossip dove past, swung around in a flat turn, climbed sharply, and stopped dead in the air, beaming.

"Fine, Towers! First rate!" he looked intently at Towers' harness, writhed around, shot one hand, then the other, through the straps, yanked the straps tight, and said, "Now, you saw what happened down there? You saw what these locals can do?"

With an effort, Towers dragged his mind onto the problem. "Yes, I—"

"Good," said Glossip. "Then, you see why I couldn't explain it. How *could* I explain it? These natives *teleport*. They can live on land or in the water, and when they're in danger—which is often in that ocean, believe me—there's a little splash as the water rushes in to fill up the space they just left, and they're gone!"

"They're gone. But where *to?*"

"That's the worst of it. As far as we can discover, they can go to *any place they've been before.*"

Towers digested this, then shook his head.

"General, it seems to me that this is a good planet to leave alone."

"Very true," said Glossip. "And when a man reaches into a barrel, thinking it's empty, and his arm sinks up to the elbow in soft tar—Why, yes, that was a good barrel to stay out of. But his problem *now* is that he's got his arm in there up to the elbow."

Towers started to speak, then paused. The natives could *teleport*. They could go *anywhere they had already been*.

Towers looked down at the Centran ship. He was high enough so that he could see, on neighboring islands, other Centran ships. And he knew that was just a small part of Glossip's force. Frowning, he asked, "What's the extreme range? How far can they teleport?"

"A very good question, Towers. That's the crux of the matter. How far *can* they teleport? We don't know. And there are a number of wrong ways we can find out."

"When you say they can go 'wherever they've been before'—"

"Let me show you."

Glossip dipped into a shallow dive, and Towers followed. They streaked high over the island, across a narrow strip of water, crossed another island and several Centran ships, then still another island, and a ship with the hatches open and unguarded.

"That," said Glossip, "is one of the ships that set down here earlier. They never knew what hit them."

They shot out over the sea, and on an island to one side and far below was another Centran ship with a pair of heavily-protected upright fins.

"Now," said the general, "stay here, and watch closely."

Towers hovered, as Glossip dropped toward the ship in a long glide, paused above it, and bellowed orders. Directly above the aft fin, Glossip slowly began a vertical descent. Below, the metal cages swung up and out. Glossip descended with elaborate caution, as if afraid he might somehow miss the hatch and get hung up on the spikes. When he was about twenty feet above that hatch, suddenly there appeared a ring of blue-green forms around the bristling fin. Their arms were uplifted, holding something. Before there was time to see what, there was a similar ring of blue-green forms above them, arms stretched up and out, where suddenly another blue-green ring materialized, completely surrounding Glossip.

Glossip blurred into motion, tore his way through the cage of bodies, slashed, kicked, punched, and left in a rapidly accelerating climb, clutching something in one hand.

Below, the blue-green figures vanished, then abruptly one appeared near Glossip, vanished, and reappeared, face twisted in pain, close beside Glossip, to scream savagely and reach out with a curved blue-white blade. This native was so close that, for the first time, Towers noticed that in place of ears there were oval membranes, now noticeably bulged out, at each side of the head.

The big muscles in the general's arms and chest stood out under the fur. His fist smashed out like a mace.

The blue-green figure dropped, turning over and over, and growing smaller and smaller as it fell toward the sea. As it hit, the water shot out in an explosion.

Instantly, a writhing nest of rubbery arms reached up, and jerked the body under. A whitish stream of bubbles burst briefly to the surface, then disappeared.

Glossip swung up beside Towers, and now Towers could see what he was carrying was a brownish shell, roughly a foot across, and very thin along one edge, where a number of small oval bits apparently had been broken off.

Glossip glanced at Towers, "Did you see how they worked that? How they showed up one atop the other?"

"Yes. But I don't see why."

"They can go anywhere they've been before. But what does *that* mean? This planet is swinging around the sun, while turning on its axis. Its *location* is changing from moment to moment, and so is the location of everything on it. What these natives teleport to is, therefore, a familiar *object*. Unfortunately, the object doesn't have to be very big."

Towers looked at the shell. "That—"

Glossip nodded. "It's big enough, or massive enough, so that they can sense its structural pattern, or whatever it is that they do. And then—they can *go* to it."

The implications hit Towers like a combination of blows. "When they teleport, they *can carry things with them?*" Glossip smiled. "That's it."

"Each of them can go to any place he's familiar with?"

"Right."

"And if *one* has been to a particular place, there's nothing to prevent him from going there carrying some object that *others* have become familiar with?"

"That's standard procedure."

"Therefore, wherever *one* can go, they *all* can go."

"Exactly."

"And one or more of them has learned the molecular pattern—or whatever they need to know—*of some part of each of your ships?*"

"Correct."

For the first time, the situation seemed to fall into place. The Centrans had an entire invasion force cooped up in its ships by a population of teleports, the limits of whose power they didn't know, and they couldn't leave because *wherever they went, the teleports might go, too.*

Towers spent the evening on his headquarters ship. After making sure the state of affairs on the planet was explained to his own men, so they could adapt themselves to the incredible facts, he spent his time studying a selection of reports ferried up by one of Glossip's landing-boats, and gingerly transferred by way of a charged container, in case the natives put in an appearance. Towers and Logan split the stack of reports, and started working their way through. They weren't long in finding that, however bad the situation looked at any given moment, it looked worse after reading the next report.

"Phew!" said Logan, "Listen to this: 'As there is no sign of local humanoid inhabitants on this planet, and as its climate is unsuitable, agricultural land severely limited, and any ore bodies apparently located at the bottom of an ocean populated by inimical forms of life, there appears to be no point in directing sizable forces to this world. We recommend that there be set up a signal-and-life-saving station on the planet, for use in the event of spaceship disasters. The climate might make the planet useful for disciplining troops, and as a punishment station for trouble-makers in general. Conditions, though oppressive here, are so free from danger that the signal-and-aid-station might well be manned by a category of troops not suitable for more exacting duties."

Towers blinked. "What report is that?"

" 'Planet A6-3EJ4166B—A Summary.' "

"One of their initial reports?"

"Yes. And stuck to the bottom is another, titled, 'Dis-appearance on A6-3EJ4166B.' Listen to the last sentence: 'No sign of any possible cause has been found. The gar-rison has disappeared without a trace. The only clue is that *most of the portable weapons have also disappeared.*' "

"That's nice," said Towers. "That adds a dimension that wasn't there before. This report follows directly after the other one you read?"

"Right. The first recommends the signal-and-life-saving station. The next tells what happened to it."

"What I've been reading is more recent. Here's one titled 'Troop Exercises After Dark.' Apparently the Centrans started out thinking they had an unpopulated planet, but listen to what they're up against now: 'We conclude, there-fore, that to prevent disciplinary problems, exercise in the open air is necessary. Since such exercise in daylight hours is precluded by the casualty rate, after-dark exercise becomes necessary. In summary, the correct procedure includes the following steps:

" '1) The armored tractors must thoroughly rake and stir the sand, discharging into the sea any object larger than a hand's breadth. The tractor crews must look over the outside of the entry ports, and clear away any enemy hidden on the blind sides.

" '2) Occupy the hatch chambers. Swing up the gun mounts and searchlights.

" '3) Sweep adjacent land and water by searchlight, to blind natives in the vicinity.

" '4) Extend ladder and slat rests beyond the spike-bars.

" '5) Send out the slat-emplacement parties.

" '6) Sweep the area again with searchlights.

" '7) Send out the troops, by teams, opening and closing the bars for each party.

" '8) The scrub and other non-sand environs of the ship must be kept well trapped and mined. This must be checked daily.

" '9) For their own peace of mind, the troops must be armed. The guards, of course, must be heavily armed. The exercising troops, however, may be armed only with *unloaded* guns. Otherwise any disorder may result in heavy losses. Since darts are easily hidden, the only way to assure unloaded guns is to remove the bolts on exit, detailing a suitable officer and party to tag the bolts.

" 'If these steps are properly carried out, night exercise becomes feasible, due to the enemy's inferior night vision. But all precautions must be *maintained*, day and night.' "

Logan shook his head. "What a mess to get into on an apparently empty planet. It seems almost like a trap."

"It doesn't seem possible," said Towers, "considering that local inhabitants were here first, and all the Centrans had to do was stay away. But—let's try this one." He picked up a report he'd briefly glanced at earlier, and opened it to the back. " 'In summary,' " he read, " 'the testimony obtained from this native, Goshal, who was found washed ashore severely wounded, and brought back to health by our medical team, clearly indicates that the locals are divided into clans or tribes, each of which is warlike and aggressive. The whole population is united only rarely, in times of emergency. Each tribe possesses a number of islands, located at intervals around the planet. Constant warfare follows from population pressure. The land area is small—only the chain of equatorial islands—while the enormous ocean is occupied by creatures of all degrees of ferocity. This leaves only the limited land space, and the shallow offshore waters thickly grown with *krunga* weed, and usually avoided by the open-sea life forms.

" 'Because of the resulting competition for more territory, the local natives have become extremely cunning in the use of their limited array of weapons and their unusual power; but they are often frustrated by this weakness of their weapons and the enormous escape potentiality of the power. The native, Goshal, agreed, saying that the initial attack on our life-saving-station was for the main purpose of *seizing weapons.*'"

Towers lowered the report. "There's *that* aspect again."

Logan nodded gloomily.

Towers found his place: "'It therefore appears that these natives fall into a category difficult to deal with: They are technologically backward, because of a lack of suitable materials on the planet. They are, however, possessed of a formidable power, which apparently developed out of the necessities of life on this world. They are subtle—from long practice—in warfare, using various forms of deception, sudden ambushes, and traps, which apparently are the only reliable ways of dealing with enemies possessed of such an effective power of escape.

"'It follows that we must be very careful to avoid further weapons captures by the natives.

"'It is also evident that to arrive at a treaty of any reliable kind with these natives involves unexpected difficulties, because of their nature and past history of deceit. The more reasonable and attractive the suggestion made to them, the more cunningly hidden and cleverly designed will seem the inevitable trap their experience tells them must be concealed in the agreement.

"'The only solution appears to be bring an overpowering force to the planet.'"

"Whew," said Logan, "what's an 'overpowering force' in a setup like this?"

Towers nodded. "That ignores maintenance and supply problems, and the fact that the Centrans have more to think of than just this one planet, which in itself is practically worthless to them, anyway." He was about to set the report aside, but frowned and separated the pages. Like all the others, this report looked as if it had been stored in a steam bath.

Logan said, "Does it tell how the Centrans carried out a conversation with this native?"

"Here we are," said Towers. "' . . . His pronunciation being imperfect but recognizable. The men, after applying tourniquets, carried him over to the aid station on the far side of the island. Goshal asked again to be put out of his misery, objecting that our methods created pain without serving the purpose, and that our troops were not right in causing him pain since he was not of the tribe that had attacked our expedition, but had learned our tongue from a wounded prisoner traded to his tribe by the neighboring tribe, the "green snakes".' "

"So the Centrans didn't know the local language. The locals learned the Centran language."

"Apparently."

"This looks worse and worse," said Logan. "The natives are intelligent, and past masters of deception. You can't beat them, because you can't catch them. You can't trust any agreement with them, because they're masters of deceit. And you can't get away from them, because wherever you go, *they* can go, too."

Towers moodily reached for the unread reports. "Let's find out if there's more bad news."

The two men read in silence for a long time, then Towers tossed the last report aside in disgust. Logan read on a while longer, then looked up. The two men glanced at each other.

"Well," said Towers, "most of this just reinforces what we knew. But there's something in this last report. The local food here is indigestible for the Centrans. And the locals get nothing from Centran food. What this boils down to is that there's a continuous supply problem, which will get worse if the Centrans bring in more troops."

Logan nodded. "That fits."

"What did you find out?"

Logan said dryly, "In an earlier expedition, a good many locals were transported in Centran landing-boats *to the prison ship.*"

"The *what?*"

"Prison ship."

Towers stared as the implications hit him.

Logan said, "If we ever start to forget these locals are tricky, these are just the reports to remind us."

Towers forced himself to sit back.

Logan said, "The first thing to remember is that Glossip is in charge of the *fourth* bunch of Centrans to hit this planet. The first was the team that scouted the planet, and recommended establishment of a signal-and-life-saving station. This first bunch *apparently* got away safely. The next Centrans came with the signal-and-life-saving station. The natives captured them and seized their weapons. This meant an unexplained cut-off of communications, which led to an investigation. This was the *third* Centran expedition. Their report, in turn, brought down Glossip and the invasion force. It was the third bunch that set up the prison ship."

"What happened?"

Logan picked up a handful of papers:

" 'The natives were quite easily captured as they floundered up out of the water swinging their crude weapons of shell. Our men disarmed them quickly, and headed them into the landing-boats, whence they were transferred to the prison ship. Several were taken aboard the Guard ship for attempted interrogation, and language studies.' "

Towers sat back slowly. "*Then* what?"

Logan leafed through another sheaf of papers. "This one is headed, 'Night Attack on the Guard Detail':

" 'The first attempt came from the direction of the Interrogation Room, preceded by a loud clatter, a hideous yell, and a sound like an avalanche. The Guard, survivors of the Earth campaign, rolled out of their bunks, guns in hand, and fired down the corridors. The stitching-guns got into action at once. Then the attack broke off, and resumed from the direction of the C.O.'s office. That was stopped by grenades, but started up again from the direction of the landing-boat ramp. This attack was broken up by the C.O., using his own stitching-gun. The attack then resumed at all places at once, with terrific intensity, and moderate casualties now resulted on our side, since the use of Centran weapons by the enemy led to the belief that our men were firing on each other. Following repeated repulse, the enemy attacks were finally broken off, and the enemy withdrew, taking his dead. The Guard reoccupied the remainder of the ship, and discovered that the hatches were all still shut and under control, but that a number of portholes had been smashed open. This peculiar fact has raised a number of questions. In the first place, it was obvious to seasoned troops that withdrawal of this sizable force, with their dead and wounded, could not have been carried out through these portholes. Moreover, while the glass from the smashed ports was on the inside, so was a quantity of sand, suggesting that the glass had fallen outside, *then been brought back inside*, purely as a deception. But if the enemy did not gain entry through the ports, and the hatches were still shut and under control, how *did* they get in? The ship was not holed anywhere. This matter deserves study.' "

Logan looked through the reports and pulled out one headed, "Analysis of the Attack on the Guard Ship":

" 'There is thus no way to avoid facing the apparent impossibility. The fact is that the portholes could not have been broken open in the beginning without alerting the guards by means of the electric alarm, which sounded later, when the attack was already under way.

" 'The electric warning system's recording drum shows the breaking of the ports to have taken place respectively at 0101, 0106, and 0112, while the attack started a little before 0100.

" 'At 0100, the hull of the ship, including all hatches and portholes, was intact.

" 'Nevertheless, at 0100, the attack was already underway.

" 'The only local natives on board, admitted by our own men, were the three taken aboard for interrogation and language study. No others had been admitted.

" 'Nevertheless, the attack was carried out by *large forces* of the local natives, *inside the ship*.

" 'In short, with only three of the enemy on board, and the hull intact with all openings shut, a very large force of the enemy gained entrance, *without forcing any of the openings*.

" 'The conclusion is inescapable that the enemy in some way *passed through the walls of the ship*.

" 'We are now faced with the phenomenon of the broken portholes. Since they were not broken to obtain entrance, why *were* they broken? The fact that nearly all the glass was placed *inside*, though much of it would have fallen *outside*, suggests that the purpose was deception. While it is impossible to infer motive with rigorous accuracy, let us consider the implications.

" 'What would be the effects of this deception?

" 'Bear in mind that an attack had been carried out, at night, on a ship fully sealed and protected, with guards on duty, but with no special reason for alertness on the part of the troops, who had just that day helped repulse with ease the "attack" of the local humanoids. Would these troops have any reason to expect trouble? The attack had been defeated. The weapons of the enemy were feeble. The enemy's physical prowess, out of the water, had been demonstrated to be negligible. The prisoners, under attempted interrogation, had showed a pathetic desire to please, and had cooperated readily in the first language studies. The only cause of discomfort was the heat. The troops were tired after a day of strain, culminating in relief that the supposed enemy was harmless. What reason was there for an attacker to expect a strong resistance?

" 'Now, then, having obtained a high degree of reassurance and presumed unreadiness on the part of the defenders, the natives delivered an *overwhelming attack*. That the attack failed is due to no neglect on their part, but to bad luck. The staff, in sending the improvised investigation force to the planet, happened to find a large detachment of the former Headquarters Guard of Horsip's Earth Invasion Force in a convenient location to be rerouted. These troops, survivors of the worst action on record, awarded the platinum nova *as a unit*, are to all intents and purposes unsurprisable. Military surprise presupposes reliance on an incorrect assumption as to the enemy's intent or capability. As a result of their past experiences, the troops of the Guard consider all such estimates unreliable. They maintain, by ingrained habit, the maximum state of readiness.

"'It was pure bad luck that brought the enemy attack up against such troops. In all ordinary circumstances, this attack would have succeeded, the troops would have been wiped out, *and the smashed portholes would have suggested that entry had been made in this way*.

"'The analysis, however, cannot stop at this point. Grant that the enemy had every reason to expect the attack to be successful. Grant that preparations were made to mislead any investigator as to the means of entrance. The question arises, *why mislead?*

"'For the answer, we need to consider outside facts, not included in the attack on this one ship.

"'On the same night, the laboratory ship, where the natives had been physically examined the day before, was attacked, and the crew wiped out. A porthole was found smashed, and the hatches open.

"'On this same night, an attempted attack was made against the headquarters ship, *from the landing-boat locker.* A disturbance there during the night was heard by the officer of the deck, who decided it was a drunken spree of formidable proportions, and left it locked up. Next morning, the locker was entered by a strong party, and found empty; there were, however, signs of an ineffectual attempt to open the lock.

"'Meanwhile, the fourth ship, the landing-forces ship, was traveling over the island chain looking for anything that might account for the disappearance of the life-saving station. By the time this ship returned, it was to be expected that the personnel of the other ships would have been wiped out. A seemingly reasonable explanation would help lull the remainder of the force.

"'We now have the final conclusion to unravel from the evidence. The attackers were able, by some means, to pass through the walls of this ship. Why, in that case, were they unable to pass through the walls of the headquarters ship? Examination of the records reveals that native prisoners were not brought into this ship, though they were ferried to the prison ship in the landing-boat of the headquarters ship, and hence *had* entered this landing-boat, *which returned to the landing-boat locker of the headquarters ship*. We are driven to the conclusion that the natives were able only to enter places *where one of their number had already been.*

" 'We are obviously confronted with an opponent possessed of an extraordinary power, and extremely capable in ambush warfare. And there still remains hanging over our heads the possibility that the enemy is concealing some new surprise. Extreme caution is necessary.' "

Involuntarily, Towers whistled. "This was a conclusion of the *third* expedition?"

Logan nodded. "The deductions of one Derk Moggil on the fourth ship—the ship that was away when the natives attacked."

"They seem to have sent some good men on that third expedition. I'd like to have a talk with this Derk Moggil. I wonder if he's still on the planet?"

Logan shook his head. "His name was on a list of those invalided out after the massacre of most of the third expedition."

"The natives sprang the new surprise Moggil was afraid of?"

Logan nodded. "The Centrans hadn't yet figured out the actual way this teleportation worked. When the soldiers found some large pretty shells lying on the beach one day, they took them on board for souvenirs. The natives then wiped out most of the troops on the headquarters and landing-forces ships."

"How about the Guard ship?"

"The Guards were apparently too busy cleaning their guns and practicing angle shots down the corridors to pay much attention to souvenirs. The locals tried another attack the same night they hit the other two ships. But the Guard ship turned out to be crammed with booby traps every place the natives had been before. For good measure, the Centrans flashed lights on and off, and bounced timed grenades off the walls while observers watching through periscopes called the shots. The bulkheads of some of these places where the locals materialized had been reinforced and holed so the Centrans could fire machine guns through them from the other side. One had a kind of dispenser that dropped Bouncing Betsy mines every time the soldier on watch saw another local show up. It was supposed to be a surprise attack, but it worked out as a slaughter. After about five minutes, the natives quit."

Towers nodded with grudging approval. "Where the situation's hopeless, they clear out."

"And come back again from another angle."

"They tried again?"

"The night after next. They showed up just long enough to bring in some things like snakes, in woven baskets, and turn them loose. Apparently these were supposed to be poisonous, but the shock of the booby traps and mines going off killed them. The next night, the locals tried again, with a kind of biting insect. But the insects didn't like the taste of the Centrans, generally wouldn't bite, and died when they *did* bite. About that time, Glossip and his invasion force were diverted to the planet, and pretty soon the natives had something to think about besides the Guard."

"How long after Glossip got here till he called us in?"

"Judging by the dates, it couldn't have been much over a month."

Towers frowned. "Just suppose, for the sake of argument, that this teleportation ability of theirs will let them reach the nearest habitable solar system? Then what?"

"They still can't *get* there until they've been there."

"I wonder where the ships of the original scouting expedition set down last? Where did they go after they left here? What other ships were at the place where they set down, and where did they go?"

Logan looked startled. "You mean, what if natives stowed away, say, on a Centran ship?"

"What if *by any means* they get off this planet, into a position to put this ability of theirs in use on a large scale? If the practical limit is half a planetary diameter, that's impressive, but it's a local problem. On the other hand, what if the practical limit is thirty light-years? This changes the scale entirely. The fact that the original scouting expedition didn't *see* anything doesn't prove a thing. The natives operate by indirection. If they would go to all that effort to deceive the *third* Centran expedition, who knows what they may have done to the *first* expedition?"

"It *is* peculiar that first expedition didn't see anything."

"Deception is second nature with these natives. They rely on it regularly in their warfare with their neighbors. I wonder if this fight with the Centrans doesn't fit right into their usual framework with no trouble at all."

"A different neighbor, you mean?"

"Correct. And a war with him, started off with maximum deception."

"Hm-m-m. The scouting expedition didn't see anyone here at all. The occupants of the life-saving station disappeared without a trace. The investigating team *almost* got wiped out. But look, if their aim is conquest on a large scale, why not *stay* hidden—only come out at night to touch the side of the ship, or whatever they do so they go to it? The Centrans would never know what hit them."

"If they'd done that, the Centrans might have given up trying to figure out what happened here, and left, taking their ships, their weapons, and their equipment with them. The locals had already fooled the first expedition. They'd easily overcome the second expedition. Why shouldn't they think they could overpower the *third* expedition? Then they'd have all the equipment, and all those weapons, and wouldn't the Centrans send a *fourth* expedition, too?"

Logan swore. "You think *they planned it this way from the beginning?*"

Towers shrugged. "As the Centran report says, it's impossible to deduce motive with certainty. But it sure seems to fit."

"In that case, whether meant that way or not, this planet was a trap, set and baited from the beginning."

"That's what I have in mind."

Logan shook his head. "God help us if the brute-force boys get hold of this one."

"Luckily, Glossip seems to have sense. Suppose you get those Centran scout ships traced, and I'll see what we can do to ease things for Glossip."

"I just hope the scout ships from that first expedition didn't go straight to some crossroads of commerce."

Towers, his mind already elaborating an idea that had occurred to him, said absently, "One way to find out."

The two men were hard at work, when the communicator on Towers' desk buzzed, buzzed again, and he flipped it on.

"Sir," said an apologetic lieutenant, "we have an emergency call from General Glossip."

"Put him on."

The screen flickered, and Glossip appeared, in full battle dress. His face was intent, and his eyes glittered.

"Listen, Towers. Can you hear that?"

In the background was the prolonged crash of small-arms fire in a confined space.

Towers, dazed by the suddenness of this, could only say, "I hear it."

"Nine out of every ten ships I've got are under attack. The remaining one out of ten can't be reached. We don't know how they got inside, and there's nothing for us to do but fight to the finish. Keep out of it, Towers. I just want you to know what's going on. Your orders are to stay completely off this planet."

"Yes, sir. But—"

"You can't help us by getting stuck in it yourself."

"Yes, sir."

The screen went blank.

Towers glanced at Logan, who was talking to someone on his desk screen. Towers shoved his chair back. *Now* what? He couldn't sit here while Glossip and his men were slaughtered. Yet he had Glossip's orders to stay off the planet. Suppose he dropped leech-canisters on the Centran ships? The canisters would attach themselves to the hulls, and bore their way through. Then they would flood the ships with sick gas. Towers reached for the communicator, then paused. If he did that, he would *certainly* put the

Centrans out of action, but who knew about the body chemistry of the locals?

Frowning, Towers reached for the communicator, and called his intelligence chief.

A harried face appeared.

"Sir?"

"What's going on down there?"

"I've been wondering whether to call you. There's nothing *visible* taking place. But in the last ten minutes, we've had two reports of a terrific racket on the sound pickups, apparently from the Centran ships."

"They've been boarded. Let me know what happens."

"Yes, sir."

Towers' mind raced through the long catalog of special weapons and devices developed in fights on other planets. Wasn't there even *one* he could use? Suppose he used close-trained lions and gorillas, with their controllers operating through the new visual linkage? Could they be counted on to attack the *locals* and not the Centrans? Was there time to do it? His mind whirled with calculations. So long to "awaken" them, so long to explain the situation to the controllers, so long to get them down to the planet. It would have to be cleared with Glossip, and the Centran troops would have to have some idea what was happening, or they would attack the animals as well as the locals.

Towers shook his head. There wasn't time.

The communicator buzzed.

"Sir," said the Intelligence chief, "now the portholes are being knocked out of the ships."

"That fits. Let me know what else shows up."

"Yes, sir."

Towers' mind was racing. Suppose he flooded the Centran ships with yellow jackets? They would sting the Centrans. But would they touch the natives? Mild methods were unreliable. But anything *certainly* lethal for the locals would finish the Centrans, too. How to strike at *one* set of people fighting at close quarters without hurting the other set?

On the desk beside the communicator, the second hand

was steadily sweeping around. If he was going to do anything, it would have to be done fast. But, with two sets of them tangled up in close combat, how—

For an instant, some remembered fact seemed to present itself, to show the problem in a clearer light; but it was for an instant only, leaving Towers blankly trying to recover what had flashed through his mind and gone on. Carefully, he groped along a vanishing trail of mental associations. Something about separating two sets of people? Something he'd seen down there? Had he ever seen anything, in the brief time since he'd been here—some instance in which the locals had reacted differently from the Centrans, been at a disadvantage, or displayed a weakness?

The communicator buzzed. Towers snapped it on.

"Sir," said the tense Communications officer. "General Glossip."

The screen showed a chaotic flash of Centran troops, drifting powder smoke, swiftly-shifting groups of blue-green forms, now here, now there, always two or three of them to one of the Centrans. Before Towers' eyes, the Centrans went down. There was no panic. The troops were fighting. But their blows didn't land. And always, each Centran soldier was attacked by two or three of his enemies, appearing in a flash from nowhere, to strike from the side or rear, and vanish.

Glossip's voice came through. "Do you see this, Towers?"

"I see it. Listen, we can drop close-trained animals down there—"

"No time, Towers. By the time you get anything here, it will all be over. Do you see how they fight?"

"I see it."

"Are you recording this?"

"Yes, sir. Automatically."

"Then there's a record, at least. They'll believe it at headquarters. I think I see what happened here. They can change position so fast you hardly see them. If, as our men went out for their night exercise, carrying their rifles, these locals simply flashed through the shadows for an instant, near the ship, long enough to contact the rifles, or do whatever they do, they would then have their homing objects, which the men would carry back into the ships with them."

Towers nodded dazedly. There it was—Yet another trap.

On the screen, Glossip straightened, and his voice came across clearly. "This is a direct order, Towers. Keep out of this. There's no time now for you to do anything. Better destroy that pack you wore down here, by the way. Good luck, Towers."

Then, with his attention elsewhere, the thought came back to Towers. He instantly focused his whole awareness on it, and abruptly the situation seemed to change form. Yes, it was too late for him to intervene physically. *But he could still send information.*

Glossip was turning from the screen.

Towers said, "General—*Lift your ships!*"

Glossip turned back. "They'll only learn—" He saw Towers' face, and whirled out of sight of the screen. An instant later, a high-pitched whistle cut through the din, in a combination of tones repeated again and again, and then the communicator buzzed urgently.

Towers, vaguely aware of Logan speaking earnestly into his own communicator, snapped down the Hold switch, put the new call on the screen, and saw his Intelligence officer.

"Sir, several of the Centran ships are lifting fast."

"Good." Towers called his Communications officer.

"Sir?"

"All the Centran ships should lift shortly. If they don't lift in the next two minutes, beam the order to lift ship, and either open hatches or smash some portholes. And keep lifting as long *as the outside air is thick enough to breathe.*"

The Communications officer blinked. "Yes, sir."

Towers snapped the Hold switch back, and there was Glossip, turned partly away from the screen, his face tense.

Frowning, Towers thought over his brief flash of insight. Everything *seemed* to hold together. Why should a mechanism develop if it wasn't needed? And hadn't it been shown by that humanoid that had attacked Glossip? But then, suppose he was wrong?

Towers snapped down the Hold switch, and called Gunnery. A major with a bulldog jaw appeared on the screen.

Towers said, "The Centran ships have been boarded by the locals and there's a chance that the locals may get control of some of them. If so, we want to be ready to destroy those ships ourselves."

"If you need us, sir, we'll be ready."

"Good." Towers switched back to Glossip, found that nothing had changed but the background noise, which was now more screams than shooting, and called the Officer of the Watch. The earnest face of Lieutenant Cartwright appeared on the screen.

Towers said, "Have you had any trouble from the active equipment locker? I left my grav pack there, and it seems to me the locals may have had opportunity to convert it into a 'homing object' while I was down there."

Cartwright's eyes narrowed. "I'll check on it, sir. It will only take a few minutes to find out."

"You don't plan to just open the hatch and look in?"

"No, sir. I'll seal the adjoining corridors before I do anything else."

"Go to it."

Towers switched back to Glossip, and at the same moment became vaguely aware that Logan was standing beside the desk. But Towers' attention was fixed on the screen.

Glossip was turned sidewise, gun in hand. His face bore the smile of the man who has been attacked by a robber, and now the robber is at his mercy. Glossip stepped out of range of the screen, and came back dragging a blue-green figure by the arm. The creature's face was twisted in agony, and both hands were pressed to the membranes, on either side of the head, that served as ears.

Glossip looked at Towers. "You were right! I'll get in touch with you as soon as we clean up the remnants."

Glossip vanished from the screen, and Towers became vaguely aware of Logan's voice saying, "Sir, we no sooner got started on this than we unearthed a query from a

Centran space depot, asking information about this planet's surface."

"Why did they ask about that?"

"It seems that a Centran scout ship broke down, and turned up at the space depot for repairs. An officer noticed a brownish shell stuck to the scout ship, apparently for decoration. It seems that some of the scout pilots will mount on their ship a plume, skull, or some other souvenir of the planet they've scouted, as a sort of trophy. This is strictly contrary to regulations, and the Centrans are cracking down on it. Well, this shell is stuck on with some kind of powerful adhesive, but the scout insists he didn't put it there. The officials at the depot want to know what the surface of the planet here is like, and what the chance is of a thing like this happening with no help from the pilot."

"Where is this stuck onto the ship?"

"On the underside, where the ship would naturally set down."

"How big?"

"Roughly a foot across."

"Sounds exactly like their favorite homing object."

"Yes, sir. We've been assuming the locals could use *any* large object. Maybe they can't."

Towers shook his head. "How much did you hear of what's going on down there?"

"Just the last few exchanges on the screen."

Towers described what had happened. Logan listened in amazement and shook his head. "Then it follows they *don't* need these shells to home on. Then why *did* they put one on the ship?"

"More peculiar yet, why did they put it where the ship would *land on it?*"

Logan said quietly: "The shell would break when they land."

"*That's* it."

Logan said in exasperation: "They apparently, in some way, familiarize themselves with the molecular structure of an object, and then they can home on it—guide themselves when they 'jump' to the place where the object is. Perhaps each object has a characteristic—call it a 'wave-state'—that the teleports can detect and use to guide themselves to the place where the object is. So, they take great pains to stick a homing object to a departing scout ship, and they stick it where it will be destroyed when the scout ship lands—*which is exactly when they will want to use it*."

"Right," said Towers. "That's it exactly."

"But how? Once it's mashed to bits in the landing, *that* will change the characteristic wave-form, won't it?"

"Yes, and tell them *that the ship has landed*."

Logan looked startled.

"Otherwise," said Towers, "how do they know when the ship has reached another planet? It's *there* that they want to come out, not somewhere in between planets."

"And then they home on the ship itself? Yes, I see it. The molecular structure of the *ship* won't change substantially. The fact that it remains uninjured, and the shell is destroyed, suggests that the ship has set down. In that case, it follows that they *did* plan ahead. Even though they weren't seen, they were active *when the first Centran expedition scouted the planet*."

Towers said, "Apparently they aren't lacking in the taste, or the ability, for conquest. All they've been lacking is opportunity."

Logan, looking stunned, sat down at his desk. "In the short space of time since that first Centran scouting expedition, these teleports have worked out a technique for getting to other planets, destroyed a Centran life-saving station, captured its crew, learned the Centran tongue, seized a quantity of Centran weapons and learned how to use them, surprised a Centran force sent to investigate, wiped out most of it, attacked an entire Centran planetary invasion force, and came within a hair's breadth of—"

Towers' communicator buzzed. He snapped it on, to see, through the open visor of a suit of battle armor, the serious face of Cartwright, the Officer of the Watch, who stepped to one side to show half-a-dozen blue-green bodies lying on the deck inside the active equipment locker—a long, high,

narrow room with rows of clamp-fastener shelves on one side,
and snap hooks on the other side. On one of the shelves lay
the grav pack Towers had used on the planet. At the far end
of the locker was the closed hatch leading to the outside air
lock. Back out of sight of the camera was the corridor to the
spray baths and the air lock to the interior of the ship. It was
possible to enter the ship by any of several routes, but as a
means to cut down the admission of germs and parasites, this
was the route taken on returning from a trip to a strange
planet, and it was the route Towers had used. On leaving the
equipment locker, he had shut the inner doors that cut down
air circulation—and the screen was now showing the view
through this doorway into the locker, where the blue-green
bodies lay like so many rag dolls. Half hidden under a
muscular blue-green arm was what looked like a large shell
inside a case of tightly-woven fiber that fit like a thick tire
on a broad wheel.

Towers looked the bodies over carefully. They all showed
plain evidence of having run into a terrific concentration of
fire.

"Are there any more to the screen?"

"Yes, sir."

"What happened?"

"We set up two mesh barriers in the corridors, in case
anything came out of the locker in a rush. The first barrier
was right outside the locker door here, and the second was
back up the corridor with the guns behind it. I came up
behind the first barrier to use a hand grapple on the locker
doors. There wasn't a rustle from the other side as I eased
the door open. Then here was a yell, a shower of darts, and
the whole net bulged back as six or eight hit it at once. I
was knocked flat on my back. A kind of shell wrapped with
fiber—there it is on the deck there—hit the net and flattened up against it, and another of these natives materialized in the air on *this* side of the barrier. He had an armload
of shells, and as I went down I could see him cast them down
the corridor. I yelled 'Open fire!' That did it, sir. But if we
hadn't suspected they were in there, we wouldn't have had
a chance."

The screen drew back, to show a metal frame tightly fitted against the walls of the corridor, with a net, now badly torn, stretched so that it blocked the passage, yet at first was scarcely visible. The view swung around, to show more blue-green forms strewn on the deck. Farther down the corridor was another frame and net, and, behind, it, a pair of short-range nine-barrel fusion guns set up side by side with armored men prone behind them, and behind them, another pair set higher on their adjustable mounts, and angled slightly upward.

Towers glanced back at the motionless forms on the deck.

"Is that all the attackers?"

"No, sir. I think we had fifty here for a moment or two. Apparently they decided it wasn't working, and left."

Towers thought it over in silence.

"Let's have a better view of that deck."

The scene tilted, and he was looking at motionless blue-green forms with many tiny oval fragments of shell scattered amongst them.

"That can't be the armload of shells you mentioned."

"No, sir. Maybe they took them back with them."

Towers fought down the urge to profanity. The active equipment locker, and that whole stretch of corridor adjacent to it, was now as open to attack as if it were part of the planet. By the same token, it was denied to Towers, except for armored men, and all that was needed was one slip, and the whole ship would be wide open. He didn't like the way the opposition traded blow for blow. It was painfully obvious who had the initiative, and there was no point stepping the fight up a little bit at a time, so as to make a staircase for them to climb by stages until they perfected their measures up to the level of Centra and Earth combined. What was needed was a blow delivered with a force they couldn't understand, from a direction they didn't expect. The difficulty was, the target could move from place to place with lightning rapidity. And since their technology was primitive, there was no way to strike at them through that. With due care, and enough shrewdness and force, over a long period of time, it would probably be possible to exterminate the whole race—provided they never succeeded in establishing themselves on another planet—but that would violate Centran principles, and deny the advantages that might conceivably come from an eventual change in the natives' attitude. And *that* was the crux of the matter. How to change that desire for conquest into something more like an honest interest in cooperation?

These thoughts went through Towers' mind in rapid succession, and he was only vaguely aware of Cartwright walking down the corridor, the visor of his armor down, to talk to the men at the fusion guns. Then an obvious fact penetrated to Towers' consciousness, and he called, "Did they touch your armor?"

"Yes, sir."

Before Towers could say more, half-a-dozen blue-green forms appeared on all sides of the Officer of the Watch. The multiple short-range fusion guns let loose a murderous burst.

The attack was over as fast as it started. But amongst the sprawled attackers lay an unusually large shell. The Officer of the Watch, protected from the fire by his armor, picked up the shell and threw it the length of the corridor. It apparently hit the net near the door to the equipment locker, bounced back into sight on the screen, and split in half when it struck the deck.

Towers studied it coldly.

Each half of this shell was as big as an ordinary shell.

Cartwright raised his visor and looked questioningly at Towers.

Towers adjusted the screen, and was fairly sure he could see traces of some dark substance along the line of the break in the shell.

"Why not walk down and just see if there isn't something like glue along the break in that shell?"

Cartwright walked down the corridor, filled the screen, and said, "Yes, sir. There's a hardened streak of some kind. Shall I smash the pieces?"

Towers thought it over. Every few minutes, there seemed

to be some new example of craft and cunning. The teleports looked more formidable by the hour. When opportunity offered, they wiped out whole military commands at once. Against stiffer opposition, they contented themselves with establishing a toehold, and expanding it by steps into a bridgehead. Towers had started out feeling an underlying sympathy he often felt for the objects of Centran Planetary Integration. But by now, the sympathy had congealed into loathing. Now there was this clever new stunt with the oversize shell. Had they tried this before, and found that the victims carried the broken pieces with other rubbish into another part of the ship, and a new section was opened to attack? Or was it a distraction, to draw attention from the fact that Cartwright's armor would provide easy access to whatever part of the ship that armor was in? Or was there some *other* clever booby trap involved?

"Better leave it where it is," said Towers. "I don't see that they gain anything by it."

"Sir, I'm just wondering, can they sense the relative positions of two objects they've 'learned'?"

"Maybe. But I don't think that's going to help them."

"But, if they could, there might be an advantage in introducing a number of such objects into a ship. Something similar to triangulation may be involved."

Towers nodded. "Maybe that was their reason. But they aren't going to get beyond this part of the ship if we can help it."

"In that case, sir, the sooner I get out of this armor, the better."

Towers' eyes narrowed, then he smiled. "And if they can tell the relative position of different parts of that armor, when do you suppose the next batch of them will come through?"

"When I've got it about half off. I won't be able to defend myself, and if the fusion guns fire, I'll get hit, too."

"Right."

"Sir, suppose we put on masks, and fill the corridor with chlorine gas?"

"First, we don't know how fast it would affect them.

Second, it would surprise them, but probably not so much that they couldn't get away—to spread the warning."

"It might make them more wary about coming through."

"That's the third reason why we shouldn't do it."

Towers considered this latest predicament. Before Lieutenant Cartwright could go back into the part of the ship that was safe, he *had* to get out of the armor. If he didn't, any part of the ship he went to would be unsafe. But to get out of the armor meant to open himself to attack.

"Sir, if you'd have them send up another suit, I could take this off piece by piece—"

"And have them come through when the piece you've got off is the breastplate? No, we'll get you out of there, but not dead, if we can help it."

At Towers' instructions, a false deck was welded into place behind the fusion guns. The fusion guns then drew back behind it, and two new nets were put up, in front of the guns. Cartwright cut away the old net, stepped up on the low false deck, hesitated, sat down inside the nearest net, and suddenly his feet were out of sight, then his legs, and he squirmed and twisted and then he was completely inside the claustrophobic space that had been left open under one side of the false deck. Since there was no room under there for anyone else, a teleport who came through there would wind up with the false deck embedded in his body. On the other hand, if he came through overhead, the false deck would serve as a shield.

As Lieutenant Cartwright squirmed out of his breastplate, there was an earsplitting yell, a shower of darts, a shell hit the first barrier, a blue-green form materialized behind it, to scatter an armload of shells, and the corridor was filled with the crisscrossing radiance of the fusion beams. The corridor was a shambles when the attack was over. A technician in armor cut through the lower edge of the net, the fusion guns made a barrier of energy overhead, and Cartwright crawled back to safety.

All that, Towers told himself, to get one man free of the attention of the "natives."

As soon as the men were safely out of the corridor, the

ship was treated as if it had suffered heavy battle damage. The air was pumped out of the active equipment locker, the corridor, and all adjacent parts of the ship, back to the reinforcing walls. The locker and corridor were then completely cut out, and, plate by plate, they were cut up and melted down, in space. At the same time, in a nearby landing-boat, a nervous surgical team dissected a number of the native dead.

While this was going on, a total of twenty-six more teleports appeared, in and around the corridor that was being disassembled, and were at once blown apart by their own internal pressure. But in the landing-boat where the dissection was carried out, nothing interfered except the surgeons' uneasy urge to look over their shoulders.

Towers now went to a separate landing-boat, to talk to Glossip.

Glossip, to Towers' surprise, was beaming broadly.

"It's all relative, Towers," he explained. "When you expect quick victory, a little delay seems like a setback. When you expect to be slaughtered, if you come out somewhere near, even, it seems like a victory. In this case, I was prepared to be finished off, following which the planet would have been subjected to methodical bombardment with nuclear weapons until that race of teleports was as close to extinction as brute force and persistence would bring them. Instead, that piece of advice of yours opens up new possibilities. It also demonstrates that Centra was right to make the alliance with Earth."

Towers looked puzzled. "Was there any question about that?"

Glossip shrugged. "You've been busy, solving problems that some people don't know exist. Therefore, you've missed a few points that we can't overlook much longer. After this is over with, if it *can* be solved, you may find yourself up against a tougher proposition."

"I never hope to see a tougher proposition than these teleports."

"Well, Towers," said Glossip, smiling, "if you're able to beat them, it stands to reason that *you* are a tougher proposition."

Towers, puzzled and vaguely exasperated, decided to drag the conversation back onto the subject.

"Sir, that's what I'd like to get cleared up: How this collection of frustrated conquerors is going to be jammed back onto their own planet."

Glossip's air of well-being vanished.

"Jammed *back* onto their planet? What do you mean, Towers? They haven't got *off* it yet."

"Yes, sir. But unfortunately, they seem to have thought that out in the beginning, before anyone was aware they existed." He described the scout ship, with shell stuck to it in such a way that a landing would break the shell. He described his and Logan's idea of how that had come about, and added, "Maybe Logan and I are wrong, but—"

"No," said Glossip. "It fits in with what's happened here. That's exactly what they *would* think of."

"Well, sir," said Towers, "we should know soon. Major Logan is tracing the rest of those scout ships. If we find, for instance, that one of them has landed on an oversize, warm, wet, roughly Earth-type planet, and if the scout ship has a few odd bits of shell stuck to its underside, then we shouldn't be surprised to find, before long, that any other ship that touches down there is likely to suffer a sudden disappearance of the crew and weapons."

Glossip shook his head in disgust, then the light of craft and shrewdness lit up his eyes. "Hm-m-m, Towers. Now, just suppose, instead of a *warm wet planet*—"

Towers smiled. "I've been thinking the same thing."

"What we want," said Glossip, "are two things. First, to get loose from this place, with a whole skin. Second, to jar the minds of these teleports onto something besides killing everyone they can reach."

Towers nodded. "Their standard procedure seems to have two stages: First, spread homing objects into the territory of the opposition. Second, attack to kill, with stunning shock-effect and overwhelming force. Considering the conditions on this planet, it must seem almost as natural as breathing."

"It seems to me that our idea, once we put it into action,

ought to do something to this automatic procedure of theirs."

"Yes. Of course, a lot might depend on what the dissection shows."

"Yes," said Glossip. "It will be interesting to see just what that turns up."

The surgeons, after several long, nerve-wracking sessions, duly submitted a report that boiled down to a statement that the natives were typically humanoid in their body structure, with certain little-understood organs somewhat more developed than in the people of Earth or Centra— but that this was well within the limits of normally-to-be-expected variations; that there was a complicated digestive system, apparently designed to handle a wide variety of local foods. An analysis of the contents of the digestive tract was appended, with sketches and photographs to give some clue to the local diet.

Towers and Logan, and later Glossip, searched backwards and forwards through the report for some explanation of the locals' teleporting ability. But there was no explanation there. There was, instead, a long statement about the development of the skeletal and muscular systems, and special adaptations for swimming, such as partial webs between the fingers and the elongated toes, eyes capable of being thrust forward under the brow ridges for purposes of better observation, a large chest with exceptionally powerful muscles, the absence of external ears, and speculation as to the hypothetical superiority, underwater, of the membrane that took the place of the external ear.

Towers skimmed over the question of streamline form typical of underwater creatures, but paid close attention to a description of an arrangement in the ear that permitted the mechanism to withstand comparatively heavy pressures, as the chair of small bones that transmitted sound vibrations came ɔ rest inside a supporting cage of bone, while most of the external membrane itself was pressed back against a porous bony surface that apparently could support it at any depths likely to be reached in the offshore waters near the islands.

There was no arrangement for adapting to low external pressures, the report went on, apparently because there was little likelihood of experiencing them on the planet. There were no high mountains to climb, the planet's axis was vertical to the plane of the ecliptic, eliminating seasonal extremes, the weather seemed uniform, and the report theorized that in the event of unusually low atmospheric pressure, a sense of "unease" would be felt, possibly leading the humanoids to teleport to another locality, or to dive into the warm waters, where the resulting pressure would promptly eliminate any discomfort.

"Too bad," said Logan, "they didn't just evolve gills and have done with it."

"Probably wouldn't have worked," said Towers. "They'd have been in competition with the sea life, and it's formidable."

Logan nodded. "But at least we'd have understood which mechanism did what."

Towers leafed back through the report. "Whatever it is, the surgeons could have the organ used for teleporting—if there *is* a special organ for teleporting—right under their hands and never know it. But what puzzles me is—as far as it's possible to tell from this—*we've* got everything they've got."

Logan smiled. "Who knows? Maybe they could show us how to do it."

"Provided they'd stick around long enough without putting a knife in us."

"There *is* that difficulty. Well, what now?"

"The first thing is to find some way to get several tons of stuff they can eat off the planet and into storage. The trouble is, they can't eat *our* food, so we may have to bring food all the way from here to feed them."

"Sir, feed *them?*"

"So we can keep them alive while we bring them back from other planets."

"I thought the whole idea was to keep them from ever *getting* to other planets."

"The idea is to keep them from carrying out their program

of conquest, without having to divert manpower from halfway around the universe to do it. What's the best way to stop someone from carrying out a program of conquest?"

Logan cast a belligerent look toward the planet below. "Flatten them out. If necessary, kill them."

"That may be the *surest* way, if you can do it. But suppose you can convince them that there's no profit whatever in their program of conquest, that there is, in the nature of things, *nothing to gain by it?*"

Logan blinked. "Well—Yes, but—"

"In fact," said Towers, "couldn't you say a conqueror is flattened out and killed *as a conqueror*, once he discovers that the result of his clever schemes is likely to be *pure agony?*"

Logan looked at Towers attentively.

"How do we do that to them?"

The next few days brought word of the other Centran scout ships. They had separated, and all but one had so far found nothing worth mentioning. That one had moored alongside a large desolate chunk of nickel iron, and by pure miscalculation on the part of the scout, the ship banged into this floating chunk of ore before the scout got his beacon and claim-plate anchored in place. On returning, he was stupefied to find eighteen blue-green bodies, a large assortment of weapons, and eighteen unbroken shells, drifting alongside the ship which had a few fragments of broken shell still stuck to it, and innumerable bits and slivers drifting around loose. There was no other ship in sight, and the big chunk of ore offered no sign of an entry or exit. The scout blinked, uttered a fervent prayer, and lost no time getting photographic evidence. He then consulted his "Manual of Official Rules and Procedures," and found that he now had no choice but to report this airless block as an "inhabited planetoid." Finds in this category were so rare as to create a sensation when the report came in, followed on closer examination by massive censorship. Only by the authority of the Supreme Staff was the lid pried loose, and then Logan and Towers looked at the photographs and glanced at each other.

"Well," said Logan, "that proves it. They *can* teleport to a great distance, once they have a homing object to jump to."

"Yes," said Towers, "and it also shows us something else."

"They're eager for conquest. This scout scarcely left the ship and came back, and there they were."

"And they have a definite technique. They come through in a flash, one wave following another. When they're winning, there's no end of them. When they're losing, they stop coming through. *How do they know which to do?*"

"Maybe one of them flashes through, then goes back and gives the word."

Towers shook his head. "What if he doesn't live to go back? No, I've studied the films of that business in the corridor, and that isn't how it works. They come in waves. In the corridor here, *one* came through, and threw out a stack of shells. To each shell came another teleport, each carrying, as far as the field of view shows us, a shell under his left arm, the thinnest edge of it gripped between fingers and thumb of his left hand, and in one swift motion of his left hand, he flung this out."

Logan frowned. "Yes, but what—"

Towers yanked a large envelope out of a stack on his desk, pulled out a handful of blown-up photographs, selected a number showing the chaos in the corridor, the air seemingly jammed with natives, the fusion beams searing into them as they flung out the shells that would serve the next wave as homing objects. Carefully, Towers examined each photograph before handing it over.

Each photograph Towers selected showed a shell in the foreground. And each shell showed in its edge at least one small curving break.

"How," said Towers, "do they know when to come through, *and when to stop?* In the corridor, we have on the film upwards of forty of them in one attack alone. Some were killed and others got away. But the Centran scout, when he accidentally let his ship drift into the ore body and smash the shell, came up against only *eighteen* of them. *Plus* eighteen shells."

Towers glanced at the report of the scout. One plate showed the shells drifting in space amongst the shambles of eighteen bodies, and assorted rifles, splat-guns, and grenades. The sight was horrible enough, but the nearest shells, lit up starkly by the flash that accompanied the shot, looked perfect and unbroken. He handed the report to Logan.

"Compare the shells that were followed by another wave of attack with those that were *not* followed by another wave of attack."

"Hm-m-m. Yes, I see."

"It's been a puzzle all along how they signaled the next wave. It *might* have been that they went back and notified them. It *might* have been telepathy. Or it might be that it's done by means of these shells. After all, why do they always use *them* when they come through? We know they can use other objects. Why don't they come through carrying a captured spanner from a Centran ship, or a captured Centran helmet? Why isn't it enough that they come through with a Centran rifle that another of them has 'learned'? What conceivable advantage is there to lugging this shell along?"

Logan said, "Let's see now. On some level of consciousness they 'learn,' or familiarize themselves, with an object. This object apparently gives off some kind of signal that enables them to home on it. If the object ceases to exist, the signal ceases, too. But, if the object isn't actually *smashed*, if a small piece is *broken off*, then most of the object is still there—maybe the signal would still be transmitted, but the *character* of it would be altered." Logan looked up in astonishment. "It might be like a radio tone that abruptly changed pitch."

"Yes."

"And *that* would explain their using the shells. It's a little inconvenient to break a piece off a rifle or a helmet. Well, if so, we've finally got a way to trap *them* for a change."

Towers nodded. "If our assumptions are right, we should be able to hit them so hard it will jar their automatic-conquest habit down into their throats—where they will choke on it."

The following months passed under the painful handicaps imposed by the fact that the locals were on the watch to take advantage of any slip, and this added complexities to the problems of dealing with an unfamiliar planet that no one had thought of before. Dredges were sent down to collect edible plants for use later, and immediately ran head on into the fact that the off shore waters were thick with a honeycomb network of coral-like structures, traversed only by various fish, the locals, and a kind of stretched-out alligator with long armor-tipped snout, numerous pairs of legs, and a highly flexible body. While the coral dulled cutters and jammed machinery, the alligators specialized in punching through the sieve-like containers that held the contents, to get at schools of small fish trapped amongst the vegetation inside.

Meanwhile, the natives pulled out cotter pins, hauled on sprockets and gears, and then swam down to locate the pieces, and tried to deduce what these things were good for. Small TV cameras attached to the machines showed what was going on. The coral was wearing out the machinery, the alligators were living a life of ease and luxury, and the humanoids were demonstrating a fantastic mechanical stupidity, as evidenced by the fact that they swam around the dredge, prodding it with shell-tipped spears, apparently seeking the heart of the beast. But their idea of damage seemed accurate enough. Anything capable of being pulled off, they pulled off, and if it was big enough, they ran their hands over it, with a peculiar expression of concentration, suggesting that they were converting it into a homing object.

It was now up to the technicians to devise a machine that could either avoid or chew through and spit out the coral, resist the efforts of the alligators, and meanwhile stand off the locals. One difficulty followed another, and before it was over the Special Effects Team had devised an armored dredge with underwater cannon and shock generators, and enough circuitry to wire a city. This behemoth was a success until it chewed a path completely through the coral-like barrier, to the outer sea.

In through the channel came a beast like the offspring of a mammoth lobster mated to a giant squid. Whatever this creature was, the dredge had apparently intruded into its territory, and by the time it got through, the dredge was scattered over a hundred square miles of ocean bottom. Then there was nothing to do but build another one.

Glossip, meanwhile, had gotten hold of a nuclear furnace and steel works suitable for converting metallic asteroids into sheets, bars and tubes, and he was slowly and methodically running his contaminated space fleet in one end of this and out the other, where his crew labored to convert the sheets, bars and tubes back into space-ships. The frustrations were maddening, and meanwhile the Centran high command grudgingly doled out items that couldn't be reconstructed, and accompanied the dole with a flood of warnings about the mounting expense. All that made it possible was that the Centrans never used anything complicated where something simple would do the job. When they finally ran into absolutely impossible problems, a crew of experts would show up with the necessary materials and precision tools, and with much shaking of heads and wise advice for the future, put the finishing touches to the work.

At the end, Glossip had a fleet that was not much worse than the fleet he'd had before, and he could walk down the corridor without the thought that half a hundred teleports might spring out at him any minute. Towers by then had large quantities of local food on the way to various planets where scout ships orbited patiently. The local natives had a large collection of miscellaneous parts they were trying to somehow fire, explode, or otherwise put to useful service. Everyone but the natives was worn out, and no one was absolutely certain that they hadn't somehow insinuated a booby trap into the works somewhere.

Glossip, however, remained as persistent as a river eating its way through a mountain, and Towers was kept busy adding refinements to what he thought might prove to be the only real surprise this race of teleports had ever experienced. But always some part of the plan was weaker than the others, so his work went on and on, until it finally reached the point where he had covered everything he could conceive to be possible, and for good measure, quite a few things he *couldn't* conceive to be possible.

The food was now at the planets, under refrigeration. The scout ships were ready to land. The planets were waiting patiently for whoever might care to come down.

Everything seemed as ready as it could be, so Towers gave the signal for the first scout ships to set down.

Seated at his multiple screen, Towers looked from one to another of the landing fields. One view showed slush a foot deep, with occasional showers of sleet lashing past almost horizontally. At the top of the screen, little images of comparison gauges showed atmospheric pressure far below that on the teleports' home world, while, thanks to a relatively small planetary diameter, the surface gravity was painfully higher.

Another planet had a heavier gravity and thinner atmosphere, with impressive ranges of volcanoes belching clouds of sulfurous fumes over a landscape of cracked earth and bubbling pits of mud, while occasional patches of scrawny vegetation gave the only sign of life.

One of the colder planets had something extra, in the form of humanoids whose protruding muzzles, and all but nonexistent foreheads, were somewhat compensated for by thick fur, exceptionally powerful jaws, and sharp teeth. Considerable numbers of these humanoids, their small eyes glinting shrewdly, were behind the protective rock walls at the edge of the landing ground. Eagerly, they were breaking bits off the edge of large brownish shells, and then carrying the shells and broken-off bits to a Centran bundled in furs, who in return handed out copper disks the size of saucers. These disks the humanoids carried through a nearby stone doorway, to emerge beaming, with handfuls of steel traps, hatchets, knives and small sacks marked with the Centran word for salt. The Centran who accepted the broken bits and the shells dropped the bits in a leather bag, and handed the shells to humanoid children, who tucked them under their left arms and darted off, the grown-ups pounding after them. As the delightful game went on, shells broke and were discarded, and the shaggy humanoids began glancing around eagerly for whole shells that might have been overlooked.

Towers, watching the scene on the screen, suddenly watched more intently.

Over the landing ground, sinking slowly through a brief shower of sleet, the first of the scout ships was coming down.

Slowly the ship settled into the slush, and its weight came to rest on the shell fixed to its underside. Beneath the slush, the shell crushed on the hard-packed pebbly surface.

Towers watched intently. How long would a warlike race stay alert for the possible conquest of a planet?

Around the scout ship, heavily-armed blue-green figures suddenly appeared, shells clutched under left arms, faces lit with a look of determination and triumph.

Then the powerful gravity took hold. The wind lashed out with a fresh volley of sleet. The slush extracted heat from bodies accustomed to equatorial waters. The thin atmosphere declined to push back the internal pressures in lungs and body cavities.

The expression of triumph vanished in a look of shock. Hands were clasped over eyes and ear membranes. Mouths opened, distended chests deflated. The look of shock gave way to agony.

From the low rock walls along the edge of the field came a shout. Shaggy figures rushed out, the sleet striking harmlessly against thick fur, the slush seeking in vain to draw heat from insulation perfected over ages of exposure to varying extremes. The heavy gravity and thin air no more troubled them than seaweed and water disturb a fish, and now the first shaggy figures reached these peculiar blue-green things, hesitated, then put their minds on what really counted, grasped the shells and broke off the first small bits.

An instant later, *other* blue-green things appeared, with *other* shells.

More humanoids came splashing through the slush, each seizing one of the precious shells, and each carefully breaking off a small piece.

More blue-green shell bearers appeared, to announce their arrival with gruff coughs and screams.

Here was wealth unending!

The landing ground swarmed with shaggy humanoids.

The blue-green figures multiplied in successive waves of horrified shock.

When an unmanageable catastrophe seemed certain, an amplified voice boomed out in the local tongue that only those who got back before the sun bit the edge of the world could trade their shells. For the time of darkness and moon, a new kind of shell was to be given out.

The humanoids squinted into the storm with practiced gaze, and left in a rush across the field.

Centran stretcher-bearers now filed out, to carry the writhing blue-green forms to a ship at the far edge of the landing ground, which was to serve as combination pressure chamber and first-aid center. Meanwhile another screen showed a landing ground on a different planet, where another scout ship was just settling down. The first scout ship now lifted, to be melted shortly into scrap, as the crushers moved out to grind up the pebbly surface where it had landed.

Towers watched thoughtfully. Now the question was, would the teleports be able to use their ability to escape?

Logan said finally, "Either they're in no hurry to go home, or they can't."

"When they're startled, they apparently can't use their power. I imagine they've never been startled like this before."

"In that case," said Logan smiling, "*we* will supply the transportation."

"And everything possible will have to be done to learn their language. Meanwhile, we may be able to find out something more about this planet."

While the ships carrying the dazed teleports were on their way back toward their home planet, the disguised pickups were already there—little things that drifted quietly down in the night. In the waters close off shore, careful reproductions of the stretched-out alligators served as reconnaissance vehicles and it became clear that the locals had a number of secrets they hadn't yet disclosed.

On the basis of all Towers had seen, it was evident that the natives teleported out of the water onto the land, or from one place on land to another place on land, but they hadn't been seen to teleport into the water. The trouble was, there were times when a number of natives vanished at once, and didn't show up elsewhere. What had happened? The obvious answer seemed to be that they had gone into the water somewhere out of sight of the pickups. But then, why were they never seen to do it? There were times when a raiding party surprised a band of locals on land, and Towers had watched fights where the sequence of shifts in position was a fantasy of rapid flickerings from spot to spot as the local inhabitants tried to convert a superiority in known local positions into an advantage that would place them behind the attackers for just a second or two. This rapid shift in position was never seen in the water, the only maneuvers there being fancy swimming or sudden escapes to a location on land.

Glossip, listening to Towers' report on the situation, sat back, frowning.

"Where," Towers was saying, "do they go? Our coverage, on land, is about perfect."

"Somewhere, Towers, they've got a cavern, or a set of hollowed-out tunnels, that we haven't found."

"If so, we can't detect them."

"They might be too deep to detect."

"Well, you may be right, sir. But there's another possibility."

Glossip looked uneasy. "What?"

"Suppose that some tens, hundred, or even thousands of years ago, another race capable of space travel landed on this planet?"

Glossip winced. "You think when these teleports vanish completely, *they're going to another planet?*"

"It's a possibility, sir. You notice how neatly they responded to the arrival of the scout ships. It almost seemed as if they'd had *practice.*"

Glossip thought it over without enthusiasm.

"In which case, Towers, we may run into them on *another* planet."

"Yes, sir."

"Then we'll have to study them continuously, to learn everything we can. We don't want to be unprepared a *second* time. But—if they *have* another planet, or several other planets, mustn't they have experienced already the shocks they came up against this time?"

"Probably some of them would have experienced them, *but those that did would have died.* Really severe conditions stop them from teleporting, and when they can't teleport, how do they get back to let anyone know what's happened? In their case, the bearer of really evil tidings can't travel."

"Then the race would end up only on planets fairly well suited to it, and would be denied knowledge of planets *severely unsuited* to it."

"Yes, sir. And with their lack of adaptability, minor changes could make a planet severely unsuited to them."

"We'll have to send out a warning on planets of this type. Luckily, we're not too anxious to acquire planets of this type. Well, Towers, I hope you haven't noticed any other little anomalies."

"There *is* one other thing that has us puzzled."

Glossip looked apprehensive. "What's that?"

"According to our picture of this, when they teleport, either from water or air, there should be a *clap*, as the air rushes in to fill the space vacated."

"There's *no* sound, so far as we've noticed. Except for a clatter, when these shells *drop to the deck.*"

"But, you seee, they vacate a space, so why isn't there a clap as the air rushes in to fill the empty space?"

"It follows the space must *not* be empty."

"But in that case, sir, they evidently *replace* the air when they depart. How? All we can think of is that they teleport in *one* direction, and air instantaneously goes in the other direction. Air from the space to which they teleport fills the space which they empty."

Glossip looked exasperated. "As soon as we work out the details of this, Towers, our troubles multiply. Look here. *If* they do it that way, it follows that they vacate the space into which they teleport their own bodies. We could do without this complication. It's bad enough that they can teleport *themselves*. What do we get into if we find they can reverse-teleport *objects* in the opposite direction?"

Towers shook his head.

"At least, we've never seen any sign that they do that. We've never known them to arrive in anything but empty space—that is, space empty so far as large bodies of solids or liquids are concerned. It seems to follow that, for some reason, they can't do it."

"Then," said Glossip, looking relieved, "that solves *that* problem."

"No," said Towers regretfully, "it just shifts it around a little.

"We've never known one of them to teleport anywhere without coming out in empty space. We've supposed that they get a signal from their homing object. That seems to make sense. But how do they know *whether the space adjacent to that homing object is clear or not?* Is the signal affected by the physical objects in its vicinity?"

"Maybe," said Glossip, "they just try to come through, and if there isn't enough empty space, they can't do it."

"Yes, sir. But no matter how you slice it, if there's *any* signal picked up, either by trial and error, or their conscious or subconscious faculties, it follows that, to that extent, they've got a kind of radar operating in the vicinity of any homing object they've managed to plant in somebody else's territory."

Glossip thought it over, and swore. "Well, we can count on it, any time a life form has an advantage, it will wring out the last drop of gain, at the expense of other life forms.

Let's just hope the return of their teleport invasion force has the effect on the rest that it ought to."

When the first of the ships arrived, Towers watched intently as a special landing boat, covered with a thick tarry gunk, set down on one of the islands.

There was an instantaneous appearance of blue-green figures surrounding the ship, and they at once smacked their hands against it. Their hands instantly sank into the gunk, and when they tried to pull loose, they were stuck fast. They promptly vanished, leaving a number of hand-shaped holes in the gunk. They reappeared with an irritated look, and changed position rapidly, apparently expecting someone to open fire. Instead, after a brief pause, a section of the ship began to exude more thick sticky substance, and a massive hatch swung open, the edges drawing out long bluey strands that broke, to hang in a curtain of large drops on threads and ropes of gunk. From the sides of the hatchway, streams of gunk oozed out. From inside, emaciated blue-green figures, bandaged around the ear membranes, some of them with bandages over their foreheads, eyes, and other parts of their bodies, staggered forward on slatted duckboards, and dropped unsteadily to the ground.

The teleports outside stared, rushed forward as if to get at the interior, got a look into a black chamber plastered top, bottom, and on all sides with a coat of thick sticky gunk, with nothing in there that *could* be touched except the easily disposable duckboards, and then several rushed forward and thrust their hands determinedly into the coating over the outside of the hull. After a few moments of pressure, they jerked back with a startled angry look. Their surprise evidently affected either their teleporting ability or their presence of mind. Instead of vanishing and reappearing at a distance, they pulled back, drawing out long strands of thick sticky adhesive. On close examination this adhesive turned out of have numerous small pointed objects in it, some straight, some curved, and many with ends like fishhooks. A quick look into the holes from which their hands had been withdrawn disclosed what appeared to be parallel hairs lying on the surface of the gunk underneath. A hard pressure against these produced screams, a sudden jump backwards, and the brief emergence of parallel razor-sharp edges. A glance at the underside of the ship disclosed short gunk-covered legs, not only hard to get at, but probably disposable. Another look inside seemed to offer no better prospects. The structure of the slowly oozing gunk couldn't be learned, because it didn't remain constant, and nothing *else* could be reached.

Meanwhile, the returning teleports were now outside the ship, and those who had stayed at home stared at them incredulously, and began to ask questions. The returnees tapped their bandaged ears. The local teleports pointed, vanished, and reappeared after a moment. The returnees spoke moodily. The locals looked shocked. They pointed at the sky, at the sea, smiled blissfully, and turned their palms upwards. The returnees looked sour, made wavy motions with their hands a foot or so above the ground, raked the air with their hands, picked up a handful of sand and hurled it through the air, coughed. They silently portrayed men freezing to death in a blizzard, with the added attraction of trying to keep their ears from bursting and their eyes from popping out of their heads.

The locals looked incredulous, and began to argue.

Just then, a loud voice issued from the ship, in the local tongue:

"Whoever wishes to visit a distant world, toss your shell into the ship. We will let you know when it's there."

The locals vanished.

The ship stayed where it was.

The locals reappeared with guns, and opened fire.

The voice spoke again:

"The darts do no damage, because what they strike is either too soft to be hurt, or so hard it doesn't matter. You waste strength you should save for enemies."

The teleports vanished.

The ship stayed there.

The teleports reappeared, ringing the ship, each bearing a shell which he pressed hard against the tarry surface.

Here was the real test of the Special Effect Team's carefully compounded gunk:

The shells fell off.

The voice said patiently, "The shells must be placed *inside*. Then we will deliver them."

For the first time, the locals looked jarred, and glanced at each other, to exchange angry comments.

Meanwhile, those who had just returned were walking around, feeling of bushes, dropping to their knees to place their hands flat on the sand, walking into the water to let it lap gently at their feet. Abruptly, one of them vanished, to reappear six feet away, beaming.

Amongst the locals who hadn't left the planet, disorder had now reached the point where some vanished, to reappear uncertainly with guns.

Glossip, watching the screen with Towers, said, "You've done it, Towers! I never hoped to see *them* in confusion."

"They've been able to fit everything else into the framework of conflict, which is apparently their specialty. But whether this confusion will spread, or—"

A large blue-green figure appeared, wearing a headdress of shells of pink and gold, raised his hands, and in the abrupt silence, spoke a single word. All of the locals, except this entity and the returnees, vanished; then one or two of the returnees disappeared. The one with the headdress remained, looking at the gunk-covered ship with no very pleasant expression.

The voice spoke from the ship: "More people may be returned from other planets later. Those who wish to travel there may place their shells within."

The entity with the headdress started to speak, changed his mind, glared, and vanished.

Glossip beamed. "Well, Towers, that may not be victory, as yet; but after what we've been through, it's highly satisfying to get a draw out of it."

"Provided we're careful, we ought to get that much, anyway. Meanwhile, they can't help but learn, from those who've come back, just what they risk when they make a jump to invade another world. Who knows? It might change their attitude."

"That's what we've been trying for; for just between you and me, Towers, by now I'd be well content to leave them bottled up indefinitely. I can do without these manifestations of psychic power, if you know what I mean."

Towers nodded, happened to glance at a scene of the planet, coming in on a screen across the room, and frowned.

Glossip was saying, "It's a relief, at least, to find that material means and devices, with some careful thought, can beat psychic power. But still—"

Towers looked at the screen again. What the deuce was that, anyway, but a kind of mechanical clairvoyance? As a matter of fact, when you thought about it, how did any of the achievements of advanced technology differ from what psychic powers were supposed to do? And, come to think of it—"

"General," said Towers, "what did you say it was that beat those teleports?"

"Why, material means and careful thought," said Glossip. "What else? Certainly *we* have no psychic power."

Towers thought it over. What did "psychic" mean but "not in the realm of the physical?" And what was "power" but "that which does work?" If a man could do twice as much work with a machine as without it, the extra work was naturally credited to the machine. But where did the *machine* come from? *First*, somebody had to *think*, and get an idea. Therefore, ultimately the extra work done by the machine could be credited to the *thought*. But thought was "not in the realm of the physical." Therefore, since it did work, it was power; and since it was not in the realm of the physical, it was psychic; and if that didn't make it *psychic power*, what would?

Glossip was looking at Towers wonderingly. "Why, Towers, what do you have in mind?"

Towers shook his head. There were *some* things it just didn't pay to try to explain. "I was just thinking, sir, these people have been operating a kind of trap, based on their psychic power. It occurred to me—it would only have been justice for them to catch a race of wizards in their trap."

Glossip smiled.

"I'd certainly enjoy seeing a thing like that, Towers. Unfortunately, such things are too good to be true. They don't actually happen."

Towers nodded. "Maybe not, sir."

But he wasn't so sure.

Part VIII:
Pandora's Galaxy

Once back at his headquarters, Horsip found it impossible to believe what he had seen with his own eyes. But his staff assured him that, as a matter of fact, Mikeril attacks were becoming common.

Moffis said moodily. The only bright spot in this mess is that Earth general we took on the Supreme Staff. Here's a report from Sark Glossip, on the teleports."

Horsip looked around blankly. "On the *what?*"

"Teleports. Glossip and his expedition were trapped by them, but Towers got them loose."

"What are *teleports?*"

Moffis handed him the report, and pointed out a line. Horsip read:

" . . . although obviously impossible, we were driven to the conclusion that these natives are teleports, and can go from one place to another *instantaneously*, regardless of intervening bars, walls, armor plate, or, as far as we could find out, anything else . . ."

Horsip looked up.

"Towers solved a thing like that?"

Moffis nodded. "He found a weak point in their abilities."

Horsip gave a low murmur.

"What is Towers doing *now*, Moffis?"

"The last report I read, he was enlarging his organization. He has it up to six divisions now, I think. Of course, using his theories of war, these are small divisions."

"Is he . . . ah . . . way off at the other end of the system?"

"No."

"This outfit is all Earthmen?"

"As far as I know. But they seem to be a special kind of Earthmen."

"They're *loyal?*"

"Absolutely."

"But would they fight against *Earth?*"

"I don't know."

Horsip thought a moment. All over his desk lay reports, and as he glanced at them, stray words and phrases sprang out at him:

. . . chaos on this planet . . . upheaval . . . Snard landed another twenty divisions this morning . . . Control Commission voted 5-1 . . . another Snard army corps has been formed . . . now identified three flying-bomb squadrons of the Earthquake class . . . hopeless . . . ultimatum was delivered by Dictator Schmung . . . combined strength of Snard and Rogebar Soviets exceeds by a factor of four available Fleet strength in this region . . . NRPA appears to have a somewhat stronger central control, despite the still unexplained postponement of the attack on Columbia . . . local disorders continue to increase . . . Morality Index published by the Brotherhood now reached (minus) -19.2, which is lowest recorded since catastrophe of . . .

Horsip's head whirled. He shoved back the reports.

"Send for Towers. We can use his whole six divisions right here."

"Wouldn't it be better to get the Supreme Staff to issue the order?"

"You're right, Moffis. And if they won't issue the order after I read them a few extracts from this mess, I'll be surprised."

The Supreme Staff, assembled at Horsip's request, listened in glum silence to the catalog of disasters. When Horsip got through, there was a lengthy silence. Then

General Maklin looked sourly at General Argit, who looked stubbornly defiant, and then Maklin turned to Horsip.

"This is what comes of that plan that was to be of such great mutual benefit, and that was incidentally supposed to split up the Earthmen so they would be *harmless.*"

Horsip nodded, but said nothing.

General Roffis glanced at Horsip.

"Well, General, you must have something in mind. What is it?"

Horsip said, "It's too late to end this mess by force. These dictators are stronger than we are. But they're divided. If we concentrate our full strength, we are still strong enough to be a factor in the situation. Moreover, there are planets that are loyal to us, or at least independent of *them.* I suggest that we send out the warning signal to the Fleet, bring in Able Hunter and his Special Effects Team, and try to work these two sides against each other."

General Roffis nodded. "We might salvage something, at least."

"If," said General Maklin, "the High Council doesn't countermand the order."

"Well, let's *do* it, and see what happens."

"All right. Let's put it to the vote."

There was at once a unanimous vote in favor of the suggestion.

"All right," said Roffis. "Now, we've got a sword. Who wields it?"

Maklin said, "Horsip has experience fighting these Earthmen."

Horsip said, "At getting beat by them, sir. No, the most capable man should be in charge."

Maklin bared his teeth in a grin. "You're more capable than you think, Horsip." Maklin looked around. "Put it to the vote. I nominate Horsip for Commander of the Fleet."

The motion passed, with Horsip abstaining and no one against it.

"Now," said Roffis, "let's not waste any time. Secretary, draw up the warning order at once, and also the designation of General Horsip as Supreme Commander of the

Fleet, and—what's the phrase?—of the United Arms of Centra. Note in the body of the designation that the vote of the Supreme Staff was unanimous."

The secretary looked unhappy.

"General Horsip didn't vote for himself, sir, so . . . ah . . . the vote *wasn't* unanimous."

Roffis said in a no-nonsense voice, "I now ask General Horsip to so state if he wishes to *not* cast his vote for himself for Fleet Commander. The vote not being unanimous would convince our enemies there was disunion among us."

Horsip kept his mouth shut. The secretary began to write.

Ten minutes later, the warning signal went out to the Centran Fleet.

Fifteen minutes after that, Horsip was officially placed in command of all the armed forces of the Integral Union, exception being made for certain minor forces such as the guard forces for the Supreme Staff and the High Council.

Horsip's ship had apparently served many purposes in the past, and was now speedily made over as a "combined-fleets command ship," rooms being opened up that Horsip hadn't known were there. Meanwhile, he kept his information agency hard at work, and awaited a possible veto from the High Council.

Horsip soon was startled to receive a message reading:

By Command
The High Council

The High Council, by unanimous vote, approves the selection of General Klide Horsip to command the United Arms of Centra, including the Fleet of the Integral Union.

The High Council warns every Centran by race and birth to obey the commands of the Supreme Commander, General Klide Horsip, on pain of death.

So long as General Klide Horsip's command shall last, his word is the word of the High Council, and from this word and this decision there is no appeal within the Integral Union.

> J. Roggil
> Chairman
> The High Council

Horsip, slightly dazed, looked up to see a trim Earthman, with quiet, businesslike manner, wearing the uniform of a Centran general, grade III, and the insignia of the Supreme Staff, cross the room amidst the electrified staff. Horsip recognized John Towers, and got up at once. He handed Moffis the message from the High Council, and then saw, coming behind the Earthman, a well-built member of the Holy Brotherhood in black robes with purple collar. The Earthman, realizing from the stares of those nearby that someone was behind him, stepped aside to let the Brother pass ahead.

The Brother halted before Horsip's desk to raise his hands and bow his head in an awesome gesture toward Horsip.

"By the word of the Council of Brothers," he intoned, some resonant quality making the words seem to ring in the head after they were spoken, "the cause of the Brotherhood is placed in your hands. Use the trust wisely, nor fear that ye may not succeed. The word of the Brothers is behind you, and the Legions of the Brothers are rising, to consume the unrighteous in a flame that will burn them utterly and to the last. Until the task is complete, your authority is the authority of the Brothers so long as your command shall last . . . that there be no division in the ranks of the Union, the authority of the Council of Brothers is vested in you alone. This is the message which I am commanded to give, and to ask the blessing of the Great One on our united cause. I bow in reverent homage to the authority of the Council of Brothers, vested in you."

The Brother bowed deeply, and in a humble voice said,

"I beg the permission of Your Excellency to report that my task is done, and the message delivered."

Horsip, with an effort, recovered the use of his voice.

"Thank you." The words came out with an echo of the brother's ringing tones. Horsip cleared his throat, and said in a carefully low voice, "Please give the Council of Brothers my thanks, and tell them that their message is delivered."

That time, he sounded more like himself, but he still had a disembodied sensation.

The Brother bowed low, backed away several paces facing Horsip, bowed again, backed another pace or two, then turned and strode with steady, measured pace to the door.

Moffis, with trembling hand, returned the message from the High Council to Horsip's desk.

Able Hunter watched the proceedings with a politely expressionless gaze.

Horsip sucked in a deep breath, and observed that his staff was looking on wide-eyed as if waiting for some spectacular manifestation.

Horsip cleared his throat.

"Back to work, men. Turn up the fans, there. Let's get a little air in here."

The trance seemed to evaporate, and a semblance of normality returned. Horsip loosened his collar and sat down. He still didn't feel like himself, but he didn't know what do about it.

Able Hunter now saluted. Horsip returned the salute, and cleared his throat.

"Pull up a chair—that pivot chair is comfortable—and tell me what you know about this mess."

Hunter eyed the pivot chair without enthusiasm, and pulled over a straight chair.

"I'll take this one, sir, if you don't mind. If I bump that lever, the whole works will go over backwards."

"Nonsense," said Horsip, absently bracing his tail against the floor as he adjusted his own chair. "All you do . . ." He paused abruptly.

Hunter said, "It takes *two* Earthmen to adjust one of these chairs . . . As for the situation, no one has told me anything. Obviously, there's a mess of some kind. Some bird calling himself the commander of the 'Shock Combat Legion of Space' tried to hold us up on the way here. I identified myself as a member of the Supreme Staff, and that didn't even slow him down. We had to slice his outfit into giblets to get through . . . The stars matched our charts, but a lot of the political units seemed new."

"You don't know *anything* about the situation?"

"Only what I've told you."

Horsip nodded. "Make yourself comfortable. This will take a while."

When Horsip finished describing the situation, Hunter looked bemused.

"This explains some comments made to me at different times. But I had no idea a thing like this was going on."

"We never thought it would turn out like this, either."

"What do you want me to do?"

"The first question," said Horsip, "is whether you are prepared to fight Earthmen."

One corner of Hunter's mouth curled slightly upward.

"This crew I'd cheerfully fight, whatever race they belonged to. *Most* Earthmen are either on Earth, or on planets like Columbia. This bunch that you're up against is the same kind that has always made trouble for us. Yes, I'll fight them."

"Would you take part in an invasion of Earth?"

"No. But we'll take on this gang you describe anytime."

"You have to bear in mind," said Horsip, "these dictators are powerful."

"Our opponents are *always* powerful. There's just one thing that puzzles me. What are these Mikerils you've mentioned?"

"I'll have to refer you to the records. What they *are* is beyond me. What they *do* is clear enough. Whenever we make progress enough to think we can settle back a little and take things easy, they turn up, and knock us halfway back into barbarism. But it's impossible to believe it until you see it, so half the time we're under the impression they're a myth."

"Where do they come from?"

"If we knew that, we'd blow the place up."

"Do they attack in one spot at a time, or on a large front?"

"It depends. Sometimes, they hit only one planet. At other times, the records show they've hit many planets at once."

"How does it look this time?"

"Worse than anything recorded since what's called 'The Year of the Horde.' The experts have charted the outbreaks, and their projected curves go up off the top of the charts. It takes extra sheets of paper to show where these curves go to, and they haven't found the peak yet."

"H'm," Hunter shook his head. "I'll have to examine these records." He shoved back his chair. "Is there anything else, sir?"

"As far as I know, that's all of it."

As Hunter headed for the records section, Moffis said hesitantly, "Sir . . ."

Moffis' tone reminded Horsip of the awesome authority he had been given, now that the opposition was so strong, and the Integral Union so weak. . . . Well, he told himself, at least the Fleet was warned. Now, the thing to do was to keep every element of strength the Integral Union possessed lined up in mutual support of every other element of strength, and the first step was clear.

"Yes, Moffis?" said Horsip briskly.

"I . . . sir, I . . ."

Moffis appeared dazzled by Horsip's presence.

Horsip cleared his throat, to make sure no trace of that reverberating tone was left over.

"Now, Moffis," said Horsip, feeling his way cautiously, "we have to remember there was just one purpose to that message from the High Council, and that visit by the Holy Brother. The idea is to unite any wavering Centrans, and make it clear they have just one choice—obey or be condemned. Since you were never a waverer, Moffis, all that wasn't meant for you. And it has no effect on the situation, either. We are still in the same pickle we were in before. So, the thing to do is to forget these things among ourselves, and keep our minds strictly on the job."

Moffis intently followed this argument to the end, then nodded.

"Truth."

"Now," said Horsip, "what is it, Moffis?"

"I . . . ah . . . was looking at these reports while you were talking to Hunter, and there are several I thought you should look at."

Horsip was by now allergic to reports, but he nodded gamely. "If you think so, Moffis."

Moffis picked up two reports that each bulked as thick as the Centran casualty list after the invasion of Earth, and one considerably thinner than the average report.

Horsip glanced at the titles:

"The Peace Wagers on Earth-Controlled Planets"

"Statistical Analysis of Armaments and Production, Fifteenth Revision"

"The Masked Planet: Columbia"

Horsip skimmed through the statistical analysis of armaments, and unconsciously hunched in his chair. The dictator planets loomed up off the pages like giants. The Integral Union dwindled and shrank to a pathetic shadow.

Angrily, Horsip straightened up. The Fleet, regardless of its relative weakness, was still a factor. *Everything*, however small, was a factor until destroyed. He slapped the massive document on the desk, and settled back to read about the "peace movement."

This report turned out to have been written by someone with an exasperating turn of phrase. Horsip found himself bemusedly reading the summary:

These individuals detest the possibility of the dictator planets taking over their own planets, and hence they—the wagers of peace—violently attack their governments for not yielding faster to the dictators, in order to avoid angering the dictators, since anger might lead the dictators to take over non-cooperative planets. This is certainly a very reasonable argument. If a man gives the robber everything he has before the robber gets a chance to make his demands, then there can be no robbery. It is always possible to prevent murder, provided the victim can commit suicide fast enough . . . The situation is extremely dangerous and uncertain. The Peace Wagers, brilliant, ignorant, unwearied by the heaviest responsibility that anyone else may bear, are not bought traitors, but a phenomenon brought on by the Earthmen's creation of plenty beyond previous dreams of wealth, and their simultaneous minute dividing of experience into numerous parts, so that one man knows only the right paw of the animal, while another spends his life studying the root of its upper left long tooth—this, and the withholding of responsibility for long periods of time, act as a rot on the sources of judgment, and here we see the result . . . These people are no part of any plot; but the plotters rely on the unwitting help of these brave cowards, these moronic geniuses . . .

Horsip became vaguely conscious of the sound of work men in the background, but his attempt to unravel th meaning of the summary had his attention riveted. Momen tarily, he would think he had it, then some new phras would snap the thing into a different shape. Horsi scratched his head, reached out, and got hold of the thin nest of the three reports—the one titled "The Maske Planet: Columbia."

He opened this up with no great enthusiasm, read th first page, turned to the second, sat up, read on, and arrive at the summary:

Summary: The planet named "Columbia" has received little attention until recently, owing to its independent foreign policy and lack of aggressive designs on other planets. Also, it is a planet of a star somewhat removed from the usual routes, and even with the latest refinements of the stellar drive, distance remains a factor. Thus Columbia was largely ignored until the recent attempt by Dictator Ganfre to "protect" the planet against Snard by taking it over himself.

Ganfre's take-over began with a warning to Snard. Four hours later, an ultimatum was delivered to Columbia, giving the choice of "voluntarily" joining with Ganfre, or experiencing "precautionary occupation." Columbia at once rejected the ultimatum, and issued a general warning placing its solar system off-bounds to any ship without Columbian permission.

Ganfre's fleet was already approaching, and leading elements entered the Columbian System. From decoding of intercepted messages, what seems to have happened is as follows:

After passing the formal limits of the Columbian system, the leading ships of Ganfre's fleet began to accelerate. The fleet commander sent a signal ordering deceleration. The ships reported that they couldn't decelerate. They continued to speed up, headed directly for the Columbian sun. As following elements of Ganfre's fleet passed the formal boundary, they, too, accelerated. The fleet commander turned the main body of the fleet and notified Ganfre. Ganfre at once signaled Columbia, withdrawing the ultimatum, on the basis that he was now satisfied Columbia could protect itself against Snard. He requested permission for his scout ships to leave Columbian territory. The Columbians granted permission. The scout ships slowed, and simultaneously begin to spin, tumble end-for-end, and overheat. Their courses changed into an arc which carried them out of Columbian territory.

Ganfre now suggested an alliance with Columbia. Columbia declined, pointing out that it was important to have uncommitted neutrals in any war, to help provide food and supplies in case the combatants wrecked each other, and also to give political refugees some place to go in case the worst happened. Ganfre accepted this reasoning.

Since this experience, Columbia has received a great deal of study, and it develops that all that is definitely known is that the planet was first settled by Centrans, and received a large influx of "Americans" after the treaty with Earth. These Earthmen claimed they were going to "rebuild the planet on basic American principles," avoiding errors made on Earth. But since the planet aroused no interest earlier, no one knows what this means, and because of the off-limits decree, it is now impossible to visit the planet to find out.

Columbia therefore is indeed the "masked planet," formidable, aloof, and powerful, a mystery to adversaries who discounted her power until too late.

Horsip looked up exasperatedly.

"Moffis, what do we have on Columbia?"

Moffis had a few thin reports opened out on his desk. "I've got it right here—what there is of it."

"Let's see the ones you're not using. We're going to have to give that place some thought. It seems to me—"

He looked around then, a pounding noise catching his attention.

Across the room, workmen were carrying off a bulkhead. This disclosed a room on the far side, where they were carrying in big spools of cable that ended in a maze of many-colored wires bearing fastening attachments. Other workmen were carrying in odd-shaped sections of some kind of furniture that fitted into recessed parts of the floor, the various wires from the cables being snapped, clipped, screwed, or bolted to mating parts of corresponding colors in the sections themselves. Meanwhile, other workmen were stuffing the cables into channels in the floor or walls of the room, and putting metal covers in place over the channels.

Since there were cables and wires being unwound all over the room at the same time, and sections of all sizes and shapes being carried in simultaneously, this room suddenly exposed to view gave the impression of a look through the wall into a madhouse.

Moffis looked up and stared speechlessly. Horsip got to his feet. An officer with colonel's insignia, wearing coveralls, and carrying a sheet of yellow paper in one hand, looked around, and suddenly spotted Horsip. He crossed the room briskly, and saluted. "At the command of the High Council, sir, we are activating the command's ship Master Control Center. The equipment has been thoroughly checked, parts replaced where needed, oiled, and refinished. It's all in first-grade condition, but if you have any trouble, just let us know, and—"

Horsip glanced from the colonel to the tangle of wires and dismantled sections of unrecognizable objects. He groped mentally for the meaning of the words "Master Control Center." Nothing came to him but vague associations.

Horsip cleared his throat.

"Colonel . . . ah . . . what *is* the 'Master Control Center?'"

The colonel looked blank.

"Well, sir, *that's* the Master Control Center. It's Sealed Section A-1. This room here is Open Section A-1. This work sheet says, 'Open communication between Sealed Section A-1 and Open Section A-1.' According to the work code, 'open communication between two sections' means 'knock out the wall between them.' That's what we're doing. Now, farther back, it says, 'Recondition all equipment and reconstitute full panoply of representation and control units.' Now, according to code—"

Horsip said, "But what does this Master Control Center *do?*"

The colonel shook his head.

"Sir, that's not my department. If we stopped to figure out what all this stuff *does,* we'd never get the sequence checks finished." He brightened, and shouted to a workman holding a clipboard in one thickly furred hand. The workman cupped a hand to his ear, and the colonel bellowed across the room.

Horsip glanced around, to observe that work had come to a stop among almost all his own staff. He picked up a pad, and duly noted who was still working. Then he waited until one of those not working glanced in his direction. Horsip fixed a ferocious glower on his face. The offender fairly sprang out of his skin. At once he began to bustle around. This hurricane of activity startled his neighbors, one or two of whom glanced at Horsip. In a flash, everyone was attending to his business.

The colonel nodded to his workman, and turned back to Horsip.

"Sir, the manual is in the right upper drawer in front of the Master Control Seat—that's that thing they're setting up now."

Horsip looked at a thing like a big pivot chair just being lugged in, and nodded.

The colonel saluted, and hurried back to work.

Horsip turned to Moffis. "Where were we?"

"Talking about Columbia," said Moffis. "Do you want the reports I've finished?"

Horsip nodded, and glanced again at the chaos in the next room.

"I wonder if the Earthmen ever have a thing like this? I suppose not."

He took the first report Moffis handed over, and sat back to read about Columbia. From time to time he reached out for others, and at last he had read them all. He sat back, baffled. These told him that the Columbians "rely on a highly developed system of rail transportation, with great care paid to the road grade, and continuous improvement of their unusually wide-gauge system . . . Highway transportation on this planet is restricted to the original Centran road network, traveled by animal-drawn transportation, plus a limited network of roads elevated above the ground surface, and requiring little winter maintenance, as the wind ordinarily sweeps these roads clear of snow . . . Production of ground-cars is limited, but the

ground-cars are exceptionally well made and durable, as
are nearly all Columbian manufactures . . ."

Horsip looked up. What did all this tell him? " . . . rumors
are that the Columbian electrical underground rail transport
system is to be further extended, but little is known about
this development, as the Columbians rarely talk about their
plans in advance . . ."

Exasperatedly, he skimmed through reports he had already
read once, trying to piece together some picture that would
explain the planet to him. He read, " . . . raising of farm
crops has not been interfered with as on other planets. The
Earthmen apparently do nothing except to introduce some
of their own farmers, these being unusual only for their
manner of dress and their exceptional skill. Like Centran
farmers, they do not use complicated highly powered
equipment, but rely on animals to draw the equipment. . . .
The Earthmen, apart from their heavily equipped factories, seem to have a great number of research
facilities . . . Notable is the fact that schooling, by
Earthmen's standards, is finished quickly, formal education
usually being completed by the eighteenth year . . . There
is said to be a large armed force. All the Earthmen serve
without complaint, certain picked Centran volunteers also
being allowed to serve, it is rumored . . ."

Horsip shook his head, and sent for a list of the uncommitted planets, and those still loyal to Centra. The lists
showed that there were still a considerable number of
planets loyal to Centra; but they were all either awkwardly
located, barren, small, or otherwise undesirable, with the
sole exception of Centra itself, the Centran solar system,
from its experience of numerous attacks, remaining a for-
tress. Here the Holy Brotherhood was so strong, and the
sense of imperial loyalty so great, that the Earthmen had
made no noticeable dent at all. Examining the list of
uncommitted planets, Horsip found that here the Holy
Brotherhood again had been active, and some of these planets were even armed. But nearly all suffered from some
degree of the dictators' influence or intimidation.

Looking over these lists, Horsip wondered if it might

prove possible to make anything out of this wreck. He longed for the ancient days, when in times of trouble the central authority imposed the *clokal detonak,* and wielded its invincible Fleet like a sword. Studying the lists and charts, Horsip searched for a reasonable strategy—and found that the Earthmen had been there before him. Without a powerful fleet, it was impossible to piece together anything out of this scatter of bits and pieces—unless he could get the Columbians to cooperate.

Horsip glanced up at the Master Control Center, where some kind of order was starting to show through the chaos, then he turned to Moffis.

Moffis, with an expression of moody hopelessness, was skimming through reports, and shifting them from one pile to another.

Horsip cleared his throat.

"Moffis, what do you know about diplomacy?"

Moffis looked blank.

"About what?"

"Diplomacy."

"Sir, I don't know anything about it. Why?"

"That's what I know about it, too," said Horsip. "But that's what we're going to have to rely on. We can't rely on force. We *have* to use diplomacy."

To begin with, Horsip sent envoys to the wavering planets, to urge their leaders to stand by the Integral Union. It quickly developed that most of leaders could not have cared less for the Integral Union, it being only the power of the Holy Brotherhood and popular sentiment that kept the planets from joining the dictators.

Horsip quietly initiated military training on a number of the planets most loyal to the Integral Union. He at once ran into shortages of all kinds. While Horsip had squads practicing with pitchforks, the dictators stood with upraised arms on reviewing platforms while troops thundered past forty and fifty abreast.

Horsip scraped together all of the Fleet that had yet trickled in, reinforced it with his own crack squadron, and sent it as a quiet show of strength to planets wavering on the edge of submission to the dictators. The dictators got word of this, and sent their own fleets around, creating unfavorable comparisons.

Horsip quietly hinted to the Columbians that they would find a warm welcome in the Integral Union. The Columbians politely explained that they preferred independence.

Horsip labored to solve the aggravating problems of infant or decrepit armaments industries on the few industrial planets under his control. Meanwhile, the dictators turned out battle fleets by mass production, and had the crews ready to board the ships as they came off the production lines.

Horsip struggled to create the impression of a quiet powerful force that might at its choice intervene decisively in the situation. The impression that came across was of a collection of antique relics manned by a team of amateur cheerleaders.

As one day succeeded the next, Horsip could sense that the tide, so far from turning, was gathering momentum in the other direction.

Meanwhile, the reports came in, more and more frequently, of Mikeril raids, and the raids were growing larger.

And now the swaggering envoys of the dictators began dropping in on diplomatic "courtesy calls," to urge Horsip with none too subtle arguments to stop trying to kid anybody, and pick out which side could do him the most good. Horsip was very polite. Next, the representatives of half-lunatic revolutionary organizations started coming around, to put forth grandiose plans that Horsip, trying to get enough straws together to make a raft, was in no position to reject. On the other hand, when he tried to combine these tiny organizations, to make something useful, he at once ran into a little difficulty: Each revolutionary wanted only his *own* revolution.

As time went, the revolutionaries grew shriller, the Mikerils more numerous and bolder, and the dictators' envoys more smilingly suggestive.

As his position wavered on the edge of disaster, with his weakness daily more plain for all to see, the governing body of Horsip's largest industrial planet met to decide which dictators to join. Horsip examined the latest reports from the Holy Brotherhood on the planet, sent iron-clad instructions on his authority from the Council of Brothers, then sent an order on his authority from the High Council, stripping the planet's governing body of all authority, and placing its troops under command of a loyal Centran officer. Horsip's ships, approaching the planet on a courtesy call, received new orders. As dawn broke over the capital, the Brotherhood, with threats of fire and damnation, sent mobs of the faithful surging through the streets, the warships of the Integral Union appeared in the skies, and Horsip's crack bodyguard massed on the steps of the government buildings, to raise the Centran flag to the roll of drums and the delirious roar of the crowd.

As the shock from this event momentarily immobilized the dictators, Horsip summoned their envoys to a specially built audience chamber. Here, seated in an elaborate chair with the Supreme Staff in a curving row behind and above him, and with sixteen of Able Hunter's men seated in a curving row behind and above the Staff, Horsip met the envoys. The envoys, incredulous and angry, glanced from Horsip to the Staff, sneered, and then saw the Earthmen. Horsip spoke quietly. "Gentlemen, the situation is not what you may think. The basis of power has changed fundamentally, and I request that you notify your principals that any attempt to interfere with the proper exercise of Centran authority may lead to serious consequences. This is all that I am free to say. I ask that you consider it carefully."

As Horsip spoke, more of Able Hunter's Earthmen came and went, conferring briefly with this or that impressively uniformed Earthman in the top row of the dais, looking down coldly on the perspiring envoys.

Swallowing nervously, the envoys bowed low to Horsip, and left the room.

No one interfered with Horsip's occupation of the planet. No one said a public word against it.

No one was at all disrespectful.

And when Horsip moved his command ship forward, to set it down in the planetary capital and make the planet the formal site of his headquarters, no one objected to that, either. The dictators said nothing at all. Only Moffis had his doubts.

"Look," said Moffis, "what happened is that the sight of Hunter's Earthmen, dressed in those uniforms, convinced the envoys that we were being backed by *Earth*, isn't that right?"

"Moffis," Horsip protested, "I didn't say that. All I said was that the basis of power had changed fundamentally—and it had, hadn't it? And I suggested that the situation was not what they might think. How can I be blamed if they jumped to the wrong conclusion?"

"What happens if they reach the *right* conclusion?"

"Let's hope," said Horsip, "that they don't."

On the days following Horsip's forward move, there followed a momentary suspension of action on the part of the dictators, as if they were waiting cautiously to see what might happen next.

Horsip used this pause to renew his offer to Columbia, to strengthen his grip on the planets that were loyal, and to bring as many of the waverers as possible into line. To reinforce the bluff, Able Hunter's Special Effects Team labored overtime to create a fleet of imitation warships realistic to the last welded seam. As the dictators, cautiously probing Horsip's position, sent little unmarked scout ships to check on what Horsip might have, this fleet was briefly exposed, lurking in the asteroid belt that ringed the planet's sun.

Moffis objected, "But they will be able to find out, from the Earthmen, that we aren't allied with Earth."

"Truth. We never said we were."

"The idea is to make them uncertain *what* we have?"

"Yes," said Horsip, "because anything they might imagine is better than what we *do* have."

Moffis looked serious, but said nothing.

Horsip, however, stayed determinedly optimistic.

The dictators, baffled by Horsip's arrangements, avoided any direct clash, but went to work to undermine him indirectly, each side bringing over to it those planets that were the most subject to coercion or bribery. Each time, they took pains to have heavy forces on hand as the planet 'voluntarily' proclaimed its change of loyalty.

Each time, Horsip, seeing the hopelessness of intervening, did nothing, but continued to study his charts and maps, and the reports of his agents on planets in and out of the dictator's worlds. Particularly, he studied the reports from one small planet where popular dissatisfaction with the local Snard ruler was combined with relative closeness to Horsip's worlds, and where the Holy Brotherhood had gone underground but remained powerful.

As the dictators' power surged ahead, and their confidence revived, one fine day Able Hunter's Special Effects Team swamped the planet's primitive detection system, the populace rose in wrath and raised the Centran flag, the new president, elected on the spot, appealed to Centra for protection, and Horsip's elite guard came down on the planet to overawe the local soldiery. Officers in the local detection center reported a gigantic fleet standing off the planet, with monster transports ready to land hundreds of thousands of troops. The local sub-dictator blasted off in his escape ship, and poured on the fuel for far places.

The news of the event was broadcast and rebroadcast on the Centran planets, and combined in various ways with Horsip's take-over of the first planet, one report emphasizing the huge fleet, another bearing down hard on the weakness of the dictators under stress, another pointing out the popular rejoicing at the event, in such a way that suddenly the Integral Union appeared the new force in the universe, and the dictators seemed almost feeble by comparison. As ringing sermons proclaimed the victory of the Old Ways, there was an outburst of popular enthusiasm for the new rise of the almost forgotten power. Abruptly, the reports from Horsip's agents began to turn optimistic, while the agents of the gigantic dictatorships began reporting a disastrous shift in public opinion.

As cheering events occupied the public eye, however, Horsip was just starting to replace new recruits' pitchforks with rifles, waves of Mikeril attacks were devastating the planet he had made his headquarters, and the latest confidential comparison of fleet strengths put him a tenth of the way up from the bottom of the page, while Snard and Ganfre were off the top of the chart.

The Columbians now again replied to Horsip, this time stating their sympathy with certain standards of the Integral Union, but again stating that they preferred to remain independent, and would not join the Integral Union under the present circumstances; but they would join no one else, either, under the present circumstances.

Moffis looked impressed. "They are more friendly than they were."

Horsip nodded, and looked confident.

Moffis said, "But the Fleet still isn't here . . . Whatever there may be of it."

Horsip looked quietly cheerful.

"It will be, Moffis. Don't worry. Remember, the High Council itself is behind us."

Moffis said uneasily, "But I wonder if—"

Horsip cleared his throat.

"No need to be concerned, Moffis. After all—"

From the corridor came a muffled tramp of feet, then a heavy rap on the door. As Horsip and Moffis looked up, a scared junior officer reported, "Sir, there's a . . . a bunch of officers and *Earthmen*, and some guards in strange uniforms. They want to see you right away. They're from Snard, sir!"

Horsip told himself this could not be an invasion; it could be the local Snard ambassador, who had a guard like a small army.

"How many guards?" said Horsip.

"A lot of them, sir. The corridor is full of them."

Horsip turned to Moffis, but Moffis already had the phone marked "Provost" off its hook. " . . . every guard you can lay your hands on down here on the run, and bring them in through the Master Control Center. Shut the automatic doors between here and the corridors, and be ready to flood the corridors with dead-gas. But don't sound any alarm—notify the sections by phone."

Horsip loosened his service pistol in its holster, and turned to his frightened junior officer.

"Tell them to leave the guards outside—but the officers can come in."

The officers of Snard came in like a conquering host, thrust Horsip's people out of the way, brushed the papers off the desks as they passed, and reached out to shove over a cooler of mineral water, which smashed to bits on the floor. Right behind them came the armed guards. Horsip, watching them stream in the door, felt a wave of relief as the last one came in.

Horsip eyed them alertly. They all had a well-drilled look.

Horsip adjusted his uniform, stood up behind his desk, and looked directly into the eyes of the leading Snard officer, a broad-chested general whose muscles stretched the cloth of his bemedaled jacket as he strode down the aisle. This general's eyes were fixed in contempt on Horsip, and looked Horsip over like some peculiar form of insect.

Moffis, bent over back of his desk, was getting something out of a crate, but Horsip had no time for that. He watched the Snard officers approach, waited until they were almost at the end of the aisle, then abruptly inflated his chest to the limit, and intoned at the top of his lungs:

"Detaaiil HALT!!!"

The entire Snard military contingent, generals, officers, and guards, looked blank and came to an abrupt stop. Half a dozen civilians, trailing along behind, slammed into the backs of the soldiers and were knocked off their feet.

Horsip, unhesitating, stepped in front of the burly Snard general, and bellowed:

"Abouut FACE!!!"

"Forwaaard MARCH!!!"

Knocking the civilians out of the way, the Snard armed

guards leading, the whole outfit, with the exception of three or four Earthmen, who looked around blankly, started for the door.

Horsip judged the moment, sucked in a deep breath, and intoned:

"Column riiight MARCH!!!"

The Snard guards, feet striking in unison, trailed out into the hall, turned the corner with precision, and disappeared.

The Earthmen from Snard looked incredulously at them, grabbed at the glassy-eyed Snard officers going past, and got them headed back toward Horsip.

Horsip drew his gun and aimed it at the officers.

The officers stopped, and glanced in confusion at the Earthmen, themselves speechless.

Horsip, listening for the arrival of his own guards, had yet to hear anything. The door to the hall was still open, and there was nothing to prevent anyone from coming in.

Horsip spotted a young Snard lieutenant, who looked more confused than anyone else in sight. Horsip snapped, "Lieutenant!"

The lieutenant swallowed at the tone of command and snapped to attention.

"Sir?"

"What the devil are you *standing* there for? Get out in that hall, and get those guards turned around. Lead them back this way, and halt them outside the door. They aren't to come in. They are to halt *outside*. Now, get out there, turn them around and halt them outside that door! *Move!*"

The lieutenant saluted, and ran out. His bawled orders echoed down the hall.

The Earthmen looked at Horsip, then at the Snard officers as if they had never seen them before.

Horsip ignored the Earthmen, and focused on the burly general in front of him. From the stupefied expression on the general's face, it was clear to Horsip that the general's assurance had been momentarily pulverized. Horsip spoke in kindly tones.

"Stand at attention, General. I am the Supreme Commander of the Integral Union, and you are inside my staff headquarters. I have only to say one word. and you and all your party will be struck dead where you stand. Protocol requires that you salute."

The burly general glanced around, looked toward Moffis, and beads of sweat took form on his forehead. He glanced back at Horsip, stood straighter, and his hand came up in salute.

A quick glance showed Moffis behind a well-oiled stitching-gun, the snout aimed at the general's stomach.

Horsip returned the general's salute.

From somewhere came the sound of running feet, and the snap of safeties clicking off on a considerable number of guns.

The Snard general shook his head, and appeared to come out of some kind of trance. His jaw set.

"All right. You're the Supreme Head of the Integral Union, but the Integral Union amounts to nothing. Your so-called fleet, hidden in the asteroid belt, has been checked by these *Earth experts*, with the latest equipment, and we know it's *no fleet at all*. It's a set of dummies, with just a few real ships mixed in. We aren't certain what you used in this latest attack, but we've checked all the likely routes, and no such fleet passed any of them. We formally checked with Earth itself, and they acknowledge no alliance with you at all. Your whole position is hollow. I doubt that you have over a thousand armed men of your own on this planet, which is your capital. Our fleet is on the way. Nothing will stop us. We'll wipe you up, and after you the whole Integral Union, which is nothing but a memory propped up with cardboard. I call on you to surrender!"

From the corridor came the low rumble of automatic doors sliding shut. Horsip, in a quick glance, saw that where the open door to the room had been, there was now a solid sheet of polished steel, which reflected the room like a slightly wavy mirror. That was a relief, but he still had the general to contend with.

Horsip said, still gently, "If what you say were true, General, would I ever have taken a planet belonging to Snard?"

"You had to, to pull your own people together."

"To pull *your* people off-balance."

"What does that mean?"

"Think it over," said Horsip, with quiet confidence. "You are sending a fleet *here*, where in your own words I don't have a thousand men committed."

Horsip looked at the general quietly, as, inside his own mind, Horsip called up charts of space.

The Snard general was staring at him. "You mean this is *bait?*"

"What do you suppose will happen to Snard while it throws its weight against shadows?"

The general stared at the corner of the room, then shook his head. "We aren't that weak. Yes, if you cut in behind—if you had the strength—but we can shift the reserve fleets to block you. You could never get all the way in."

Horsip looked disappointed. *"Think."*

The general looked baffled.

Horsip nodded. "It's as I thought. You *don't* have the information."

"What information?"

"It's a question of *timing,* General. The Integral Union has long experience with timing. We have had to let Snard and Ganfre become large, because of the difficulty with—but you don't know about that. Well, I certainly won't explain it. But we don't need you or Ganfre any longer to defend this region. One or the other of you is bound to attack first, and make the necessary opening. It's immaterial to us which one we clean up. It's only reasonable that we ally ourselves with one side to finish the other . . . You see, General, you still don't realize who is with us, *do* you?"

The Snard's general's eyes darted this way and that, as if trying to follow elusive objects that flitted just out of his range of vision. He swallowed, and took a hard look at Horsip, who looked back at him with quiet confidence. For an instant, the general looked shocked, and said, "Ganfre wouldn't . . ." then stared at Horsip in horror.

Horsip smiled, and said, "General, I don't need you any longer." He glanced around, to see a line of his own armed guards, with General Maklin beside them. The guards looked all business. Maklin had a look of wondering awe on his face. Horsip stepped aside, to give the guards a clear line of fire, if necessary. The Snard general thrust out his jaw and faced the guards.

Horsip shook his head. "Relax, General. I need good men. It should be possible to find quite a few after Snard is smashed up."

"Ganfre will turn on you afterward!"

"If Snard attacks here, the chain of events can't be stopped."

"You can't trust Ganfre! He has no principles!"

Horsip shrugged. "It's too bad it has worked out this way, but you don't think we can permit an attack without striking back? You can understand this. It is exactly what you would do, isn't it?"

Horsip glanced at Moffis.

"There is no reason for us to hold the general prisoner."

Moffis looked agreeable.

Horsip looked back at the Snard officer.

"How many armed men do you have with you here, all told?"

The general was staring straight ahead, beyond the line of Centran guards, at the big screens of the Master Control Center. He had a look of fascinated attention, but turned with a shake of the head to face Horsip.

"How many? About two hundred and fifty—the staff of our embassy, plus the guards." He looked apologetic. "It seemed like enough."

Horsip nodded. "Just get them all together, and get them back to your embassy." His manner was open and generous. "We will overlook all this." Horsip glanced at Moffis. "Instruct the provost to open up the doors one at a time, to let the general and his men out." Horsip glanced at the general. "You agree, of course, to get all your men back to your embassy, without delay?"

"Yes, as soon as I can. I thank Your Excellency for your kindness."

Moffis got busy on the phone, the automatic door at the end of the room slid open, the Snard general saluted, and marched out with his officers.

There was a silence in the room.

Horsip let his breath out slowly.

He groped around, felt the edge of his desk, and found his chair. He sat down slowly.

Moffis said soberly, "What happens when the Snard fleet gets here?"

Horsip took a deep breath. "If he can get a message off fast enough, maybe it won't. When does Hunter get back here with his Special Effects Team?"

"He was due the day after tomorrow. I sent a message through the Communications Section as soon as this started, to speed him up. He *should* be here tomorrow."

"Good." Horsip glanced at the stitching-gun beside Moffis' desk. "I appreciate your forethought, Moffis."

Moffis nodded, but he had the expression of someone adding up figures and not liking the total.

"What happens," he said, "if there *is* an attack? Hunter can't stop them. We don't have time to get our own guard back here soon enough. And practically every man we've got *here* is in the next room. We can no more stop Snard than tissue paper can stop an avalanche."

Horsip tried to think. The trouble was, he had next to nothing to work with. It was reaching the point where it took strokes of genius and special dispensations to keep going from day to day. The only sensible thing to do was to assemble the strength he *did* have in one place, so that he could at least act with decision. But, as soon as he did that, the dictators would take over the rest of the Integral Union. The only place Horsip could hope to hold was the planet of Centra itself. But once he let the dictators know his real weakness, even Centra wouldn't be able to hold out for long.

Moffis was saying, "At least we could go down fighting. This way—"

"Sir," said the lieutenant who had announced the arrival of the Snard general, "the emissary from the NRPA is outside, and demands to see you. He says he has orders from Guide Ganfre himself."

Horsip sucked in a deep breath. "How many guards does *he* have with him?"

"None, sir. He has three officers."

"Send him in."

Moffis said, "What do you want me to do?"

"Ignore the whole thing. It's beneath your notice."

"I suppose I should put this gun away? But with Ganfre . . ."

Horsip looked at the stitching-gun, its ugly snout pointing at the spot where Ganfre's emissary would have to stand.

"Leave it there, Moffis. I hope you have the safety off?"

Moffis reached over, and there was a dull click.

"It's ready to fire. You only have to touch the trigger."

Horsip nodded, pulled out a report at random, and a chart showing the strength of Ganfre's fleet looked up at him.

As he shoved this back into the pile, he heard the rap of heels striking the floor in unison. He glanced up to see four gray-uniformed officers, their caps at jaunty angles, approaching down the long aisle. Their uniforms were pressed into knife-like creases. Small emblems glittered on their chests. Their heads were tilted back, their expressions arrogant. Horsip ignored them.

With a click of the heels, they halted before his desk.

Horsip swiveled his chair, and bumped the gun.

There was a little gasp. Horsip looked up.

One of the lesser officers was eyeing the gun nervously. The other three ignored it.

Ganfre's emissary stood radiating contempt, then raised his hand in a formally correct salute.

Horsip looked him over without enthusiasm, then returned the salute.

Ganfre's emissary took one step forward, slapped an envelope on Horsip's desk, stepped back, and snapped his hand up again to salute, as if about to leave the room, his whole manner contemptuous.

Horsip rested his left hand on the gun, and said coldly,

"I'd appreciate it if you would stay here while I read this. There may be an answer."

The emissary glanced from the gun to Horsip, and snapped his arm down. When he spoke, his voice carried:

"For that, I will have you hanged by your feet in the market place, to be ripped to pieces by wild dogs."

Horsip had a sheet of crisp paper out of the envelope, and had got it pried open enough to see what it was—an ultimatum with a half-day limit. He was balancing how to convert this colossal disaster into something useful when there was a harsh rap of heels. General Maklin, his uniform spotless, leather and medals glittering, stepped out, jerked the NRPA emissary around, and smashed him across the face. As the emissary went down, Maklin yanked him to his feet again.

Maklin's voice rang with confident good cheer:

"You piece of stinking garbage! *You* will have the elect of Centra hanged! That statement gives me the pleasure of doing what I've wanted to do since the first time I saw you! General Horsip, by your leave . . ."

Horsip, still absently trying to calculate what to make out of this mess, said, "Do anything you want with him, General, it's all the same to me."

Maklin booted the emissary down the aisle. Then he threw him out the door.

Horsip dropped the ultimatum in the waste basket, and looked up at the three paralyzed officers, still opposite the desk.

From the corridor, Maklin's voice carried loud and clear:

"Guards, take this subhuman garbage, carry it outside, and dump it beside the main steps. Careful, or you'll soil your uniforms."

The three NRPA officers stirred, as if struggling to come out of shock.

Horsip, still trying to make something out of the mess, concluded it was so far beyond hopelessness that maybe he could do something with it, after all. He spoke irritably.

"Well, what are you standing there for? Isn't there any

sense in the whole NRPA? Get out there and help your molk of a commanding officer back to his quarters before I change my mind and have the lot of you shot."

The highest ranking of the three drew himself up stiffly, and tried to speak. But the shock of this treatment caused his words to get jammed up in a general congestion:

"You cannot . . . we . . . the insult . . . our mighty fleet . . ."

"Does it ever occur to you," said Horsip irritably, "that we can get tired of trying to save you from yourselves? We could smash your fleet anytime. Unfortunately, things are not that simple. Now, we have had about enough for one day. Get out there, and take care of your emissary. Believe me, he is in better shape than your fleet will be in if we attack it. Now get out. *Move!*"

The officers, shocked and incredulous, saluted and started out, the highest ranking one first, the other two behind. Though they walked stiffly, there was a jerking quality to their stride so that they appeared to be tiptoeing.

Meanwhile, General Maklin came back in. Maklin did not move an inch out of his path, so the NRPA officers had to jump aside.

Moffis watched their departure with pursed lips, then put the safety on his stitching-gun. He aimed the snout of the gun steeply upward, but kept it handy.

Horsip settled back in his chair, and tried to sort things out. There were now two fleets on the way. Ganfre and the Snard Soviet were *both* coming to wipe him out. All he had was a handful of troops, his own command ship, an imitation fleet that was already known to be imitation—plus the Earthman Hunter, and *his* imitation fleet, which was already suspected to be imitation. That should get here sometime tomorrow. Horsip shook his head.

General Maklin, with a look of grim satisfaction, strode up the aisle.

Maklin beamed.

"A great day, General Horsip."

Horsip looked around to see who might be in hearing distance that Maklin might want to bluff, turned back, and thought again of the approaching enemy fleets, which for all he knew might be acting together.

Horsip said politely, "Why?"

Maklin looked intently at Horsip. Suddenly Maklin burst out, "Great hairy master of sin! Was that all bluff?"

"Would you tell me what else there is around here to work with?"

Maklin clapped Horsip on the shoulder, and pointed toward the Master Control Center.

"The Fleet's coming in!"

Horsip crossed quickly to the screens of the Master Control Center, and stopped in his tracks. Staring down at him was a huge array of ships stretching across the screen, with enigmatic symbols above and beside the screen, to give details of distance, fleet strength, and direction.

Horsip dazedly feasted his eyes on the mighty ships, emblazoned with the emblems of Centra. The array seemed endless. The symbols detailing the numbers of the Fleet staggered the imagination.

For an instant, Horsip was carried back to the days of his youth, when Centra ruled the universe, when the Old Ways were backed by unyielding might, when the power had all been taken for granted, because it was always there. Tears came to his eyes. An instant later, he was alert, sentiment blasted like pretty flowers in a frost. He glanced at the figures beside the screen, then at Maklin.

"Do I read this correctly? These ships will get here *tomorrow?*"

"That's right, General Horsip." Tears were streaming down Maklin's cheeks. He banged one fist into the other. "*No one* beats the High Council! That's where the corruption stops!"

Horsip glanced around at Moffis. Moffis was carefully oiling his stitching-gun.

Horsip took a deep breath, went back to his desk, and sat down. In a low voice, he murmured, "What do you think, Moffis?"

"About what?"

"That fleet on that screen."

Moffis kept his voice quiet.

"*Able Hunter* is supposed to get here tomorrow."

Horsip nodded.

"At least, it *looks* convincing."

"So did the fleet in the asteroid belt—until the Earth experts went to work on it."

Horsip tried to think of some way to back up Hunter's bluff. Unfortunately, he could find nothing to work with.

Maklin spoke from the Control Center.

"General Horsip, the Fleet Commander wishes to talk to you."

Horsip got up. The "Fleet Commander," under whatever guise he appeared on the screen would almost certainly be Able Hunter. And very possibly the conversation might be intercepted and monitored by Snard or Ganfre. That might even be the purpose of the call.

Horsip straightened his uniform, and strode to the screen, where a tough-looking Centran general in battle dress snapped to attention, and brought his arm up in a stiff salute, after the fashion of years gone by.

Horsip, impressed with Hunter's realism, returned the salute stiffly.

The Centran on the screen barked, "Nock Sarlin, Commander Battle Fleet V, reporting to United Forces Command Headquarters. Where is the enemy?"

Horsip thought fast. This must be a request for information.

Horsip gave a quick resume of what had taken place that day, with his best opinion of the likely location of the approaching fleets of Snard and Ganfre, and their probable strength.

"Sarlin" saluted, made a quarter turn, and barked, "Fleet course: lock-on Target B. Close at maximum fleet maneuver acceleration, opening out by divisions to depth 3 plus 1. Heavy bombardment squadrons numbers 1 through 40 to the right wing, angular concentration plus 20 to minus 20; heavy bombardment squadrons numbers 40 through 50 to the left wing by groups; numbers 51 through 100 to Fleet Reserve. Fleet conform by squadrons. Number 99 heavy bombardment squadron will detach from Fleet Reserve with accompanying medium and light squadrons as escort for Landing Force Ships, which will remain in this system under direct control of the Supreme Commander. Numbers 1 through 4 ships of the guard will land near the United Forces Command Headquarters subject to approval of the Supreme Commander, to act as the Supreme Commander's guard. *Execute!*"

Horsip, dazed as "Sarlin" turned to face him, returned his salute. Horsip's imagination was still catching up with the "Fleet Commander's" orders. Everything seemed technically correct, but it implied an even more gigantic force than appeared on the screen. Snard or Ganfre might easily have concentrated such a force. But would they believe he, Horsip, could do it?

With "Sarlin's" salute, the screen went blank, and before Horsip had time to recover there flashed on the screen the image of a younger officer, who saluted briskly.

"Nar Doppig, Guard Force Commander, reporting to the Supreme Commander for landing permission."

"Granted," said Horsip automatically, and an instant later, while returning Doppig's salute, it occurred to Horsip that he should have refused. How could Hunter land nonexistent troops?

Horsip stood looking blankly at the screen, then, there being nothing else he could do, went back to work. He seemed hardly to have gotten started when Moffis' voice reached him.

"Sir," said Moffis dryly, "the emissaries from Snard and Ganfre want to see you again. Now they're here *together.*"

"Send them in," snarled Horsip.

"One at a time?"

"However they want to come."

Moffis spoke into the phone.

A minute or two later, there was a sound of heels and the two emissaries, one broad and burly, the other tall, haughty, and heavily bandaged, started down the aisle toward Horsip's desk. They halted before the desk, glanced at Moffis' stitching-gun, which Moffis had again lowered, so that they were looking down its muzzle. They cleared their throats, looked at Horsip, and, as if remembering something, saluted.

Horsip returned the salute.

They stood looking at him, but said nothing.

Horsip said, "Gentlemen, if you have something to say, I am listening."

The burly Snard emissary looked faintly regretful.

"You can't get away with it."

Horsip smiled.

The emissary from Ganfre spoke almost reluctantly.

"After what you have done to me, I should hate you. But, I have to admit, you almost convinced me. Let me extend to you the compliment of my professional admiration. I never saw nothing made into such a convincing appearance of might."

The Snard emissary spoke almost sadly.

"You overdid it."

Horsip shook his head regretfully. His voice was assured.

"You have been warned. There is nothing else I can do for you."

"It is impossible," said the Snard emissary, "for the Integral Union to have such strength. It is therefore obviously a clever trick. With a third or a half the number, you *might* have convinced us."

Horsip sat back and looked confident. There must have been some reason for Hunter to use that number of decoys.

Horsip said, "And what do your trained Earth specialists have to say *this* time?"

"Only that your technique of mass production of dummy ships is highly advanced, and that this batch might have fooled them, except for the excessive and uneconomical use of what reads out on the detectors as belt armor on the ships."

Horsip looked blank.

Belt armor was one of those things that the Centran Fleet had always made abundant use of—until the Earth specialists had proved by statistics that it was not economical.

But Hunter was as familiar with the present lack of armor belts as Horsip was.

Horsip spoke carefully.

"Let me be sure of what you just said. Except for the belt armor—"

"The *appearance* of belt armor—as our detectors, and data analysis, show it."

Horsip nodded. "Except for this appearance, you would now be here offering peace instead of threats?"

Ganfre's emissary said condescendingly, "And the numbers, General. But the point is, we are separately prepared to offer you considerable benefits if you join us willingly."

"Why?"

The emissary cleared his throat.

"We have agreed to unite with each other—our leaders, that is, have so agreed—in order to finish off . . . ah . . . Columbia—in an economical way. We are stronger even than you realize, but in dealing with the Columbians— who have peculiar weapons—our wise leaders choose to apply the maximum force. With your realistic dummy fleets, General, we believe we can deceive the Columbians as to our actual intentions. We propose to open the psychological attack against Columbia by the total defeat of the Integral Union. We will not reveal your actual weakness, but will give out reports of a great battle, which we have won by better leadership, in order . . ."

Horsip could feel the loathing rise up inside him, but kept his face expressionless until the emissary was through. As the emissary went into rapturous detail over the particulars, it took him time to finish. Then he looked expectantly at Horsip.

"Well, General, you see you have no choice, and Columbia has no chance, correct?"

Horsip's voice came out in an ugly tone.

"If my fleets were made of tinfoil, I would fight." He smiled, and the smile was such that the emissaries looked jarred. "But," said Horsip, "they aren't." He leaned forward. "I advise you to get in touch with your leaders, and explain that the true fleets of the Integral Union *have always used heavy armor*, and have crushed their enemy in every war throughout recorded history. That you should be outnumbered is exactly what you should expect. You have challenged the *Integral Union!* Now, get out of here. There's work to be done."

For a moment, the emissaries stood paralyzed, but then they relaxed. They glanced at each other with tolerant smiles.

The emissary from Snard said, "You will hear from us again, General. Soon."

On the way out, Horsip could hear Ganfre's emissary say wonderingly, "Amazing. He almost did it again!"

As the door shut behind them, Moffis said, frowning, "Could it be?"

Horsip said stubbornly, "We *always* used armor belts until these Earthmen proved it was a waste. But it wasn't a waste! I never saw a ship yet where the men weren't happier behind a good solid shield. And if you have to go down into the atmosphere to get somebody out of a pickle, that armor backs up the meteor guards when they go to work on you with the artillery."

"But the *numbers!*"

"Maybe it is *part* bluff. But . . ." Horsip shook his head.

Moffis said, "Could we use the Control Center to get in touch with them?"

"And what if it is all bluff, and the transmission is picked up?"

"Truth," said Moffis.

Horsip said exasperatedly, "There's nothing to do but hang on tight and hope for the best. But if that fleet is fake, and these dictators punch right through it, then there isn't any good we can do here. We'll have to get out."

"At least, we can do *that* without too much trouble."

Horsip, who had had the command ship set down in the big courtyard of the planet's main administration building, said, "All we have to do is blast loose the connecting corridor, cut the auxiliary power cables, and leave." He paused, thinking that over.

Moffis said, "And . . . if the enemy fleet is closing in when we leave?"

"That's not good."

"Suppose we left now? Then, if the dictators turn away, we can come back."

"If we leave, that news will be broadcast to them, so they will see through the bluff. We have to stay here until we're sure, one way or another."

Horsip, none too hopeful as to what the morning would bring, took a hot bath, and went to bed early. During the first part of the night, he was awakened by the provost marshal, who explained that there was rioting in the streets, and the local police were calling for help, but the provost marshal was afraid that, if he sent any of the few men he had, the command ship couldn't be protected.

"Tell them," said Horsip, "that there will be all the troops on the planet tomorrow that they can ask for. But they will have to get through the night on their own."

The provost marshal beamed. "I *heard* the Fleet was coming in."

Horsip grunted noncommittally. "Meanwhile, double the guard in the connecting corridor, disconnect the auxiliary power cables, and be ready to get your men in the ship on a moment's notice."

"Yes, sir. Ah . . . sir, if the Fleet is coming in . . . ah . . . why would we want to get out of here?"

"Because," snarled Horsip, "we don't know *whose fleet it is.*"

Horsip fell asleep, was awakened by the sound of shouting and the rattle of stitching-guns, then fell back into a fitful doze interspersed with nightmares in which various dictators, ten times normal size, swaggered around a room in which Horsip had to jump and run to avoid getting squashed underfoot. The dictators were arguing over who was to get this or that piece out of what was left of the Integral Union. By morning, Horsip, who had gone to bed early to get a good rest, was worn out. He got up, washed all over in cold water, and was just rubbing himself dry when a thundering roar passed overhead.

Feeling that the day could not be worse than night had

been, Horsip buckled himself into his uniform, and went into his office.

Moffis was already there, cleaning and oiling his gun. The provost marshal, a portable stitching-gun under one arm, was directing Horsip's staff as they turned their desks into a barricade. Wounded men were lying on folded blankets, with medical aides taking care of them. In the corner, behind a white cloth, a surgeon was working.

Horsip paused by each of the wounded to say a few words, turned his holster-flap under his belt so he could get his gun out in a hurry, opened up the locker behind his desk, got out a thick emergency ration bar, sat down, and spoke on the phone to the officers in charge of the ship's engines and navigation. They could leave anytime, but space off the planet was filled with ships, and one of them had just landed. As Horsip was talking, there was a roar overhead, and another one came down.

Moffis said, "We might as well fight it out on the ground. If we take off, we'll never get past them. But suppose we started out as if we were taking off, then landed and dispersed in rough country? They could have trouble getting us out of there."

Horsip shook his head. "We can't abandon the command ship. Centra needs every ship."

"We couldn't get through."

"Some way may turn up."

The provost marshal came over.

"Sir, request permission to abandon the administration building, down to the connecting corridor."

"Granted. Who are we fighting?"

"Up to the second watch it was vandals, then the Mikerils took over till halfway through the third watch, and we got three men out with pretty bad bites. Since then, it's been something called the Ahaj Revolutionary Army."

"What side are *they* on?"

"I don't know, sir, but it isn't ours."

Horsip nodded, and the provost marshal went off to direct his men.

Horsip glanced at Moffis, who was talking on the phone.

Moffis glanced up inquiringly, and Horsip said, "Moffis, is there an armor belt on this pot, or isn't there?"

Moffis put his hand over the mouthpiece. "I think there is. I think it was made over from one of the old Warrior class. Sir, there's the Snard emissary on the wire. He wants to speak to you."

Horsip got out of the way of two men carrying a flame-thrower from an exhibition case of weapons used in the war with Earth, held the phone to his mouth, looked confident, and said cheerfully, "Good morning, General."

"Good morning, General. I call on you to surrender. Our troopships are landing in the capital. Our fleet is overhead."

"I've warned you of the consequences, General."

"Are you insane? I am calling on you to surrender."

Horsip put his hand over the mouthpiece. "Has anyone seen the markings on these ships?"

"No, sir. The men had to be taken off the detectors to hold the corridors."

Horsip spoke confidently into the phone.

"I advise you to pass my message on to your rulers. You are in grave danger."

Two more wounded were set down gently across from the white sheet in the corner of the room.

There was a harsh rasp from the phone. "Have you taken leave of your senses? Your situation is hopeless!"

"Nonsense. We are in no trouble here."

"I hear the firing in the background."

"Reinforcements have arrived."

A huge black creature bristling with hair burst in the doorway. There was no one in sight there, and Horsip's staff were still heaving desks into place. Horsip held the phone in one hand, his palm covering the mouthpiece, and aimed with his other hand. The Mikeril jumped over the desks. The gun leaped in Horsip's hand. The Mikeril went down, then staggered up. Horsip fired again.

Just then, half a dozen grim-looking guards came out from the direction of the display case of Earth weapons, wheeling a squat gray object on a heavy cart. Across the room, the Mikeril was getting up. The phone was shrill:

"I call on you to surrender! You have no chance! My troops are marching on you at this moment!"

Horsip hung up, eyed the lettering on a placard stuck at an angle to the thing on the cart, tilted his head, and the lettering suddenly was clear:

A-Bomb, circa 1955 (Earth-style) U.S.A. manufacture.

Across the room, the Mikeril got up and headed for the wounded.

Horsip swore, fired again, the Mikeril went down, and Horsip jumped over the desk, grabbed the arm of the nearest soldier, and pointed across the room.

"Get that thing out of here. How the devil would you like to be over there by the butcher's tent and have *that* take a bite out of you?"

"Sir, we want to blow up the Glops with this."

"You can't use it on the Glops. It's too strong. It will blow us all up. *Get that Mikeril. . . .* Who's guarding that door? *There's another one!*"

Moffis put that one down with a short burst from his stitching-gun.

Horsip got a phone down, but at once a little flag on a different phone popped up. He took it off its hook, and the voice of the Snard emissary sprang out. Just then, Horsip spotted another Mikeril and hung up.

The provost marshal appeared in the doorway, looked around incredulously as the soldiers chased the Mikeril around the room, stepped back into the corridor, looked up and roared, "Who left the hatch open?" He aimed his portable stitching-gun straight up, and opened fire.

Horsip heard a thud from the direction of the Master Control Center.

A Mikeril appeared in the doorway.

Horsip shot it, then shook the empty shells out of the gun, and worked in fresh bullets. The provost marshal approached.

"Sir," said the provost marshal, "request permission to arm the staff and put them on guard duty."

"Granted."

The Mikeril, red eyes glaring, black fur weirdly on end, rose to its feet, clawed hands lifting out.

Horsip aimed carefully and shot it between the eyes.

The provost marshal glanced around, put a short burst into its neck, looked back, and said, "When they disconnected the power cables, they didn't lock the hatch. All that saved us is, a bunch of them tried to come through all at once, and got jammed in the hole."

The Mikeril struggled to its feet.

Another appeared in the doorway.

Horsip shot the first Mikeril in the head, and the provost marshal stepped aside to get a shot at the next without hitting the Control Center.

Horsip reloaded, scooped some bullets out of the top drawer of his desk, and looked around.

Across the room, weapons were being issued to the staff. Smoke was drifting in from the corridor. Several guards ran in, holding cloths to their faces, and set up a stitching-gun just inside the doorway.

Another Mikeril appeared in the Master Control Center.

Horsip aimed carefully, and shot it.

Moffis was speaking into one of the phones: " . . . the last automatic doors. Get ready to pull in the boom of the communications and control cables. Don't go out after them—it's thick with Mikerils out there. Be ready to start the take-off as soon as I give the word."

More guards came in, dragged out the Mikerils, then there was a rumble and the smoke from the corridor abruptly stopped coming in. Horsip looked around, saw no immediate trouble, crossed the room to the Master Control Center, to work the viewer controls.

In quick succession, there sprang onto the screen a view of an empty control room, then a gangway crowded with troops, then a view down a broad avenue that Horsip at once recognized as the capital's main thoroughfare. The scene shifted.

Now Horsip was looking at big grayish-brown traveling forts, even larger than those he had seen on Earth, moving slowly down the wide avenue. Behind them came full-tracked armored troop carriers with troops in battle dress standing on the tops of the vehicles holding small microphones, and glancing watchfully around. Abruptly there came into view several soldiers carrying automatic rifles, then a solitary drummer whose steady, slow monotonous beat suddenly filled the room, then an officer in battle dress with a trumpeter to his right and a sergeant carrying a portable communicator to his left.

Immediately behind these three came a soldier carrying the flag of Centra.

Behind the flag, strictly aligned in rank and file, twelve abreast, moving in unison to the beat of the solitary drum, marched six ranks of silent drummers, drumsticks turned back under their arms.

Abruptly, there was the piercing blast of a Centran trumpet. The tone changed swiftly, to end on a single high note.

The massed drummers brought down their drumsticks. The crash of the drums filled the room.

Horsip snapped off the volume control.

From outside came the roll of massed drums.

On the screen, dense formations of heavily armed Centran troops filled the avenue, sunlight glinting on their guns, helmets, and the interlocked plates of their battle tunics. Overhead flew small ships, similar to spacecraft in appearance, but apparently built around one large gun or rocket-launcher that protruded from the front of the ship like the tip of a sword thrust out from behind a shield. In the background, at the far end of the avenue, out in the distance beyond the limits of the city itself, could be seen a looming tower, and behind it another and another lined up at the city's spaceport. Climbing steeply from the distant spaceport came slim needle shapes that glinted in the morning sun.

From overhead came the roar of another huge ship passing over toward the spaceport.

There was a flashing yellow light to Horsip's right. Horsip snapped on the communications screen.

The same general who had reported to Horsip the day before saluted.

"Nock Sarlin, Commander Battle Fleet V, reporting to United Forces Command Headquarters. Sir, the enemy is destroyed as a fleet. Isolated enemy units are drawing away from us with acceleration slightly superior to our fleet maximum. Our detectors show the second fleet on our plot yesterday is withdrawing at high speed on a diverging course. A third fleet, approximately 20 percent superior in numbers to our own, is appearing on our remote pick-ups, approaching at high superlight velocities, beaming the command code of Able Hunter, and the identification of a Battle Fleet 46. We have Able Hunter on our books, but no Battle Fleet 46. These ships show characteristics contrary to Centran standard construction, but have beamed the correct recognition signal. Shall we maintain concentration and block Fleet 46? Or shall we continue the pursuit?"

From outside came muted sounds of a tramp and rumble, and of the shrill blast of whistles signaling orders.

Horsip fought his way out of his daze.

"Fleet 46 is a special unit and their ships are of non-standard construction. This is normal for this unit. Continue the pursuit, but don't get too spread out."

On the screen, Sarlin saluted, made a quarter turn, and spoke briskly, "Slow units form on the axis of flight. Pursuit units to the front by flotillas, wings, and squadrons. Unit star with wreath to the outfit that brings down the most ships!"

The screen went blank. Horsip turned to find Moffis listening wide-eyed and staring at the screen.

"These are our men?"

Horsip said warily, "If not, Able Hunter has tricks I never heard of. But we'd better take a look before we count on it."

Surrounded by guards, they reopened the door to the corridor.

Amidst dead Mikerils and the corpses of the Ahaj Revolutionary Army, heavily armed Centran troops saluted. From outside came the deafening roll of drums.

From a window of the building, Horsip looked out on massive columns marching through heavy clouds of dust, followed by traveling forts, launchers, troop transports, and motorized cannon.

Moffis looked down in choked silence, then turned to Horsip.

"The High Council *has* come through!"

Horsip nodded. The High Council must have drawn on the resources of the huge Sealed Zone, and now put forth its concealed strength.

But Horsip, thinking of the charts he had seen of the two monster dictatorships, drew a mental comparison. Although victorious here, the Integral Union was in fact still not the equal of either of the two dictatorships.

Moffis said, "This will change things."

"Not enough. They're still stronger."

"What about Hunter's fleet?"

"*If* that were real, we'd be stronger than either alone, but not both together."

"As far as they know, it *is* real."

"And that gives us our chance. Well, Moffis, let's see if we can dig these dictators a hole and shove them into it."

During the next few days, Horsip, like an accident victim after a gigantic transfusion and the most expert treatment, found himself in better shape than he would have dared believe possible. The loyal planets were swept by waves of enthusiasm. The uncertain hastened to his banner. The disloyal trembled. Dictator Ganfre earnestly talked peace, while the Snard Soviet and its allies were gushingly friendly.

Horsip, calculating the odds, and observing that Ganfre was now noticeably diminished by the outcome of the battle, was very agreeable to the heavily bandaged and crestfallen NRPA emissary. Horsip explained that the Integral Union had *had* to protect itself, that everything he could have done to warn of the danger had been done, that really it wasn't Ganfre that he wanted to fight, but certain "degenerate elements." The emissary, listening alertly, at once identified

Snard. If, Horsip suggested, Ganfre and the Integral Union could get together, it might be possible to do something about these degenerates. The emissary swallowed the bait, and at once went off to get in touch with his master.

"Ganfre," Moffis objected, "is as bad as Snard—and Ganfre attacked us!"

"Yes," said Horsip, "but if Ganfre will go along with the idea, we should be able to beat Snard. With Snard out of the way, the threat that holds Ganfre's pack together will vanish. Then if we can get a few of Ganfre's people to go along, we can eliminate Ganfre."

Moffis followed this line of reasoning.

"Truth."

"Meanwhile," said Horsip, "we have to get Columbia allied with us. Somehow, Moffis, we have to get more of these Earth-controlled planets on our side. We aren't strong enough to win by ourselves, and the worst of it is, while we have a good-sized fleet *now*, these dictators have a big production to fall back on. We need to beat them quick."

Unfortunately, Ganfre sent a new emissary to make a pact with Horsip, by which Ganfre and Horsip could finish Snard *after* Snard and Ganfre, now secretly allied, polished off Columbia.

Horsip hid his disappointment. "Columbia is a minor power. We should finish the source of the trouble first. Columbia would be easy later."

"I am inclined to agree with Your Excellency," said the emissary, looking sincere. "If only your offer of alliance had arrived sooner! But the end of hostilities left us in temporary disarray, and it seemed wise to unite momentarily with the common enemy of both of us. We did not at that time realize, of course, how you felt . . . Now"—he looked pious—"we must honor our commitment."

"How," asked Horsip politely, "does this attack on Columbia enter into the commitment?"

"It was Snard's price for agreeing to hit you from behind if . . . ah . . . that is, for agreeing to stand by us in our hour of crisis."

"I see."

"But once we have fulfilled that sacred pledge, *then* your forces and ours may combine to eliminate the common enemy." The emissary looked earnest.

Horsip looked agreeable, but regretful.

"It may be that there will be nothing left for us to be allied with."

"But I thought Your Excellency was of the opinion that Columbia is a minor, if somewhat dangerous, power?"

"It is not your *enemy* that gives me concern, but your ally. In such an attack, there could be many opportunities for"—he searched for the word—"*errors.*"

The emissary looked moody.

"I think we have thought of all of them. But, it is true— with such friends as that, there is no telling."

Horsip said, "If you come out of it with a whole hide, *then* offer us this agreement."

After the emissary had left, Moffis said, "Once they finish Columbia, then what?"

"Then," he said, "they finish *us.* After that, they eat each other up."

"Then we should help Columbia."

Horsip nodded, and sent for Hunter, who had come after sending the bulk of his mysterious fleet on "maneuvers."

Hunter entered the room looking faintly dazed.

Horsip, who had never seen Hunter like this, sat up in alarm.

"What's wrong?"

"I've just been in your Records Section, studying reports on Mikerils."

"Bad as they are, we have a worse problem. If we don't help Columbia, Snard is likely to win this war."

"Not Snard. The Centrans will win."

Horsip, knowing the way Earthmen used the word "Centrans" to mean anyone of Centran descent, considered the various dictatorships, revolutionaries, maniac faddists of all manner of cults, and said, "*Which* Centrans?"

Hunter glanced toward a rugged guardsman recently arrived with the Fleet.

"That's the kind. It won't be long before there won't be any other kind."

"Why?"

Hunter started to speak, then shook his head.

"To explain *that* would be complicated, sir."

Horsip shrugged. "Snard and Ganfre have ganged up against Columbia. Unless we help, I think Columbia will get beaten. But we aren't strong enough to intervene openly."

"If we waited until they are right in the middle of the attack—"

Horsip shook his head.

"The commander of Fleet V tells me that there are other 'fleets,' so-called, which I think must be mostly for deception purposes—like your 'fleet'—but they must have some real strength, and, as I calculate it, the united real parts of these fleets would make us much stronger than we are now."

Hunter said, "You want to gather your strength, so you need time for these units to come in?"

"Yes."

Hunter looked thoughtful.

"There are a few stunts we've worked out that we'd like to try on these birds. Sir, if we could have permission to operate completely on our own—"

"Granted," said Horsip promptly

Hunter saluted, and went out with a look of creative enjoyment.

Moffis put down a phone, and turned to Horsip.

"*Another* Mikeril attack! The commander of the guard says ten thousand have hit the outskirts of the capital in the last hour. They avoid the troops and hit the populace. Fifteen thousand more *went by overhead*, to attack the outlying districts."

"*Overhead?*"

Moffis said, "It's impossible, but they do it."

Chills ran up and down Horsip's spine. A verse from school days went through his head:

By day, by night,
In eerie flight,
Their shadows pass across the sky.
They stoop, they dive,
Their numbers thrive.
Through air and space in hosts they fly,
Drawn by unseen cords that tie
Sinners to the Mikeril hive.

Moffis said, "If it gets any worse, we're going to have
an invasion on our hands. You can't call it anything else,
when they start coming in like this."

"Where do they come from? Moffis, you know that
poem . . . ah . . . 'Through air and space in hosts . . .'"

Moffis shivered. "I know it."

"That part about 'space'—that, at least, should be
impossible."

Moffis nodded. "It *should* be. But how do they fly
through air?"

Horsip considered it. How *did* they fly through air? It
was impossible. The Mikerils were big, hairy, clawed creatures, as large as a man, hideous to look at, and according to legend they could tie a man up in invisible strands.
He had seen at least part of it confirmed. But . . . the
creatures had no wings.

Horsip shook his head. They had troubles enough without this complication.

In the following weeks, the Mikeril attacks didn't slacken.
They got worse. They swept over the planet like a hurricane. As the reports flooded in, Horsip found it impossible
to separate fact from panic, chose a newly arrived brilliant
staff officer, and let *him* read the Mikeril reports. Horsip
went out with Moffis to visit the troops.

"Here they come, sir," roared a sergeant in charge of
a squad with a big splat-stitcher.

Straight ahead, low over the trees, came a thin grayish
blur. Swiftly it enlarged into countless black dots.

The sergeant shouted, "Ready! Here they come!"

Somewhere there was a blast of a whistle.

The sergeant shouted, "Loaders back! Aim high and sweep! *Fiiire!*"

The gunner shook in his seat, the numerous belts of ammunition fed up to their separate guns, the frame blurred, streams of glowing tracers arced out. All around Horsip was a hammer and rattle that deafened him. Then the nearest gun ceased fire, and the loaders ran up with fresh belts of ammunition.

In the distance, the dark cloud sheared off.

The sergeant bellowed, *"Ceeease fire!"*

Horsip and Moffis went up with the colonel in charge of the unit to look over the slaughter. The Mikerils were strewn in grisly heaps . . . And not one had wings.

Horsip returned from his inspection tour to find that, while the population was being decimated by the Mikerils, the balance of force between Centra and the dictators had again shifted.

The dictators, locked in their savage battle to exterminate Columbia, were being diligently sabotaged by Able Hunter, whose brief battle reports spoke of fine strong wires that opened up the Snard ships like pea pods, and of undetectable leech-mines that sought out the enemy ships and blew them up. But Hunter could only inflict painful bites on the gigantic mass of the enemy fleets.

What altered the situation overnight was the unexpected arrival of Battle Fleet II of the United Arms of Centra. Battle Fleet II, it quickly developed, was as powerful as Battle Fleet V. Even allowing for the mushrooming production of the dictators, Centra was now very nearly as strong as either of them.

Horsip at once lifted his command ship from its landing place, and led his fleets against the enemy at the height of its siege of Columbia.

The big screens in Horsip's command ship showed the situation plainly. The outer planets of the Columbian system were under the control of Snard and Ganfre. The system had an asteroid belt, in which the battle for control was apparently going against the outnumbered Columbians. The dictators had also succeeded in seizing a huge satellite closely circling the Columbian sun. The inner planets remained under Columbian control, but a huge invasion fleet was preparing to attack the home planet itself.

Horsip was promptly challenged by one Supreme Commander Strins Rudal, a subordinate of Ganfre's, who ordered that the 'dummy fleet' be withdrawn at once.

Horsip, wishing to defeat the dictators separately, listened politely as Rudal delivered his warning from the communications screen.

"I am aware," said Rudal, "of your deception fleet, General Horsip. I suggest you put it back in your asteroid belt before we blow it up."

Horsip looked stern, but kept his voice level. He selected the name of a powerful Snard dictator none too popular even among his fellows.

"I am not interested in attacking *you*, General. My quarrel is with Q. Schnerg, who is, I think, in this group of ships somewhere."

"High Leader Schnerg is a member of the Coalition. What of it?"

"I have told you, General. I have a quarrel with Schnerg."

"High Leader Schnerg."

"I don't care what you call him. I want him."

Rudal looked blank.

"Surely, General Horsip, you can see we are occupied here. High Leader Schnerg is not available."

"Schnerg will either come out, or I will go in and get him."

"You do not have the ships to challenge the Coalition."

"I don't challenge the Coalition. I want Schnerg."

"Would you mind telling me why?"

"I would mind. I will tell Schnerg."

"General Horsip, I will pass the word to the High Leader. It is not fit that one of his rank be approached by—"

Horsip said coldly, "Do *you* now question the power of the Integral Union to defend its honor?"

Rudal looked uneasy. "I didn't mean that. I meant I would take your message personally. But—"

Horsip looked Rudal in the eye. "My message for Schnerg is not something you can *hand* to him. It can only be *fired* at him. Where is he?"

Rudal lowered his voice.

"General Horsip, I mean no offense, of course, but the real portion of your fleet cannot defeat High Leader Schnerg. Besides, the Coalition is one solid force. We are as one. We will defend each other as if we ourselves were attacked."

Horsip smiled and said nothing.

Rudal looked uneasy.

Horsip said politely, "I have no quarrel with you, or with the Coalition. But I am going to get Schnerg. Now, don't tell me you are going to stop me. I can see the situation you are in as well as you can. If you let go of Columbia to stop me, the Columbians will take back everything you have won. Don't tell me my ships are dummies. Just show me where Schnerg is, and I will show you what my ships are made of. Now, either you get me Schnerg, and get him fast, or I will go in and get him myself."

Rudal looked browbeaten and exasperated. His feelings showed on his face. Why, he was obviously asking himself, had this mess had to come about at *this* moment? Horsip, calculating that anyone with Schnerg's traits would be bound to make enemies, was not surprised to hear Rudal say, "General Horsip, I . . . ah . . . must admit I am not surprised that the High Leader has given you offense in some way . . . But, could you not possibly wait until some more propitious moment?"

"I want Schnerg," said Horsip, "and I want him now."

"To separate his ships from the rest will create chaos!"

"That is too bad," said Horsip, straining to look regretful, "but if Schnerg does not come out, I will go in after him."

"Just a moment, General. I will take this matter to our leaders."

There was a short delay, which Horsip used to beam messages at the Columbians, pointing out that he was neutral in that fight, and interested only in getting Schnerg. Since Schnerg was one of Columbia's main enemies, the Columbians were only too happy to recognize this kind of neutrality. Then Dictator Ganfre came on, to offer to mediate the trouble between Horsip and Schnerg. Schnerg, said Ganfre, claimed that he had never had anything to do with Horsip, *or* the Integral Union, and was not interested in either of them.

"Ah," snarled Horsip, "he is not interested in either of us, eh?"

Ganfre made an earnest plea for Horsip to wait until the battle was over, then he could do anything he liked with Schnerg. Schnerg apparently intercepted that message, and didn't like it, as Horsip promptly received a note from Moffis that the Coalition Fleet was breaking up, large units pulling out in the midst of the battle. Ganfre obviously learned the same thing at the same time. His eyes narrowed and a look of calculation passed across his face. Horsip thought he could follow his train of thought. Schnerg was temporarily allied to Ganfre, but that alliance would break up as soon as Columbia was defeated. If, therefore, Horsip beat Schnerg now, Ganfre would not have to beat him later. If Schnerg beat Horsip, that would simplify the calculations too.

"May the best man win," said Ganfre.

"Thank you," said Horsip. "I hope to."

Then he led his fleet against Schnerg.

Horsip had a sizable numerical superiority over Schnerg alone, but did not dare to use it. If he got into a vulnerable position, the other dictators might decide to rid themselves of this nuisance by letting go of Columbia to attack Horsip. Schnerg maneuvered as if to take advantage of this possibility, and Horsip had to use a large part of his fleet to guard against a possible attack by the rest of the

dictators. Halfway through the battle, a huge host of
Mikerils, their bodies rigid and unmoving, passed through
empty space around his ships as if traveling on unseen
wires. Shaken by this sight, Horsip was none too sure of
victory or anything else; but his tactics worked, and the
Centran Fleet destroyed the dictator's fleet.

Horsip now found himself in the rear of the other
dictators, with a fleet approximately half their size, while
their attack on Columbia was out of gear because of
Schnerg's withdrawal.

The dictators at once offered Horsip a share of the spoil
if he would join the attack on Columbia.

Horsip declined.

The dictators proposed a mutual accommodation. Horsip,
certain they would stay together against him now that their
own danger was clear, considered that he had done all he
could for the moment, and was inclined to agree, as they
outnumbered him two to one. He asked for time to consider, and as the screen went blank, Moffis, looking pale,
stepped forward.

"A message," said Moffis, "from the High Council."

Horsip unfolded the yellow slip of paper. He looked at
it, and chills ran up and down his spine. It read:

By Command
The High Council

We, the guardians of the essential strength of our
race, in accord with the ancient law, do hereby pro-
claim throughout the Realm of Centra the edict of
the clokal detonak.

We hereby vest in our loyal servant Klide Horsip
that power gathered to us from all the race, to reduce
the aberrant of the Realm to obedience, or by death
cleanse them of their abomination. Let the sinful lay
down their arms, abase themselves before the Great
One, admit the error of their ways, seek the aid of
the Holy Brotherhood in again finding the True Way,
and the sword of chastisement will be withheld.

If they fail so to do, we require General Klide Horsip, Commander of the United Arms of Centra, to destroy the traitors utterly and without mercy.

This command is absolute and binding, it cannot be questioned or negotiated, its effect is immediate, and its term shall last until the submission or death of the last traitor.

> By command
> The High Council
> J. Roggil
> Chairman

The hair at the back of Horsip's neck bristled. He glanced at the battle screen, which showed in stylized symbols the strength of the enemy, and his own strength. He glanced at Moffis.

Moffis looked helpless.

Horsip glanced back at the message. There in front of him were the words "it cannot be questioned." Horsip straightened his tunic. "Get Ganfre for me."

High Commander Strins Rudal appeared on the screen, trying to look cordial.

"Well, well, General Horsip, we are very busy, of course, but always glad to talk to an old friend. I am sorry we will have to make this quick, but—"

Horsip said evenly, "Are you *still* convinced my fleet is made of dummies?"

Rudal looked uneasy. "We all make mistakes—"

"I have just received a message from the High Council which requires—"

Rudal burst out, "We all know, General, that you *are* the Integral Union. We have to admire the way you have pulled the pieces together, but spare us this play-acting!"

Horsip observed Rudal's nervousness, and hid his own. "I am merely the tool of the Integral Union," said Horsip, "and if I break, I will be tossed aside, and another chosen to do the work. I am the servant of the High Council."

Rudal struggled to cover a look of long-suffering.

"Of course, General. Certainly. I will pass the message on at once."

Horsip spoke slowly and distinctly.

"By command of the High Council, the *clokal detonak* is proclaimed throughout the Integral Union. By this command, an absolute obligation is imposed upon you, and upon every living person of Centran blood, to lay down your arms, abase yourselves before the Great One, and seek the aid of the Holy Brotherhood in again finding the True Way. If you fail to do this, you will be destroyed without mercy. You cannot negotiate. The command is absolute."

Rudal swayed on his feet.

Horsip looked at him steadily.

Rudal opened his mouth, closed it again. "I will inform our leaders of this, General Horsip. Now, excuse me."

The screen went blank.

Moffis said uneasily, "It doesn't say anything in there about persons of Centran blood. Maybe it just means . . . well . . . in our *own* territory . . ."

Horsip smiled.

"I know what it means, Moffis. The Council isn't commanding the people in *our* part of the universe to lay down *their* arms. The Council is commanding the 'aberrant of the Realm.' I know who the 'aberrant of the Realm' are."

Moffis nodded unhappily, and looked at the battle screen, where a new large force of the dictators' ships was separating from the battle with Columbia.

Moffis said, "It didn't say we should attack them at once."

"Truth," said Horsip, "but we can't wait until Columbia is captured."

The screen came on again, to show Dictator Ganfre, backed by a vague, out-of-focus semicircle of figures. Some trick in the transmission made Ganfre look larger than life, and his words came out with subtle undertones of power.

"I am surprised, General Horsip, that one victory over a fraction of our forces should create such . . . presumption."

Horsip said, "I will read the command of the High
Council." Horsip read slowly and distinctly, then lowered
the paper. "I can't question it, I can't negotiate it. I can't
soften it. You have two choices—obey or die."

Ganfre looked blank.

There was an uproar behind Ganfre and for the next
fifteen minutes Horsip monotonously beat down offers
of partnership, threats, attempts to buy him off—until
at last the incredulous dictators saw he meant exactly
what he said. Then there was a change in the atmosphere.

The communications screen at once went blank.

On the battle screen, the entire battle fleet of the dictators began to break free of Columbia. At this distance,
it appeared a slow movement. But Horsip knew what it
meant.

Horsip didn't wait for the enemy to take the initiative,
but attacked at once, to pin a portion of the dictators' fleet
back against the Columbians. As Horsip drove this enemy
force into the eager grip of the Columbians, the rest of
the dictators' fleet curved around behind him, so that he
was between two enemy forces.

Horsip, eying the battle screen, turned to his communications officer.

"Ask permission of the Columbians to enter their territory."

"Yes, sir."

The enemy in front of him was being slowed by the
missiles, beams, and drifting minefields of the Columbians,
while the enemy behind was gaining steadily.

A staff officer at another screen called, "Sir, we have
a fleet showing up here."

"What recognition signal?"

"None, yet, sir."

There was the rap of a printer.

The staff officer said, "Here it is . . . Fleet 99, United
Arms of Centra . . . Bogax Golumax, commanding."

Moffis said, *"That's* no Centran."

Horsip's communications officer spoke up.

"Sir, the Columbians grant permission to enter their territory."

"Good." He looked at the long-range screen, where an enormous fleet was beginning to loom into view, then glanced back at the battle screen.

Between Horsip's Centrans and the Columbians, the trapped section of the dictators' fleet was melting away like a light snow in a hot sun. But the main force of the enemy was gaining relentlessly.

Horsip spoke to his communications officer.

"Signal to Ganfre: 'You are trapped. Surrender or be destroyed to the last ship.'"

Moffis grimly studied the screen. "That won't scare him."

"It will if he looks around."

The battle screen now showed symbols on both sides flaring up and winking out as the enemy fleet thrust into range.

Meanwhile, "Fleet 99" loomed even more gigantic, a monster phalanx whose numbers suggested a traveling galaxy.

Horsip said, "Signal to Fleet 99, both in code and in clear: 'We have the enemy in position. Close and destroy them.'"

Horsip's ships were beginning to get the worst of it. Not only were they heavily outnumbered, but with rare exceptions they could bring beams, missiles, and other weapons to bear better to their front than to their rear. As long as Horsip fled, which he had to do, his disadvantage in fighting power was worse than his disadvantage in ships.

But now the enormous Fleet 99 began to appear in the background of the battle screen.

The enemy symbols on the screen abruptly underwent a peculiar writhing motion.

Horsip spoke sharply, "*General order:* 'Reverse course. Turn by squadrons.'"

The screen showed Horsip's fleet undergoing the same peculiar motion. Now he was pursuing the enemy. Though still outnumbered, this disadvantage was offset as his heavier armament came to bear on the dictators' ships.

The gigantic Fleet 99 closed at high speed, with a smoothly flowing ease of maneuver that put the other fleets to shame.

Horsip said uneasily, "What are the characteristics of Fleet 99's ships?"

"Still not clear, sir."

"H'm . . ."

On the battle screen, Fleet 99 was moving with an ease which suggested something supernatural. The desperately fleeing ships of the dictators were getting the worst of it as their overloaded fire-control centers tried to deal with both Horsip and Fleet 99 at the same time.

On the screen, the enemy's ships winked out, but now the ships of Fleet 99 began to disappear faster.

The communications officer shouted, "Message from Fleet 99, sir! Bogax Golumax to Commander United Arms of Centra: 'The enemy is armed. Now what do I do?' "

Horsip kept his voice level:

"Transmit general order: 'Reverse Course. Turn by squadrons. Maximum acceleration.' . . . Signal Fleet 99, Commander of United Arms to Bogax Golumax: 'Go back and get your guns.' "

There was an astonished murmur in the room. Experienced officers were looking around as if they had lost faith in their senses.

The screen showed Horsip streaking for the protection of the Columbian system, while the dictators tore into Fleet 99, which folded up with only the most pathetic resistance. While part of Fleet 99 was still coming forward, another part was leaving faster than it had come. Still other ships were vanishing while out of range of the enemy.

Moffis said suddenly, "That must be Able Hunter's deception fleet!"

Horsip growled. "Who else would send a message like that?"

The officers at the long-range screen shouted, "Another fleet, sir. Approaching on the same course as Fleet 99!"

"How many ships?"

"Too distant to be sure, sir. It looks big."

"What characteristics?"

"Lead squadrons seem to fit Centran standards."

Horsip glanced at the battle screen. The enemy had given up pursuit of Fleet 99, and was coming after Horsip at high speed. But Horsip now had too great a lead to be caught. Once in the Columbian system, the dictators had the little problem of dealing with Horsip *and* the Columbians.

There was the rap of the printer.

"Sir, message from Gar Noffik, Commander Battle Fleet VII, to United Forces Commander: 'Shall I join you, or attack them from the rear?'"

"Signal: 'Join me.'"

Moffis snarled, "Is *that* fleet real?"

"I hope so. But I'm not planning to take chances."

The battle screen showed Horsip drawing within range of the Columbian defenses. The dictators' fleet was well behind him. Fleet VII loomed up solidly on the long-range screen, though by comparison with Fleet 99 it looked modest.

"Sir," shouted an officer, "ships of Fleet VII have Centran characteristics!"

Fleet 99 had now vanished entirely.

An officer at the long-range screen began reading off numbers and types of ships.

On the screen, the enemy ships shifted position, and Horsip, watching closely, could see the possibilities. Ganfre might lead his whole fleet against Fleet VII before it reached the protection of Columbia. To save Fleet VII, Horsip might have to leave the Columbian system. Ganfre could then turn and attack Horsip.

Watching alertly, Horsip could see that, without Hunter's deception fleet, the position was clear enough. Ganfre still held the advantage, and obviously intended to use it. Already the dictators' fleet was swinging around to get between Horsip and the reinforcing fleet—if it was a reinforcing fleet, and not another of Hunter's phantoms.

Horsip, studying Ganfre's movements, and the continuing approach of Fleet VII, cleared his throat, and turned to his communications officer. "*Signal Fleet VII:* 'Enemy force outnumbers our present combined fleet strength. Stand off until you see a chance to join us.'"

Fleet VII answered, "While they attack us, you can attack them from behind."

Horsip smiled. "Send: 'I like your spirit, but they could split their fleet in two, and outnumber both of us.'"

"My men are impatient to kill traitors."

"There are too many of them. We need some advantage before we hit them."

"Fleets IX and XV are coming behind me."

Horsip looked blank, and turned to his staff officer at the long-range screen.

"Well, sir, there is *something*. Just what it is, we don't know yet, but—"

The harsh rap of the printer interrupted him.

"Sir, message from Sark Roffis, Commander Battle Fleet XVI, to United Forces Supreme Commander: 'Where is the enemy?'"

The printer gave another rapid-fire burst.

"Sir, message from Brok Argil, Commander Battle Fleet VI, to United Forces Commander: 'Which ones are the traitors?'"

Horsip looked around blankly.

"Sir, there are more coming in from another direction!"

Chills ran up and down Horsip's spine.

"Are they ours?"

"Ship characteristics match, sir."

The printer went off again.

"Sir, message from Nark Rokkis, Commander Battle Fleet IX, to United Forces Commander: 'Show us the enemy!'"

Horsip stared at the long-range screens, then turned to look at the battle screen.

Ganfre, with the equivalent of four battle fleets, was sliding his ships past the Columbian solar system, where Horsip waited with Centran Battle Fleets V and II, and he was already between Horsip and Battle Fleet VII. Ganfre could not attack Horsip without coming into range of the Columbian defenses, while Horsip could not attack Ganfre without leaving the Columbian defenses, and fighting at odds of one against two. Battle Fleet VII, meanwhile, at odds of one against four, belligerently faced Ganfre as Ganfre eased forward to get this fleet into his grip. As the dictators' fleet reached out for Battle Fleet VII, Battle Fleets XVI and VI approached at high speed, with Battle Fleet IX looming up ever more solidly on the long-range screen.

Now Ganfre had his ships almost in position, and at any moment might begin his attack on Battle Fleet VII, which if anything was edging forward to hasten the moment.

The printer clacked.

"Sir, message from Gar Noffik, Commander Battle Fleet VII, to United Forces Commander: 'Do I have permission to attack?'"

Horsip, calculating the odds, said, "'Refused. Avoid contact with the enemy until I give the word.'"

Ganfre now chose to begin the attack on Fleet VII.

Each individual ship in Fleet VII simultaneously pivoted 180 degrees and accelerated sharply.

Ganfre closed the gap, to run into a ferocious barrage. Then Fleet VII drew out of his reach.

Battle Fleet XVI now began to show up on the battle screen, along with a gigantic Battle Fleet 88, "Snar Gorible" commanding.

Horsip had seen enough. Fleet VII was unquestionably real. And if the Concealed Zone of the Integral Union could put forth three such fleets as II, V, and VII, it followed that there was every reason to think the approaching Battle Fleet XVI was also real—and that fleet, for the first time, made the odds even.

Horsip at once gave his commands to the Centran battle fleets.

The ships of Fleet VII simultaneously turned ninety degrees, to bring their main fore and aft armament into action, the entire fleet moving in a wide lattice toward the right edge of Ganfre's fleet, which was approaching them head-on.

Out from the Columbian system came Horsip, with Centran Battle Fleets V and II opening out into a thin lattice, and heading for that same right wing of the dictators' fleet.

At high speed, Battle Fleet XVI raced for the juncture where the other three Centran fleets should join, approaching the "upper" edge of that right portion of the enemy fleet.

Ganfre, his right wing suffering under the simultaneous fire of the main fore and aft armament of Battle Fleet VII, while his own ships could bring only their forward beams, missiles, and other weapons into most effective use, and with his left wing completely out of action, had ordered a ninety-degree turn to the right by his ships, to equalize the rates of fire on the right wing, and hopefully to enable him to curve his left wing around behind Fleet VII.

But now Battle Fleets V and II were approaching his right, so that it would be sandwiched between two Centran forces, and struck simultaneously from both sides.

Ganfre at once saw his mistake, and signaled a 180-degree turn to withdraw from the Centran trap.

Ganfre's fleet, however, was a coalition, not trained to the same level. Where some of the ships obeyed with precision, others turned late, and some had rejected the first order to turn ninety degrees by ships as being too difficult in this situation, and instead had turned by squadrons. When the second order, to turn 180 degrees, followed on the heels of the first order to turn ninety degrees, the ships turning by squadrons were caught with the first maneuver uncompleted. Again the response varied. Some units elected at once to turn back the leading ships of the squadrons, while others elected to finish the first maneuver before beginning the second. In the resulting chaos, Horsip did not even turn his ships to conform to the new enemy direction, but instead exacted the full toll of his advantage on the enemy's right wing.

Ganfre now swiftly curved back the left wing of his fleet,

turning this wing 180 degrees, the huge fleet formations curving around to take Battle Fleets V and II in the flank, and hopefully to sandwich Horsip's left wing as Horsip had sandwiched Ganfre's right wing.

Horsip turned the ships of Battle Fleets V and II ninety degrees "down," each individual ship now headed at right angles to the ships of Ganfre's fleet, as Centran Battle Fleet XVI, slightly altering its course on Horsip's command, approached the "upper" edge of Ganfre's formation.

Battle Fleet XVI, already spaced for maximum effect, threatened to bring to bear on the thin upper edge of Ganfre's fleet the concentrated fire of all the forward weapons of its ships. The ships on the upper edge of Ganfre's fleet could not hope to equal that concentration of fire. The danger existed that Battle Fleet XVI might chew its way through the whole of Ganfre's fleet from top to bottom, taking the whole fleet in the flank.

Ganfre, seeking to avoid the chaos that had come about before, signaled a ninety-degree turn by squadrons, to swing his whole fleet "down," paralleling the direction of Horsip's Battle Fleets V and II away from Fleet XVI.

Horsip, meanwhile, turned Battle Fleet VII 180 degrees, by ships, aiming it from the right of the formation back toward the left.

The accumulated momentum of the various maneuvers now exacted its price.

Battle Fleet XVI was already moving at high speed before Ganfre gave the order to turn. As Ganfre's ships turned, Battle Fleet XVI passed down through the gigantic lattices of ships, working murderous execution on the enemy, but finally ceasing fire because of the intermingling of the other ships, enemy and Centran, once the upper wing of Ganfre's fleet was passed.

Battle Fleet VII, moving to the right of the other fleets, continued in that direction even after the order to turn had been obeyed. While Battle Fleet XVI was still passing through the formation, Battle Fleet VII was fighting its own inertia, and slipping farther to the right—out of the way. Then, gaining speed, it slid back across the decimated formation of the dictators' fleet while their ships were gathering momentum downward.

Horsip, totally concentrated on the job, now reversed the direction of Battle Fleet XVI.

Ganfre, clubbed and battered, the condition of his fleet varying from iron discipline to chaos, now had the added treat of seeing Centran Battle Fleets IX and XV loom up on the screen.

Horsip brought Battle Fleet IX in from the original left flank of his fleet. Battle Fleet XV he had stand by, on the far side of the battle from the Columbian system.

Ganfre at once: (a) offered sizable concession to Horsip; (b) threatened the use of new secret weapons if Horsip did not accept the concessions; (c) signaled Earth, calling for help; (d) gave orders for the disposition of new reserve forces of the NRPA; (e) proposed a permanent alliance with Snard, until Centra should accept his terms.

Horsip repeated the original demand of the High Council, and brought in Battle Fleet IX to sweep the enemy formation and be out of the way before Battle Fleet XVI should pass back through the remnants, while Battle Fleets V and II, parallel to the enemy formations, were laboring at the task of destruction, and Battle Fleet VII was getting into position for another pass.

With this in store for it, the enemy coalition abruptly broke into fragments, each fragment suffering multiplied destruction as it clawed for safety, the surviving enemy groups splitting into small formations, and even into individual ships.

Horsip at once signaled Battle Fleet XV, which divided into pursuit groups to run down those enemy ships unfortunate enough to be within its reach.

The other fleets Horsip kept out of the pursuit. Fleets IX and XVI he turned against the home planets of Snard. Fleets VII and VI he sent against the home planet of the NRPA. Fleets V and II, together with Hunter's formidable-looking Fleet 88, he kept together as he watched to see if there should be any truth in Ganfre's threats of new fleets and secret weapons.

Off the home planet of Snard, the Centran fleets met and smashed a reserve fleet half their size just setting out to join the battle.

Near Ganfre's home planet, the leading ships of the Centran fleet began to vanish in bright explosions, out of range of any known weapons.

Horsip suddenly found himself in a war of attrition. The enemy, with the advantage of his weapon, tried to pick off Horsip's ships from a distance. Horsip sought to seize the enemy planets still unprotected by the weapon, and meanwhile used Able Hunter's phantom fleets to get some real ships close enough to pick off Ganfre's sniper-ships. Meanwhile, watching quietly on the far fringes of the action were ships Horsip suspected to be from Earth.

Not liking the looks of things, Horsip got in touch with the High Council.

"Don't worry," said Roggil. "The Concealed Zone is working at its highest pitch, and has been for years, while the Earthmen in the Integral Union have had every opportunity they might want to waste their effort on extravagances."

"This new weapon," said Horsip, "makes it impossible to finish the job."

"We expected something like that. Keep working on them and don't worry. More reinforcements are on the way."

As Ganfre multiplied his weapon, Centran Battle Fleets XVIII, XI, III, and X came in. The *clokal detonak* still applied, the power of Centra was rolling in like a tide, the Mikerils in gigantic numbers ravaged the main planets of the enemy—but Ganfre's factories labored night and day, turning out new ships armed with the new weapon.

Horsip could see the end of the Integral Union. He had Able Hunter multiply his deception apparatus, and prepared to lead the massed Centran Fleet, masked by Hunter's phantoms, against Ganfre's new fleet. At once, the changing balance showed up as Ganfre slid out of reach, his improved detectors ignored Hunter's phantoms, and with easy mastery he destroyed Centran ships in rapid dazzling flashes of blue-white glare. In the midst of the slaughter, with all hope lost and nothing left but grim persistence, several squadrons of ultrafast Centran ships ripped through the edge of the enemy fleet, their passage marked by the dull glow of enemy ships fading off the screen . . . Centran laboratories and workshops had produced their own new weapon.

The Centran ships armed with this new weapon proved also to be carrying cargoes made up of the new weapon, and Horsip lost no time distributing it. Then, as Ganfre's fleet avoided battle, Horsip led the attack on his main planets, capturing them one after the other to deprive Ganfre of nearly all his base. Horsip was about to finish the job when, once again, his ships began to be destroyed beyond the effective range of his own weapons.

Horsip resorted to tricks and subterfuge, using Hunter's improved phantom fleets to screen his movements. But Ganfre was exacting a heavy toll. Horsip again got in touch with the High Council.

"We are," said Roggil, "sending you an improved version of our own weapon, but it will take time to reach you. Don't worry. They have lost too much of their base to recover."

Nevertheless, Horsip's ships were vanishing.

Trying to trap Ganfre, Horsip sent a fresh fanatical fleet head-on against the dictator's main fleet, with the order to simulate panic. Ganfre's ships, mercilessly destroying the fleeing Centrans, followed them into a region filled with an improved version of Able Hunter's multiplied phantoms. Hidden by these phantoms were Horsip's massed fleet, which surrounded the enemy fleet, and closed in at high speed. The enemy went to work with his long-range weapons, and the outcome wavered in the balance as the printer clacked, and Horsip's communications officer called, "Sir, message from J. Smith, Major General, Columbian Space Force: 'Request permission to join fighting units of the Centran Fleet.'"

"Granted," snapped Horsip. "Ask their course, relay it, and warn our ships not to fire on the Columbians."

As the little force of Columbian ships showed up on the screen, abruptly the enemy weapon stopped working.

On the screen the enemy fleet turned almost as one ship and attacked the thinnest portion of the Centran fleet. But now the Centrans' ordinary weapons, as well as their long-range weapons, came into action.

Horsip broadcast his surrender ultimatum, to receive no reply.

Faster and faster, as the Centran Fleet brought its full strength to bear, the enemy collapsed.

Suddenly it was all over.

Horsip and Moffis stood looking at the screen.

Moffis said, disbelief in his voice, "We've beat them."

Horsip nodded. But all he said was, "Maybe."

The collapse of the remaining territory of the dictators followed like an avalanche. With only remnants of a fleet to guard them, with the *clokal detonak* backed up by still mounting Centran power, with hordes of Mikerils already over-burdening the defenses, the remaining enemy planets earnestly returned to the True Way.

Then, the conquest complete, and the Holy Brotherhood laboring to get the survivors on the right track, the Mikerils were the next problem. But as Horsip turned his enormous military machine against them, they were already dwindling. Before his attack, they vanished.

Horsip found himself looking around among the ruins for an enemy. But there was no enemy. All that was left was the wreckage, the dead, wounded, and maimed, and a populace of survivors devoutly attending worship. The Mikerils were gone.

Horsip grappled with the problem.

"Moffis, do you understand what has happened here? *Where are the Mikerils?*"

Moffis was frowning over a lengthy report headed *The Real Enemy—Projected Mikeril Numbers—An Assessment.*

"According to this, we've only started to fight them."

Horsip glanced at the report, which was full of words

he had never seen or heard before, and which relied heavily on mathematics, summarized in a formidable array of charts. He tossed the report on the desk.

"Do you remember that nursery rhyme—let's see— 'When the sun of right' . . . ah . . ."

"I know the one you mean," said Moffis. "My mother used to put me to sleep with the poem that rhyme is in. Let's see . . ."

Moffis nodded suddenly, and cleared his throat.

"As the sun of right sends forth his rays,
  Dark shadows flee.
  So the evil band, Great One,
  Flees thought of Thee."

Horsip said, "That's it! . . . Moffis, it is almost unbelievable, but I think that is what is happening—*has*—happened. As soon as the people went back to the True Ways, the Mikerils started to let up!"

Moffis looked doubtful, started to speak, then stopped, frowning.

"There may be something to this. It seems to match up. But how *could* it be?"

"Hunter knows. He predicted that we would win, after studying some reports on Mikerils."

"Well," said Moffis, "when we see him, we can—"

They looked around at the steady approach of footsteps. A messenger, escorted by armed guards, saluted.

Horsip returned the salute, and took the message, to read:

By Command
The High Council

We, the guardians of the essential strength of our race, in accord with the ancient law, do hereby decree:

(1) Throughout the Realm of Centra, the inviolable edict of the clokal detonak is lifted.

(2) The power vested in our loyal servant Klide

Horsip, to reduce the aberrant of the Realm to obedience, is hereby withdrawn, as the task is done.

(3) The actions of General Klide Horsip as Commander of the United Arms of Centra are approved by unanimous vote of the High Council, and have attained that purpose which was intended. This appointment is therefore withdrawn.

(4) Command of the armed forces of the Integral Union is hereby returned to the Supreme Staff, except for certain units which shall be held under control of the High Council.

(5) By unanimous vote of the High Council, General Klide Horsip is created a Full Member of the High Council.

(6) By unanimous vote of the High Council, two individual citizens of the planet Columbia, to be selected by the legitimate leaders of that planet, are created Full Members of the High Council.

> By command,
> The High Council
> J. Roggil
> Chairman

There was a hush in the room, and the approach of solemn footsteps. Horsip looked up. A strongly built member of the Holy Brotherhood, in black robes with purple collar, strode up the aisle, bowed his head before Horsip, raised his hands, and said solemnly, "Your Excellency, I bring to you a message from the Council of Brothers. The trust vested in you by the Council of Brothers, and the authority, has reached its fulfillment, and the Brothers, with gratitude, withdraw now this awesome power, lest its presence in a sole human vessel might work some harm to the wielder of so mighty an authority. But know this, that the gratitude of the Council of Brothers is no light thing in this world, and if you desire counsel, or aid spiritual or worldly, you have but to ask, and the Brothers will be at your side. That is the message I have been commanded to give, and I now beg the permission of

Your Excellency to report that my task is done, and the message delivered."

Horsip drew in a careful breath. "Please give the Council of Brothers my thanks, and tell them that their message was delivered."

The Brother bowed, backed two paces, then turned and strode down the aisle and out the door.

After the Brother went out, the door opened up, and another messenger came in.

Horsip braced himself, returned the messenger's salute, and a few moments later found himself reading a message commanding him to attend a special meeting of the High Council.

"Well, Moffis, it looks as if we're not the only people who think the trouble is over with." He handed him the two messages.

Moffis looked relieved.

"But I still don't know *how* they know."

"Able Hunter knows. . . . If I can get a chance to ask him."

Since the High Council, for some reason sufficient to itself, was now situated far from where Horsip would have expected, the trip involved special transportation. Horsip soon found himself on an ultrafast ship with simple arrangements, a minimum of luxurious appointments, a well-equipped gymnasium, and a library with a highly unusual selection of books. Horsip, who did little reading—aside from reams of hated reports—found that any volume he picked up in this library held his interest, regardless of the subject. It dawned on him that these books must have been culled from the entire production of all Centra.

"H'm," said Horsip, eying a book titled *The Essence of Combat—Tactics, Strategy, Policy, and Basic Principles*.

He settled down in a comfortable armchair, and was deep in the book when he vaguely heard the door shut, read on, became dimly aware of someone moving around, looked up, and saw Able Hunter frowning as he examined

the titles on the shelf from which Horsip had gotten the
book. Hunter looked up, and saw Horsip.

"Ah, General Horsip, how are you? You haven't seen
a . . ." He paused, noting the book in Horsip's hands.

Horsip smiled genially.

"I will be through with this in a few days. Perhaps I
could finish it sooner if I could get a distraction out of
my mind."

Hunter laughed.

"If there's anything I can do to help . . ."

"What are Mikerils?"

Hunter glanced around. Save for the two of them, the
room was empty.

"Mikerils are Centrans infected with a microorganism
passed on to them by the bite of another Mikeril."

Horsip looked blank.

Hunter said, "A study of the comparative anatomy of
the two proves the relationship. It should have been obvious. How do these attacks start? Few and far between.
Then they become gradually more numerous, and finally
overwhelming. Why? Because *the more of these creatures
there are, the more Centrans they can bite.* And the more
Centrans they bite, the more Mikerils there are. But to
be susceptible to the disease, a Centran's body chemistry
apparently has to be upset in a certain way. What we used
to call 'sin'—and what your priests call 'not following the
True Way'—upsets a Centran's body chemistry in such a
way that he becomes susceptible to the attacks of the
microorganism. *That* is what causes the Mikeril attacks."

"But—what started them in the first place?"

"I don't know. Possibly it began as an infection on an
early colony planet. Certainly there must be some other
host, to act as a reservoir of infection."

Horsip thought it over.

"Their size isn't much different from ours, but . . ." He
thought of the creatures moving trancelike through empty
space, and sweeping overhead by the thousands—without
wings, "It just isn't possible."

Hunter nodded. "I know. We've seen it, but in a few

decades people will doubt our reports. All I can say is, mystics on Earth claim that men can 'levitate'—that is, in effect, fly—and can do a great many other things, by following disciplines that control certain nerve currents, as I understand it."

Hunter looked exasperated. "That's their *claim*. But they generally refuse to demonstrate. Now and then there are reports of demonstrations, but are they true, or aren't they?" He reached up to a different shelf. "Here's a book I found yesterday titled *The Powers of the Disciplined*. When I open this book, I find that it is written in a kind of script I can't read. But the publishing house is the Self-Development Society. If this were Earth, I would be sure this was a mystic book of some kind . . . Now, if there are such powers, then perhaps Centrans *can* exercise them, but only after so much self-discipline that for most people it just isn't worth the effort. Perhaps the disease strengthens these powers temporarily, just as an insane man shows unusual physical strength."

"Do your people have anything that corresponds to Mikerils?"

Hunter looked uneasy. "Not that I *know* of."

"Then you, at least, can enjoy the fruits of your labor."

"You mean, after we have a good system set up, then we can settle back and take things easy?"

Horsip nodded.

Hunter moodily shook his head. "What happens then is that we get soft—and get overthrown. Centra has had *one* empire. We've had hundreds. They all got soft."

Horsip suddenly saw how it all fitted together. The Mikerils, hideous as they were, were what kept the Integral Union from falling apart. Every time the Centrans started off on the wrong path, the Mikerils turned up.

"Are you," said Horsip, "the first to learn this?"

"Don't think it for a minute. If I'm not mistaken, the Holy Brotherhood knows all about it. And I imagine the High Council does too."

❖   ❖   ❖

By the time their ship had reached the headquarters ship of the High Council, Horsip and Hunter had each read *The Essence of Combat* several times. Horsip detected what seemed to be a faint air of wondering respect in Hunter's manner toward him, tried to unravel the cause, and concluded that possibly Hunter was surprised that he, Horsip, could read such a transparently clear and well written book—and could understand it. This thought put Horsip in a bad frame of mind. While in this bad frame of mind, they arrived at the High Council's headquarters ship, were escorted aboard, and, without delay, decorated with a variety of ribbons and shining emblems in gold, silver, and platinum. The citations were impressive, and Horsip should have been beaming with pride. Instead, he was conscious of the blank expression on the face of Able Hunter as the decorations were hung around his neck.

Horsip's mood got worse. Then the ceremony was over, and Horsip was invited to the big H-shaped table. Hunter, bowing with outward respect, went out.

Horsip let his breath out in a hiss, and sat down. He had reached the height of power, had held the most exalted position open to anyone in the Integral Union, his name was a household word, and just one of the decorations he had received should have made him eternally grateful. As a matter of fact, he was in an ugly frame of mind.

Horsip looked around narrow-eyed, his dissatisfaction dying down somewhat as he looked at the faces around the table. They all showed intelligence and strong character— and then Horsip saw the two representatives of Columbia.

They appeared to be out of much the same mold as the Centran members, but the sight of them made Horsip wonder. The authority of Centra had been solidly upheld— but could it have been done without the help of the Earthmen themselves—those of them who opposed the dictators? Meanwhile, Earth was still there. Who could say when the next batch of enterprising individuals might come out from Earth? And now there were two of them—these two Columbians—on the High Council itself.

Just where was this going to end?

It still seemed to be headed toward the same solution—the Earthmen were going to take over the Integral Union.

Across the H-shaped table from Horsip, Roggil growled, "The ceremonies are now over, and the recorders, photographers, guests, and honored citizens may withdraw."

There was a rustle and murmur, then finally several doors shut, Roggil glanced around, and said shortly, "That's over with. All right, gentlemen, we have business to attend to, and it looks like a mess of the first order. Now—"

One of the two members from Columbia said in a low voice, "Just a minute before you get started on the new business."

Roggil glanced around, none too pleasantly.

"What?"

Horsip looked on blankly. Was this the legendary High Council in action? Where was the air of smooth functioning he had noticed before?

The member from Columbia said, "We've just been through quite a convulsion. We want to know what it was all about."

There was a chilly silence.

Horsip sat up.

Roggil said in a flat tone, "The convulsion was brought on by Earthmen, my friend. Do you have any more questions?"

The representative from Columbia smiled—it was an unpleasant expression, as if he contemplated slicing off Roggil's head.

"Why, yes," said the Columbian, "I *do* have more questions. Why did you let it get out of hand to start with? You could have held all that nonsense down. You had power enough. Instead, you withdrew your strength, and let the maniacs run wild. Then, when the whole mess had blown up into huge proportions, *then* you came back in and flattened all those people who should never have been allowed to seize power in the first place. What was the point of all that?"

Roggil favored the Columbian with an equally unpleasant smile.

"When you open up a box of incomprehensible oddities such as we found on Earth, *how do you know how they work until you try them out?*"

The Columbian blinked. After a considerable silence, he glanced at his companion.

The companion nodded slowly.

Roggil, with no special look of good humor, waited.

The Columbian looked back at Roggil, and spoke carefully.

"Do you mean to say you deliberately exposed millions of your citizens to a horrible death—in order to *test the value of various Earth attitudes and procedures?*"

"Yes," said Roggil, "that's exactly what I mean. We deliberately *found out now* what these Earth attitudes and procedures were, rather than wait three centuries and have them rammed down our throats step by step, on your Earth installment plan."

The Columbian smiled suddenly.

"So, for mere *principles,* you risked lives?"

"We'll risk lives for the sake of principles anytime. As soon as you lose principles, your lives are first worthless and next lost."

"But could you have won without us?"

"You were part of the calculation. We had to assume that somewhere in the incredible diversity, there was *something* on Pandora's Planet that made sense."

"So you let everything out to show what it could do, so you could pick the best of the lot? Well . . . all right. But why in such a hurry?"

"Very simple," said Roggil. "If we had held the Earthmen back, they would have had time to multiply. Their undesirable systems would have developed more slowly, and been backed up by Earthmen from top to bottom. Therefore the Earthmen were permitted to expand rapidly. While they held most of the positions at the top, the body of their organizations were made up of Centrans—*who are subject to Mikeril attack.*"

The two Columbians nodded, and looked agreeably at Roggil, and the spokesman of the two said, "Your reasons make sense. We just didn't want to ally ourselves with a selection of . . . ah . . ."

"Dullards," supplied Roggil, smiling.

The Columbian nodded. "That's the word . . . Well, what's the business? This mess you speak of?"

Roggil drew out a thick report, eyed it a moment, and now there *was* that sense of working in harmony.

The members waited intently.

"Here," said Roggil, "we have a report on a new race discovered at a location . . ." He touched a button, and a star map appeared on the ceiling of the room. A ghostly pointer moved around it, to pick out a star Horsip was not familiar with.

"This," said Roggil, "is at the edge of our latest advance into new territory. Here we have run into a humanoid race which poses for us a peculiar problem." He glanced at the two Columbians. "We will be interested to learn your suggestions."

The Columbians looked interested.

"What's the problem?"

Horsip leaned forward intently.

"The problem," said Roggil, "is that we have discovered a race," he looked at the Columbians quizzically—"which is more intelligent than we—or *you*."

The Columbians sat up.

Roggil went on, "They are, in effect, a race of geniuses—by your standards as well as ours. On the average, we would say, their general intelligence is as far above yours as Earth's general intelligence is—on the average—above that of Centra."

The two Columbians looked profoundly blank.

Roggil sat back and smiled.

"Now, gentlemen—what do *you* suggest?"

SWEET REASON

Editor's note: Although it is not directly connected to the Horsip/Towers stories which constitute *Pandora's Legions*, "Sweet Reason" is the one other story which Christopher Anvil wrote set in the Pandora universe. We are therefore including it as an appendix to this volume.

I

Captain Karp Moklin, Centran assistant psychologist at the local prison camp, nodded to the perspiring Earth psychotherapist who was his visitor.

"Yes, Dr. Garvin. As you say, such cases as these are for the specialist."

Garvin drew a shaky breath. "I certainly do feel privileged, Captain, to come and watch a Centran psychologist at work. I'm very anxious to meet Major Poffis. My own—ah—efforts certainly don't seem to have accomplished much."

In the cell behind him stood a large Centran soldier, his fur unbrushed and untrimmed, tail thrashing in triumph, a sneer on his face, and a chunk of Dr. Garvin's sport jacket in his hand.

"Of course," said Garvin, "really deep psychotherapy is a very slow process. This is why I am so anxious to see one of your own people, and observe his methods. Possibly if we could—ah—pool our resources it might be possible to considerably accelerate the course of treatment."

Moklin nodded. "Major Poffis himself has often complained that the work takes too long."

"Is the—ah—the incidence of relapses—" Gavin hesitated, then rephrased the question to fit the less developed Centran mentality. "I mean, do the patients have to come back very often for a second course of treatment?"

The Centran seemed startled at this idea. "No, of course not."

"The treatments are usually *successful?*"

"Oh, yes."

"Does the major also treat those suffering from—ah—battle fatigue—"

The Centran looked puzzled. "Everyone is fatigued in battle. No, the major's treatment is not meant for that. He handles mostly these uncontrollables, the ones with—"

"Severe neuroses?"

"With the—ah—with the violent—ah—" Moklin paused as if mentally searching for some word or phrase that he had memorized once with the intention of using it later for effect. He straightened, and said learnedly, "With the 'violent antisocial tendencies.'"

Garvin blinked. "This is Major Poffis' specialty, then?"

"Yes," said Captain Moklin. "He does a lot of this work."

"That is precisely what we find most difficult." Garvin glanced uneasily at the prisoner, who with coy gestures was now urging him to come closer to the bars. "We find," he coughed slightly, "that these are often the most obstinate cases. They are difficult to reach—to contact—to form any common—"

The captain glanced at the wall clock.

"Major Poffis can reach them. He will be here soon. He is always on time. Then you will see how he does it."

The prisoner methodically tore his piece of Garvin's jacket to shreds, and leered at Garvin through the bars.

The clang of an outer door and the sound of voices heralded the arrival of Major Poffis.

Dr. Garvin said anxiously, "Is the major, ah, quite high in your academic hierarchy? In civilian life, I mean."

The Centran captain looked blank. "He has a Qh.Q."

"Ah, I see. Of *course*. Well—I'm not really familiar with the niceties of Centran—ah—academic protocol. Shall I call him 'major,' or 'doctor'?"

The Centran looked blank. "He is a major."

Garvin had the sensation of coming up solidly against a blank wall. He nodded hastily, and barely stopped himself from saying, "Silly of me to ask." Such comments, he had found, were likely to cause the Centrans to agree. Instead, he prepared himself to greet the Centran academic.

From the man's record of cures, he was a veritable master psychologist. Some of Garvin's colleagues, of course, did not consider the record of cures really significant. For them what counted were the methods used and the theoretical justification of the methods. But Garvin personally found it a little embarrassing to do no better than unaided nature. From Major Poffis—in his mind he decided to call him Dr. Poffis—from Dr. Poffis he would learn the best of Centran practices, then combine it with the highest Earth theory, and perhaps thus create a universal treatment superior to any hitherto used.

A murmur just outside the door told of Dr. Poffis' approach.

Garvin prepared his smile and readied the comment, "I hope that a useful cross-fertilization of our mutual concepts may bear fruit in a more successful treatment, Doctor." Just where he would put this into the conversation Garvin wasn't sure, but he wanted it to be ready when the time came.

The door latch clicked, and Garvin extended his right hand. He was on the alert to approach the tall distinguished Centran who would come in, who would perhaps be impressively silver-furred, with a slightly wry smile, or perhaps with a look of blazing incandescent genius demanding the instant submission of lesser intellects, and—

The door opened. A Centran major of above average height, broadly built, with muscles up both sides of his neck under the fur, walked in and growled, "All right, Moklin, what's on the sheet for today?"

Captain Moklin bawled, "Atten*tion!*"

The prisoner raised his right hand to his forehead, as if in salute. Then he lowered the thumb and forefinger to the sides of his nose and blew out hard. In case the idea didn't get across, he spat through the bars onto the major's tunic.

The major showed no sign of noticing anything unusual. "At ease. What do we have today, Moklin?"

"This is the first one, sir, in the cell right here."

The major nodded, started to speak, then frowned at Garvin. Garvin had his phrases all set, and now heard himself say stupidly, "How do you do? I am Dr. Garvin from Rolling Hills Rest and Recuperation Center. I—er—had hoped that a—ah—a useful cross-fertilization of our—ah—mutual—"

Major Poffis took a closer look at Garvin.

Garvin paused, groping around for some way to give a more conventional ending to this opening gambit.

Poffis glanced at the captain. "Is *this* a patient?"

"No, sir. This is the Earth psychologist from Mental Institution 16."

Garvin cleared his throat, and said gently but firmly, "We find it more appropriate to designate it 'Rolling Hills Rest and—' "

Poffis looked him over coldly. "What the devil's the matter with them out there?"

Garvin looked blank. "What?"

Poffis said shortly, "Why don't they get their thumb out of their mouth and give us some action? I sent half-a-dozen cases of combat nerves in six months ago, and so far we've gotten just one back. The boy was worthless. What the devil do you do to your patients?"

He turned to Captain Moklin. "I notice this fellow has a chunk out of his jacket. *Has he been administering treatment in my absence?*"

"Not actually, sir. He just walked over and tried to reason with the patient, that's all."

Poffis looked mollified. "That shouldn't do much harm." He glanced at the cell. "Now, then, this fellow hasn't been in combat yet, has he?"

"No, sir. He isn't out of training yet."

"You're sure we've got the *right records?* This isn't a damned administrative bungle like that last mess?"

"No, sir," said Moklin grimly. "I checked that myself, sir. This is the right man, all right."

"What's the recommendation?"

"Court recommended death. Patient's commanding officer pleaded for leniency."

The patient laughed out loud, as if witnessing a peculiarly silly scene in a play.

Major Poffis looked the patient over appraisingly, then glanced at Moklin. "On what grounds did his commanding officer plead for leniency?"

"He thought the fellow could be made into a good soldier, sir. With the proper treatment."

Poffis scowled. "Yes, there's *that* again. What's on the sheet, Moklin. *How many* of these cases have we got for today?"

Moklin looked apologetic. "Three more for this morning, sir. Now, about this prisoner—"

Poffis stared at him. "And this afternoon?"

"Sir?"

"*How many* this afternoon?"

"We've got—that is—" Moklin swallowed. "Sir, there are *six* of them."

Poffis's brows came together.

"That's too many. Put some of them over till tomorrow."

"Well, sir, tomorrow—"

Poffis snarled, "It takes time to get a cure started. I'll handle *three* this morning, and *three* this afternoon. From there, it's routine. But I'm taking *six* new ones a day and that's that."

"Sir, at that rate, they'll pile up from here all the way back to Training, and the colonel will—"

Poffis's eyes glinted.

"I know how many new patients I can handle in a day, Moklin. If the colonel wants me to take on eight a day, ten a day, twelve a day, then *I* am going to end up on the other side of these bars, and the colonel can see how *that* works out. Let them pile up. That's better than sending back fake cures. There's a cause to this mess somewhere. The sooner that dawns on them, the quicker they'll slap the *clokal detonak* on this whole region, and burn out the pus. Now let's have the keys to the cell so I can get started."

Moklin dazedly handed over the keys to the cell.

II

Garvin, stupefied, was grappling with the idea that the Centrans thought *six new patients a day*, with routine follow-up treatment, was about right. If Garvin got six patients really cured in a year, it was cause for celebration. Baffled, he took a fresh look at the patient Poffis was ready to treat.

The patient had watched with interest the exchange between Poffis and Moklin, but now stiffened as he saw Poffis come toward the cell. He threateningly approached the bars, bared his teeth and suddenly reached out through the bars to take a grab at Poffis's uniform.

Garvin watched intently, wondering what Poffis could possibly do now.

Poffis instantly seized the out-stretched hand, whirled and yanked downward.

The patient screamed and slammed against the bars.

Poffis promptly kicked him back against the opposite wall, then unlocked the cell door, went in, banged the door shut and tossed the keys to Moklin. The patient shook his hand dazedly, felt his shoulder, glared, let out a roar of rage and sprang across the cell at Poffis.

Poffis whirled, shot out a leg, tripped the patient, and sent him smashing head-first into the far corner of the cell.

The patient lay on his face for about fifteen seconds, then sat up dazedly, stared at Poffis and sucked in a deep breath. His voice came out loud and ringing.

"I got a *right* to go to a rest home! I'm *crazy!* I'm a

patient! I'm *sick!* You can't touch me! I got a *right* to go to a rest home!"

Poffis said angrily, "If I knew where that idea came from, I could get this work-load down to normal. All right, Moklin. Read the charge."

Captain Moklin unfolded a long sheet of paper and read in a clear sober voice:

"Prisoner committed following acts, which have been proved by careful and thorough inquiry. He:

"1) Threatened to beat up his own mess-mates, and then took their food from them by force.

"2) Threatened his squad-leader with a knife, when reprimanded.

"3) While off-duty, struck an elderly man who happened to step in his way, thus bringing disgrace on the armed forces.

"4) On being charged, as above, laughed in the face of his commanding officer, Lieutenant Boggis, and referred to Lieutenant Boggis as a 'molk.'

"5) Struck Lieutenant Boggis on the face with his open hand.

"6) Threatened Lieutenant Boggis that if Lieutenant Boggis defended himself, he (the prisoner) would state under oath that Lieutenant Boggis struck first.

"7) Resisted the guards summoned to the scene.

"8) While under detention, announced to everyone within hearing that he would receive a medical discharge and be home living on a pension while those who did their duty would be eaten up by Mikerils for their pains. Prisoner taunted all the law-abiding soldiers within hearing that *they* would soon be at the front defending *him.*

"9) By voice and act, abused everyone in authority who came near him during detention.

"10) Refused to cooperate with properly designated authorities in curbing his undisciplined actions. This refusal was compounded by disrespect and insult and reflects no detectable principle or ideal, but merely an undisciplined, willful, ill-governed nature, which is urgently in need of correction."

Captain Moklin lowered the paper. "That's it, sir."

"I see," said Poffis. "Well, well. Here we have a full-blown case of it." He studied the patient, who got to his feet, looking apprehensive and defiant.

"Now, then," said Poffis, "the first thing to realize is that how you got here doesn't matter. This is the trap right next to the drain. Either *we* cure you, or *they* shoot you. And we aren't given much time to cure you."

"I'm *sick!*" cried the prisoner. "I want to go to a rest—"

"Luckily," said Poffis, "we've got just the way to cure you. We've developed it over several thousands of years. There are only two things you need to know about this cure: It's quick. And it hurts."

The prisoner opened his mouth, and shut it again. Poffis was moving right along like a planet in its orbit, and showed no sign of stopping for anything.

"There's one reliable way," said Poffis, "that Nature teaches what's right and what's wrong. When you do right, you get rewarded. When you do wrong, you get hurt. Our method is the same, but more condensed."

"Look," said the patient exasperatedly, one hand outstretched, "I'm not *responsible.* You can't blame me for—"

"The basic idea of the cure is very simple," said Poffis briskly. "It is based on the observation of sages, that there is a real inner self, which is not subject to the phenomena of the physical world, and an outer self which is."

A succession of expressions crossed the patient's face, and ended with a look of defiant outrage. "To the *Mikerils* with all this stuff!" He followed that with a piece of profanity that took Garvin's breath away, but that left Poffis and Moklin visibly untouched.

"The real inner self," said Poffis, "is conscious of events, because it is 'connected,' by resonances and various nerve-tracts, with the outer physical self that exists in the physical world, and is a type of living protoplasmic machine, serving the inner spiritual self which is not physical."

The patient shouted, "I'm *crazy!* I WANT TO GO TO A REST HOME!"

Poffis moved steadily along. "To properly treat the

patient, it is necessary to distinguish between the true inner self of the patient, the outer physical self which is the medium through which the patient contacts and is contacted by the physical world, and the various traits, habits and emotions which manifest outwardly through the physical body, and inwardly by coloring the information passed to the brain and thence to the real self."

The patient stamped his foot. "Ah for—"

"The real self," said Poffis, "is strictly blameless. The trouble comes from wrong traits and attitudes having been established, usually in childhood, and by their habitual presence having generated emotions which falsely color the information passed to the brain. The cure for this is best administered early by the parent. By inflicting pain without damage, the parent breaks the grip of the wrong emotion, destroys its effects in distorting the information passed to the brain and demonstrates that emotions are temporary and changeable. Seeing the wrong emotion flee before the hand of the parent, the child is emboldened to strike down the wrong emotion himself, and takes the first step towards becoming master in his own house."

The patient ground his teeth, and looked around like one seeking sympathy for the heavy burden under which he labors.

"Punishment," said Poffis methodically, "'should be swift, intense and fleeting, with proper suggestions for future improvement, and should be ended without vindictiveness when the right attitude is firmly established. That's the theory. Now for the practice.'"

The patient leaned against the bars in an attitude of exaggerated boredom, and looked ready to fall asleep anytime.

"The practice," said Poffis, "is even simpler than the theory. By appropriate action, we first permit the undesirable traits to manifest themselves and promptly deliver painful consequences on each occasion. Next we administer a general treatment designed to loosen up bad traits and induce a cooperative frame of mind, during which we urge improvement. Following this comes formal punishment, then the actual recovery. All this is basically very simple, the difficulty being to properly suit the treatment to the individual patient. That's the practice. Now you have it, and your mind will retain enough so that it may be of use to you later. It's time. Prepare for treatment."

Outside the cell, Moklin opened a faucet that filled a bucket half-full of water. He tossed a sponge into the bucket, picked up a clean towel and a first-aid kit, set a chair just outside a corner of the cell and dusted off the seat of the chair with a whisk broom.

The patient glanced around with a scowl and gave the cell door a quick shake. The door was solidly locked.

Poffis glanced at the wall clock, then cleared his throat with a somewhat pompous, false and irritating sound. He said, "Now, first, permit me to point out—ah—that this method, while it *could* be used for wrong purposes, is in fact only used for the real *good* and the *genuine*—"

Dr. Garvin, outside the cell, squinted at Major Poffis, and tried to get him back into focus. By some trick of vocal wizardly, Poffis began to project such an air of sweet reasonableness that even Garvin felt the urge to get Poffis by the throat and bang his head against the wall. Garvin had no trouble overcoming this impulse, but the patient abruptly ceased looking for a way out, and eyed Poffis.

"—*welfare* of the patient," Poffis was saying sweetly. "The entire treatment is *meant* for the patient, who, deprived of proper parental assistance in the initial stages of character-formation, is thus disadvantaged by his defective self-control. We assist the deprived patient in many areas—"

"*G'r'r*," said the patient. His tail flicked back and forth, and his lips drew back to disclose large sharp teeth.

"—always," said Poffis piously, "to aid in whatever measure may be granted to us the unfortunate, under-privileged—"

The patient blurred forward, seized Poffis around the waist and slammed him to the floor.

Poffis landed stretched out, his forearms taking much of the impact, rolled aside fast as his patient took a flying kick at him, bounded to his feet and landed a blow that sent the patient sprawling.

As the patient stumbled, dazed and fearful, to his feet, Poffis seemed to undergo a delayed action from the fall he'd suffered. He gripped his side and tottered around the cell like someone in the last stage of physical deterioration.

This was too good an opportunity for the patient to resist. He hastened over to start a blow from the floor up, aimed for Poffis's jaw.

Poffis, however, recovered with miraculous speed, moved aside as the blow whistled past and smashed the patient on the jaw.

Garvin watched in stupefaction as Moklin stepped forward with the water bucket.

Poffis was now bent over the unconscious patient, tenderly bathing his bloodied face with a wet sponge.

III

As the patient came to and looked around dazedly, Poffis at once began to plead. "Now look here, I am your *officer*. You can't—"

The patient at once caught the pleading tone, and the words "I am your officer." He reacted with still-fast reflexes.

"Oh, *can't* I?" he snarled. He staggered to his feet with Poffis's help, and immediately tried to plant his knee in Poffis's groin.

Poffis turned too fast, and sank his fist in his patient's midsection.

Dr. Garvin watched the patient collapse and lie motionless.

Poffis now dumped a bucket of water on the patient, brought him to, and as the patient looked around dazedly Poffis bent over him and said sympathetically, "Understand, none of this is meant for the *real* you. We have to retrain your *habits* and *attitudes*, and this is the quickest way. I realize what you're going through, because I've been through the same thing myself."

The patient sat up dizzily. Some instinct for self-preservation apparently prompted him to keep Poffis talking. "You—you did?"

"Yes," said Poffis reminiscently. "I've been through the whole thing. You see, I had bad habits." A tinge of regret entered his voice. "And wrong attitudes, and I didn't even know it. That's how it works. No one could *reason* with me, or get through to me by anything that boiled down to reason, because, you see, this wrong attitude of mine distorted everything, and I couldn't *understand* things right."

Garvin was staring, wondering what would happen next. Poffis's voice was starting to grow heated.

"So," said Poffis emotionally, "they stuck me in a cell, and for these bad habits and wrong attitudes they *beat me up,* and slammed me all around." He sucked in a deep breath. "*Sure,* I had it coming. I *deserved* it. Because of the bad habits." His voice dropped. "But I felt every blow. It was meant for the bad habits. But *I felt it.*"

There was now an impression of smoldering resentment building up behind Poffis's expressionless face. The patient glanced around nervously.

"Bad habits," said Poffis flatly. "*They* got me in all that trouble. And *I* suffered. I *hate* them!"

"Sure," said the patient nervously. "I can appreciate—"

"I *hate* bad habits, bad traits, bad emotions," said Poffis, his voice rising. "But they've been beat out of *me,* so now there's only *one way I can get back at them.*"

The patient tried a quick shake of the cell door. It was still locked.

"And *that,*" said Poffis, "is to *find them in someone else.*"

The patient's eyes were wide-open. "Hey now. Wait a minute. Listen, now!"

"Right *here,*" snarled Poffis, gazing intently at the patient, "I see conceit, arrogance, carelessness—"

Poffis's voice, already charged with emotion, took on a tone suggestive of rending flesh and popping bones. He tore off his tunic and tossed it toward a corner of the cell, where Moklin with one deft motion snapped it out through the bars and laid it on the chair, neatly folded.

Patient and psychotherapist were suddenly flashing around the cell in a blur of speed, the prisoner screaming at the top of his lungs. "You can't! *Help!* You're *responsible!* STOP!"

WHAM!

The cell was one flying tangle of furry arms, legs and tails, with the prisoner's horrified face in view, and now

Poffis's grim visage. Grunts, screams and gasps resounded like the sounds of a medieval torture chamber.

Captain Moklin, watching, grinned and nodded.

Dr. Garvin looked on in horrified stupefaction, staring at the chaos resolved momentarily into grim scenes.

For an instant the prisoner was flattened out on the floor.

Then he was slammed motionless against the bars.

Next he was suspended in midair, one outstretched arm against the ceiling.

A fraction of a second later, it was one chaos of violence all over again.

Interspersed with the violence was Poffis's grim voice:

"You *will* listen.

"You *will* try!

"You *will* learn!"

There was a sudden crash, and the prisoner was saying rapidly, "All right! I'll do it! Sure, *I'll do it!* Anything you say!"

Poffis stared intently into the prisoner's eyes. "You look crafty. You don't *mean* it."

The cell exploded into chaos.

The prisoner screamed, "I *promise!* I *mean* it!"

Poffis stared deep into his eyes. "Close, but you're not there yet."

The violence ended the next time with a cry of despair. Then Poffis straightened. "Moklin!"

"Yes, sir! The lash?"

"The board."

Moklin handed in a medium-sized solidly made paddle.

The prisoner stared as Poffis took it, and said in a kindly voice, "Bend over, son. Grip the bars."

The prisoner swallowed, tore his gaze from the paddle, bent and took hold of the bars with both hands.

Poffis took the paddle in a practiced grip.

"You have committed ten serious offenses. For each offense, there must be a blow. The blows must be hard, or they will not be punishment. Hold on tight. *Moklin!*"

"Yes, sir?"

"Read the offenses."

Moklin raised the list, and read slowly and distinctly. At the end of each numbered offense, Poffis delivered a staggering blow.

Toward the end, as the list went on and on, the prisoner began to sob, but continued to tightly grip the bars.

At last, the list, which seemed to Garvin, watching dazedly, to be ten times as long as when it was first read—at last this list came to an end.

Moklin said soberly, "That is the end of the list of offenses, sir."

Poffis said, "So be it. Take the board." He handed the paddle out through the bars.

The prisoner collapsed on the floor, sobbing uncontrollably.

Poffis waited a moment, then said, "Prisoner, that ends the *punishment*. But punishment is not necessarily the same as *repayment*. You have, by your actions, done grave damage to the Integral Union itself. Yet the Integral Union feeds and shelters you. You have attacked what defended you. Are you sorry?"

"*Yes,*" cried the prisoner.

Poffis nodded. "Good. Look at me. *Are you going to do better?*"

"*Yes!*"

Poffis nodded slowly. "Yes, I see you mean it. *Moklin!*"

"Yes, sir?"

"This prisoner has hard work in front of him. He will need to sleep, but first he needs something to ease the pain, and he also needs a little warm thin gruel. Take care of this at once."

"Yes, sir."

Garvin, still watching in a sort of daze, saw Poffis help the prisoner to his feet, to ease him, very carefully, warning him where to put his hands and feet, onto the cot. To Garvin's astonishment, the prisoner, still sobbing, gripped Poffis's hand in what appeared to be gratitude.

Poffis said gently, "Don't worry, son. You may think we're going to half-kill you. But we'll get you out of it."

Moklin stepped into the cell, carrying a small bowl in one hand, and a jar of bandages in the other. Poffis stepped out of the cell and beckoned Garvin into the next room. Uncertain what to expect, Garvin followed with unspoken reservations. Poffis shut the door behind them.

"Now, just what the devil is going on at Mental Institution 16?"

Garvin said, "Why, just standard treatment."

"*Whose* standard treatment?"

"Well—"

"What *is* it?"

Garvin drew a slow deep breath, and described it.

Poffis shook his head.

"Conceivably that may work on *Earthmen*. But a thing like that won't work on Centrans."

"Is that so?" said Garvin, his professional pride touched. "Well, all I can say is, it certainly is more scientific than the procedure *you* use!"

"Obviously," said Poffis, "that's exactly what's wrong with it. The techniques of *Science* were developed for use on *inanimate objects.*"

As Garvin grappled with this statement, Poffis said, "Observe what has happened. Science came into existence to solve purely physical problems. To solve these problems it was necessary to exclude emotional considerations. The forces operative in this physical world are different from the forces operative in the emotional world. It is as if one were land and the other sea. The seafarer who goes ashore has little need for nets, lines and a knowledge of the tides, winds, and currents. But when he has built up his structure on solid land, is he then automatically fitted to go *back to sea, relying exclusively on land methods?* It won't work, Dr. Garvin, except where, so to speak, the emotional sea has been frozen over, turned to ice on the surface. In the emotional world, to say, 'My methods are entirely scientific,' is similar to saying, 'I have made an entirely scientific proposal of marriage.' It is a cause for alarm, not confidence."

Garvin hesitated, distracted by the uneasy suspicion that there might be some truth to Poffis's point, but stung by the implications. If psychology wasn't a science, then wasn't he, Garvin, a charlatan of some kind?

Poffis said earnestly, "Why insist that your study *must* be a science? Should everything be jammed into the same mold, and any parts that don't fit be thrown away? Just because a hammer is useful, should we throw away screwdrivers, wrenches, pliers and every other tool, and *force the hammer to do work it isn't meant for?* Or, by some kind of verbal wizardry, have we got to represent screwdrivers, wrenches, pliers and other useful tools, as *different kinds of hammers?* They are not hammers, my friend, any more than all useful studies are sciences. If you let such a distortion enter into your thought, you may not only blur your picture of the subject you are thinking of, but also your picture of Science itself."

On thinking it over, it seemed perfectly clear to Garvin that if psychology was not a science, then he, Garvin, must necessarily be a fake. If psychology was not a science, then it followed that he was no scientist, and this meant that he was less than, for instance, a physicist, or a chemist, and if he admitted to being not a scientist, it followed that he would *seem* to be less than one of those incredible creatures, the *political* scientists who, everyone agreed, were actually no scientists at all.

All this went through Garvin's head in a flash, and at the end he said coolly, "Psychology, Major Poffis, whatever it may be among *Centrans*, is universally recognized among Earthmen as the 'science of the mind.' I certainly don't intend to argue this proposition."

Poffis was watching Garvin's expression intently. "Psychology," said Poffis, with the air of one who reluctantly concedes a point, "may *deserve* to be a science; it may have distinct scientific *elements;* but if you say psychology is *and is only* a science, then I say that in your respect for your subject, it appears to me that you are mistakenly throwing half your tool kit into the nearest ditch. The essence of Science is the Scientific Method, and the essence of the Scientific Method is the Repeatable Experiment. To have a repeatable experiment requires first that the object experimented upon be comparatively *constant.* If atoms could argue, fight back, run away, sulk, plead, throw tantrums, learn our terminology and use it against us, then we might reasonably have some doubts as to just how strictly scientific the study of atoms could be. But in that case, would the study of atoms be any the less important?"

Garvin said hesitantly, "I came here to learn your method, so that I could combine your methods and ours—"

Poffis looked doubtful. "Your method, as you have described it, suggests to me the attempt to fix a malfunctioning ground-car by the use of analytical chemistry."

"And how would you explain *your* brand of psychology?"

"Very simple. To begin with, we believe in sympathy, power of will, character, habit, love, association, contrast, the power of example, the soul, the spirit—"

"What a hodgepodge! You've got religion in there! You've got—"

"What we got in there," said Poffis, "is Truth, and we accept Truth from *any* source, including religion."

"But, of all the unscientific—"

Poffis momentarily paralyzed Garvin with a poke of his long forefinger.

"The one advantage of Science is that it enables us, where it is applicable, to reach Truth. Truth is the goal, my friend, and Science is one means of reaching Truth, where Science applies. Don't forget your quest. You are seeking Truth. *Don't mistake the means for the goal.*"

Poffis went out, leaving Garvin open-mouthed. Dazedly Garvin considered Poffis's last two sentences.

"You are seeking Truth." Certainly this was so. Why had he ever been interested in Science in the first place? *He was seeking Truth.* And that warning, "Don't mistake the means for the goal." Could he, Garvin, possibly be like a boy who spent so much time laboring over his finicky but beloved car that he rarely actually went anywhere?

The rest of Poffis's argument was borne in on him. How the devil *did* you have a science when the thing you were working with was as unstable and changeable as the human

personality and the human intellect? *Science!* Was it an
example of Science when the object of the experiment got
up and tried to strangle you, as had happened twice now
to poor Hardison? Was it Science when the experimenter
fell in love with the object of the experiment, as had
happened to Pangeist? And what about Hergeswalther, who
got sucked into the patient's fantasy, and was only gotten
out again because the patient realized what was going on?

"Science!" snarled Garvin. "My foot, it's a science. Only
parts of it are scientific." And in that case, how was it going
to get him to Truth?

For the second time, it dawned on Garvin that Poffis
was really a master psychologist. How the deuce had *Poffis*
known what he, Garvin, had turned to Science for? And
how had Poffis been able to drive his idea across with such
effect that, just a few minutes later, Garvin was accept-
ing them as his own? But the main thing was—how was
Poffis able to make cures while he, Garvin, spent his time
floundering through the dark, and as often as not accomplished little more than to give the patient a knowledge
of the underlying theory, which might or might not work.

Garvin hesitated, then went to the door.

Captain Moklin glanced up and smiled. Across the room,
the patient slept peacefully.

Garvin said in a low voice, "Does the major *always* use
the same treatment?"

"No. It depends on the patient."

That was helpful, thought Garvin sourly.

Moklin said, "Major Poffis looks to see what is wrong
with the patient, then he fixes it. Down the corridor is one
who is here because it is against his *principles* to obey
orders. Major Poffis will break his arguments into little bits
and pieces. He will make it all so clear that the prisoner
will go out seeing the question in a new light. But most
of these uncontrollables have a treatment more like this
one here. Only, each treatment is different in the details,
because the prisoners are different."

Garvin nodded. He was still getting nowhere. At random, to keep the conversation going until he thought of

a new approach, he said, "No wonder the major complained about the work-load."

"Yes," said Moklin, "the work-load is piling up, and the major hasn't even an apprentice to help him."

Garvin nodded sympathetically, then blinked, "Apprentice? You mean you teach psychotherapy by the *apprentice system?*"

"Not I," said Moklin, block-headedly literal minded.

"No, no," said Garvin, "I mean is that the *Centran* system for teaching psychotherapy?"

"*The* Centran system?" said Moklin blankly. "Why should we have only one system? Also, there are schools that teach it."

"Yes, but you can't have *both!*"

Moklin looked at him. "Why not?"

"Well, the results wouldn't be uniform, for one thing."

"So?"

Garvin looked blank. Here he was again. The Centrans, block-headed fellows, did some silly thing, and when Garvin tried to explain *why* it was silly, the reasons evaporated, and he was left with this foolish feeling.

"Well," he said stubbornly, "*obviously* a man taught at a special school would know more than a mere apprentice. By the results not being uniform, I mean that the apprentice would be *inferior.*"

"Oh, you think so? With Major Poffis to teach, you think the apprentice would be laggardly in his efforts?"

"Well, no, I can see the major would keep him working, but—after all, there are a lot of things to be taught. At a school, there would be special teacher for each subject."

Moklin nodded agreeably. "And this special teacher will have a class with many in it, and split his efforts among the class."

"All right," said Garvin angrily, "if this apprentice system works, why do the students go to school *instead of apprenticing themselves to the major?*"

"Because," said Moklin promptly, "they are *afraid* to apprentice themselves to the major. Once they apprentice themselves to him, he will not let them go until they are almost as good at cures as he is, and he is one of the best there is. It will be nothing but work, work, study, practice, practice, and the major will see through excuses, punish laziness, stimulate earnest hard work, and judge with merciless accuracy. And we have been unable to find any students who are anxious to go through this."

Garvin thought it over. "But at the end, his apprentice will be *almost as good at it as he is?*"

"Oh, yes. Major Poffis will see to that."

"H'm." Garvin paused to consider. He was totally fed up with floundering around. Among other kinds of patients, Rolling Hills Rest and Rehabilitation Center, where Garvin worked, got a good number of uncontrollables. The frustration in dealing with them was terrific. "Ah," said Garvin, "is there any limitation—on age, race and so on—would the major take a—ah—an *Earthman*, past the usual student age—"

"With this work-load," said Moklin, "the major would take anyone, provided the apprentice was in earnest, and, of course, showed some promise."

"How many apprentices can the major take at once?"

"I don't know. I've never known him to take more than three at one time."

Garvin thought hard. He would like to have a record of cures like the major's. On the other hand, he certainly did not want the major's undiluted attention focused on him alone. It followed that he would need to interest *someone else*. How about Hardison? After that second strangling attempt, Hardison had sworn that he had always wanted to be a corporation lawyer, and the director had practically turned himself inside out to keep Hardison from quitting, right on the spot, and heading for law school.

Then there was Hergeswalther. His brief sojourn in fantasy-land had given him a new outlook. Who among the staff hadn't heard him muttering, "I could go nuts myself, any time. *Any* time." What wouldn't Hergeswalther do to get a better grip on sanity?

Here are two additional prospective apprentices, if

Garvin could only sell them on the idea. He glanced at Moklin.

"How much do apprentices get paid?"

"Not much as apprentices, beyond room and board," said Moklin, adding at once, "But they get *very* high pay when they have acquired their skill."

"H'm," said Garvin, "that's very interesting."

In his mind, he was saying to Hardison and Hergeswalther, "It's a tremendously exciting idea to me, from a *scientific* viewpoint. Here was a method that works, that turns out cures like clockwork, and it's never really been scientifically analyzed."

"Yes," he could hear Hardison say, "But, for God's sake, Garv, to apprentice ourselves to this Centran witch doctor—"

"I know, I know. But that's the only way to really get his methods. We could write a book afterward, detailing the underlying scientific elements of the cures."

"Hey, we could, couldn't we?" Hardison had always wanted to write a book.

Hergeswalther said uneasily, "And, meanwhile, what do we eat?"

"Well, we get room and board, and I guess not much more. But afterward we've got the ability. And then they really pay. Believe me, there's plenty of business there. The patients are piling up fast. And we could *cure* them."

"Yes," said Hardison, with a smile. "That *would* be a change, wouldn't it? If our treatment would *work.*"

There was a thoughtful silence.

"Just think, Walt," said Hardison, "we could call the book, *Elements of Centran Psychotherapy.*"

Hergeswalther's lips repeated the title, and he added softly, "By Hergeswalther, Hardison and Garvin."

"Yes," murmured Hardison, half-aloud. "By Hardison, Hergeswalther and Garvin."

Garvin came out of his fantasy. *Actually,* he told himself, the book should be "By Garvin, Hardison and Hergeswalther." Any fool could tell that it sounded better that way. Not that *that* argument would get anywhere with the other two. Let's see now: A, b, c, d, e, f, g, h, i . . . Of *course!* It was alphabetical! Garvin could rest his case solidly on that argument.

Beaming, Garvin got his coat and turned to thank Moklin for a very pleasant visit.

Moklin said, "I am sorry, Dr. Garvin, that you must go now. Shall I say good-by to the major for you?"

Garvin shook his head.

"Don't bother," said Garvin. "I'll be back!"

Afterword
by Eric Flint

Pandora's Legions has a complicated history.

The Pandora "cycle" began with the publication in the September 1956 issue of *Astounding* magazine of a novelette entitled "Pandora's Planet." (That novelette is included in this volume as "Part I.") In the years which followed, Christopher Anvil pursued two separate lines of development from that original story.

In one line, following the career of the Centran character Horsip who stars in "Pandora's Planet," he expanded the original novelette into a novel with the same title— *Pandora's Planet*, first published in 1972. The novelette "Pandora's Planet" constitutes the first seven chapters of that novel.

Periodically, in the course of that novel, references are made to the adventures of a human character named John Towers—but the adventures themselves remain entirely offstage. Towers' part of the story was recounted instead in a series of stories published in *Astounding/Analog* during the 1960s: "Pandora's Envoy" (April 1961), "The Toughest Opponent" (August 1962) and "Trap" (March 1969). The first was a short story, the later two were both novellas.

In addition, in June 1966, the short story "Sweet Reason" also appeared in *If Science Fiction*. Although it is placed in the same setting as the other Pandora stories, "Sweet Reason" is not directly part of the Horsip/Towers cycle.

When I set out to edit this volume, I re-read all the Pandora's stories for the first time in many years. As a teenager, Christopher Anvil had been—along with James H. Schmitz—one of my favorite authors appearing regularly in *Astounding* and *Analog*. But in the intervening years, I had forgotten how closely connected the series of Towers stories were to the novel version of *Pandora's Planet*.

I was a bit mystified, in fact. Why hadn't those stories been included in the novel? The Horsip and Towers stories fit together perfectly! And the end result of combining them would be a single story which was (in my opinion, anyway) better than either "branch" of the story published separately.

When I put that question to Christopher Anvil, his explanation reminded me how much the world of SF publishing has changed over the decades. My own fiction has all been published beginning in the mid-90s (a short story in 1993 and my first novel, *Mother of Demons*, in 1997). Like most full-time professional SF writers nowadays, I'm a novelist who (as a rule) only writes shorter pieces on invitation for anthologies. Anvil, on the other hand—like almost all professional SF writers of earlier generations—made his living primarily from short form fiction.

The decade of the 1970s, roughly speaking, was the period when SF underwent the sea change from being a short form genre to a novel genre. And many authors who lived and worked through that transition often found the seas choppy. As Anvil explained, in a nutshell, he'd originally *intended* the entire story to work as a whole, but . . .

By the time he sat down to write *Pandora's Planet*, the Towers stories had already been published in *Analog*—which meant that re-issuing them as part of a serialized novel in the same magazine seemed unworkable to him. And when he negotiated the rights to the Horsip story from a novel publisher, the Towers sequence got left out of the equation.

"For what it's worth," Anvil told me, "John Campbell told me later he thought I'd made a mistake by not including the Towers adventures in *Pandora's Planet*." But by then the novel contract was signed, and it was too late to do anything about it.

John Campbell was the editor of *Astounding* (later renamed *Analog*), and is generally considered the greatest editor in the history of SF (an opinion which I share, by the way). He was certainly right on this issue. *Pandora's Planet*, without the Towers episodes, is a workable novel. But it lacks the flavor and zest of the original novelette ("Pandora's Planet") which constitutes its opening episode.

The reason is obvious. Beginning with Chapter VIII of the novel, Horsip has enjoyed a major promotion. And while promotions are a splendid thing in real life (well . . . usually), they tend to be a problem in fiction. Put simply, admirals and four-star generals don't have as many hair-raising scrapes as lieutenants and captains. So, after the first eight chapters, *Pandora's Planet* winds up recounting a story which is almost intellectual in nature. While Horsip's story gives the overall framework for the Pandora cycle, his adventures, for the most part, are those of the boardroom, not the battlefield.

And it's *such* a pity—because, meanwhile, Towers and his crew are having as many hair-raising scrapes as you could ask for! Off-stage!

Can't have that . . .

So I proposed that we take John Campbell's advice, long after the fact, and Christopher Anvil agreed. As editor, I "broke apart" the various episodes of *Pandora's Planet* and combined them with the Towers episodes in a single story. Anvil then worked over and polished the manuscript, which resulted in this volume. (Since "Sweet Reason" was part of the setting, we included it more or less as an appendix.)

To sum up, after several decades, *Pandora's Legions* gives the reader for the first time the *entire* Pandora story.

—Eric Flint
July 2001

ERIC FLINT

ONE OF THE BEST ALTERNATE-HISTORY AUTHORS OF TODAY!

1632	31972-8 ◆ $7.99	___
Mother of Demons	87800-X ◆ $5.99	___
Rats, Bats & Vats (with Dave Freer)	(HC)31940-X◆$23.00	___
	(PB) 31828-4 ◆ $7.99	___
Pyramid Scheme (with Dave Freer)	(HC)31839-X◆$21.00	___
The Philosophical Strangler	(HC)31986-8 ◆$24.00	___
	(PB) 3541-9 ◆ $7.99	___
Forward the Mage (with Richard Roach)	(HC)◆$24.00	___
The Shadow of the Lion (with Lackey & Freer)	(HC)◆$27.00	___
The Tyrant (w/David Drake) (available in April 2002)	(HC)◆$24.00	___

The Belisarius Series, with David Drake:

An Oblique Approach	87865-4 ◆ $6.99	___
In the Heart of Darkness	87885-9 ◆ $6.99	___
Destiny's Shield	(HC) 57817-0 ◆$23.00	___
	(PB) 57872-3 ◆ $6.99	___
Fortune's Stroke	(HC) 57871-5 ◆$24.00	___
	(PB) 31998-1 ◆ $7.99	___
The Tide of Victory	(HC) 31996-5 ◆$22.00	___

James Schmitz's stories back in print!—edited by Eric Flint.

Telzey Amberdon	57851-0 ◆ $6.99	___
T'ɴT: Telzey & Trigger	57879-0 ◆ $6.99	___
Trigger & Friends	31966-3 ◆ $6.99	___
The Hub: Dangerous Territory	31984-1 ◆ $6.99	___
Agent of Vega & Other Stories	31847-0 ◆ $7.99	___

Keith Laumer's writing, back in print—edited by Eric Flint.

Retief!	31857-8 ◆ $6.99	___
Odyssey	0-7434-3527-3 ◆ $6.99	___

If not available through your local bookstore send this coupon and a check or money order for the cover price(s) + $1.50 s/h to Baen Books, Dept. BA, P.O. Box 1403, Riverdale, NY 10471. Delivery can take up to eight weeks.

NAME: _____

ADDRESS: _____

_____

I have enclosed a check or money order in the amount of $_____